John Gibbons

The Shadows of Peace

The Shadows of Peace
©2024 John Gibbons
All Rights Reserved

This is a work of fiction. Names, characters, places, and incidents are either products of the Author's imagination or are used fictitiously. Any resemblance to actual persons, living or dead, or actual events is purely coincidental

No part of this book may be reproduced, distributed, or transmitted in any form or by any means, including photocopying, recording, or other electronic or mechanical methods without prior written permission of the author, except in the case of brief quotations used in reviews of certain other noncommercial uses permitted by copyright law.

ISBN: 9798341364127

For inquiries, please contact: www.StellarDigitalStudios.com

First Edition: November 2024

Printed in the United States of America

To every dyslexic dreamer: may this story remind you that no barrier is too great, believe in the power of your voice—your story matters.

Prologue

Aboard the Pax Aeterna, a flagship of the Galactic Assembly, Captain Frederick Langfield charts a course home from the Wolf system. His mission, though routine in appearance, carries the weight of sustaining the fragile peace that defines the Assembly's rule—a beacon of hope and prosperity in the eyes of its citizens. The Assembly shines as a model of unity and progress to the wider galaxy, its guiding light reaching the darkest corners of space. Beneath this luminescent facade, however, the gears of bureaucracy grind slowly, and the shine has begun to tarnish. Among the Assembly's outer colonies, whispers of independence stir, and factions yearning for autonomy feel the weight of the Assembly's rule weighing them down.

With each broadcast of propaganda, the Assembly citizens remain blissfully unaware of the freedoms that have steadily eroded over time, a slow decay hidden beneath a veneer of advancement. The Pax Aeterna makes its return journey to Earth, and all the while the historical shadows of the Eastern League loom large. As instigators of World War III, Earth's most destructive conflict, the Eastern League ravaged ninety percent of Earth's population in just under three years. Eventually they were defeated, and this led to a century of enforced servitude: they were pressured into rebuilding the planet they had scarred. Segregated and marginalized while simultaneously denied basic necessities like food and shelter, their humanity diminished with each passing generation. Later, Earth healed and prospered on the backs of their labor, and a resolve formed among them: to make Earth and the Assembly atone.

Their desperation culminated in the hijacking of humanity's first colony ship, the Odyssey, so that they might conquer the unknown horrors of space rather than endure the terrestrial ones. The story of the Odyssey marks a pivotal chapter in human exploration: once heralded as a triumph of human ingenuity in galactic travel between the stars, the true fate of the Odyssey and its encounter with the League has been obscured by layers of official records and sanitized accounts. This manipulation of history serves the Assembly's agenda: the League was relegated to just a whisper throughout the years. The League's history has been whitewashed, scrubbed clean from the minds of Assembly citizens, and their role in the Assembly's near destruction fell from mind as humanity looked to the future.

Regardless of the League's forgotten past, those who were wronged never forgot, fueled by the most powerful force in the galaxy: unchecked emotions. Humanity's hunger to expand had never been stronger, and a century of prosperity followed the so-called destruction of the Odyssey. The factions that held dominion relinquished control of their home, Earth and the Solar System, to the Assembly as the seat of power for humanity. They signed the Codex, an interstellar agreement stating that the Assembly would provide protection while the factions expanded into their own sections of space.

As Captain Frederick navigates through the starry void, he contemplates this complex web of politics and power as well as his own internal struggle to believe in the existence of a perfect utopian existence—force fed to him by the Assembly. Unbeknownst to him and his crew, the echoes of forgotten wars are converging, ancient fires soon to be rekindled. In the depths of space, old enemies await, their resolve forged in the crucible of remembered injustices. The Pax Aeterna, from the ancient Latin phrase *Peace Eternal*, strives to uphold her namesake. The Pax's safety is more precarious than it seems, threatened by secrets that, if unearthed, could ignite the flames of war across the galaxy once more.

ACT I

"Discovery brings light—but casts long shadows. Respect the balance."

— *Galactic Assembly Codex, Article VI: Exploration*

Chapter 1

The engine of the ship rumbles as it makes its way through space. In the year 2402, life is lived mainly among the stars, and fleets of ships move sleekly and silently around one another. The Earth and its Solar System sit and wait, each planet holding life in the form of colonies populated by citizens of the Galactic Assembly. During World War III there was chaos, ruin, and wreckage; the Galactic Assembly brought peace and order, protecting those who fell in line with their ideology—and casting out those who didn't. They've maintained peace, but at what cost? While the Assembly is able to manage their sizable collection of planets and people, some believe they've now expanded too far, reaching well beyond their jurisdiction and bringing assimilation with them, yet no one and nothing has yet impeded their progression.

As the craft passes through hyperspace faster than the speed of light, its full length is a marvel to behold. At six hundred meters in length and two hundred fifty in width, its large hull is a shining silver accented by the blue glow of gargantuan engines below. Glass windows gleam along each side. Staring out of one such window is Jane Mitchell, glad to be heading back to familiar territory. She looks at the passing blur of space, her heart divided by hidden secrets. How long can she keep up with this charade? It's been three months since she's been back home on Mars, having embarked on an expedition to the Wolf System to discover the new and strange. As a physicist, it's her job to explore the unexplored and chart the uncharted; the Wolf system still holds secrets despite the small colony living on the fifth planet.

Although humans have colonized this planet relatively recently, not every nook and cranny has been explored. In an attempt to expand their outpost, a group of colonists traveled to an uninhabited planet within the system and discovered something interesting: a cache of what appeared to be ancient ruins. This discovery was quite shocking—the colonists believed themselves to be the first inhabitants of the Wolf system. In fact, humanity as a whole believed itself to be alone, having had no contact with aliens throughout their explorations of space. Apparently, they were wrong. Thus, an expert opinion was sought and Jane was tapped by her superiors as the right explorer for the job.

Naturally shy, Jane is nevertheless confident in her abilities and education in a great many scientific fields. She's lived most of her life on Mars, which was fully colonized in the year 2039 as the first non-Earth settlement, and Mars University, an institution of education and learning, was founded shortly thereafter. Jane obtained the highest degrees offered by Mars University and is now largely recognized as a thought-leader in the Galactic Assembly. Around the galaxy, scientists respect her opinions and the conclusions she draws from her expeditions to far-away planets. This recent exploration to Wolf has been no different, and Jane has found something to spark questions, excitement—and maybe even a little fear—in the hearts and minds of her fellow Assembly citizens. All will be revealed at the meeting today, and she's buzzing with anticipation about her news.

"Janey, are you even listening to me?"

At the sound of her nickname—only used by one person in the entire galaxy—she snaps back to attention, pulling her small eyes away from the window. "Yes, of course I am, Marcus," she says with a laugh. "You know I'm easily distracted." She runs a hand through her hair, letting it fall back against the midpoint of her neck.

"That I do, and how could you not be? Look at that cabin! They've really rolled out the red carpet for you," Marcus rejoins with a slight upturn of his full lip. His bust takes up the majority of Jane's holodisplay.

Jane looks around at her spacious accommodations on the starship Pax Aeterna, an aptly named ship with an undaunted crew. Her cabin is light and airy, with metallic bulkheads and gleaming metal fixtures, designed with visitors in mind—designed to impress. It's large and spacious with enough room for a double bed, a comfortable lounge, and a full shower. The only thing missing is a kitchen, but she doesn't mind this omission. This way, she can mingle with her crewmates in the mess halls and enjoy their cajoles and laughter.

"You're right, it's nice, and it's been home for so long now. I can't believe our expedition is actually over. Am I tearing up?" she jokes, and Marcus can see her straight, white teeth.

Marcus laughs, and Jane watches as his broad shoulders move up and down with humor. "You academics, excited about books and ruins and dust. But today's the big day, Janey. You can gloat—I mean, tell the world about your findings. Looking forward to the meeting with the admiral?"

"Ha ha, very funny." Jane is too thrilled for words, much more ecstatic than Marcus could ever understand. Her findings—the details of her long foray into the unknown regions of Wolf—will finally be shared with anxious Galactic Assembly members at her upcoming meeting with Senator Corvex and Admiral Pacifica. "I think…well, I *know* they'll be amazed at what I have to tell," she says, thinking back to those odd and ancient ruins.

"And I'm so proud of you, Jane, it's all truly enthralling. Your research and theories are finally coming to a head, and I enjoy hearing about your discoveries. Though honestly, I'm glad of anything to take my mind off Anatoly—he's getting on my last nerve. I've never met anyone so–so–."

"Conceited, annoying, pretentious?" Jane finishes his sentence, as she's heard this complaint before. In fact, she's met Commodore Anatoly Petrov, and this is an accurate summation of his character. The commodore is arrogant and difficult to get along with, though his high status ensures everyone does in fact get along with him. He's in his early forties, with long blond hair that he wears loose around his shoulders.

"I think his big, strong nose suits his character well, don't you? I've never met someone who cares so much about his appearance," says Jane with a laugh, reflecting on the last time she encountered Anatoly. He couldn't stop brushing off his shoulders, ensuring his uniform was neat and clean of invisible dust at all times.

Many think highly of Commodore Anatoly, but Marcus can't be sure if it's out of love or fear. Led by Commodore Anatoly, Marcus and his crew are currently patrolling near an Assembly outpost in the Colorado system in the United Coalition territory. It's been an excruciating experience for numerous reasons. The biggest reason, according to Marcus, is the commodore's ego, though Marcus knows without a shadow of a doubt that it's worth it for his own career advancement.

"All of the above. I'm just…looking forward to the end of this patrol, you know I am. We spent hours yesterday searching for ghosts—a crew member swore he saw something out of the ordinary, a disturbance of some sort, during our patrol, but it turned out we were chasing our tails. It was odd, Jane…almost as if an echo showed up on our sensors. We checked it out extensively, but there was nothing there," Marcus says, a faraway look in his eye. He shakes himself and brings his thoughts back to the present. "All I can think about is seeing you." Marcus beams and Jane's heart swoops.

"I feel the same. I've been missing home, friends, colleagues, you. I'm glad both our missions are coming to a head. Much as I've enjoyed the company of the crew, it'll be nice to move at a leisurely speed." As she finishes her sentence, she can feel the ship begin to slow, and she knows it's nearing its destination.

"And I'll still see you after the meeting with Senator Corvex?"

"Yes, of course. At our usual place. I wouldn't miss it for the world." They gaze at each other, both reminiscing about the past, before patrols and expeditions got in the way of their time together.

"There's something else I wanted to discuss with you, Marcus, before you go. You and Captain Frederick have known each other for a while, but his commitment and loyalty to the Assembly concerns me. It could just be that he and I have two different views on the world—I want to act fast at times, and he can be far too cautious. Isn't that frustrating to you?" Jane asks.

Marcus appraises her thoughtfully. "He's an assembly captain Jane, and he's at the helm of the pride of the fleet, no less! He's got a lot of eyes on him, so naturally he'll feel bound by his duties as a captain. Any quick action he takes has endless possibilities and consequences," he says, knowing the full weight of his own command of the Intrepid and what he carries.

"Out here, every captain is alone, and that knowledge can be overwhelming," Marcus continues.

Jane considers this for a moment. "Perhaps, you're right... I still think of him as a friend, but he vexes me. Just like you do sometimes," she says, returning once more to happy thoughts. They share a knowing look.

Jane's musings are interrupted by a message from the captain himself, Frederick Langfield, which pops up in red letters on the narrow screen above the holodisplay.

ALL COMMAND CREW REPORT TO THE BRIDGE FOR A BRIEFING.

With a sigh, Jane begins her goodbyes. "I should get to the bridge, Marcus. It feels like we're almost at the shipyard. I'll be home before you can blink."

"See you soon, Janey." With a curt wave, Marcus is gone, and the hologram goes blank. Jane stands up and opens the door to her cabin, making her way to the bridge, her captain, and her crew. Later, she would regret not telling Marcus she loved him one more time.

Chapter Two

Jane makes her way down the brightly lit corridor of deck four, passing other members of the crew, both young and old. This deck contains her quarters, the captain's quarters, and those of other VIPs, as well as neat conference rooms and cheery alcoves. She passes nondescript, rectangular doors inset within the deck walls; plaques have been placed in the middle of the doors proclaiming whether the room is occupied and by whom. The low heels of her shoes glide along blue carpet, plush and ornate with intricate golden motifs. Its softness ensures the sound of her steps don't reverberate down the hall. Beneath the carpet is metal galvasteel decking which speaks to the strength and fortitude of the Pax's foundation.

Jane hurries past the observation lounge as she makes her way; it doubles as a mess hall for the crew. Just as she passes its doors, two crew members step out, jostling one another happily.

"Dr. Jane, hello!" Mika Rios, Jane's cryptographer, calls, attempting a wave with hands full of lunch leftovers. Next to her Hina, Jane's archeologist, quiets his laughter and he, too, begins to raise his hand in formal greeting.

Jane stops mid-step. "Mika, Hina, greetings! There's no need for formalities–we've been on this ship with each other far too long for that."

Mika smiles. "Care to join us for an after-lunch snack?"

"Unfortunately, I can't, I'm headed to the bridge. Maybe next time!" Jane calls, walking backwards. She turns and continues on her way until she reaches the ship's NovaPath which will take her up, sideways, and around the ship—wherever she needs to go with simply the touch of a button and a thought.

Jane presses her thumb to the NovaPath's call button on the wall next to the doors. With a ding, the double doors of the NovaPath slide open, and Jane walks through. She turns to the control panel, consisting of one singular button. It glows blue, ready for activation. Pressing her finger to the activation button, Jane mentally envisions the location of the bridge to enable the elevator's motion. As soon as the image is firmly fixed in her mind, she feels the floor of the NovaPath jolt just slightly, and she knows she's off, traveling through the ship at an incredible speed. Up, then sideways and slightly to the left; the movement ceases and the doors of the NovaPath slide open smoothly, and the interior of the NovaPath glows blue once again in anticipation of its next traveler.

On the bridge, pandemonium is in full swing, and crew members rush around their stations. Out of those on the bridge, six high-ranking crew members, Captain Frederick among them, talk to each other about their impending arrival at the shipyard, multiple voices raised in a cacophony of sound. Alarms beep from speakers, and Jane realizes this is what it means to be on such an important Galactic Assembly ship in hyperspace; she marvels at the controlled chaos playing out before her eyes. Captain Frederick is the conductor of this symphony, relaying orders to his crew, many of whom he considers friends.

"We'll be at the shipyard shortly. Renee, anything out of the ordinary on our sensors?" Frederick asks. His voice is strong yet not too deep.

"Nothing to report, Captain. That strange sighting from the other day seems to have completely disappeared, but I'll run a full diagnostic when we arrive at Gaia," says Renee Girard, the ship's scientific advisor. After speaking, she gazes with wide set brown eyes at the speed of passing nebulas through the windows on the bridge. Renee absentmindedly tugs on the end of her long French braid of russet-colored hair. The awed look on her heavily tanned, slightly freckled face portrays her love of open spaces.

Frederick grins and says in reply, "I know you're never one to sweat the small things, Renee! You'd be much happier enjoying the fun and free side of life rather than the dull, intense regime on this starship, eh?"

Renee closes her eyes for a brief second, and her mouth relaxes into a slight smile. "That might be true, Captain, but unfortunately for me, my expertise is always needed!" She replies lightly. Her capability with astronomy and science means her talents are consistently requested.

Jane overhears this, happy to call Renee a friend. She admires Renee's appreciation for the great black unknown of the Solar System.

"Too true, Renee. And Mikhail, enjoying the respite? No reason to use our weapons at this time, hm?" Captain Frederick clasps his smooth, slender hands together in contentment, already knowing the answer is yes, and his blue eyes shine with pride.

"We may find some asteroids, I could use a test fire, sir!" Mikhail, the weapons officer, shouts, his face intense. "I am ready to use any weapon at any time."

Brutality, immense strength, and full force: all words Mikhail applies to himself and his tactics. He's a mountain of a man, well over six feet tall with closely cropped salt and pepper hair, always wearing a crisped and clean uniform starched within an inch of its life—he takes seriously the Assembly phrase *harmony in form reflects harmony in function*. There's no time for jokes, only explosions of heat, shrapnel flying; this is Mikhail's modus operandi when it comes to war—and even peace if necessary.

As a skeptic of the universe and most entities within it, Mikhail has no diplomacy and would rather avoid small talk with his fellow crew members—most despise him for this. He has few true allies, consistently preferring to see the bad in people rather than the good. He trusts his captain, however, always willing to board a ship with Frederick in command.

"Wonderful, wonderful." Captain Frederick is collected and calm despite the noise and movement around him. His eyes roam from Renee to Mikhail, happy he's been given such a competent crew.

From the pilot's seat comes the quick staccato of Leo Draven's voice, reminding everyone of his youth. "Man, oh man! Can't wait to be home soon!" Leo loves the adrenaline, the rush of fear and excitement which accompany flying ships much smaller than the Pax. "Flying—what a rush it used to be," he mutters, ending in a slight grimace. His chestnut head of hair bobs and his foot taps, dancing along to the music of his daydreams; if only he'd been born in the twenty-first century.

Frederick begins to explain the details of their arrival at the dock and shipyard, as he and Jane will soon meet with the commander of the highly regarded Assembly Solar System fleet. Though officially named the Solar System, Assembly citizens that work among the stars refer to it simply as Sol. All the while, Leo fidgets impatiently, thinking of the small metal box hidden away in his quarters, the only thing on this ship he cares about. He glances wistfully at the clock on the wall of the bridge, mentally willing it to move just the slightest bit faster.

Time itself is infinitely complicated in space, Leo thinks to himself. Everyone typically conforms to time on Earth, synchronizing their watches and clocks to align with the mother planet, though other planets in the galaxy align with the different factions. The Assembly uses a twenty-four-hour clock, counting 365 days in a year. Despite the fact that there are no planets other than Earth that rotate at this exact speed, it was deemed the best for humans to continue this cycle, even when not on Earth.

"And Captain, how do *you* feel?" Renee asks. "Ready to be back in Sol for rest and relaxation?"

Frederick cuts her off. "No, no rest for me, I'm afraid. There's always another mission."

"Exactly!" Mikhail agrees. "No rest for me either. In fact, once we make it to the dock, it will be the perfect time for weapons practice. Perhaps try out some new rifles—."

"Whoa, Mikhail!" Leo laughs. "It's always flames and sparks with you. Why not join me and Jane for some drinks, take a load off—."

Frederick closes his eyes, reveling in the jovial sounds of camaraderie, and turns from his crew as they chatter amongst themselves. As he opens his eyes again, he spots Jane waiting at the entrance to the bridge, and they share a look.

"Captain!" Jane allows herself a slight smile. She clips down the short stack of stairs leading to the bridge floor and stands before Frederick.

"Jane, good to see you." Frederick's long face relaxes into relief. He turns back to glance at his crew. "Very glad you could join us." He leads Jane to the huddle of his crew, and she follows his physically fit, powerful form—befitting of a captain—as he walks across the bridge.

Leo announces from his seat, "We'll be arriving at Sol in ten minutes, sir."

Frederick nods at this remark, and he and Jane pass Leo's station to convene nearby, quietly discussing matters that don't interest Leo. Instead, Leo focuses on the system ahead. The ship slows as they near Sol. To enter the system, Leo uses the navigation sensors to scan ahead and make sure nothing is in his way, expertly avoiding any collisions with rogue rocks or space debris. Because of the intense speed involved with traveling between the stars, Leo would only have a few minutes at best to avoid a catastrophe if he were to strike an object. He shudders to think about the damage that would cause and checks the ship's sensors. As he realizes he has no work to do, he breathes a sigh of relief, knits his fingers together, and places them behind his head.

While relaxing, Leo mentally takes note of the jump points, which are at the very edge of the gravity well of the star. They lay just outside the orbit of the last planet and provide a defined entry and exit point per system; this makes galactic travel a little predictable. When ships exit Sol, they end up slightly beyond Pluto. This means the Pax must navigate through what's known as Sol's starway—this starway will push them the rest of the way past Pluto and right to their destination: Gaia, the shipyard.

The entry point into the system is clear, and the Pax smoothly enters normal space. The lights and color of hyperspace stabilize, shimmering stars filling the windows of the bridge for everyone to see. Crew members briefly cease their actions and collectively gaze in wonder and awe. Through the window, the Colossus can be seen sitting silently in wait for pirates or other interlopers. The Colossus is an Assembly battleship that patrols the stars and makes sure no persons of ill intent threaten the peace and security of space, peace that the Assembly has spent much time attempting to preserve—they wouldn't appreciate any usurpers entering or disrupting their home system.

"Leo, another smooth transition!" Frederick pauses his conversation with Jane to focus on Leo's flying prowess. Frederick hands out compliments and punishments in equal measure, but in this moment, he praises Leo like the prodigal son, grateful that his pilot has such skill and dexterity.

"Thanks, Cap." Leo moves his hands out from behind his head and straightens his posture, drumming his fingers on his leg. He's happy for the praise but never quite sure how to react to a compliment. "Next stop: home," Leo responds, slowly moving the lumbering bulk of the Pax away from the jump point and towards the entrance to the starway. He enters a myriad of commands on his keyboard, striking buttons on his console as he's done countless times.

The starways are composed of two small satellites which project an intense light; the light creates a tunnel that instantaneously moves ships thousands of miles and clear across Sol. It was actually Jane who brought this marvel of celestial starways to life. Through her many expeditions, Jane endured slow, painstaking journeys from planet to plant; one could grow old just traveling from Pluto to Mars.

On a particularly long journey, she began to run out of reading material to keep her busy. As she flipped through a tome about the ancient roadways of Earth, genius struck. Jane mapped out the trajectory of the starways and called Marcus to tease out her thoughts—once he understood the implications of such fast travel, he wholeheartedly supported the idea. Jane then brought her plans to the Assembly and its leaders who saw the merit in the starways and established it that very same year.

While the starways are quick, on busy days they can be filled and clogged with travelers and traders hoping to reach their destinations in the blink of an eye. As far as Leo can see, there's only one civilian ship, its name the Golden Key, between the Pax and the entrance to the starway. Ahead of them, the Golden Key enters the jump point, and Leo keeps his distance. He navigates the Pax behind the Golden Key, waiting for his turn to enter the jump point.

"Curious, Captain..." Mikhail grumbles, squinting as he looks at the Golden Key through his console.

"What is it, Mikhail?" Frederick asks.

"The Golden Key, sir," says Mikhail, still staring with a frown.

Frederick senses Mikhail's energy and turns to him with a warning. "Mikhail, you're not testing anything on a civilian vessel."

"Hm, perhaps another time, a different place." He strokes his chin with large, blocky fingers. "It is strange to see a ship of the Horizon Class. Surely, they're now obsolete," Mikhail muses, desperate to test his weapons out on a ship of that class.

Frederick considers this statement, but he isn't perturbed by the Golden Key's presence. "You know civilians hang on to relics if they work."

"True, Captain," Mikhail replies. "I just think it is unusual—that rust bucket seems to have seen better days…"

Frederick and Mikhail watch as the Golden Key transitions through the starway gate. As they look on, the Golden Key appears to be swallowed by the light. Then, in the blink of an eye, it's gone. Frederick snaps back to attention. "Leo, looks like we're next. No time like the present." He gestures to Leo to move the ship forward.

"Captain," Renee chimes in, "I'm seeing that same sensor ghost again. Something is leaving hyperspace."

"I see it too, but I'm not reading a GFF," says Operations Officer Marie Linnea. As the crew knows, the term GFF stands for Galactic Friend or Foe, and it's used throughout the galaxy to assist ships in identifying each other. Vessels can determine whether nearby ships are friendly, an enemy, or simply unidentifiable based on the ship's associated serial number, which is transmitted constantly to any ships in proximity. All serial numbers are stored in a central database for quick retrieval by officers.

Frederick looks to First Officer Xavier Reynolds. Xavier cringes as he says, "Must be pirates."

"How can you be sure? There are hundreds of vessels arriving daily in Sol," Jane pipes up next to Frederick.

"Every vessel in the Assembly uses a GFF to identify themselves. Pirates usually don't have a GFF since a ship's serial number must be renewed every few years. Sometimes pirates will manufacture a fake. If a ship doesn't have a GFF, it's likely operated by pirates," Frederick replies.

"Maybe its GFF is malfunctioning…?" Jane muses, thinking out loud.

Frederick turns down his lips. "That's highly improbable; there hasn't been a known GFF malfunction in decades," he says.

Jane knits her eyebrows together. "Shouldn't we give them a chance to explain?" She asks stubbornly.

"No Jane—this is the way of our world. You understand the ways of the galaxy through your books, but this is *reality*. We have to read the obvious signs and react accordingly," Frederick says curtly.

Marie interrupts. "Captain, I'm getting a message from the unidentified vessel. It's text only."

"Read it out to us, Marie," Frederick commands.

Marie clears her throat and says, "Cease all actions immediately. You are carrying a dangerous item, and its destruction is required. We will force you to comply, if necessary," she says and looks up from her screen.

"There you have it," says Frederick as he looks sideways at Jane. His expression is flat as he turns to Leo. "Bring us about face so we can see that vessel." Leo acknowledges his captain's command and does as he's told.

Xavier shakes his head, bemused. "What are they thinking? Can they actually believe they can take on the Pax and the Colossus?" He asks rhetorically.

Frederick gives Xavier a rueful look, thinking about what he fights to protect on a daily basis: his home planet, Titan. "We won't let them make that mistake," he says, "Mikhail, you might get your wish—raise the shield and charge our weapons. All hands to battle stance." At that, Marie sounds the alarm on the bridge.

Next, Frederick turns to Renee and Marie. "Why couldn't we detect them until now?" He asks, clearly irritated.

"I don't know, Captain," says Marie as she shakes her head and stares intently at her screen. "Everything's in working order, but they appeared out of nowhere. I can't detect any hyperspace trails."

Pirates are of little threat, but their sudden appearance now—and so close to the end of this mission—feels too convenient to Frederick. Too planned. Is someone trying to set them up?

"We are ready, sir," Mikhail reports, and his tone carries its typical arrogance.

Renee says from her seat on the bridge, "Captain, it's an older cruiser of the Nova class."

"A Nova class? Hm, I haven't seen one of those in a while," Xavier says, stroking his chin.

"The Colossus is turning to engage the cruiser, and I'm receiving a message from its captain, Talia Varrick. She's requesting we leave the combat to the big boys and continue on our way," Marie states.

"Send an acknowledgement to Captain Varrick, please. They're more than capable of dealing with this ragamuffin. We'll hold our position though, just in case," Frederick replies.

"Yes, sir," Marie says, and she does as she's told.

"I'm glad to know Talia is still in command. I haven't seen her in years… You know, she was one of my mentors when I was fresh out of the academy," Frederick says to the bridge at large.

"I hope you can see her again soon," Xavier responds.

"Perhaps I will," Frederick says and opens his mouth to say more. Before he can start another sentence, however, he's interrupted by the sight of the Colossus; she's rapidly firing her ion cannons at the unidentified vessel.

Jane watches from her place on the bridge. Based on the conversations swirling around her, she knows the firepower from the Colossus will be more than enough to stop the pirates and their ancient cruiser. She watches the explosions in awe but wonders at the outcome. Was she right to question Frederick? He's made her feel as if she's not as smart as she thinks she is, but as Marcus said, Frederick has a lot on his plate. Despite this thought, his command style and dedication to his so-called duty doesn't sit right with her…

"Like dust they rise, and like dust they fall. In the end, all that remains is the silence of space." Mikhail solemnly recounts a line from a poem he's recently read and enjoyed.

Explosions and ion cannons cease their fire: the Colossus has dealt with the pirates. Frederick ushers his crew back to their original mission. He points to his pilot. "Leo, get us through the starway," he says.

"On it, Cap," Leo responds.

Chapter Three

Leo proceeds to the center apex of the starway, and the Pax glides through the gate. A bright light envelopes the front of the ship, sliding over the exterior. As the Pax passes fully through the gate and onto the other side, the starway deactivates behind them. Leo navigates the Pax toward the largest human-made stellar structure to date: the Gaia shipyard. Gaia is magnificent in size and home to the Assembly's admiralty. It serves as the main hub of construction and repair services for the entire Assembly fleet. Lining the dock of the shipyard are next generation peacekeeping vessels under construction, along with others undergoing repairs from minor skirmishes—typically fights with raiders in the less civilized parts of the known galaxy and controlled by the factions.

Jane moves to one of the windows on the side of the bridge and takes in the technological marvel. Grand in size, the shipyard seems to go on forever in every direction—sprawling like a spider's web with a central column jutting out and multiple sections for vessels to dock. The shipyard is a military facility, she remembers, thus clearance is restricted and very few civilians are permitted.

"Been to Gaia before?" Frederick wants to move away from the incident with the pirates, and so he joins Jane at the window, standing shoulder to shoulder with her. He observes the station, too.

Still gazing, Jane replies, "No, never. I've always wanted to, but I've never had a reason to get clearance before."

"Well, I'm glad to give you something you've wanted." Frederick smirks.

Jane glances at Frederick and notices his smug expression. She turns to fully face him, her side towards the window. "This mission has been amazing Frederick, I'm so glad we were able to work together."

Jane is emphatic—she's enjoyed her time overall on the Pax and is grateful to have spent the voyage with a competent captain and close friend. "I've missed home—and Marcus—but I'm glad to have called this crew family for the last three months." Jane's eyes go misty as she realizes the journey is finally coming to an end.

"You're not getting rid of us that easily, Jane. We still need to present what you've found—evidence of life on Wolf before the first known colonists left Earth. Where the hell did they come from?" Frederick asks rhetorically as he raises his eyebrows. "We have to get back out there eventually," he says, replying in earnest.

"I could use additional time to study my findings. There's always more to research." *Maybe there's a way to continue this expedition after all*, Jane thinks. She hates goodbyes.

Movement on the bridge continues around Jane and Frederick, and their conversation is overheard inadvertently by a few nearby crew members. The crew try to keep mostly to themselves and their assigned tasks, though some are curious as to the intimacy their captain seems to have with Jane.

"You can continue your research on the Pax, and we can return to the stars and see what else we can find." Frederick is excited at the prospect of another mission despite the fact that they've only just returned from this one. "And perhaps we'll find another clue—we can't sit on our hands and waste time while we have a galaxy's worth of exploration, mysteries to uncover."

Jane is slightly taken aback by Frederick's vigor, but she recognizes the urge in herself, too. "Frederick, we don't have all the facts. Just think—the ruins could've been left by the League. If that's the case, we don't know anything about them. What if they're dangerous?" Jane asks the question rhetorically, as she knows the rewards of this knowledge far outweigh the risks.

"You're preaching caution now? Jane, usually you're telling me to be more open to new ideas," Frederick says, feigning a relaxed tone. Internally, he's annoyed.

Jane purses her lips. "What I want is for you to be less loyal to the Assembly—don't just accept the status quo! Open your eyes to possibilities, whatever they might be," she says.

Frederick sighs. "The Assembly is all I know—I was raised on Titan and spent my life in the Sol fleet. I've seen the good we do. My duty—both as Captain and to my crew—will always come first, but I know the Assembly is far from perfect," he says, his constant internal conflict peeking through.

Frederick goes on. "I'll be honest with you, Jane—I was hoping when you first came to me that your theories were wrong. I didn't believe in you, though Marcus convinced me to give you a chance," he says and sighs. "I've since realized the darker side of the Assembly, and upon reflection, I think I've received some questionable orders over the years."

Jane is silent at this outpouring. The truth, and all its implications, are of the utmost importance to her. She despises lies, and being lied to, for that matter. As a student, she's been taught to follow Assembly rules: don't step out of line, and you'll be rewarded for your obedience and good behavior with safety and serenity.

Throughout her studies she couldn't help but feel she'd been duped—some details from her history books just hadn't seemed to match up. And if her conspiracy theory is true, if the Assembly covered up some sort of big, historical secret, how can she live within a society like that? Blissfully follow the rules knowing the peacekeepers do more than simply enforce the law? She'd be forced to expose their deception, calling everything the Assembly has built into question. A chance to discover these truths is the reward she's seeking.

While everyone else on the bridge continues about their responsibilities, Mikhail has kept one ear in the conversation between Frederick and Jane, unabashedly eavesdropping. At Frederick's last remark, Mikhail interjects as if he were speaking with them all along. "The darker side, Captain? Pah! The Assembly is what stands between us and complete anarchy." Mikhail leans forward in his chair with a growl.

Jane jumps as she realizes Mikhail is speaking to her and Frederick. *His confidence in the Assembly is stifling, his loyalty knows no bounds, too*, she thinks to herself. Jane turns to him and her eyes flash, a rebuttal on the tip of her tongue, but Frederick beats her to it.

"You need to release that aggression, Mikhail." Charming as ever, Frederick's words distract Mikhail from his ferocity and fixation on their conversation. Frederick leans toward Jane and says under his breath, "I didn't realize we had an audience. Let's continue this later." He moves away from the window, Jane, and thoughts of the Assembly.

Mikhail replies, "No arguments from me, Captain. I always look forward to target practice."

Frederick nods in acknowledgement but looks at Leo. "Do we have docking instructions?" He stops to stand at the command table he shares with Xavier Reynolds.

"Yes, coming through now." Leo presses buttons on his console. "Berth fourteen. You know, I'm not sure if I should be insulted—I could park three Paxs there. Do they think I'm incompetent?" Leo smirks, his hubris rivaling Mikhail's.

"Just make sure we don't chip the paint on one of the newer carriers. There's no room for mistakes, you know that, Leo." Frederick says this sternly, but his eyes tell a different story. He likes to pal around with Leo, taking the edge off an otherwise tense and tedious docking procedure.

"Hah, no pressure," Leo mutters to himself.

Berth fourteen, part of one of the larger docks of the shipyard, plays host to a number of frigates and destroyers, as well as the cruisers Paladin and Empathy Echo of the Honor class. Both are sister ships of Frederick's last command, the Resilient Fortitude, and typically take on simple patrols, investigations, and smaller caliber missions. Frederick's ambition was greater than that—he longed for more substantial missions and received exactly what he wanted with the Pax.

Leo approaches the dock, maneuvering the Pax to align itself with the berth. He positions the Pax perfectly straight.

"Think you could've done better?" Leo pokes at Mikhail but never takes his eyes off his controller.

Behind Leo, Xavier begins mentally reviewing his docking checklist. "Alright, let's get everything sorted out. Marie, ready to dock?"

"Just finishing up now," Marie says from her station. Her long fingers and immaculate nails press the appropriate buttons to assist with the docking process. "It's nice to be home." She tucks a wisp of curly, dark brown hair behind her ear.

Marie is an older member of the crew. She's been quiet at her station, watching and listening as she always does. She has no family or romantic partners, so she's used to relying on herself: she worked from the gutters of a rigid hierarchy all the way to the rank of lieutenant— higher than an ensign but beneath a legionnaire and commander. All this work has made her a bit hard.

With a small shudder, the Pax docks with Gaia, and the crew collectively relaxes.

"Marie, let's turn those reactors off and let the Pax have a nap. She's earned the rest." Xavier continues to ensure everything is on track. "Limit the power, turn off what we don't need—weapons, shields, anything noncritical."

From her station, Marie begins to shut things off. "Reactors powering down to minimal, Commander. Everything noncritical has been put to sleep," she reports from her seat.

Frederick accesses the internal communications system of the ship to make an announcement. He raises his voice to get the attention of everyone on board.

"Crew, we've now docked with Gaia. Please make sure each legionnaire has the rotation orders, and don't forget to enjoy some rest and relaxation."

"Captain." Marie stands and faces Frederick. She puts her hands behind her back. "Admiral Pacifica sent over instructions just before we docked. He requests you and Jane report to Gaia's command deck."

"Thank you, Marie." Frederick dismisses Marie with a curt nod, and she heads toward the exit of the bridge, following the rest of the crew in the NovaPath and off the ship.

Turning to Jane, Frederick says, "It's time for your fifteen minutes of fame."

Jane blushes, nerves and excitement battling for dominance inside her. "Is it?" She asks, wringing her hands. Frederick pats her on the shoulder, sensing her emotions. He waits until the NovaPath is empty of other crew members before heading towards its doors. They'll need to travel to deck twenty-three to disembark the Pax and reach the command deck.

"Everything will be fine. Let's not keep the admiral waiting."

Jane follows Frederick up the short stack of stairs. Together, they enter the NovaPath which will take them on a journey through the corridors of the Pax. Frederick takes the lead and pushes the button on the NovaPath's panel, thinking of deck twenty, section C. This deck and section will place them close to the airlock leading to Gaia. The NovaPath whirs and begins to move swiftly.

A thought crosses Jane's mind as they wait for the NovaPath to deliver them to the correct deck. "I wonder... well, I know the interworking of the starways—I suppose I should since I built them. But Frederick, do you know why we use the jump points around Sol?"

Frederick indulges Jane's nervous chatter and answers her question with a question. "Have you ever seen a ship entering or exiting hyperspace?" The thought brings just the slightest amount of discomfort to Frederick's mind. The action of entering subspace through hyperspace is beautiful but dangerous. A ship entering subspace creates a shockwave with the potential to damage everything around it, a ripple effect of destruction. He'd rather avoid that at all costs.

Jane shakes her head slowly. "No, I haven't," she murmurs.

"It's quite a sight, Jane. Imagine forcing a ship out of this universe and into an area of subspace where the laws of physics don't work." Frederick has a faraway look on his face as he thinks about the incredible existence of subspace. "I'm sure you remember the ancient works of Einstein?" He asks. "Einstein set the groundwork for your wormhole starways."

"I drew inspiration from him and others, yes," Jane agrees.

"You know, we've never been able to overcome that—can't go faster than the speed of light and all—but it's possible we can find a way *around* by using the tunnels between systems and entering hyperspace. That gets us around that galactic speed limit by ripping space apart—albeit violently."

Frederick continues, "Hyperspace is affected by the gravity of the local stars, so we need to get to the edge of the system before we can safely enter and exit, or there's no guarantee where the hell we'd end up." He sighs and shakes his head. "If that wasn't bad enough, an entrance wave would act like an explosion, damaging any other ship in close proximity."

Jane knits her eyebrows, slightly alarmed at the prospect. "I need to do more research on this phenomenon, maybe it'll help me refine the starways." She rubs her forehead before continuing. "Honestly, it's been quite a marvel to see another world—before we went to Wolf, I'd never left Sol at all."

"That's understandable—you've spent most of your time at university studying!" Jane rolls her eyes at this and Frederick grins.

"I've had a few commands in my career, as you know. On the Resilient and the Pax, I've had the luxury of leaving Sol. The system may seem calm and soft, but don't be fooled," Frederick says.

He pauses, unsure if he should speak the rest of his thoughts, but Jane should know the truth. Frederick presses on and says, "The rest of the galaxy is different. The Assembly directly controls only a few systems outside Sol. The factions have jurisdiction in most of space, they have their own rules and their own ways of enforcing those rules… Some of those methods of enforcement are more *effective* than others.

"Life is harder out there than it is here—it's more of an open frontier, and resources are difficult to acquire, piracy is more of an issue. It's nothing the Assembly hasn't been able to deal with, but the wild beyond Sol keeps us busy. More than our admiralty might want the general population to know." Frederick blows out a breath, surprised again at his sudden outburst of truth.

"Frederick—," Jane starts.

With a ding, the NovaPath doors fly open, cutting Jane off. Frederick doesn't reignite the conversation, and the pair exit the NovaPath, walking along a short corridor adorned with multiple monitors for various uses. This deck contains most of the airlocks on the Pax, as there are many on both the port and starboard sides of the ship. As they walk, Jane notices one of the monitors that looks to be a map of the ship, displaying the scale of the Pax in magnificent colors. There are other, smaller monitors next to doors, and these monitors list the crew members' names and ranks. Jane presumes these doors lead to crew quarters.

Their feet quietly pad on the soft blue carpet of the corridor; lavish lighting illuminates their path overhead. Soon, they reach a much larger corridor at the very edge of the ship with wide windows on one side. Jane can almost spot Gaia's personnel through the windows and from this distance. She spies the walkway they'll use to disembark.

Frederick picks up his pace, walking slightly faster than Jane; she quickens her steps, too, to keep up. As Frederick walks, he turns his face slightly to Jane and asks, "Do you know when you'll see Marcus again? Is he returning from his patrol anytime soon?"

"Hopefully in the next few days," Jane says. "We plan to meet on Mars after I finish here—we have a spot we love to go to. Currently, he's in the Colorado system at the edge of the United Coalition." Jane hesitates, trying to determine whether she should continue speaking. She decides to tell Frederick the whole truth. "Marcus—he never told me what he was doing there…and I never asked."

Frederick is genuinely concerned at Jane's words. He feels for her and doesn't like to see her confused, upset, or unsure. "Once we're done here, I can get a pilot to take you to Mars," Frederick says, hoping to be a white knight. "I'm sure we can spare a shuttle for a quick journey. Or, maybe I can take you myself, see this so-called lovely spot."

"If that's not too much trouble?" Jane asks, a delighted smile brightening her face. "That's very kind of you."

"Of course—it's my job to protect the Assembly and her citizens," Frederick replies with a half grin.

They reach the end of the corridor and arrive at the open airlock. Jane and Frederick cross the path of two Pax guards standing staunchly on each side of the entrance leading to Gaia. Both guards salute Frederick as he passes. The guards' uniforms are colorful and elaborate, the insignias on their arms show their low rank. Large automatic rifles rest on their backs, along with other equipment around their waist as part of their kit; Jane isn't able to identify it all. Frederick reciprocates their salute and continues down the bridge, Jane following behind. Metallic, interlacing designs creep up the windows on each side, and Frederick can see his reflection in the glass.

They exit the airlock of the Pax and enter the bridge of the gangway which leads to Gaia. At the end of the bridge, two Gaia security personnel stop Jane and Frederick to request retinal scans for verification before entry into another airlock, this one opening into Gaia station. Like a seasoned captain, Frederick walks over to the device held out by one of the guards and places his face closely to the scanner. A bright white light shines in Frederick's eye, rapidly changing to green. Once his retina has been scanned, Frederick steps aside.

"You're next, Jane," Frederick says as he moves away from the scanner.

Jane is a bit nervous—she's never experienced a portable retina scanner before. She musters up her courage and follows Frederick's lead, placing her face close to the scanner. Once again, the light turns from white to green, and Jane backs away from the device.

"You're both cleared and may proceed," the guard says, and Jane breathes a sigh of relief.

"Thank you, ensign," Frederick responds.

The airlock opens, and Jane and Frederick begin their trek through the station to the command deck of the shipyard once again. Gaia has been the Assembly's main shipyard for the nearly two hundred years since the Odyssey incident and mankind's first intergalactic voyage into the stars. The Odyssey was the first ship completed at Gaia in 2223; since then, Gaia has expanded to accommodate a growing fleet, evolving into the sprawling marvel it is today. Some areas of the station are beginning to show their age, a distinct difference from the modernity of the Pax.

Jane doesn't feel like the station is falling apart, but she does feel as though she's stepping back in time. In some ways, she's right. She stares at panels on the wall that have obviously been recently updated—they're shinier and in stark contrast to their worn surroundings. Instead of the plush carpet she's used to, the floor is a dull metallic—patches of it are dark and scuffed, a result of the thousands of inhabitants that have walked these halls over countless years.

Jane notices many slowly flashing lights on the metal walls of the station. In fact, there's one behind her: displayed on a small screen embedded in the wall and underneath the flashing bulb is the name "Pax Aeterna" with the serial number ASC-CC4576. The status of the vessel is next to its name and serial number—**DOCKED** in green letters. She looks down at the floor again and notices many lines in several colors: red, green, and blue. Each line veers off in a different direction. Jane is happy Frederick knows the layout of the station so well; she could easily get lost.

"It's a maze in here," Jane says as they stride along. "Thank god I have you to lead our way." Jane smiles, looking down at the lines herself. This makes her slightly dizzy, so she looks up to Frederick instead.

"If you ever get lost, just ask someone," Frederick says, gesturing to the scattering of people milling around them. "Anyone would be happy to help you."

They continue their walk until they reach a large, open space bustling with people. There are bars, restaurants, and other amenities for the crew of the station.

"I had no idea how busy it would be here," Jane remarks.

"There are probably tens of thousands of people here now, at the very least," Frederick says, looking around without seeing any of it—he's been to this station dozens of times and isn't awed by the visitors from different vessels taking respite.

The pair finally reach the NovaPath that'll take them to the command deck, a quick journey up the central spine of the station. From the NovaPath's high vantage point, they can see much more of the station, including the docked vessels and the many production facilities creating everything the assembly fleet needs, from frigates, cruisers, and battleships to fighters, weaponry, and shields.

"I never realized something so dangerous could be so magnificent," Jane muses on their ride up to the command deck. "I know everything here can be used to kill," she continues. "Honestly, I can't help but be inspired to see what we can accomplish, hopefully for the good of civilization. But there's always a price."

As they've walked and Jane has been given a tour of sorts, she's been thinking. Up until now, Jane has spent most of her time at Mars University, first as student, then as an exploratory researcher, carefully studying, not realizing how sheltered her life has truly been. She knows the Assembly has an impressive armada of vessels, but she's never seen them up close. The damage they could do in the blink of an eye, coupled with her quest to discover the Assembly's hidden truths… Jane isn't sure whether she's proud to be a citizen of the Assembly or frightened of the alternative.

Frederick's interest has been piqued, and he asks, "Why do you say that?"

"Do you not see those huge cannons on your own ship, Frederick?" Jane's question is rhetorical, her eyes wide.

Frederick raises his hands, palms up in mock surrender. "Okay yes, we might have powerful vessels, especially in comparison to other factions like the Russian Conglomerate or the United

Association's fleet, but Jane, we're peacekeepers." He firmly believes their job is to make sure the violence of the past doesn't reemerge.

"Don't you think that implies the Assembly is keeping everything in check by holding the largest stick?" Jane challenges Frederick with a level stare.

"Where is this coming from, Jane?" Frederick looks confused. After touring the station, he assumed Jane would be filled with awe, not aggression. "We've seen an unparalleled level of peace. As part of my studies, I remember reading about the twenty-first century. Two global conflicts, and from what I understand, constant unrest," he says ardently. "We—you and me both—are trying to protect against the return of dark human urges. And I'll protect our peace with every fiber of my being." Frederick heaves a big breath after his fervent speech.

Somewhere in Jane's brain, an alarm signals, and she relents. She looks down at the NovaPath floor. "Good that we haven't had a major conflict in hundreds of years." She looks back up at Frederick, raising just one side of her mouth in a sheepish expression.

Frederick visibly relaxes and leans back against the NovaPath wall. He shrugs his shoulders. "My crew will be ready for whatever the future holds. But realistically, there's nothing that can oppose the fleet of the Assembly. We might be using the barrel of our guns, but it's working."

He pauses for a few seconds, then says, "We've talked before about my previous missions, right? Fleet command sent me to Tolaria on my first solo command as part of a convoy escort. You're familiar with Tolaria, yes? On the outer rim of the French Star Union?" At Jane's nod, Frederick continues.

"The populace has no love for the Assembly there. We were bringing aid to the Star Union since they were running out of galvasteel. We were happy to oblige, but next thing we knew, they'd opened fire on us! Though their old vessels were inferior in every way and of little threat, my convoy leader demanded their complete destruction. Thousands of people lost their lives needlessly that day. So yes, the Assembly stands for peace, but as I said when we were unceremoniously interrupted by Mikhail, there's a darker side. My faith and loyalty aren't so blind, you know…"

Frederick casts his eyes down, and Jane remains quiet for the remainder of the ride.

Chapter Four

The NovaPath ceases its movement, announcing their arrival at the command deck. This deck is located at the top of the central spire of Gaia; it provides an excellent view of the entire station. The doors of the NovaPath open, revealing the command deck, and the first thing Jane notices is the deck's construction—apart from most of the floor, the room is made of glass so the command crew can see all operations of the station. Jane guesses there are around one hundred people busy working, the space filled with overlapping conversations; there are a few small groups of crew each, and other, larger groups are engrossed in operations around the station.

Gaia is the beating heart of the Assembly fleet, with several hundred docked vessels, a large percentage of which are able to respond quickly to any mission Admiralty deems important. Sector Admiral Novalis Pacifica is commander of the shipyard, second only to Fleet Consul Admiral Thane Krios. Frederick and Jane exit the NovaPath, and Pacifica himself steps forward from his place on the command deck to welcome them.

"Captain Langfield, welcome back to Gaia," Pacifica's powerful voice booms, and he gives a salute. He's an older man with crinkled, dark brown eyes, and the wrinkles on his face denote a long career of service in the field. His once jet-black hair is now white, and he wears it slicked back. Still trim, his uniform fits neatly over his torso and long legs. He's been looking forward to debriefing with Jane and Frederick.

"Thank you, Admiral," Frederick responds, saluting in return. "But really, it's Jane who's the star of this show." He places his hand on Jane's back and gently pushes her forward.

"Yes, indeed. Welcome, Jane!" Pacifica reaches out to clasp Jane's small hands firmly in his own larger pair. With a warm smile, he says, "Your reputation precedes you. And I'm sure you have much to tell us."

Jane blushes, the center of attention. "I think you'll be very interested in what I have to show you. It could be the start of a whole new era," she says with a note of confidence. Nervousness tries to creep up, butterflies in her stomach, but she pushes them down. This is the admiral, after all, she chastises herself.

The admiral lets go of her hands. "You made good use of Frederick and his ship?" He asks, and Jane nods. "Splendid. Let's fetch the senator and get started. We'll discuss it in my office." Pacifica leads the way, and as he passes a young man on deck, he says, "Ensign, send a comm to Senator Corvex, and tell her to join us in my office immediately."

"Of course, sir," the young ensign responds. With dogged loyalty, he obeys Pacifica's every order.

Frederick and Jane briskly follow Pacifica the thirty meters from the middle of the command deck to Pacifica's office. One side of the deck is filled with light from the sun, streaming in from the large windows.

As they enter Pacifica's office, both Frederick and Jane can tell it's the office of a high-ranking official. It's spacious and could easily accommodate many people at once. A large office chair sits behind a work space at one end; here, the admiral can work in peace. There's also a long table that can seat eight to ten people. Frederick stands near the door quietly with his hands behind his back, waiting for the arrival of the senator. He says nothing and allows Jane to take center stage.

Jane notices a number of small replicas sitting atop the admiral's desk. Intrigued, she remarks, "Quite the collection you have, Admiral."

"I've worked hard to get here." Pacifica sighs. "To be honest, most of the time all I do is approve damn reports." His face lights up. "But Jane, you've given me some excitement recently!"

"And these models on your desk—what are they?"

"Ah, these." Pacifica walks to his desk and picks up one of his figurines. "Memories from a more exciting time in my life, when I was out in the deep dark and all I had was the ship and its crew." He holds the figurine up close to his eyes. "This one is my favorite. A tiny replica of one of my old commands, the Resolute."

He continues, "I was on that ship for a four-year stint, one of my last before I joined Admiralty. We were able to save one of the French Star Union primary worlds, New Paris."

Jane remembers hearing about it—a terraformer went rogue and was spewing out poisonous gasses. Pacifica shakes his head, remembering the chaos, the fear. "If it had continued, we would've lost the entire planet in the blink of an eye. We had to destroy it from orbit. Luckily, we were nearby... We lost too many that day, but we saved far more." Pacifica closes his hand around the tiny replica and carefully places it back on his desk.

Since she's got his attention, Jane decides to pry a little. "If you don't like being behind a desk, why don't you return to being a captain, get back out there?" She asks.

"That's not for me anymore." Pacifica's hand slices through the air, denoting the finality of his decision to remain behind the desk rather than return to the unknowable blackness of space. "Plus, I can do better for the Assembly and its people here." He wanders over to one of the glinting windows and looks out to the fleet below. He points to the Pax.

"What did you think of your chariot, Jane?" Pacifica asks.

Jane says from behind him, "She's the largest vessel I've ever seen."

From his spot near the door, Frederick can't help but boast. "The best ship in the fleet with the finest crew—that's for sure. We were all glad to have Jane on board, to help with her expedition. And I'm certainly glad to say I had a hand in the Pax's original design."

This is news to Jane. "Did you both design her?" Jane questions.

"We both headed up the project, but others were involved," Pacifica explains as he leaves the window and heads over to the large table. He gestures for his guests to join him, and they do, Frederick and Jane taking seats next to each other and across from the admiral.

"A large portion of our fleet is beginning to age, and space is expanding by the day. Between the factions spreading in every direction and the Assembly trying to support them, we're getting left behind. Our ships are too slow, and the missions they were designed for are outdated." He pauses and places both hands flat on the table, leaning forward towards his guests as if he's letting them in on a secret.

"The Pax is meant to be the first of a new generation to support our growth amongst the stars. We have more than enough citizens who want to join our four academies spread out across the entire Assembly." There's West Point, Lunar, Sandhurst, and Nunziatella, each at a different location but offering the same education. Students who matriculate at these academies aren't just taught military tactics—some may not go into the fleet but instead will be employed in other areas like production, research, or logistics.

Pacifica sighs. "It takes a long time to build a ship from scratch." The truth, unspoken but still there, is that Gaia isn't able to fulfill everything the Assembly requires, and additional infrastructure is sorely needed, sooner rather than later.

Senator Vivian Corvex walks in just as Pacifica finishes his sentence, and she closes the door behind her.

Frederick leans over towards Jane as says quietly, "Vivian's the senator for the Unusual Occurrences arm of the Assembly. She's the former governor of Titan, so she's accustomed to influencing people and getting her way. Keep in mind that her headstrong attitude has made her a formidable foe in the war room, and she knows it."

Jane gazes at the senator. Though she's small in stature, she's strong, and she doesn't allow her young age—*a mere forty-five years*, Frederick whispers—to impact her. Many don't know she has both a nineteen-year-old son and a partner of her own; whether this is due to the fact that she's good at hiding parts of herself or she seems too icy to bother with love, one can only guess.

Vivian walks over to the admiral first and shakes his hand, glancing briefly at Jane and Frederick. She barely acknowledges their presence, as if they're both beneath her. Vivian sits next to Pacifica and smooths the full skirt of her dress; her outfits are always colorful, usually including vibrantly hued fabric and gold threading. On her ears dangle big, teardrop, ruby red earrings. She wears her black hair in a severe bun atop her head, like a heavy crown of her own making. "Admiral, I hope you're well. How are your partners?"

"Both Judith and Gabriel are fine, thank you. And Leandro, how is he?" Pacifica asks in return.

"Good, thank you. Back on earth now, so once we're done here, I'll look forward to going back to see him," she says loftily, as if her partner is the most important person in the world and beyond. "But," she continues with mock sincerity, "I suspect we have something crucial to discuss today."

Vivian finally turns to look directly at Jane and Frederick. She tilts her head, inspecting them from across the table. Vivian is a powerful woman, a long serving member of the Assembly. She's a senator with a great deal of influence, simply put, and Jane begins to feel a little intimidated by her stare. Deep down, however, Jane knows she herself is competent and is confident in her own abilities.

"Indeed," Jane says as she nods. "Frederick, can you bring up my findings?"

While Frederick interacts with the terminal which controls the nearby display screen at the end of the table, Jane begins her explanation. She stands and moves closer to the display.

"This all started a few months ago when Wolf colonists found something surprising and called for support from the Assembly. What we found was the remains of an artificial structure."

Vivian purses her lips and narrows her eyes. "A structure…" Vivian's distaste is clear. "You… you brought me all the way out here for a structure," she deadpans.

"Some of the most important discoveries start with the smallest of things," Jane says, trying to regain control of the conversation.

"And what was so special about this little *structure*?" Vivian asks sardonically.

"Technically, our findings came from the third planet in the Wolf system. For those unaware, the colonists of the Wolf system are located on the fifth planet in the system," Jane continues, putting on her professorial voice. "It's a little far out from the Goldilocks Zone and a bit on the cold side, but we've begun terraforming operations."

Jane points to the monitor on which images of her findings are displayed. "The planet has an atmosphere and oxygen, so we can breathe outside, but you would do well to bring a warm jacket. The important part is that the colonists have limited resources—only one vessel able to do extra-planetary operations.

"From what we understand, they've only just started exploring the third planet. It's uninhabitable, so there was no real reason to explore before. The colonists noticed a small area on the planet that showed signs of life, which was a little strange. It was an exact one mile by one mile square—and that doesn't happen in nature. Only man-made objects are that precise." Jane opens her mouth to continue but is interrupted by Vivian's harsh tone of voice.

"Just to make sure I've got this clearly," Vivian says with annoyance, "The newest Assembly carrier was tasked with a mission to a far-flung system…because there was an interesting patch of *dirt* and you found a *structure*." She makes a steeple of her fingers and places them beneath her chin, giving Jane a withering look.

"And that structure contained nickel-titanium dated to at least one hundred fifty years old."

Vivian quirks an eyebrow. "I don't understand?"

Finally, a break. Jane smiles and says, "We colonized the Wolf system on only two planets over fifty years ago, yet we've found evidence on the planet that materials were used one hundred fifty years *before* our colonists arrived."

Frederick pipes up from beside the monitor. "We also don't have any vessels in the fleet or any colonists' equipment that contains nickel-titanium."

"So, the question is, if we didn't put it there, who did?" Jane asks rhetorically.

Vivian pauses for a beat before she starts to giggle. "You…you really think a tiny piece of metal in a glorified patch of grass under a box is that significant? Pacifica, please talk some sense into these two! Are you serious?" She puts one hand to her mouth and tries to stifle her laughter.

Pacifica swivels in his chair to face her. "And how do you think it got there?" He questions.

"Just because I don't have the answer doesn't mean you're right," Vivian shoots back at him. She wonders now whether one of the Assembly's most important resources had been wasted on this expedition, and the thought makes her livid. She looks at Jane and says, "Presume for a second that I believe in your analysis—I don't, but let's say I do for the sake of this argument." Vitriol drips from every word. "So what? What would you have us do about it? You obviously didn't find little green men or anything spectacular."

Jane stares back at her and says firmly, "We need to see if it's just a one-off, deploy the Pax to discover if there's more to find. We can go from system to system and look for anything out of the ordinary or additional nickel-titanium signatures."

"There are several hundred explored systems in the known galaxy now, let alone unexplored—what you're proposing could take years, if not decades," Vivian says, thinking of the response members of the Assembly would have to this news.

"We calculate five or so years for the Pax to check everything" Frederick adds.

"So, let me get this straight. You want to go on a *wild goose chase* for the next half a decade, or probably longer, for a little piece of metal that may or may not be a red herring? In the hopes of finding the unexplained. Have I summed it up accurately?" Vivian asks with venom.

"That sounds accurate to me, Vivian. Frederick and Jane—this is great! When do you anticipate beginning this new expedition?" Pacifica says with excitement.

Vivian sputters, incredulous. "Are you really going along with this, Admiral? Don't you see how crazy it is?"

"Of course, there's a very low likelihood of success, but if we stopped every time we had a low chance, nothing would ever be done," Pacifica says lightly. "We also need to think about other variables and elements. It would be good to showboat the Pax in front of the factions so they can see the finest of the fleet is being used—and used for good. Plus, we haven't done a mission of this length before." He leans back in his chair, assuming the matter is closed.

"Well, Admiral, it's your decision," Vivian says, spreading both her hands in feigned civility. "But…it seems like a waste of time to me."

"As you say, it's my decision." Pacifica's tone is a reminder of who's really in charge in this room. "The matter is closed. Frederick, when can you and your crew leave?"

Frederick is ready with an answer. "Thank you, Admiral. We'll need a few days—our supplies are low and need to be replenished. And the crew could use some rest and relaxation to recover. We'll also need to resupply during the mission," Fredericks says. "It wouldn't be good to return to the shipyard just to restock, so we'll want to resupply further out in space. Maybe the factions can help us in that regard."

"I'm sure we can sort something out." Pacifica is content in his decision and wants nothing more than to see his intrepid explorers on their way. He stands and begins to usher them towards the door. "Get everything sorted, and leave as soon as you can, Captain."

"Yes, sir," Frederick replies, and excitement tinges the edge of his words. He stands up and prepares to head out.

Jane is stunned at their expedition's new fate. She and Frederick had discussed the possibility of another, longer exploration, but she hadn't been sure their wish would be granted. She notices Pacifica's and Frederick's movements and doesn't want to be left behind.

"Admiral," she says, following them both toward the door, "I'd like to join Frederick again. My team and I would be a helpful addition to the mission." In the back of her mind, an image of Marcus surfaces, but she blinks it away.

Pacifica stops short and turns to her. "I was thinking the same! So long as Frederick allows it?" He looks between Jane and Frederick.

"Absolutely." Frederick says it so fast, as if it were obvious. Of course Jane would be coming with the Pax—how could he not have her on this expedition? Frederick and Jane leave Admiral Pacifica's office glad to be continuing their exploration, both looking forward to another extended voyage together.

Vivian watches this departure impassively, waiting for the privacy of an empty office. Once their guests have exited, Vivian resumes her conversation with Pacifica.

"Are you sure you want to send them out?" She begins anew, a warning in her voice. "You know what they might find out there."

"Likely nothing more than additional planets for us to colonize, or interesting new materials." Pacifica returns to his seat and attempts to placate her.

"You know, we never found out what happened to the Odyssey... What if this comes back to bite us in the ass?" Vivian grates out of gritted teeth.

"More than likely, the Odyssey was a victim of a freak accident, instantly vaporized in a tragic hyperspace incident. Let's leave it there, Vivian." Pacifica looks grim. Saying more would just create confusion, and Pacifica is confident Frederick and his crew won't find anything the Assembly hasn't seen before. "Trust me, this'll be a glorified PR stunt for the Assembly."

Vivian sucks her teeth and says, "I hope so… I have a bad feeling about this one. Jane is impulsive and we haven't fought a war—a real war—in centuries…" She shakes her head and looks down at her hands, multiple gold and diamond rings glittering on her splayed fingers, lost in thought.

"We've prospered for hundreds of years, working with the factions to produce our version of a utopia. Think on that, Vivian," Pacifica says in a reasonable, albeit patronizing, tone. "Crime has all but been eradicated, every citizen has a job, and poverty is a long distant memory. Just like the Odyssey."

Pacifica makes a "poof" gesture to drive home his point. The Odyssey is in the past, and that's where it'll remain. He gets up from his seat once again and walks slowly towards an antique side table next to one of the room's windows. On this table sits elaborate glass decanters and bottles. He chooses a container of whiskey, picks it up, and pours the amber liquid into two pristine crystal glasses.

Pacifica walks back and hands a glass to Vivian who gladly accepts. The other he holds in one hand, inspecting it closely. "This whisky, like the Odyssey, is so old, its origin is like a faraway, faded memory. A fifty-year-old bottle of whiskey from when they began distributing it out of Perth—one of the planets deep into the British territories. I was given it by the governor when I took command of Gaia, and I've been slowly rationing this particular bottle for years. I drink it when I feel I need some faith." He chuckles and looks away from the glass in his hand to Vivian, slowly sipping her drink. "I feel you need a bit of faith now. Let's have a drink together, to calm your nerves."

"Hear, hear," Vivian says and raises her glass. Pacifica reclaims his seat and clinks his glass with hers. They look out the window together as they slowly sip, savoring the smooth taste of finely aged whisky—and hoping the Pax's voyage will be just as smooth.

Chapter Five

Safely in the NovaPath and away from listening ears, Frederick and Jane begin a discussion. Frederick starts. "We should get the command crew together on the Pax. I'll send a message to everyone." He paces the NovaPath floor. "Let's reconvene in the operations room in an hour."

Jane puffs her cheeks and releases a shaky breath. She sags against the NovaPath wall, adrenaline leaving her body. "We need to figure out where to go from here…" She still can't believe this is really happening. "But we have some time. I'm meeting Leo for a drink to blow off some steam. Care to join us?"

Frederick drops his shoulders. He smiles, and for a minute Jane thinks he'll accept her invitation—and what would inevitably come after. But instead, Frederick says, "No, no. I couldn't impose. Have a good time with Leo, and don't give it another thought until we meet in the operations room." He brushes his knuckles against her arm briefly, and she looks down at the contact. Before she can reply, the NovaPath ride is over, and Frederick strides out. He spares Jane a parting glance. "Do you know where you're going, Jane?"

"I'll find my way. See you soon, Frederick." And with that, she steps out of the NovaPath, rounds a corner, and is out of his sight.

Jane follows the green line on the floor which will take her to the social area. From there, she can enjoy all the amenities, like the MindScape stations that use tiny quantum computers attached to a headset to send the user into a pseudo dream state. As she walks, she passes the familiar logo of MindScape. All MindScape stations across the Assembly are similar; some are larger or smaller or might have unique features. Generally speaking, they're all recognizable. In the MindScape, a computer allows the user's mind to generate vast landscapes, games, or whatever creative activity the user would like to engage in, whether it be entertainment or work-related.

Because of the neurolytic interaction of this technology, the recommended use is only short bursts no longer than an hour. People who use it beyond the recommended time suffer significant neural injuries. On the positive side, it's also possible to share one instance, so users can partake in a dream state to collaborate on projects or just relax. Jane enjoys the MindScape; she and Marcus used it often when he was stationed at Mars. They spent their time enjoying the lush green plains of Earth, the deep caverns of Smolensk, and the calm seas of Tofino. They could spend many an hour enjoying each other's company in these virtual worlds, retreating from the pressures and realities of their lives.

Jane figures she has a little time to spare before meeting Leo, and so she considers taking a few minutes to enjoy this station's MindScape. If she heads straight to the bar, she'll be early. Then again, she thinks to herself, this was a special, sacred experience she's only ever shared with Marcus. It doesn't feel right for her to enjoy it without him, though it slowly sinks in that, considering her new mission, the Pax will probably depart before Marcus and the Intrepid return.

A wave of sadness flows over her as she takes one last glance at MindScape before continuing past and on her way. When will she ever see Marcus again, feel his physical touch? The question echoes in her head, a painful reminder of her longing for his companionship. Perhaps a drink might help her forget just how long it's been since she's felt the comfort of real, human connection with a significant other.

As she reaches the entrance to the section twelve bar, Jane is astonished at its size. The station seems to go on forever, and everything inside is grand with an elegant yet industrial feel; metallic walls and surfaces gleam—Jane knows they'd be smooth and cool to the touch if she reached out and brushed her hands against them. The doors of the bar slide open with a rush of warm air, and Jane steps though. The bar is crowded and the lighting is dim with a speakeasy ambiance; she bobs and weaves through tables and people, struggling to find her friend in this sea of new faces. She feels a little overwhelmed and heads to the bar top, thinking she might still be early. If that's the case, she'll message Leo and ask *him* to find *her*. She takes a miraculously empty seat and orders a Paraty rum from the bartender.

Jane glances around one last time for Leo as she waits for her drink. She scans faces and uniforms, looking for Leo's familiar chestnut hair and slim build. There! She notices him near the far end of the bar talking to someone she can't quite identify, someone who doesn't seem to be in military uniform but instead wears a large hooded cloak. She doesn't recognize this someone from the last three months on the Pax... Jane's gut feels uneasy. As she continues to watch Leo with this strange hooded figure, she notices Leo pocket a small package. The hooded figure swivels its head—surveying the room, Jane thinks. It all makes for a very suspicious scene, and her head fills with questions.

The bartender sets her drink down on the counter, interrupting her thoughts. Prying her gaze away from Leo, she turns to the bartender to thank him. In this short amount of time, Leo has moved on. Unbeknownst to Jane, Leo has already seen her; he slithers off his barstool and slides through the crowd, tapping Jane on the shoulder opposite to his former location. Jane jumps at his touch, startled.

"Jane! You sure are jumpy. Didn't mean to scare you." Leo grins and leans against the counter next to Jane. He holds two of his long fingers up to get the bartender's attention, then orders the same drink as Jane.

Jane laughs an uneasy laugh. "You were over there, talking to someone." She points to where she thought Leo had been speaking to that hooded figure.

"Me?" Leo pokes himself in the chest. "Nah, I only just got here. Sure you don't need glasses?" He says sarcastically. His other hand surreptitiously fingers the tiny package in his pocket, hoping Jane won't notice.

Jane doesn't believe him for a second, but what could Leo have been doing? Who was that hooded figure? She thinks back to a conversation she had with a former, now tragically deceased, professor—the discussion revolved around the idea that crime has all but been eradicated. While this is technically true, the Assembly decreed that every person is responsible for their own decisions. A number of very powerful psychoactive drugs are available, and though they're not actively distributed by the Assembly, they're not technically illegal. Challenging to find and still not accepted amongst the populace, yes. And those who seek the drug must locate a special contact to accommodate their request. But if caught, the user isn't fined for illegal possession nor the dealer for distribution. Jane has often wondered how something can be both harmful, possibly even damaging, yet legal. It's easy to claim crime has been eliminated when only certain crimes are reported...

Maybe that's not what's happening here. Rather than driving herself crazy with assumptions, Jane decides to ask outright. "Please tell me that's not Zenithar," she says curtly.

"And what if it is?" Leo responds with a smirk. "Not like it's illegal."

"It might not be illegal, but why take the risk of drug use at all? Do you think it's smart to buy it from a creepy figure in a hood at a crowded bar? I thought you had common sense," she says with distaste.

Leo rolls his eyes. "A creepy hooded figure?" He makes air quotes around the words. "His name is Lucas; I've known him for a long time. He always helps me when things get... scarce."

Jane shakes her head and begins to rebut, but Leo holds up a hand.

"Yeah, yeah, I've heard the stories, but it takes the edge off when the pressure gets to me. I'm sure *you* have moments when you just need some help—this helps me. That's all," he says defensively. "Besides, I've seen you pound stim drink after stim drink. Why is it that when it's in caffeine or alcohol, it's okay? But not for my little pills." Leo is suddenly hot, his tirade causing a sheen of sweat to break out on his forehead and upper lip.

Jane senses his anger, and her expression softens. "I'm just trying to look out for you, Leo. I don't want anything bad to happen to you."

"I know what I'm doing, and I'll be fine," he sighs. "Just let it go, please?"

Jane nods in defeat, still hoping Leo will one day see what's right from what's wrong. And this is clearly wrong. But she's not his mother, his significant other, or his wife. She can't tell him what to do, and she'd rather not risk destroying their friendship. She decides to raise the white flag and offers her hands to Leo, palms up in surrender.

"Alright, alright. I'll let it go. Just...look after yourself." Jane lowers her hands and sips her drink.

Leo brushes off her concern. "Yeah, sure. So, what's the deal? Are we getting back out there again, going to look for your aliens?" He drains his glass and signals for a refill.

"Yes," Jane says triumphantly. "We're going to be gone for a long time."

"Damn! But what exactly does all that mean?" Leo scratches his head as the bartender sets down his second glass. "Actually, we're going to need a few more drinks in that case. Keep 'em coming." He says to the bartender. "Gimme more details, I'm dyin'. I need more than just 'a long time,'" Leo pleads.

Jane says, "You'll find out more later, I can't steal Frederick's thunder! But here's something for you: though the senator was less than impressed with our findings, the admiral seemed to be very interested in getting us out there again."

"Isn't that what politicians do? They're always skeptical unless it helps them get reelected," Leo says as the bartender brings fresh glasses. Jane hasn't even finished her first.

"Maybe, but there seemed to be more to it," Jane says pensively, looking to her rum for answers. Finding none, she slurps the rest and reaches for the fresh one.

"I've never trusted politicians. You know, since the senator was so…uptight about the new mission, maybe it means you're onto something—on the right track." Leo shrugs a shoulder.

Jane agrees. "Perhaps…I mean, so long as the admiral has our back, we'll be fine. But the sooner we plan it out and get this expedition underway, the better."

"You've gotta admit though, Jane, it's a leap. A small structure of unexplained metal? Doesn't really mean something else has to be out there." Leo isn't trying to be mean, just truthful. He believes in this mission and in Jane, and he'd do anything to just keep going, flying, moving.

Jane hedges, pausing for a beat to think before responding. "Between you and me…you're right. It's a stretch." She dips her head and wonders if she should continue this line of conversation with Leo. It would mean revealing her master plan. Leo patiently waits for her to decide. She huffs, takes a sip for courage, and plows on.

"Do you remember the disaster of the Odyssey?" She asks.

Leo is caught off-guard, certain she was going to say something else. "You mean the first hyperspace colony ship? Yeah, that was, what, hundreds of years ago? What's that got to do with anything?"

Jane doesn't know if Leo is intentionally playing dumb, and she questions again whether she should be having this conversation with him. She tries one more time. "Do you remember what happened to it?"

"Uh huh. Some freak hyperspace issue. But I'm sure you know more about it than me."

"I wish I did." Jane puts her elbow on the bar top and cups her chin. "Something never sat right with me. The official story was that, when the ship entered hyperspace, it immediately disintegrated, and well over a hundred thousand souls were instantly killed—all without any wreckage."

"Yeah, and…? What's the issue?" Leo continues sipping his drink, seemingly unperturbed by Jane's insinuations.

"No wreckage at all, Leo. Nothing! Not even a particle of debris. Doesn't that sound, I don't know, suspect to you?" Jane asks him forcefully. "What if we've been lied to and the Odyssey just left and has been out there all this time?"

"Why lie to us? That would've been good news and worthy of celebration back then, right?" Leo clearly doesn't see it the way Jane does, but maybe she can convince him.

"I haven't got a clue, but I've studied that ship for a long time. You know the one thing I *do* know? A large component of the ship was nickel-titanium, just like the piece we found. Carbon dating would put it around the same age as the Odyssey as well." With that, Jane raises her eyebrows, hoping she's finally awoken something in Leo.

"So, you think the incident with the Odyssey, one of the biggest disasters post-WWIII, never really happened, and the Wolf system was where they originally landed…? Then what? They moved on?" Leo no longer sounds quite so skeptical.

"Wouldn't it be interesting to find out?"

Leo considers. "Well, I've got nothing else to do." He downs the remainder of his current drink. "Last round?" Jane nods, and Leo tells the bartender. They agree to see Frederick after their last drink.

"So, missing Marcus?" Leo says, slyly changing the subject. "How long's it been since you've seen him?"

"It's been a while. We speak on the holodisplay when we can, but it's been a struggle," Jane says with a somber expression. "The crew has been great, though. Really made me feel right at home."

"Has anyone been able to help with your needs? Frederick likes you, right?" Leo asks mischievously. He has a knack for prying into the private affairs of his crewmates.

"Uh, he's been a good friend for the last few months, but I've never thought about him in that way. I'm not sure Marcus would approve." The last round of drinks arrives, and Jane is grateful she can hide her blush with her fresh glass of rum.

"C'mon, Jane. That sounds archaic!" The rum has made Leo bolder, and he continues to pry. "Everyone has needs and wants to act on them. I myself have two partners on the ship, and there's my primary partner, Alex, on Earth." He ticks them off on his fingers. "I get to speak to Alex pretty often—most weeks usually. Yolanda and Kaelan, I see them regularly. It's not the Middle Ages any more, Jane. You can date whoever you want, set your own boundaries."

People are no longer confined to monogamy—in fact, having only one partner is rare these days. Humans still have needs, of course, and primary partners fulfill them. But when you're out in space on a long journey, away from your primary partner, it makes sense to develop a relationship with others that can satisfy your wants, who are with you physically rather than only through a holodisplay. Gone are the days of jealous boyfriends and girlfriends. Instead, people live harmoniously with multiple significant others.

"I'm not sure about that," Jane says slowly, "but I suppose I could be more open to the possibility..."

Before Leo can ask her what exactly she means, their cos-links begin to hum. They simultaneously pull their cos-links out of their pockets and check the screens. A new message from Frederick is illuminated, requesting the command crew return to the Pax's operations room. The pair quickly finish their drinks and leave the bar, making their way back to the Pax.

Chapter Six

While Jane and Leo are busy talking and drinking, Frederick heads back to the Pax's bridge to begin preparations with Xavier. They'll need to work tirelessly to restock the ship for its impending departure. Xavier is on the bridge at their joint station, waiting patiently.

"Xavier, we'll be going out sooner than expected," Frederick says.

Xavier looks up from his screen, surprised. "The admiral approved the longer mission?"

"He did," Frederick says proudly. "The senator seemed less than convinced, but it was the admiral's decision. Five years! The admiral wants us to do a long-term mission—it'll be a first for us and the Pax, as you know."

"No other Assembly crew has done anything close to five years." Xavier is incredulous. "We can only carry a year's worth of resources," he says, worry creeping onto his face. "Where do we get the other years' supplies? Do we come back every year to restock?"

Frederick taps the side of his head. "We're going to need to be smarter than that, Xavier. I'm wondering if we can try and either restock at some of the further out Assembly outposts… Or a long shot: perhaps the factions will help us, though they can be deceptive. Technically, the mission is for *all* humanity, not just the Assembly," Frederick muses.

"We can always ask, what's the worst they can say? No?" Xavier shrugs.

"Hopefully we won't need to stock up on ammunition too often, and we can limit our wares to food and other consumables." Frederick pauses for a second to think. "We'll also need to find a few asteroids with deuterium since we'll need to refuel the reactor every so often."

Xavier makes a note of that on his screen. "That should be easy. We won't need to plan too much for that. I'm more concerned with obtaining provisions, food. But Marie and I will work on that, as well as obtaining ammunition and vehicles." Xavier continues to make notes, writing out lists of items they'll need to gather and tasks they must complete before departure.

Frederick nods slowly, lost in thought. He agrees with his first officer on all counts and is ready to leave these machinations to him. "Once you're done, report to the operations room. I want the command crew to agree on a plan for the next few days. Bring Marie with you."

"Yes, sir," Xavier answers. He leaves his station and walks over to where Marie is sitting, presuming she's heard his entire conversation with Frederick. As he walks, he glances out at the scene in the shipyard; he's always loved watching the precise dance of small shuttles and repair crew moving between large warships of the fleet. The bridge isn't a big room on this ship; in its entirety, it's only around one hundred feet by one hundred feet. With glass taking up most of the wall space, it's easy for the crew to see the rest of the Pax as well as other vessels moving around the shipyard. It's a mesmerizing scene, ships flying at incredible speed and only inches from disaster—with help from the station's command deck, their navigations seem so effortless.

"Marie, we have a new mission, and we need to be ready to leave as soon as we can. We've got to restock everything: supplies, ammunition, vehicles, the works," Xavier says to her.

"You got it. And how long are we going to be out this time?" Marie asks.

Xavier shrugs his shoulders. "I think the captain wants to announce the timeline, and I wouldn't want to spoil anything," he says, "you know he likes his surprises. We're going to be out much longer than we've been before, meaning we'll need more supplies than our cargo holds can, well, *hold*," Xavier says, perplexed. How will they bring enough rations with them to survive so long out in the great, empty, unknown of space?

"Understood. I'll work with Gaia's attendants to get us restocked." Marie nods curtly and begins to make a list of her own. "It normally takes a full day to retrieve everything—besides the deuterium, we're low on practically everything else. Marie clicks away on her device, using her skill with organization to orchestrate the restock request.

Xavier watches over her shoulder as she ticks the appropriate boxes; she finishes her frantic tapping in triumph. The order for a full restock is complete, and Gaia will accommodate their request. Marie glances behind her with a small smile. "Done, commander. And it'll only take a day or so for Gaia to provide our requested supplies." She turns back to her screen, assuming Xavier has moved on.

As a more experienced member of the Pax command crew, Marie has been in the Assembly fleet for a long while and has moved from vessel to vessel, crew to crew. As she prepares the ship for its next long journey, she thinks to herself that this'll be her last assignment; she's looking forward to retiring soon. To her, the Pax is just a job, not a lifestyle.

Then again, she ponders the question of what to do next. No family, no partners, no real future plans. This is a sort of freedom, but it's crippled her ability to make a decision. She'd rather some external force make the decision for her.

"Alright Marie, let's head to the operations room." Xavier lightly taps Marie on the shoulder to get her attention and she startles a bit, lost in her own thoughts. He waits for her to rise from her seat.

Together, the two proceed to the NovaPath at the back of the bridge, riding until they reach their destination. They enter the large operations room. Gigantic, semi-circular windows cover the far wall, and monitors with terminals stand at either end; a holotable sits at its center. Xavier and Marie see Frederick, Renee, and Mikhail already standing at the table. All three are bent over, peering at a map of the galaxy: it portrays the Assembly systems and Sol at its center, plus the factions which include the British Territories to the southwest, the United Coalition to the southeast, the Russian Conglomerate to the north, and the German Association to the west.

"See there? Nestled between the Russian Conglomerate and the United Coalition sits the French Star Union. After the third world war, and the period of harshness that followed, it was clear to all humanity that the factions of old needed specific areas to call their own." Frederick says, pointing at the map.

"Because of this, the leaders of the factions decided there was plenty of space for everyone. Once each faction decided upon a planet to harness, they claimed it and brought their choice to the Assembly to ratify ownership." Frederick continues, and the others nod in agreement. This process is still currently in effect, and as such, conflict is rare. However, it allows the Assembly to keep control over the factions.

Mikhail responds. "The Assembly holds domain over Earth, does it not? The industrial powerhouse that propelled them into the stars in the first place. Even though the factions may have a significantly greater population density, they are spread far and wide over hundreds of systems and countless worlds."

"Isn't it true that, to make sure the balance of power holds firm and doesn't sway out of their favor, the Assembly restricts what can be acquired by the factions and limits usage to the previous generation's technology? This way, the Assembly always has an advantage, right?" Renee asks.

Frederick shrugs and says, "Yes, but regardless of the power of the Assembly, the factions *do* have their own in-house technology and vessels, but they're low quality when compared to those created by the Assembly. The GAC Odin, for example, is the flagship of the German Association and widely regarded as one of the most powerful faction ships. Nevertheless, it would be little more than an annoyance to the Pax should we ever find ourselves at odds, like a fly buzzing around, waiting to be swatted." This last sentence is said with arrogance.

Frederick stops speaking to turn at the sound of footsteps; he acknowledges Marie and Xavier's arrival. "Ah, Marie. How are our restocking plans going?"

Marie inclines her head. "It should take about a day or so until we're fully restocked."

"Perfect." Frederick replies as Commanders Torrin Vale and Elara Dorne enter the operations room.

Torrin, the commanding officer of the Pax marines, comes to stand by Frederick and view the map; Torrin is responsible for more than five hundred marines and their equipment. He has authority over the assault forces on the Pax, and as such, he's a tough man—he has to be. He's seen many skirmishes, so he always makes sure the Pax is ready for whatever mission her captain throws at her. As usual, Torrin is wearing his traditional military garments, complete with a light gray camouflage jacket and trousers.

Next to him is Elara, the commanding officer of the Pax's Air Wing which comprises four squadrons of Eagle class fighters and two squadrons of Hornet attack craft, twenty fighters each.

Frederick turns toward the new arrivals. "Ah, Commanders! Good of you to make it. We're just waiting for Jane and Leo to join us," he says, ushering them to spaces around the table. Everyone shuffles, making room and quietly greeting one another.

"Have we received a new mission?" Torrin inquires, not quite able to keep the eagerness out of his voice.

Frederick nods. "Indeed, but let's wait for Jane to arrive before we continue discussing. She'll have some details to add."

At that very moment, Jane and Leo step off the NovaPath. Everyone turns their head at the sound of Jane and Leo entering the room.

"Good timing! Now that Jane and Leo are here, we can get started. Join us," Frederick says, beckoning them to the congregation.

Chapter Seven

The four-foot tall holotable fully accommodates the eight highest ranking members of the command crew. It displays holograms which replicate different features, from maps to internal systems and objectives. Everyone finds a space around the table with a clear view of its contents.

Frederick raises his voice so they can hear him around the room. "I know you were looking forward to having a few days' rest, but we've got a new mission. As you all are aware, we found something interesting at Wolf, and we brought nickel titanium for analysis here at Gaia."

Mikhail grumbles from the opposite side of the table. "Sir, a small amount of unexplained metal—can this really mean aliens exist? Bah! I said this as we left, but I have to say it again…" He huffs with defeat after repeating himself. This time he hopes his disbelief doesn't fall on deaf ears.

"And you'd be perfectly right to question it, Mikhail," Frederick replies. "I'm sorry to say, but this whole thing has been… Well, it's been a little bit of a ruse. We aren't going after aliens," he says cryptically. Those around the table begin to murmur amongst themselves.

"So, why not tell us the truth? What were we actually doing out here?" Marie voices the question of the entire group. Her expression is disconcerted at the deception, and it's mirrored on the faces of many of the command crew.

"I know, I know. I lied to you all—," Frederick begins to explain himself, but Renee cuts him off.

"Did you not trust us, Captain?" Renee asks heatedly.

Frederick directs his gaze at Renee, feeling like he's lost control of the situation in just a matter of minutes. He must show his authority—they have to listen to him. "Settle down everyone," Frederick says, raising his hands with palms downwards, hoping to placate his crew. "Let me explain. Jane was looking for evidence that the Odyssey might've actually survived. She and I thought it best to hide that fact until we could talk to Admiralty and get their support in continuing our expedition." The crew goes silent, and many give Frederick a questioning look.

"Sir, were you expecting a fight?" Torrin asks.

Frederick shakes his head slowly. "It's been hundreds of years, and the story seems to be stable, though Jane came to me with a theory. She purports that the ship was taken over prior to the hyperdrive test, and the vessel left successfully. It's possible that, for the last hundred years or more, it's been lost out there in the void."

Jane takes over in agitation, sensing the crew's disbelief. "From my research, I believe one of the more radical factions in human history—the Eastern League—might've actually taken control of the ship just prior to launch, then went radio dark. They could've left at just the right moment, charged up their hyperdrive, then made it appear as if the hyperdrive entry was unstable. After that, of course observers would believe the vessel was destroyed in an instant." She lets out a heavy breath, relieved that she's finally able to explain her theory to the crew.

"I'm not sure what I believe more, aliens or this," Marie says, laughing sarcastically and shaking her head.

Xavier looks around at other members of the command crew, unsure what he believes, too. "Are you sure Jane? It seems your imagination has taken over…" Xavier trails off.

"When have you ever known something to be destroyed with no clue as to what destroyed it?" Jane asks vehemently. "There was no wreckage—no nothing! That's not how our current understanding of hyperspace works. Every other instance that resulted in the loss of a ship had wreckage... As the story stands now, it just doesn't make sense." Jane brings a hand to her forehead.

"Why would they cover up something like that? It was the dawn of the Assembly; we were striving for greatness. Why would this be swept under the rug?" Elara bombards Jane with questions to soothe her own confusion. She's usually one of the most intelligent people in the room; always watching, yet slow to comment. When she talks, however, everyone listens—even the captain.

Jane is exasperated. How can they not see the truth? She begins, "This whole thing reeks of political meddling, don't you think? During that period, ninety percent of the population was wiped out."

She brings one hand down onto the other in a chopping motion. "Most of the factions we know today originated after World War III, the fall of the Federation, and the rise of the Assembly.

"The rest of Sol, which was in its infancy of colonization, left Earth on their own, with destroyed cities, a crippled infrastructure, and a decimated population." She lectures the crew, reminding them of the Assembly's destructive past. "Life was incredibly hard from what I've gleaned from my history lessons. The Eastern League took the worst of it, and since they started a nearly planet-ending war, they're seen as the enemy. If the Eastern League *did* take the Odyssey and its crew, they could've had enough people and resources to start somewhere new, start again." Jane finishes her speech. Her words don't seem to have the desired effect.

Marie begins to speak, her words a peace offering. "I... I see what you're saying, Jane. But we can all agree this is a longshot. Let's say we believe you—then what? If I understand correctly, you propose we follow the trail of the Odyssey and try to find these forgotten people?" She asks, not unkindly. "Don't you think that trail has gone cold? Where do we start? They could be anywhere... It's a needle in a galactic-sized haystack," she says gently.

Jane cuts her eyes to Marie. "Wolf was the first evidence of anything. The nickel everyone is dismissing matches a piece that could've been on the Odyssey's reactor. It was commonly used as a conductor around that time period. We can start there and map out a course to investigate the nearby systems, see if there's anything to find."

"We haven't heard so much as a whisper," Xavier says, looking around at his fellow crew members for validation. "Should we go out looking for trouble? I'm not sure I want to see what we find."

Frederick has grown tired of the back and forth between his crew. His next words pack a meaningful punch. "The admiral recognizes the importance of such an endeavor, and our mission is to seek and find any other evidence. We've been granted five years to search," he says with finality.

Leo's jaw drops. "Did you say, uh, *five years*, Captain?" Though he and Jane discussed this earlier over drinks, the reality is just starting to sink in. He almost didn't believe Jane when she mentioned it would be a longer stint, but hearing Frederick confirm, he knows it to be true.

"Yes, and I know—it's going to be a long mission, everyone. We'll need to think about how we resupply and where we go, and we must be efficient." Frederick looks each one of his crew members in the eye. "We need to make sure there's nothing waiting to pounce when we least expect it."

Renee shakes her head and mutters to herself. "What about my family—my primary partner? I can't go without seeing him for so long…" Others around the table incline their heads in agreement, murmuring to each other and thinking of their own loved ones.

Leo still can't believe this, and he rubs his neck nervously. He thinks about his supply of Zenithar and wonders how he'll restock once they leave for the great unknown.

Frederick points at Elara, giving her instructions. "Make sure your Air Wings are fully operational."

Next, he points at Torrin. "Same goes for you. I want the Pax ready for anything. Work with Marie to get whatever you need, and maybe a few things you don't as well."

Marie shakes off her discontent from earlier, realizing her duty to the Pax is much more important than her distrust of Jane's plan. She pushes those feelings down deep, deciding to deal with them later. "I've already requisitioned the regular supplies, Captain. Elara and Torrin, let me know what you need, but it'll take a day or two to accommodate your requests." Though she's not exactly friends with Elara and Torrin, Marie is glad to do her duty, and if that includes extending a helpful hand to them, then so be it.

Frederick continues to dole out instructions. "Xavier, come up with a search pattern of the systems around Wolf for our first phase, and work with Leo to make sure it's optimized. We don't want to stop every five minutes for deuterium."

"Not a problem, sir," Xavier says.

"Always remember this: we're ambassadors for the Assembly, so remain on your best behavior." Frederick claps his hands together. "Get to work everyone. When you have some timelines, let me know. We'll need to relay that to Admiralty." With a gesture of dismissal, Frederick ends his speech.

The crew acknowledge their orders with a nod and begin to exit the room, eager to start their tasks. Xavier hangs back, wanting a quiet word with his captain. He understands the chain of command and would rather keep difficult conversations away from the crew. Frederick has turned to look as his crew enter the corridor and head towards the NovaPath, his back to the operations room. Xavier clears his throat.

"Still here, Xavier?" Frederick turns around to see Xavier standing at the table. Frederick is proud of his first officer, and he likes that Xavier feels comfortable speaking his mind and giving his opinions. He assumes Xavier wants to share some of those opinions now.

"With all due respect," Xavier begins, "I worry we're wasting our time."

Frederick sighs. "You sound like Senator Corvex."

"She didn't see the benefits of the mission?" Xavier asks.

Frederick nods. "You presume correctly, but I expected that from her." He pauses for a beat and purses his lips. "You don't believe in what we're trying to accomplish?" Frederick is genuinely asking.

"I see the premise, as far-fetched as the evidence might be," Xavier says slowly. "I see that it's possible, but why send the most valuable vessel in the fleet on a five-year long mission? Shouldn't we be doing…something else?" He asks.

Frederick gestures to a chair, offering his first officer a seat. He'd rather they were at least slightly relaxed while talking about such a polarizing topic. Xavier takes Frederick up on his offer and walks from the holotable over to a row of chairs near the computer terminals.

"Xavier, my friend," Frederick says as he settles into his chair. "If we don't find anything, we can always cancel the mission. I'm not sure whether the admiral actually expects us to find something, and I know it's a long shot. But what if we *do* find something? What if, after all this time, we could bring a long-lost group of people back into the fold? Is it not worth the try, even if the percentage is small?" He gets up from his chair, excitement rolling off him in waves. His hands are animated as he paces in front of Xavier.

"What else are we going to do, go back out on patrol? Maybe we go to the faction capital systems, or maybe we see the Inarian

Nebula! The Assembly has kept the peace for so long, I can't remember the last time we were needed..."

Frederick stops pacing and looks at Xavier. He can't tell if his first officer is on his side or not; Xavier's face is impassive. Frederick would rather keep Xavier close, so he settles on a compromise. "I'll tell you what—if we don't find anything after a year or there's something else we're needed for and we must return, then we can talk. Would that ease your worries?"

Xavier considers for a moment. "That's a fair compromise," he says. "If you think this is the right thing to do, I'll follow you. I trust you, Captain, and I know you'd tell me if you felt we were wasting our time and capabilities."

"Of course, Xavier, and thank you for bringing your concerns to me. It's why I've kept you around so long." Frederick smiles and chuffs Xavier on the shoulder in an attempt to diffuse the tension.

Xavier scoffs in mock annoyance. "I thought you kept me around because I was the good looking one," he says, rising from his seat.

"That's just a bonus," Frederick replies. As if his cos-link knows he's available, it begins beeping and buzzing, receiving an incoming message. Frederick takes it out of his pocket and reads his latest message from Mikhail which requests his presence on the bridge.

Frederick heads toward the NovaPath, Xavier by his side. They ride together to the bridge, and all the while Frederick is curious as to what Mikhail has found. Once there, they exit the NovaPath, and Frederick strides over to Mikhail who's sitting at his station staring at a holodisplay of an old freighter.

"Mikhail, what've you got?" Frederick asks as he reaches Mikhail's station, Xavier on his tail. They congregate around Mikhail's command screen.

"About that freighter we saw earlier, it is still on my mind, Captain." Mikhail continues to stare intently at his display.

"You mean the Golden Key? Why are you thinking about that flying pile of scrap from earlier?" Xavier asks dismissively.

"Well, I took some detailed scans of it while we were in range," Mikhail explains, "Our records show that it was lost to pirates, presumed destroyed nearly a year ago."

"Destroyed?" Xavier questions, perplexed, and knits his eyebrows together. "Are you sure? It looked to be in one piece." Frederick and Xavier glance at each other in confusion, then back at Mikhail's display.

"That's what the records show," Mikhail says, dubious.

"Did you cross reference with Gaia's records?" Frederick asks. The Assembly keeps meticulous records, and the shipboard computer is updated with the status of all known military and civilian ships, including crew history and technical details.

"I'm not that green," Mikhail grumbles arrogantly. "Yes, I double checked. Every record we have confirms this ship was destroyed."

"Find anything else out of the ordinary?" Frederick feels a prickle of nerves creep up his spine. Danger is coming.

"Its configuration doesn't match anymore," Mikhail says, tapping at his console.

With a few clicks, he's able to overlay the original configuration of the vessel in blue with the configuration from the sensors in red. The Golden Key is an older Horizon class freighter, and this class is highly modular; ships like these could be configured in a number of different ways whether they're mineral haulers, fuel tankers, or cargo carriers.

Just several shipyards around the known galaxy have the blueprints to assemble these types of ships. Once built, most look the same: long, slender, very sophisticated, and several hundred meters in length, all with a central spine, as well as customizable modules. Only a few of these vessels still exist now, though they were once the workhorses of the civilian fleet.

"You see here in the cargo bay area; they are very different. The building schematics show that the middle modules should be much, much smaller than my scans show. It looks like she has gone through some major changes since production," Mikhail muses.

"I haven't got a clue what that bulge on the side is," Xavier says, squinting at the display. "If I didn't know any better, I'd say it was a hidden ion cannon emplacement… A transport like that would never be able to power a weapon of that size."

"They shouldn't have the power to fire a potato, let alone anything bigger," Frederick says in agreement, flabbergasted. He wonders if anything is in the classified files—more detail would shed light on this deceptive freighter with its hidden cannons. Perhaps Nova Corp is involved.

Nova Corp, the invisible hand that manipulates the Assembly fleet, designs innovative ship configurations to align with their objectives. They're a small division of the fleet, with just a handful of ships themselves, and their mission is to protect the Assembly at any and all cost. They're only deployed during the most critical of issues, and with good reason—their tactics can be a little unorthodox and extreme. Their homebase, aptly named Shadowpoint Station, is one of the most secretive installations in the Assembly; only commodores or high-ranking officers know the true location. To most Assembly citizens, and even the majority of fleet members, Nova Corp is but a whisper. Many only feel their effects but never see their actions.

"Keep looking through your scans, Mikhail, see what else you can find." Frederick turns to walk back to his place at the central terminal. He pauses mid-stride, addressing Mikhail once again. "Inform Gaia of your findings. Maybe they can keep an eye out, and we can investigate." Frederick continues on his way to the terminal.

"Of course, sir," Mikhail answers. "I will keep my eye on it."

Chapter Eight

Meanwhile, Jane returns to her quarters, walking slowly down the corridor from the operations room, thinking to herself. She's had such a long day and could use a conversation with Marcus to assuage her feelings of weariness and annoyance at the crew for not believing her theory straightaway.

She pulls her cos-link out of her pocket while she walks. With one tap on the glass screen, she brings it to life. There are multiple functions available to her, but she chooses to message Marcus and ask if he's free to chat. Jane is hopeful Marcus will be able to celebrate the good news and understand the unfortunate consequences of the five-year-long stint. As she approaches her quarters, her cos-link vibrates and lights up with a response.

The sensors on her door recognize her as their occupant, and they open for her automatically. She rushes to her holotable and plugs in her cos-link to call Marcus. The holotable beeps as it attempts to make the intergalactic connection. She waits patiently, knowing it could take a minute or two to connect. As she waits, she looks out her favorite square window. From this angle, she can't see much but the dark, empty blackness of space. She can, however, see a starway satellite blinking in the distance.

Staring into the abyss brings a certain odd comfort to Jane; it calms her and lets her think. She ponders what she'll say to Marcus—though she's reeling from excitement at the prospect of finding out the truth of the Odyssey, she doesn't know what this means for their relationship. It's already been so long, and their partnership has been under strain ever since Marcus took command of the Intrepid. Remaining lightyears away from each other for an extensive period of time has made it seem to her that intimacy is beyond her grasp.

The call finally connects, and Marcus's voice is tinny yet strong. Though she'd only spoken to him a few hours ago, the day has been a blur, and she feels like it's been much longer since their last call. She's happy to see his holographic face and hear his voice.

"Twice in one day? I should feel so honored," Marcus says.

Though the holotable is limited in its functions, it's still ideal for this type of one-on-one cross-galactic communication. There is, however, a slight delay; the transmission goes through subspace to reach its target, and so Jane and others using the holotable communication need to at least know the system in which the receiving ship resides. Every Assembly ship is aware of the exact location of every other ship in the fleet for just this reason. Prior to the subspace communication system, small couriers relayed messages from ship to ship, and it was incredibly resource-intense as there are more carriers in the Assembly fleet than warships.

"You should, it's a treat for you," Jane says playfully in response, a smile on her face. She thinks of how to start this conversation, and the smile slips. "We met with the senator and the admiral earlier today," Jane hedges.

"That was quick! They must've been keen. What did they say?" Marcus asks eagerly, his rich voice pulsing through the holotable's speakers.

"Well, the senator didn't seem to get it at all, and she acted the part of the typical politician. I think she was covering her own ass, but I understand why you speak so highly of Admiral Pacifica. He seems like a very good man, and he agreed that we should continue the mission," Jane says.

"That sounds like great news! And that's what you wanted, eh Jane?"

Jane looks down. "It is, and I'd love to continue."

"Why do I get the feeling you don't want to tell me something?" Marcus asks, concern rippling through his voice and expression.

Jane looks up at him and decides to just tell the truth point blank. "The mission... It's going to be five years long," she says nervously.

"Oh, I see. That's going to be quite the expedition for you, Jane."

"Yes, it's very exciting, Marcus. But... we'll be apart for a long time," she says sadly.

"I'll be there in just a few days, we can talk more once we're face to face," Marcus replies.

Jane takes a breath. "We'll be departing Gaia in the next day or so. Frederick is anxious to get underway." Jane's lip trembles just the slightest bit, and she swallows hard. She can't cry, not now.

"A captain is always eager to start a new mission," Marcus says, understanding finally sinking in. Feelings of dismay penetrate his usually tough military mask. "I suppose this means I won't see you soon after all?" Marcus's voice is low, and he's doing a terrible job at hiding his dissatisfaction.

"It depends how long it takes for us to get ready, but Marie thinks it'll only take two days. We'll just miss each other. I'm sorry, Marcus. I was really looking forward to seeing you," Jane says, defeated.

Marcus doesn't speak for a few seconds, and Jane is afraid the connection has frozen. When he does speak, his tone is grim, his expression cold. "It's been a long time since we've seen each other."

"It has, and it's been a struggle for me," Jane agrees.

Marcus's mouth is a hard line. "What do you think this means for us?" He asks.

"To be honest with you, I'm not sure," Jane says, stroking her chin as she frowns at the holotable. "I've been thinking about it, and I don't have any answers—only that I enjoy being with you. It seems our relationship is fading into the past now," she says, her voice breaking, and she almost chokes on the words. Marcus and Jane have been each other's primary partner for five years.

"I need to go, Jane. Anatoly is grating on my nerves and I've got a lot of work to do. We'll talk later." Marcus ends the call.

As his face drops from the holotable, Jane's head is filled with more questions, though her heart feels empty. Did Marcus still want to be her primary, and did she want him to be hers? Should she find someone on the Pax? She may be an almost-member of the crew for a long time; perhaps it's best she examines her options.

Chapter Nine

Back on the bridge, Mikhail has continued his research on the Golden Key. He reported the findings to fleet command on Gaia, and they were just as confused. After receiving Mikhail's scans, they decided to begin their own research.

A length of time passes, and Mikhail receives an incoming communication from Gaia fleet command. Sitting at his terminal, he accepts the communication. With just his fingertips, he easily moves the scans of the vessel out of the way to connect the call. Because of the proximity to the shipyard, Mikhail uses a standard video and audio connection instead of the holotable. It's limited to inter-system communication which makes for much smoother contact.

Tristan, a member of Gaia's fleet command, is on the line. "Mikhail," he says, "I've been looking over the copious amounts of data you sent. It's strange—we detected this same ship exiting the starway."

Mikhail is flabbergasted. "What?" He sputters. "Is it here?" Mikhail's booming voice rises in a crescendo, loud enough for all other crew members to notice.

"What's going on over there?" Frederick calls from his terminal, alarmed.

"It is—it is the Golden Key, sir," Mikhail replies to the room and to Tristan, still on the line. "It is approaching Gaia…"

With more than a little surprise, Frederick leaves his shared station to stand behind Mikhail. His curiosity is piqued, and he joins the conversation with Tristan in earnest. "Did you say the Golden Key is here?" Frederick asks.

Tristan's voice crackles through the connection. "Yes, sir, it just entered the station's perimeter sensors after exiting the starway. You know, if Mikhail hadn't mentioned the ship earlier, it wouldn't have even registered," says Tristan.

"Perhaps it's a good thing you actually listened to me for once," Frederick says as he raises his eyebrows at Mikhail. He turns serious again. "Where is it now, and what's its course?"

The sound of Tristan's tapping fingers can be heard through the speakers. "It's moving very slowly towards the shipyard. But everything looks to be in order. There's nothing wrong with the codes it's sending out, and the registry is correct… I don't see anything out of the ordinary," he replies.

Tristan's words have caused the atmosphere on the bridge to become tense; everyone is curious as to the bewildering appearance of the Golden Key. Frederick points at Marie, his gaze focusing intently on her. "Is that ship showing up on the sensors?" He asks.

"Yes, sir," Marie says as she scans her screen and squints. "I have it here—as Tristan says, nothing looks out of the ordinary." She continues to scan her screen.

The entire crew is now engaged, enthralled with the mystery of the Golden Key. They listen with one ear while completing their tasks to prepare for the Pax's next journey. Xavier strides over to join Mikhail and Frederick.

He addresses Tristan. "Can you contact the Golden Key, see if they need any help? I'd like to understand why their configuration doesn't match what we have," Xavier says, somehow able to keep his calm and collected demeanor despite the increasing intensity of the situation.

"I can indeed," replies Tristan. "Please hold."

Frederick and Xavier both look to be collecting their thoughts. They turn to each other in unison and begin a quiet conversation, speaking low so as not to attract the attention of the rest of the crew.

"I have a funny feeling about this, Captain." Xavier is uneasy, his calm facade has begun to crack.

"You and me both, Xavier," Frederick replies. "Perhaps it's best we prepare Commanders Dorne and Vale—alert them of this odd occurrence and tell them to be on alert."

"Do you think it'll come to that?" Xavier begins to sweat, a cold sheen of damp dread shining on his forehead.

"No, no, not necessarily. If we don't need their help, we can always downgrade it to a drill, but… Let's just say I'd rather err on the side of caution." Frederick breathes out; he's nervous.

Xavier nods and hurries back to his command station. Tristan rejoins the conversation at that moment. "Excuse me, Captain

Frederick. This is Tristan, back on the line. I didn't get a response from the Golden Key. This is very irregular," he says in consternation.

Frederick nods at Tristan's reply. Addressing Marie, he asks, "Where will their course take them?"

"They're moving very slowly, much slower than all other traffic," Marie says, the upward inflection of her voice belying her confusion. "They look to be approaching Gaia, and that shouldn't take them more than a few minutes, however, the amount of freighter traffic is very high."

Renee has been on the bridge this entire time but hasn't wanted to join the conversation. She's been keeping her ears open and can suppress her thoughts no longer.

"Mikhail, I'm looking at your scans of the vessel." She raises her voice to be heard over the chatter, both human and electronic. "Did you check the material composition?" She asks.

Mikhail hesitates. "Ah, no. I was too focused on the other parts," he admits.

"You missed an important detail, in that case. Sensors detect that the altered sections seem to contain trace amounts of nickel-titanium." Renee looks up and realizes most of the crew is staring at her, wide-eyed. There's audible confusion around the bridge. This is impossible, unusual—it has to be a mistake.

Xavier runs his hands through his short hair. "How the hell did *that* get on that vessel?" He demands. No one answers.

"Another interesting question—this day seems to be full of them," Frederick mutters quietly to himself. He turns to Mikhail's command screen where Tristan is still on the line. "Alright, I've had enough of this," Frederick says, determined to get some answers once and for all. "I'm going to take the Pax, park it in front of the Golden Key, and insist on a response. Any issues with that?" He addresses Tristan with force, hoping to trigger a reaction.

Tristan shakes his head no. "I see no immediate issues. Please report back on your findings as soon as possible, and I'll inform Admiral Pacifica of any developments. Be forewarned that we have considerable traffic today since we're receiving raw materials," he says curtly. With that, Tristan cuts communication, and the bridge falls silent. Everyone is breathless, waiting for their next orders.

Walking slowly back to his place at the center of the bridge, Frederick begins to plot the Pax's next move. He knows something is off—he's well within his rights to board the Golden Key and see what's what, just to ease his mind and conscience. This was far more tension and agitation than he was anticipating when he woke up this morning, far more than he was used to, in fact. Frederick makes a decision.

"Xavier, alert the crew. Tell them we're going to depart, and we'll return to Gaia later today," says Frederick sternly. "Leo, detach us from the station. Now."

Both men recognize the tone of Frederick's voice and quickly commence their duties.

"All moorings detached, and the gangways are retracting," Leo announces after a few seconds of button-mashing on his command display.

"And the crew have received a message about our departure, Captain. A number of them are still on Gaia. We currently have about nine hundred crew members on board," Xavier states. Worry has weakened his voice.

"Ninety percent of our crew should be more than enough. Hopefully this is just a misunderstanding," Frederick replies.

Leo reports from his station. "Reactors cycling up, Captain, and I'm powering up the sub-light drive." The lights on the bridge flicker as the vessel starts to wake from its slumber, and a large, blue glow radiates from its rear.

"Captain, the reactors are coming online, and the engines are building power," Xavier says. "We have enough to intercept the Golden Key, but everything else will take a few minutes. Weapons and shields will be down; we're unable to use them until they're fully powered," he warns.

Frederick's voice cracks like a whip. "Get us underway, and intercept the Golden Key's course, Leo. Put us right in the way of that freighter." He slashes his hand through the air for emphasis. "Xavier, get Commanders Vale and Dorne to prepare a boarding party, and give them a fighter escort."

Sweat beads at Xavier's temple; he hates to disagree with his captain. "Do you think that might be a bit much?" He asks. He was hoping to avoid conflict.

"Just have them prepared, Xavier. Let's hope we don't need them." Frederick's tone is ominous, and Xavier does as he's told.

Leo does, too. The colossal engines of the Pax are now fully powered up, and the vessel begins to slowly depart from Gaia; its huge mass makes slow progress at first. Any wrong move could spell doom for both the vessel and the shipyard. He expertly maneuvers the Pax, pushing away from the shipyard in a flash. He's free to navigate to the location of the Golden Key; by this time, it's only ten kilometers from the shipyard.

"Everything ready with the boarding team?" Frederick looks to Xavier.

"The team is already in a landing craft. Two Hornets and two Eagles will escort them to the target if needed," Xavier says, his heart beating a fast rhythm in his chest. What will they find?

"Marie, keep trying to get the captain of the Golden Key on the line. He *will* answer for this." Frederick begins to pace in a small circle.

"The vessel has come to a stop now, sir," Marie says, noticing the Golden Key has ceased all movement.

Xavier remarks in wonderment. "They're just sitting there..." His voice trails off in concern and confusion.

"'I've had enough of the questions—let's get some answers." Frederick turns to Xavier with a piercing stare. The desire to understand this unusual happenstance has overtaken him. "Xavier, give the order to Dorne, and get that boarding party underway." Frederick's voice is gruff, and the remaining crew on the bridge hold their breath, anxious to see how this mystery unfolds.

Xavier once again turns to his command station and sends the order to Commander Dorne who's piloting the landing craft personally. Because of their size, landing craft are relatively slow and often aren't deployed unescorted. The craft can hold twenty-five soldiers plus carry equipment, should the need arise. It's highly versatile and well-suited for a myriad of different missions, a utilitarian tool for ferrying the power of the Assembly from place to place.

This time, Commander Dorne will be escorted by members of both Alpha and Tiger squadrons. Alpha squadron is composed of twenty Eagle fighters, the latest generation of Space Superiority Fighters—single-seat fighters with two rapid fire gauss cannons each.

These fighters are highly maneuverable but lack shielding or heavy armor. Alpha squadrons, like other squadrons on the Pax, are highly trained but devoid of real experience (similar to everyone in the Assembly fleet). Tiger squadron is designed to hit hard and fast, using Hornet class strike craft; these craft have quite an old design when compared to Eagle fighters, but the Hornets are reliable and built to last. They carry an array of missiles and other heavy weapons designed to deal with severe threats.

Now that Frederick has given the green light and Xavier has alerted Torrin and Elara, the hangar bay is abuzz with activity. Aircrew run around the flight deck, which is located towards the aft of the ship, taking up nearly thirty percent of the internal space on the vessel. This deck boasts two large openings under the bridge, protected by huge doors that keep the flight deck safe when the crafts aren't being launched or retrieved. When opened, a low power shield allows for the crafts to launch without exposing the deck to cold, hard space.

The landing craft launches, and Frederick looks on through the window. He walks slowly towards the right side of the bridge. Some of the excitement has died down, and his crew return their focus to their tasks and terminals, barely noticing the launch. Frederick watches the landing craft's trajectory, flanked by two Eagles and followed by two Hornets. It only takes a minute, though to Frederick it seems like an eternity.

"Captain, the boarding team is approaching the Golden Key. It looks like the main hangar is still shielded and pressurized," Xavier calls from his station.

As the landing craft approaches their target, Elara notices the Golden Key's size—the freighter is larger than most ships but still only half the size of the Pax. The lower aft section has a large hanger that could accommodate the team. The Hornets and Eagles break off and pair up, orbiting the Golden Key with hopes to provide support and see what can be found from the exterior. They're all expecting to find a landing area bustling with activity—there should at least be a few people. Not one can be found.

Commander Torrin Vale personally leads his marines on this mission. He and his marines run from the open hatch on the landing craft, launching themselves onto the Golden Key. They immediately spread out around the front of the craft in sharp formation. Torrin and the rest of the marines are adorned in the same military uniform they've donned countless times: heavy body armor covering their flesh from head to toe and helmets atop their heads.

One marine fiddles first with the camera attached to his helmet and next his microphone to ensure he can be heard. Another taps the speakers on his helmet which allow communication to flow between the rest of the squad and the Pax command crew. Most of the marines believe this mission will be a cake walk, which is why Torrin feels his soldiers don't require the dreaded EVA suits—they've complained to Torrin that the suits are a real pain to put on, despite the fact that they protect the marines while out in space and other hazardous environments.

Once Elara unloads her precious cargo, she pilots the landing craft back out into the void and rejoins her group to observe from the outside. On the bridge, the command crew can only watch in astonishment as the events unfold on the Golden Key. The front of the bridge has turned into a large display, overlaying the glass of the window. The display shows a number of camera views from Torrin and his marines which allow the command crew to see the action.

Frederick connects to Torrin's cos-link for an update. "Commander Vale, can you hear me clearly?" Frederick asks.

The speakers vibrate with Torrin's answer. "Yes, Captain. You're coming through loud and clear."

"Where is everyone on the Golden Key? Have you seen any signs of activity?" Frederick asks.

"I have no idea—not a trace of anyone, but we have gravity and air at least," Torrin says with a note of trepidation, waiting for the other shoe to drop. Underneath his armor, he can feel a bead of sweat trickle down his spine.

"No one there at all? How can this be...?" Frederick wonders aloud. "You and the team have the schematics," Frederick says. "Make your way to the bridge and find the captain."

Torrin and his team glance around the landing area. Here, they see obvious signs of modifications, similar to the exterior. Exposed wires, bulges, and new materials are evident, none of which match neither the aesthetic nor the original schematics.

A crease forms between Torrin's eyebrows as he recalls the schematics he viewed prior to entering the Golden Key. "I have the original blueprints we downloaded before we left the Pax," he says, looking around the landing bay. "I'm not sure how accurate they are since this boat seems to have modifications. We'll make our way forward and see what we can find."

He leads his team in close formation, and the group makes their way out of the landing area with weapons drawn. Frederick watches as they find the lights of the craft to be off initially, only coming to life when sensing the boarding team's presence. An abnormal, eerie silence causes feelings of unease, and everyone watching the team's exploration is puzzled. The team's mission was to gather answers to their questions—not create more uncertainty.

They move slowly down numerous metal-clad industrial corridors, and they still don't see a single soul—or any signs of life, for that matter—on the freighter. Shouldn't they have seen someone by now? One person left behind at least, or soldiers waiting to ambush any interlopers. They weren't expecting this void, this feeling of emptiness. After a few minutes, the team reaches a NovaPath.

Standing at the entrance, Torrin addresses his team. "I want you all to split up. This way, we can quickly search the remainder of the ship for any personnel, however unlikely that seems to be at this moment. Joe, take the second squad and head to the engine room," he says with strength he doesn't quite feel. "Keep me in the loop about what you find. I'll take the first and third squads to the bridge."

Joe nods, a quick and curt acknowledgement, and leaves with his squad in the NovaPath which will take them to the engine room. This NovaPath is smaller than the version on the Pax, and the team isn't used to such confinement; it can barely accommodate the six of them. They stand shoulder to shoulder and await the opening of the NovaPath doors. With a quiet whoosh, the doors slide open on well-oiled hinges, and the team emerges to find the engine room. Again, no lights and no people.

The main reactor is powered on, buzzing and rumbling at a low pitch which gets louder as they enter the room. The reactor is larger than expected, and Joe thinks it must be able to handle much more deuterium than a vessel of this size needs; the freighter is overpowered without an obvious reason, given there's no crew. The deuterium injectors, and every other major component required to handle the astronomical amounts of energy produced, appear to be undamaged and intact. This only serves to continue the theme of strangeness, and the team is getting accustomed to their perpetual state of confusion.

"What rating is this reactor meant to be capable of, Martin?" Joe addresses a member of his squad, an ensign under his command. "Does it say on the schematics?"

Though there's no clarity to be found in this situation, Martin pulls up the schematics on his cos-link, comparing them against the reactor in front of him. "It was built with a one-gigawatt class reactor, which is more than enough for a freighter of this size and function," he answers. They all stare at the reactor, a stark reminder of the abnormality of this entire mission.

Another ensign pipes up "If it were one gigawatt, wouldn't this ship only need one deuterium injector? Why does it have *three*?" The ensign asks, knowing he won't receive an answer.

Joe shrugs, a look of consternation visible on his face. "This whole thing is strange. There's nothing more to be found here, let's report back to Commander Vale," he says, pressing the button for the NovaPath.

While Joe and his team have been exploring the engine room, Commander Vale leads the Alpha squad into a different NovaPath. This NovaPath, too, is small, unable to accommodate both teams. The third squad remains behind while Torrin takes his team to the bridge of the ship.

As they ride the NovaPath, his cos-link vibrates, indicating a communication from Joe. Torrin accepts the communication, and Joe's voice reverberates through Torrin's helmet speakers. "Commander, you wanted stranger things on this mission, right? We still haven't found a single soul as of yet, and the original reactor has been either upgraded or replaced. It has three injectors rather than one."

Torrin pauses before he responds to Joe, thinking to himself. Why would a freighter need that amount of power to operate? "I'm not liking this," he says with unease. "Joe, get your ass up to the bridge. We need to regroup."

"Yes, Commander," Joe responds and clicks off.

Torrin and his team arrive at the bridge, and the NovaPath doors swoosh open, again revealing no one. "Where the hell is everyone?" Torrin raises his voice in frustration mingled with anger and not a little bit of fear. His shout echoes into empty air. He switches his line to speak to the Pax crew. "Captain, are you seeing this?"

"Yes, I'm seeing it. No one on board, and modified components… What the hell is going on?" Frederick wonders aloud, stroking his chin.

Xavier zooms in on his copy of the schematics. "Are any of the terminals active? Torrin, can you find out where all the power is going?" He asks.

"We can give it a try." Torrin points to two of his ensigns and tells them to try and use the terminals. They scurry over and get to work. Within a matter of seconds, both ensigns shake their heads at Torrin.

"No such luck—all the terminals on the bridge are deactivated," Torrin reports back to Xavier.

"If all the terminals are deactivated and there's no one on the ship, how did it *get* here?" Xavier's query goes unanswered.

Frederick passes a hand over his face and releases a pent-up breath. "Marie, get me Admiral Pacifica," he says. "He and Mikhail are going to like my solution to this."

"One moment, Captain," Marie responds as she frantically pushes buttons. She's able to connect with fleet operations at Gaia. Tristan is on the line again in a second, ready to hear a description of the Golden Key and what they've found.

"Yes, Marie, how can we help?" Tristan asks calmly, unaware of the horrors unfolding on the Golden Key.

"Captain Frederick needs to speak with Admiral Pacifica. Can you connect us?" She asks, then tacks on a "please" as she remembers her manners.

"Sure, I can. Hold on." Tristan goes silent as he makes the connecting call. A few moments pass, and Frederick paces in anxious little steps. He finds himself absentmindedly wandering over to Marie's station as they await Admiral Pacifica.

Finally, Pacifica's voice booms over the line. "Captain, what's going on out there?" He asks.

Frederick takes a deep breath and launches into an explanation of the situation. "Admiral, I've got a team on that freighter, the Golden Key, now. There seems to be no crew on board, and there are no obvious signs of damage. I have multiple craft orbiting the Golden Key, and they've reported nothing strange except some apparent post-production modifications. The reactor on the ship is three sizes too big, and the team is locked out of all terminals."

Pacifica huffs out a short, sardonic laugh. "Why is it that you always get the easy missions, Frederick?" He chuckles without humor and asks, "What's the vessel doing now?"

"Sitting there… It stopped just short of us when we got in its way." Frederick says his next words carefully. "Requesting permission to use the Golden Key as target practice, sir." Mikhail's ears perk up at this, and he instantly feels better about the potential outcome of the situation.

Pacifica's answer is swift, his verdict final. "It's well within the defense perimeter, so use your best judgment, Captain. If you determine the vessel to be a threat, then take action. Just make sure there truly are no personnel on board first."

"Yes, sir." Frederick nods. "That was all I needed. Thank you."

"Good hunting, Captain," Pacifica says, then disconnects the call.

Frederick returns to his position at the center of the bridge. He pauses for a beat and takes a second to collect his thoughts. The bridge falls quiet, everyone awaiting the next course of action. The only sound that can be heard is ambient noise, and the atmosphere is thick with tension. Frederick closes his eyes for a brief moment, preparing to make an announcement.

"Xavier, get the team back from the Golden Key," he says, opening his eyes and pointing to Xavier.

Next, Frederick points to Leo. "Bring us around and give me a side view of the Golden Key so Mikhail can take a bow shot with the ion cannons."

Finally, it's Mikhail's turn to receive instructions. "Mikhail, you get your wish," Frederick says, "Bring power to weapons and shields. You wanted target practice, eh?"

Mikhail laughs gruffly. "Perhaps next time we can get something that fires back."

As the Pax slowly relocates away from the bow of the Golden Key, the freighter's engines begin to power up. The Golden Key's reactivation causes the landing party on board to jolt forward, and they realize the freighter is moving with them still on it. They each look out the front window in astonishment.

"Uh-huh, sir? The Golden Key has begun to move again," Leo says with incredulity.

"What?" Frederick demands. "Which direction?" He turns sharply to witness the Golden Key's progression toward an as-of-yet unknown destination.

"Forward," says Leo. "While we were in its way, its movements were paused, I guess…" Leo trails off, not believing what he's seeing.

"Commander Vale," Frederick opens the line back up to the landing party. "The vessel is on the move; someone has to be controlling it. Get back here, Vale. Now!" Frederick shouts the last word, hoping Torrin understands the urgency.

"We'll make our way to the hangar and will be on board the Pax shortly. I can assure you of that, Captain," Torrin replies. "Elara, back to the hangar bay for pick up."

Elara chirps, "I'll be ready for you. We're on our way." She begins to pilot the landing craft around the rear of the Golden Key.

As if the ship were waiting for the perfect moment, warning alarms on the bridge begin to whine, and a red glow encompasses the space. The shock of siren sounds fills the team with dread. A red glow pulses, announcing impending doom.

"Time for us to leave," Torrin shouts to his three squads. They move as one to the same NovaPath. Torrin frantically pushes the call button, but the NovaPath is no longer responding. He pushes down his nerves, knowing if he shows any sign of hysteria or distress, his team will crumble. Though he tries to remain calm, his team will soon descend into chaos if the sirens don't stop wailing, if they can't get off the bridge. Who's controlling this freighter?

The reinforced glass windows on the bridge slowly begin to descend, opening the bridge to the harsh realities of space. On the Pax, the crew on the bridge can only sit and watch in wonder, horror, and shock as Torrin and members of his team are exposed to the vacuum of space with no protection. Torrin wheezes along with his team, understanding finally that the ship has been remotely controlled by someone, some*thing*, this entire time.

They gasp for a breath that will never come. Most are quickly sucked out into space, and those further away from the window are thrown off their feet by the sudden rush of it all. They begin to lose air, and some hold their breath and attempt to run—down corridors and hallways, looking for a way out. Others sink to the floor, knowing their mission has come to an end. Torrin beats the call button on the NovaPath again, and again, and again, but it's no use. It remains silent and stoic, refusing to be of any use to him and his team.

One by one, each team member's blood vessels freeze, expanding and standing out on their necks and foreheads, angry red lines which show how hard their bodies are working to avoid death. Members of the Pax's command crew cry out, and Renee bursts into tears. All Frederick can do is stare blankly at the screen, having witnessed his crew's lifeless bodies slumped over themselves. He's paralyzed, mouth slack in abject horror at seeing his crew dead.

Chapter Ten

Xavier attempts to collect everyone. He says loudly, harshly, "This isn't the time to grieve! We have work to do first. Leo, get us onto their side. Mikhail, put those shields up now. We aren't alone out here." He attempts to get the Pax into a battle stance. "Elara, return to the Pax as soon as possible."

Now, the true nature of the Golden Keys reveals itself. The vessel comes to a stop once again, only a kilometer from Gaia. The station is unaware of the events that have just unfolded, the seemingly senseless killing of valuable Pax crew members—the team on Gaia had every reason to believe the Pax could and would handle the Golden Key, despite its curious appearance and lack of personnel.

Once at a full stop, the Golden Key generates a huge energy wave, so bright and strong it looks like a lightning storm in space. It expands rapidly, engulfing all nearby ships, as well as Gaia.

Xavier shakes himself; they have work to do. "Mikhail, you'd better have those shields up!" Xavier says with more force than he had previously. This catastrophe is weighing on him, but he has to keep in control of his emotions. He's finding it harder and harder to do so with every passing second.

"Got them up, sir," Mikhail announces, and just in time—the wave engulfs them now, and the shields spark as the energy makes contact. The crew looks on, mute with shock, as the wave takes them over.

"That was quite a hit, Commander, and it caused heavy damage to the shields. They are at only forty percent, so let us hope there is no second wave—we cannot take another hit like that." Mikhail's gruff attitude has now turned to remorse—at losing shield power and witnessing the loss of so many lives.

"Haven't had too much luck today, though, have we?" Leo says, and his humor comes across as crass, given the circumstances.

Mikhail shrugs it off. "We are in position, Captain, and the cannons are charged."

Up until now, Frederick hasn't been able to see or hear anything clearly—he can feel his own blood pulsing in his ears, a nonstop beating that won't allow him to concentrate on anything else. Tapping along to the beat is the phrase, "They're dead, they're dead, they're dead." His brain won't stop the mantra. He knows he has to shake himself out of this trance, but how? He hasn't seen combat like this, what's he meant to do?

"Captain?" Mikhail shouts loudly. This noise penetrates, and Frederick breaks his own spell. He comes back to life and out of his trance, and as he does, anger flows through every part of his body, replacing the pounding blood with pure ice.

"Obliterate the ship, Mikhail," he grits out.

Mikhail readies the cannons. "Aye, Captain, certainly. Cycling up and firing." The ion cannons are the main armament of the Pax, a pair of dorsal and ventral particle beam weapons that accelerate hydrogen particles close to the speed of light. They appear to be a solid beam over small distances. Over larger distances, targeting becomes impossible, and so combat happens within short distances. Located mid-ship, the cannons are large, visible emplacements—obvious bulges on an otherwise smooth, elegant hull.

A blue light fills the area immediately in front of the cannon, increasing in intensity. The light expands for a second until two large twin beams fire at the Golden Key. From this distance, the beams instantly hit the front of the ship, causing copious amounts of debris and damage to the vessel.

"Firing again, Captain." Mikhail's voice is dull and tired, as if he's merely going through a routine. The ion cannons fire again, and although they're powerful, one drawback is the length of time required to recharge the capacitors.

"The Golden Key is shedding some of its modules," Marie says from her post at her station.

"Shedding? Marie, what do you mean?" Frederick asks, bewildered.

"I'm seeing small pieces of debris from the aft—nice shot Mikhail—and some of the cargo modules have been unlocked and are just…floating," says Renee, who up until now has been silent with shock and dismay.

"What the hell could be next?" Frederick wonders aloud, afraid of the answer.

Tension on the bridge remains palpable—they've never been through something like this before.

"The power levels of the Key are going through the roof," Renee says, eyes glued to her display.

"Confirmed. Its power signature is about three times what a freighter that size should be. It definitely wasn't that high a minute ago," says Marie.

Frederick and his command crew have been so focused on their immediate target, they've failed to realize the incapacitated status of Gaia shipyards—it, too, has been impacted by the EMP blast. Unfortunately, the fortress shield wasn't powered up, allowing the EMP to wreak havoc. Four other freighters were keeping their distance from the station, both oddly equidistant. This is far too convenient—their appearance, the Golden Key's empty shell of a vessel: it all speaks to someone's well-orchestrated operation.

"Mikhail, enough of this! Destroy that ship," Frederick demands without one iota of patience. He's ready for this to be over.

"Almost recharged, Captain."

A few moments later, the ion cannons rage once again as Mikhail fires, sending ionized destruction to the Golden Key. The cannon fire hits her mid ship this time, resulting in smaller explosions that culminate in a violent eruption. The threat from the Golden Key is over at last…but the threat to the Assembly is only just beginning.

Frederick watches the explosions with hope, assuring himself that they've won the day. He must make absolutely sure. "Status report?" Frederick asks, taking a breath to calm himself.

"The vessel has been completely destroyed, but the explosion was too big for a freighter. I'd sure love to have a look at the debris," Renee answers.

Throughout this entire tumultuous series of events, Jane has been in her quarters, unaware of the death and destruction happening just outside her window. When the wave hit the Pax, however, the light was so bright, it was hard to miss, and she saw the explosion through her window. Alarmed, she got up from her lounging spot in her quarters and ran out of her room.

The Shadows of Peace 77

She bursts onto the bridge. "What the devil is going on out there?" Jane asks, heaving and sucking in air from her run up and down corridors.

"We're…handling a situation," says Xavier with all the tact he can muster.

"Handling a situation?" Jane strides over to Xavier's command station. "Did I see what I think I saw? A wave of light hit the ship!"

"It was some sort of EMP, and it did a number on the shields. But everything else seems fine," Renee says, and many of the crew look at her quizzically. After the time they've had, can anything really be described as "fine"?

The Pax is part of the next generation of warships with one major advancement: the shielding. It's nearly impossible to mount such a sophisticated system to a starship, and most rely only on their armor for protection because of the huge power requirements. For the Pax, these requirements are lower and use exotic materials to power the shield generators. As a result, there's a much greater output of shield protection.

Even still, the shield on the Pax is much weaker than the fortress shield produced by Gaia which utilizes four distinct generators spread around the station. Once activated, the shield provides the shipyard with a protective sphere, able to absorb a tremendous amount of incoming fire from even the most powerful armaments.

"What about the shipyard and the rest of the Assembly? The civilian vessels out there?" Jane asks, placing her hands on her hips. If only she knew what had happened not but a few moments previously. Witnessing that could change a person, and no member of the command crew decides to fill her in just yet.

"Gaia has taken a heavy hit—I'm seeing damage across their systems, and the power signature is much lower than usual. The Assembly vessels in the area are producing distress signals, so whatever that was, it immobilized every ship on our scanners. There are many civilian ships, but I'll check them, too. It's going to take some time," Marie answers in dismay.

"So…we're the only operational Assembly vessel in the area?" Jane is incredulous.

"For the moment," Frederick answers, trying to maintain a sense of calm. "Let's help them get back on their feet. Contact the captains of the other ships—." Before Frederick can finish his sentence, Marie cuts him off.

"Sorry sir, but without power they have no communication outlets. We'll need to do this the old-fashioned way, with transports, and speak to them face-to-face."

Frederick huffs out a frustrated breath. "Alright, in that case, get the Air Wing ready. Leo, move us to the closest ship."

Leo checks his screen to confirm. "The closest ship is the Guardian; it's a small frigate."

"Well, that's as good a place to start as any," says Frederick, weary but pushing through. He looks around the bridge and sees his crew—he's always been proud of them, and this crisis solidifies this belief in them. Everyone is maintaining their professionalism, running to and fro to complete their tasks and responsibilities, following his direction. The Pax will assist the fleet, but it was *his* leadership that allowed them to dispose of the threat.

"Captain, I'm checking the civilian ships, and there's another huge power spike on a different freighter... It's as high as the Golden Key's," Marie suddenly announces from her station.

Frederick's thoughts are interrupted. He assumed the threat was over. "What, another one? How?"

"Actually, I'm seeing four freighters with much higher power levels than normal," Renee adds.

"Four in total? What the hell...? Where are they?" Frederick's quick line of questions belie his panic.

"Spread out around the shipyard. And, including the previous position of the Golden Key, all four were equidistant around Gaia," Marie says, her tone tinged with fear at the realization that this has been a coordinated action... and it's far from over.

"I really don't like where this is going," Frederick says. He turns sharply to Mikhail. "Get a lock on those freighters."

Mikhail is ready for this. "I have all four in our sensors, but only two are in range," he replies.

Xavier jumps into action, anticipating their next move. "Leo, why don't you rotate us so the ventral and dorsal cannons can fire at both targets in range?"

Leo laces his fingers together and cracks his knuckles. One could almost see the nervous energy rolling off him like sparks when a match is struck. "You want a barrel roll, you got it!" He gets to work, pushing the appropriate buttons on his console. His quick flying maneuvers give Mikhail the clean shot he's looking for.

"Captain, I have a clean shot on two other freighters now," Mikhail reports.

Jane has been watching this scene unfold with a mixture of agitation and anxiety. She chooses now to speak up before they can inflict any damage on other ships. She steps closer to Frederick and says quietly, urgently, "Are you sure we should destroy those two freighters? Do we know they're a threat?" Jane attempts to speak as covertly as possible so the crew can neither see nor hear her doubts.

Frederick shakes his head once. "No, Jane. I've already lost too many good people today; I won't let us lose any more. Gaia is practically defenseless now; we need to protect her."

As if to illustrate this point, the Astrohauler—the freighter furthest away—displays exactly why its power has spiked so high. The power has been generated to fuel an ion cannon of its own, and the operators of the freighter have decided to unveil it at this very moment. The freighter fires directly at Gaia shipyards, a blinding white beam that completely destroys one of the shipyard's shield generators, the most potent defense against a threat.

Another beam hits from a different freighter—the StarLift—and it smacks directly into Gaia's command deck, shattering the glass and sending debris in every direction.

The crew of the Pax can only look on in shock, taking in the catastrophe. Everyone falls quiet. Frederick gives Jane a piercing stare, as if to say *Now do you see?* His look burns into Jane, and her cheeks go hot with shame. She breaks the stare first and looks down at the floor.

Frederick turns to Mikhail with a cold fury in his voice. "Destroy the other two freighters. Now."

Mikhail doesn't hesitate. "Firing," he says.

As the ion cannons spool up once again, Frederick moves to the glass window of the bridge and watches the large cannons rotate to face their targets. He hopes these two freighters are the actual threat—he'd never be able to live with himself if he'd unwittingly killed civilians. He tries to shake this thought away, forcing his sense of honor and duty to overtake any feelings of uncertainty and abashment. Through the window, he can see the freighters have already immobilized the rest of the fleet and crippled the shipyard. He only has one option.

The great cannons fire. Within a few blinks of an eye, they hit their targets and cause major damage. The StarLift immediately detonates in a fireball, and the Astrohauler is heavily damaged but somehow still in one piece.

"Fire again, Mikhail," Frederick says.

Xavier asks, "Marie, what's the power level on the Astrohauler?"

Marie checks her screens. "It was as high as the others, but Mikhail has taken the wind from their sails," she replies with gratification.

Mikhail makes a sound of satisfaction. "Ah yes, well perhaps they are too damaged to do anything else," he says.

"We should investigate. Right?" Leo asks, tapping his fingers on his leg.

Frederick nods. "I agree. Get us closer, Leo, and let's see what we find."

"Aye, Captain," says Leo as he makes the move. He positions the Pax right alongside the freighter within moments. Leo sees no movement or power readings from the vessel, and he assumes she's dead, a corpse of a ship.

Renee hums from her station. "Um, again, the configuration doesn't match what we have on record for that vessel, Captain."

"At this point, I'm not surprised," Frederick says. "Someone has tried to destroy the fleet. And without our shield protecting us, they would've easily destroyed us, too."

"Is there anything we can do about the shipyard?" Xavier asks. "Members of Admiralty might've been on the command deck, and we have no way of reaching them."

Frederick turns to his trusted first officer. He knows they must spread their resources thin to recover from this attack and help those on Gaia.

"Xavier, take a transport and some power generators and go help them. Assess the state of the command structure while you're there." Almost as an afterthought, he adds, "And take some marines with you. Inform them of what's happened to the boarding party." He hates to say this last remark, but he knows his marines are strong; they'll have time to deal with the loss later.

Frederick continues with, "Put us in a defensive position around the shipyard, Leo. We can lick our wounds better there."

Xavier prepares to carry out Frederick's order, arranging for a transport and gathering a group of marines so they can investigate what's left of Gaia. The shipyard is barely visible at this range, but the powerful engine of the Pax propels them forward, briskly traversing the distance. The glow of the engines shines as bright as tiny suns. As the Pax begins orbiting the shipyard, the crew can better see the horrible damage—debris floats around the shipyard, and large, glowing plasma clouds have formed at the site of impact. There's a distinct lack of lights from the station.

Frederick paces over to the window to see the shipyard. He stands next to Jane who has wandered here after their heated exchange. They both stare with amazement at the remains of Gaia—something that stood the test of time as a monument to human tenacity now looks to them like a tomb. Both see entire chunks missing from the station, its mangled remains. Frederick thinks of the dead: likely a vast number of people on the command deck, friends and colleagues, wiped out in a second. By whom, and why?

Quickly and quietly, so as not to stoke the flame of emotion within him, he tells Jane of the horrible scene on the Golden Key, now compounded by the destruction at Gaia. He'd rather she hear it from him instead of through the whispers and rumors shared amongst the command crew. Or worse still, if she'd asked about Torrin, oblivious to his fate—that would surely break Frederick. Jane continues to stand at the window, stunned, and Frederick thinks of the painful losses they've just endured.

Renee interrupts his thoughts. "Captain, there are a number of unidentified ships coming through the starway," she says.

Marie corroborates Renee's report. "I see them too, and they're not Assembly. The number's increasing every second."

This sequence of events can't be ignored. Someone or something has shut down every operable ship in the area, destroying the defenses of the shipyard and cutting off the head of the Assembly fleet—all in one effortless action.

"Ships are coming through, but I'm not getting any transponder readings. It's as if these ships don't exist," Marie says in wonderment.

"What do you mean? I can see them plain as day on the sensors." Xavier had been preparing to leave with the marines, finishing his tasks at his command station before heading down to gather the troops. At this remark, however, he stops in his tracks.

"She's right, I count twenty new contacts on sensors, none of which have any transponder codes or configurations that match our records. This entire fleet must've been built outside the Assembly…" Renee is puzzled, much like her crewmembers.

"Who'd have the resources to build a fleet like this?" Jane asks from the window. She hasn't moved a muscle since she saw the destruction of Gaia.

"No one that I know of, unless…it was one of the factions," Xavier says slowly.

"Well, that's a very scary thought," Leo says, verbalizing the fears of the crew as a whole.

"The flow of ships has stopped, and I count fifty," says Marie.

"An even fight, if that is what they want," Mikhail grumbles. This entire episode has ignited his warmongering spirit like never before. He longs to fire another cannon, fingers itching on the proverbial trigger.

"Is it possible they're here to help?" Jane says timidly and gulps, realizing at once how naive she sounds.

Frederick barely looks at her and brushes off her weak attempt at humor. "Considering today's events, Jane, that seems very unlikely," he says. "Mikhail, what's the status of our weapons and shields?"

"All primary and secondary armaments are ready; shields are back up to eighty percent. They could use more time to recharge," Mikhail responds.

"That'll have to do," Frederick says and purses his lips. "I don't think you're going to get much more time."

"Captain," Marie says, sounding a bit uncertain, "We're getting communication from the lead ship. Strangely enough, the communication is coming through in an older format—holographics won't work, only audio."

"Add that to our list of questions for today, but go ahead and send it to me," Frederick says, striding to his station on the bridge. Marie does as she's told, and he's able to answer the voice call within seconds. He says to the speaker, "I'm Captain Frederick of the Assembly vessel Pax Aeterna. Identify yourself."

A male voice on the other end of the line crackles to life. "Captain," it drawls, "you seem tense... Is something the matter?"

Frederick doesn't know the speaker and tries to recall the accent. "I get the feeling you already know what's happened here," he says.

"Do *you* know what's happened here—what's happened to the once proud and illustrious fleet of your great Assembly?" The voice continues sarcastically. "I wonder, if I had fifty warships bearing down and threatening me, I may perhaps send more than just one ship to respond. Are you really all that's left?" The voice asks with obvious fake concern.

Frederick responds with, "You're trespassing in restricted space, and I'm going to insist you turn your armada around and leave." He puts as much power into these words as he can.

"Well, if you insist, of course... But I was thinking, before I leave, as you so specifically requested, I should finish the job." A menacing tone has crept into the disembodied voice's tone. It doesn't sit well with the Pax crew.

"What exactly do you think you're going to finish?" Frederick asks.

"The destruction of the Assembly fleet, of course," the voice says, as if it were obvious. Everyone on the bridge falls silent, waiting with bated breath for the next words from Frederick and the voice.

"Why would you want that? We don't even know who you are." Frederick says, knitting his eyebrows together in bafflement.

"Did I not introduce myself? Ah, where are my manners? I am Imperator Shen Sato," the voice says slowly, ominously. "I rule the Eastern League, and we've been waiting for this day for centuries, preparing for the opportunity to cause the same pain to Earth as they've caused us," Shen says, and members of the bridge gasp.

Frederick needs more information. He mutes the call and says to Xavier, "I want as many scans as you can get on those ships; everything, right now." Turning back to the speaker, Frederick unmutes and attempts to stall, as every extra minute he buys might allow Xavier to gather more information on his opponent.

"And you think killing hundreds of innocent men, women, and children will accomplish—what exactly?" Frederick asks, trying to throw Shen off and keep him talking, to desperately buy some time.

On the other end of the line, Shen continues speaking. "Pain, only pain is what we want. After the third world war, we suffered immeasurably. We became the lowest of the low, only privileged enough to be your slaves, your workers. You worked many of our people to death."

"That was hundreds of years ago, the Eastern League hasn't had a worker on Earth since we lost the Odyssey," Frederick replies.

Shen laughs, and everyone can hear his contempt. His next words express what they all suspect. "You didn't lose the Odyssey, we took it. We went far away with a glorious purpose: to return one day and educate you on what that pain and suffering created. We simply want to feel the warmth of Earth burning as we ascend to guide the galaxy into a new era."

"You'll have to get through us first," Frederick replies with ferocity. "You may have crippled the shipyard, but our forces are numerous, and they're spread far and wide. Do you expect the rest of the fleet to just wave a white flag?"

Shen seems to have an answer for every one of Frederick's questions. "Of course not, Captain!" He says with mock civility. "I expect them to explode violently under the weight of our resolve. If you don't think we have the location of every base and facility, then you don't understand the level of our determination. We've been gone for centuries—what did you think we were doing?"

Shen suddenly sighs as if the whole conversation bores him. "But alas, I grow tired of this now. I will, however, show you a kindness and allow you to watch as we destroy your precious shipyard, the remnant of your infallible fleet, before we put you out of your misery. I'll make it quick." Before Frederick can respond, Shen cuts communication.

The Eastern League warships must've been awaiting his cue. Most of them are small, nimble destroyers with a few larger cruisers, all of which are diminutive when compared to the Pax. They begin to break formation, launching missile weapons and high caliber ballistic cannons at their targets. Inexplicably, they don't fire at the Pax.

One large warship of similar size to the Pax sits at the center of the fleet. Frederick presumes this must be Shen's flagship, and so he makes a decision: this'll be their target.

"Mikhail, are we in range of the central warship?" Frederick asks.

"Yes, Captain, but regrettably he has positioned other vessels between us. We must destroy those vessels first," says Mikhail.

Exhausted and running on pure adrenaline, Frederick scrubs at his eyes. Nevertheless, he knows what must be done. "Then do so, Mikhail. Target the nearest vessel and fire with the secondary batteries. Keep trying to hit that ship, give it everything you've got."

Mikhail engages all the Pax's weapons, though Frederick knows this is a hopeless stand. Maybe they can inflict as much damage as possible on the Eastern League's ship. A part of him wonders if he should save the fight for another day.

Too late for such thoughts. The ion cannons fire with a blinding flash of light, and both shots impact the two vessels protecting the large battleship at the center. Shen is taunting him, sitting barely within weapons range, still just out of reach.

"Keep firing, Mikhail! Leo, get us moving," Frederick says, letting the anxiety take him over as he senses the potential for total annihilation of his beloved ship and doom for his crew.

Mikhail waits for the ion cannons to recharge so he can fire again, and Frederick has plenty of time to observe the decimation befalling his once glorious fleet: disabled ships take hit after hit from the Eastern League, and explosions engulf vessels one by one. The vessels docked at the shipyard are now nothing but scrap metal. With every second that passes, Frederick's position becomes more dire. Though he's reluctant to do so, he has to make the call.

"Leo, charge the hyperspace engines, we have to get out of here," Frederick says heavily. His anxiety is now peppered with shame.

"What about the fleet?" Leo asks in bewilderment. "We're the only ones standing between them and annihilation!"

"We'll be no good to anyone dead. If we stay here, we all know what'll happen." Frederick closes his eyes. This is the toughest decision he's had to make in his entire life.

Xavier hates to go against his captain, but he concurs with Leo. "There might be a lot of them, but we have the better ship. I believe we should stay."

Mikhail sides with Xavier and Leo, too. "I have already taken out a couple," he says, hoping to change Frederick's mind. "I will make them pay for this," he mumbles, more to himself than anyone else.

Fredcrick shakes his head no. "We must save ourselves," he says. "Leo, get us out of here now."

"This isn't right," Leo says, hesitating to fly the ship; this is a new experience for him—going against his captain, no eagerness to fly. "We shouldn't leave people to die."

"Would you rather join them?" Frederick's nerves are brittle, and he's almost at a breaking point. He shouts at his crew. "I've given my orders—carry them out!"

Jane tries to reason with him from her spot at the window. "Are you sure this is the right thing to do, Frederick?"

Her words only add fuel to Frederick's fire, his temper unfettered and unfiltered. "Don't you want to see Marcus one more time, Jane, or would you rather he attends your funeral instead?" He sneers.

Jane falters, taking a step back. She understands Frederick is in the heat of the moment, but she's unable to forgive his harsh words.

"Mikhail, you get one more ion cannon shot. Target the closest ship and fire when ready," Frederick says. Mikhail mutely does as he's told, firing another shot at the Eastern League. This last shot causes a few Eastern League vessels to detonate, creating massive explosions.

"Leo, jump. I don't care where, just get us out of here," Frederick demands.

"Blind jump it is, let's see where the hell we go," Leo says, trying to shake off the earlier dispute. "I hope you know what you're doing," he mutters under his breath.

Frederick hears this and mentally says, *Me too.*

The Pax opens a hyperspace entry point and is soon swallowed by the portal, exiting Sol. The crew has no idea what's in store for them next, nor where they'll end up. The only thing they know for sure is they'll be going to war.

ACT II

"Loyalty binds the stars together; without it, there is only darkness."
— *Galactic Assembly Codex, Article II: Inter-Faction Relations*

Chapter Eleven

Glowing pulses from the hyperdrive engines recede into the dark void of space. The Pax has escaped from her imminent doom, and Shen looks upon her retreat from his position on the bridge of his ship, the Harbinger of Dawn. He sits in his elaborate throne overlooking the operations of his ship, and his officers scurry around carrying out his previous orders: cripple the warfighting capacity of the Assembly, starting with its beating heart, Gaia shipyard. Shen has been careful to keep the presence of the Eastern League concealed to the universe and out of the limelight. Until now.

He'd accounted for countless possibilities but not the Pax's presence at the battle; he thought the ship was still occupied in the Wolf system. He watches the rest of the one-sided battle unfold; eyes glued to the scene as vessel after vessel of his sworn enemy blink from existence with a brutal flash of destruction. He can sense his success and victory—a victory generations in the making—looming closer. Soon, only the defenseless shipyard is left.

Shen signals his trusted Prime Juan Logian, crooking his index finger lazily. Juan is, as always, at attention, awaiting his next order, and he sees Shen's gesture in an instant. Juan quickly covers the distance of the bridge to join Shen.

"Imperator, the Assembly fleet has been completely destroyed, and the shipyard is defenseless, as you ordered," Juan reports.

"That's good news, Juan," Shen replies, a smirk unfurling from thin lips. "Everything is going according to plan."

"What about the Pax Aeterna?" Juan asks with a crinkle in his brow. "Should we go after them? They weren't meant to be here; they might come back..." He trails off, not wanting to overstep.

Shen strokes his chin. "Their retreat, while seemingly hasty and uncoordinated, reveals their fear. They abandoned their allies, and we've significantly depleted their forces—by a third, no less. This provides us with an advantageous position for our approach towards

Earth. However, it would be a critical oversight to underestimate their capacity for a counter-movement."

He continues, "Upon their attempt to consolidate what remains of their forces, they'll confront a reality far grimmer than any they might've anticipated. Our centuries of patience will culminate not in rash action but in calculated retribution. This moment, strategically awaited, heralds the culmination of our long-sought justice," Shen ends his fervent speech, a light sheen of sweat evident on his brow.

Juan feels he must press his point. "Imperator, the Pax is the last threat to your dream of retribution... Her survival casts doubt on your success, does it not? There are traitors among us who may use this against you—are you sure it's wise to let them go?" He asks.

Shen considers for a moment in silence. Eventually he shrugs, steadfast in his original approach. "A risk we'll take," he says, "because Earth is the prize, and we *will* focus on it."

Juan nods and asks eagerly, "What are your next orders, Imperator?"

Shen pauses as if to mentally run through his playbook of sequential steps. His plans are slow but deliberate, and his mind is his most dangerous weapon. For the Eastern League, the last two centuries have been a fight for existence, and Shen has armed himself with strategy, precision, and confidence. His acuity in these areas ensures he's at least ten steps ahead of every problem.

After another beat of silence, Shen says, "It's imperative that we dismantle the Assembly's strategic foundations, commencing with this shipyard. By methodically compromising its infrastructure, we ensure its transformation into nothing more than debris. This'll significantly undermine their operational capabilities and mark the beginning of their end." He smiles to himself, his mouth a sharp semi-circle.

"As you wish, Imperator," Juan says with a curt nod.

At Shen's order, all guns are trained on every inch of Gaia. The shipyard is already engulfed in flames, a darkness where light once abounded. Debris crashes from the annihilated fleet. Shen considers it an act of mercy to put the crippled facility out of her misery. Like a chorus of base instruments, the barrels of the Eastern League's fleet light up once more; shots impact Gaia. The foundation of the shipyard absorbs hammer blow after hammer blow, and the once mighty station is reduced to smolders. Almost poetically, the shipyard that was constructed to build the Odyssey is destroyed by the return of its crews' descendants.

Juan once again looks to Shen for his next orders. "Imperator, the shipyard has fallen to our guns. Your plan is one step closer," he says with both deference and awe.

"Excellent!" Shen claps his hands together loudly, barely able to control his glee. "While we anticipate the Pax and her captain's next move, we'll cleanse this system before moving on to Earth."

"Of course, Imperator." Juan bows his head in deference once again.

Though Shen usually chooses to remain stoic, he can't help but let his happiness show. Another menacing smile pierces his facial features, inadvertently lowering his defenses for a short moment. His confidence is as high as it's ever been, and he thinks of every possible permutation of what the Pax crew would and could do next, believing it likely that they'll seek out any allies to help them return to Sol.

Rising slowly from his throne, Shen makes his way to the rear of the bridge. He passes walls adorned with relics of the past—relics from another time when the Eastern League was nothing more than a workforce for Earth. These are painful reminders of the Eastern League's history, including a signed copy of the peace declaration that ended the third global conflict which decimated Earth's population—a war instigated by the Eastern League, in fact. The declaration was signed by the major powers that survived, and today those same powers hold dominion over the stars…and relegated Shen's people to second class citizens in the past.

Shen regards the relics as he walks, considering their presence as reminders of a past that's best left forgotten: an ancient bow from the Mongol empire, part of the Heiji Monogatari Emaki scroll, and a jade seal once thought to belong to an emperor. Members of the Eastern League use them as fuel to their flames—propaganda that inspires blind devotion. The rest of the galaxy wouldn't understand these relics as they can barely comprehend the Eastern League's history. Shen pauses his steps for a brief moment to remind himself what he's fighting for, the meaning behind all this destruction. He shakes himself out of the past and, nonplussed once more, continues on his way.

Chapter Twelve

The crew of the Pax are reeling from a scenario for which they were never prepared, an enemy that shouldn't exist...and a captain that may very well have doomed their friends and colleagues to certain death. The ship may be safe from its newfound enemy while in hyperspace, but the crew is certainly not immune from each other's judgment. Anger and uncertainty, thick as a thundercloud, swirl around the bridge as the crew continue to their unknown destination. The ambience of hyperspace provides a glow over the bridge officers as they voice their thoughts.

"So...now what, Captain?" Leo asks sharply. He doesn't quite know what to say without sounding callous, and he's afraid his voice might break. He clears his throat and adjusts the collar of his uniform, seemingly too tight.

"I... I have no idea," Fredrick says with an element of nervousness. He's lightyears away from the confident man he was but a day ago. He must become a new, different sort of man.

Leo is agitated; he expects his captain to be more direct, to simply *know* what to do, never mind that this situation is anything but expected. "You have no plan," Leo says. Everyone on the bridge can hear an undercurrent of distress in his voice.

"Not yet, no," says Frederick slowly, trying to keep his composure. It's taking all his strength and concentration to balance his own emotions after their devastating loss. If only Leo would stop pummeling him with questions.

"You let our friends and colleagues die for no reason!" Leo's voice rises in pitch, hysteria threatening to take him over. He bangs his fist on his console.

Frederick is taken aback. "Does your own life mean so little to you?" He asks in consternation.

Xavier considers interjecting at this point, but the words don't come. His mind is abuzz with thoughts of Gaia, members of the crew that didn't make it back. No rousing speech from him could make this situation better. He remains quiet, listening to this exchange unfold while standing stiffly at his and Frederick's shared terminal.

Now the tears do fall, tumbling down Leo's cheeks. "I would rather die knowing I tried to save as many as we could."

Jane sees the tears and pushes herself to move. She walks toward Leo and places her hand gently on his shoulder, giving it a squeeze in solidarity and comfort. Leo doesn't shrug it off, grateful for the human contact.

Frederick shakes his head. He can't let his authority continue to erode. He trains a steady, direct gaze at Leo. "If *we* were among the dead, what would stand between the fleet and Earth?" He's not expecting an answer.

"We have the greater firepower," says Mikhail delicately, the gruffness having been sucked from his tone after the past few harrowing hours.

"Do you really think you could've taken on their whole fleet, Mikhail?" Frederick puts his head in his hands. "How delusional—."

Mikhail cuts him off, jutting out his lower lip in defiance. "I would have tried, at least."

"We're cowards, you've turned us into cowards...," an enraged Marie says from her station.

"Alright, that's enough!" Frederick's face has turned a bright, tomato red. "I get it. You all wanted to stay and do what you could, very honorable," He sneers. "What then?" He pauses to look around the room at each officer individually like a predator about to pounce on its prey. "What then?" Frederick repeats himself, his speech a crescendo. The silence of the crew makes his voice seem even louder.

Frederick enunciates each word, hoping reality will sink into the minds and hearts of his crew. He lets this moment resonate with them before continuing, saying sternly, "I made a decision. It may not have aligned with your views, but it afforded us an opportunity to avert a dire outcome. As long as the Pax remains operational, we retain the capability to resist!" Frederick brings his right fist down on the open palm of his left hand for emphasis. "Our recent encounter likely only scratches the surface of Shen's arsenal. We have to anticipate other unforeseen challenges—this battle is only the beginning. Starting today, we're at *war*, and our immediate course is to regroup and heal our wounds." Frederick finishes with a touch of arrogance, daring anyone to contradict his authority.

Marie swipes at her face roughly, hoping no one has seen her look of anguish at what's just occurred. The devastating loss, Frederick's decision, her own feelings of unease. She speaks up now, clearing her throat to remind Frederick of their harsh reality.

"Captain, we're dangerously low on resources, we barely had any time to restock. We've only got, at most, a week's worth of food and water…"

Renee jumps into the conversation, having sat mutely up until this point as her fellow crew members exchanged harsh words over and around her head. "We're going to need to find out where we are first. Captain, do you remember that you…*requested* we do a blind jump…?" Renee emphasizes the word *request* knowing full well it was an order, one she feels was given without enough thought and consideration for the unknown. "We could be headed, well, anywhere." A crinkle forms between her eyebrows.

Frederick sighs but knows what Renee says is logical and true. He asks, "Leo, any idea where we might be heading?"

Shaking his head, Leo looks at his console, not wanting to meet Frederick's eye just now. "It was a blind jump—we won't have any idea where we are until we transition back into normal space. And without the navigation computer prepared, there's no way we'll be able to see ahead." Leo runs one hand through his hair and mutters, "We're basically blind, maybe you should've thought about that."

Frederick catches the undertone of bitter annoyance in Leo's tone and raises his eyebrows. He's certainly not used to this petulant version of his pilot. "Today is full of surprises," Frederick says to no one in particular.

At that very moment, the Pax transitions into normal space. Perfect timing. Frederick and the crew stare out of the bridge's window and behold the sight: they appear to be at the edge of a binary star system with two raging suns at its center.

"Alright, let's try that again," Frederick says, turning to look at his pilot. "Leo, where in God's name are we?" He demands.

Leo interacts with his console, trying to pinpoint their location "It's taking a second, hang on." He peers at his screen. "Uh, looks like the Lumina Dyad system," he adds begrudgingly, "sir."

"Well, at least we'll be alone for a moment." Frederick takes a breath and says quietly, "There's nothing out here but asteroids…"

With watery eyes rimmed red, Jane speaks from her place on the bridge. She hasn't really been able to breathe since everything happened, since the sting of Frederick's words and his decisions changed her entire world. "We should get ahold of Marcus," she says, a slight warble coming through. "See if Gaia was just the beginning. If anything, his battlegroup can help us."

"Having the support of some friends right now would go a long way," Marie pipes up in agreement, giving Jane comfort in the little way she can. The atmosphere on the bridge is electrically charged as everyone begins to process the here and now. Emotions are still high, and Marie can sense that. Whatever she can say or do to calm her crew mates, she'll do it willingly.

Frederick tries to catch Jane's eye, but her gaze slides away toward the floor, the wall—anywhere but at him. "I agree," Frederick says. "We'll contact Marcus and request he rendezvous with us so we can determine a viable strategy against this new foe of ours." Jane nods in response, still avoiding eye contact with Frederick.

"Marie," Frederick continues, optimistic that things are getting back on track. "Can you put them through to our holotable?" Frederick is beginning to feel like his old self again.

"They're still in the Colorado system, Marie, so you know how to contact them," Jane says, looking over at Marie's station.

Marie responds with, "I'll attempt to contact the ship now." She begins to make the connection, tinkering with her console, and the call finally goes through to the ASC Intrepid.

The Intrepid is Commodore Anatoly's flagship, a Protector class cruiser currently leading a small flotilla comprised of a variety of vessels in the sector defense fleet: one other cruiser, the ASC Valiant; three destroyers called Shadowblade, Iron Wrath, and Lightning's Fist; and two frigates named the Celestial Spear and Speculator Aetheris. Frederick thinks to himself, if he could assemble these forces, it would be a strong start to forming a resistance against the Eastern League.

Marie announces to the bridge from her station, "I have a connection, Captain. Patching Marcus through to the central command console."

Marcus's head and shoulders appear on the holodisplay, close to Frederick and Xavier's shared station. Jane hovers nearby.

"Frederick, it's been a while. I hope you're looking after the pride of the fleet," Marcus says tightly, remembering his conversation with Jane not but a few hours ago.

"Marcus, have you had any communication from Gaia or any other Assembly vessel in the last few hours?" Frederick asks curtly.

"Straight to the point, I see." Marcus's mouth twists into a frown for a split second before he remembers his audience. He spies Jane in the background, behind Frederick and Xavier, and he knows he must appear aloof and strong, relying on his strict military training to smoother all emotion. He transforms his facial features into a mask of neutrality and detachment. "No, I haven't heard anything. It's been quiet over here, and in fact, we haven't had any communication from the Assembly for at least a week or so. We were scheduled to return to Gaia in a few days…" Marcus sees the stricken looks on Frederick, Xavier, and Jane's faces. "Why do I get the feeling I'm missing something?" He asks.

Frederick doesn't answer immediately, pausing to compose himself before unloading the horrible truth on Marcus. He tries to remain professional, putting on a brave face for his fellow officers. "It seems our history books are, how can I put this…not as accurate as we would've liked. The Eastern League has returned en force, and Gaia—as well as the supporting fleet—were obliterated within minutes by their armada." Frederick picks his words carefully.

"What are you talking about, Frederick?" Marcus wants to laugh, so sure this is a joke. His look is one of disbelief. "You're insane, there is absolutely no plausible way—."

"It's true," Jane interjects before Marcus can finish his sentence.

Marcus blinks in bewilderment. "Jane, is that you?" He asks.

Jane nods, a sympathetic look on her face. She hopes Marcus will listen to her and believe. "Everything Frederick said is true—we just witnessed each vessel at Gaia, as well as Gaia's defenses, get completely annihilated within moments. We're likely the only survivors."

"What do you mean, the only survivors…?" Marcus refuses to comprehend, a knot of dread forming in the pit of his stomach. He knows Jane wouldn't lie to him, but he can't just trust these outlandish claims. It's Gaia, for God's sake! How could anything dismantle the Assembly's stronghold, their beacon of hope?

"Did you see the shipyard destroyed or not?" He asks harshly. Marcus is confused and feels overloaded with information.

"We were the only operational vessel, we had to blind jump before we were overwhelmed… There was nothing else we could've done," Jane replies solemnly. She casts her eyes down in remembrance of those who have recently fallen.

Marcus nods, contemplative. "I see." He clears his throat, business-like once more. "Let's say I believe you—what happens next?" He poses the question to all of them, looking at Jane, Frederick, and Xavier.

Frederick takes this moment to speak. "Marcus, I talked to a man named Shen before the battle. He announced himself as the leader of the Eastern League. This act of violence is only the beginning." Frederick tries to remain as calm as possible while speaking, though dredging up memories of the destruction of just a few moments ago is cracking his cool exterior. He goes on, saying, "You don't waltz into Sol with that large of a fleet and not continue to Earth. There's much more going on here than we currently know." Frederick heaves out the last sentence, emotions getting the better of him.

"Spit it out Frederick, what do you want from me?" Marcus is visibly agitated, but there's not much he can do via the hologram but watch, listen, and wait for Frederick's response.

Xavier places his hands on either side of his station and leans forward towards Marcus's holographic bust. He says intently, "It's clear we're at a disadvantage. The Pax is the strongest vessel in the fleet, but Shen is sure to try and take us off the board. It'd be best for you and the rest of the Colorado sector defense fleet to join us since we can assume the Eastern League already knows the location of our forces. It's only a matter of time before they come for you." Xavier's eyes are wide open, imploring Marcus to listen and fearful for what might happen if he doesn't.

"You want us to leave our post, now? There are billions of people here we're meant to be protecting!" Marcus's voice is loud.

"And *who* will you be protecting if the Eastern League ambushes and destroys you, Captain? Who will you protect from beyond the grave?" Frederick's crass words do their best to antagonize Marcus, his questions lingering in the air like a bad stench as his peer hooks him with a level gaze through the holodisplay.

"If they do show up, I'll answer their aggression with my own." Marcus raises his chin in defiance.

Frederick grunts and says, "If *I'm* wrong, you get to say I've been an idiot and I've dragged you out of your position for a few days. If *you're* wrong…well, I suppose then *you* would be responsible for the death of every living soul you're meant to be protecting." Frederick's eyes flash. "We need to act sooner rather than later."

With a deep sigh, Marcus contemplates his decision. He runs his hands down his face and attempts to mentally quell his confusion. Does he abandon his post, disregard his duty, and follow Frederick, placing his career in Frederick's hands? He continues to think.

Decision made, he replies to Frederick and the crew of the Pax. "You know, when I woke up this morning and wondered how my day would go, this wasn't even close to what I envisioned. But, I hear your comments and your earnest tone." Though he doesn't show it on his face, he's impressed that Frederick was able to persuade him. Of course, Jane's presence might've helped with that…

"Alright Captain, we'll join you. The Intrepid will make its way to your location, but I'll need to talk to Anatoly and convince the whole fleet. You understand, that's not my call to make, but I'll recommend the fleet leave as soon as possible. Where the devil are you now?" Marcus sits back, relieved he's made a decision with a doable action.

Frederick nods at Marcus's response, inwardly glad and relieved, too, for the help. "We're in Lumina Dyad, and we seem to be the only entity here. You've made the right choice, and we'll debrief you on the Pax. We have recordings of our communication with Shen—we'll let you and Anatoly listen once you arrive, but we'll go radio silent now so as not to not draw any unwanted attention."

"I look forward to our meeting in person. Intrepid out," Marcus says. His face and shoulders disappear as the connection is cut.

The bridge is quiet. Frederick looks around and realizes his crew were watching and listening to the conversation unfold. He reminds himself that they're inexperienced, having been thrown into this situation wholly unprepared. They acted on raw emotion rather than relying on their training.

Turning to Xavier, Frederick says, "Let's get some food. We have a few things to discuss." At this point, Frederick thinks Xavier might be his best and only ally. His request for a meal companion was less a question than an order.

"Lead the way," Xavier smoothly replies. He knows Frederick is trying to be cautious, hoping to both reconfirm his authority and reassure his crew.

Frederick points sharply over to the next highest-ranking officer, Mikhail, and says tightly, "The bridge is yours."

Mikhail blinks slowly, nodding faintly in acknowledgement. Both Frederick and Xavier move with vigor to the NovaPath at the back of the bridge. Frederick selects deck four, his favorite of the mess halls on the Pax as it boasts wondrous views for crewmembers to behold while enjoying gourmet meals. Frederick thinks back to his memories of the mess halls, crew members filling every seat. He wonders how many chairs will now sit empty, their former occupants unable to ever take in the beautiful views again.

Xavier uses this short ride as an opportunity to speak candidly. He has a lot to get off his chest. "It's been a long few hours, Captain," he begins.

"Xavier, please—we need to talk honestly. Drop the 'captain,' would you?" Frederick implores.

Xavier hangs his head. "You're right…Frederick, I still feel very uneasy about what we did at Gaia. All those people, colleagues, friends! It doesn't sit right with me that we survived while they were given no choice, no chance."

"I feel your pain, Xavier, and know that it wasn't an easy decision for me. It's my job to do what's best for our crew," Frederick replies emphatically. He thinks about all the people he saw that day and the service members he called friends. "We need to organize something for Commander Vale. The rest of the marines are surely grieving after the loss of their commanding officer and fellow soldiers." Losing them is still a hard truth to swallow.

Xavier pulls out his cos-link to make note of the items Frederick wants completed. He also sends instructions to the officers in his command, ensuring the captain's orders are carried out. "I'll organize the crew to assemble on the flight deck before the Intrepid arrives," he says. "It might be best for you to address the whole crew, let them know what's going on. I'm sure there will be whispers…" Xavier's job as first officer is first and foremost to be a sounding board for his captain, making sure Frederick is held accountable. It allows Frederick to focus on the big picture.

"Thank you, Xavier, and I'll write a speech." Frederick pauses and taps his chin, thinking of other items that need doing. "I also need you to get me an inventory of everything we have, a full list. I know we're low on supplies and we weren't able to restock, but I need to know how bad it is. When we fight the League again, we need to be ready."

Xavier types away. "Marie can help me with that," he says.

The doors fling themselves open, and Xavier looks up from his cos-link, pocketing the device for now. The pair walk with purpose to the observation lounge; it's only a short jaunt from the NovaPath, and they pass the occasional crew member along the way.

Frederick breaks the silence. "Xavier, did you know Marie was planning to leave the Pax and retire from the fleet once we finished our last mission? I'll find a moment to speak with her. She likely isn't feeling great about being stuck with us indefinitely now."

"We're all going to need more time to adjust to this new reality. No one is prepared, and emotions are high. Regardless, we all of us understand our duty, and we want to protect our way of life." Xavier replies.

They enter the empty lounge; the aesthetic mirrors the rest of the vessel. A large piece of glass at one end shows the forward view of the vessel positioned several decks below the bridge. Lumina A and its sun provide a stunning backdrop, and the pair stop in their tracks to gaze at the beautiful scene. It's a timely reminder of the positivity and beauty yet to be found in space, though both feel ill at ease at this notion, considering what they've just endured.

"Isn't *this* what we're meant to be doing out here?" Frederick asks, musing.

"What do you mean?" Xavier questions, still staring at the picturesque scene.

"I'm not sure I've ever told you this, but all I ever wanted to do was become an explorer," Frederick says wistfully. "I wanted nothing more than to gallivant across the stars." He breaks himself away from the stunning sight and his imagined future, Xavier following a few steps behind.

They walk over to the other side of the lounge, filled with pre-cooked meals the chefs have prepared for the day, to collect their food. Frederick selects a steak meal, and Xavier picks the chicken. They proceed to sit at one of the many small tables that fill the room.

Xavier continues the conversation thread from earlier. "I think you told me a while ago that you'd prefer to be an explorer. Didn't you want to try and find a new planet that'd be perfect to colonize?"

Still fixated on the view of the sun, Frederick replies distractedly, "I wanted to do something that would make a difference, somewhere I could help humanity." He waves his fork around, a mouthful of steak dangling from its end. "All I've ever wanted was to feel like I've been of service. I thought the unknown wonders of space would present something to me, and the longer I looked, the more optimistic I became. Until today, I've held out hope that the universe would present an option to me. I guess, in an odd way, it has…" Frederick stops talking to chew his food.

Xavier wipes his mouth, neat and tidy as always. "We have the most powerful ship in the galaxy, and Shen will hunt us. He knows while we exist, we're a threat. Before this saga is over, there'll be a lot of people that need our help. It might not be the way you want to be remembered, but we have the opportunity to do some good now."

Frederick looks down at his plate. "I fear you might be right." He laughs a sharp laugh. "My thoughts of exploration thus far have been nothing more than a young man's day dreams. I doubt Shen's sudden appearance will be the last surprise in store for us. I'm not sure I've ever asked why you joined the fleet, Xavier." Frederick changes the subject mid-chew and looks up.

"I've never liked bullies," Xavier says primly. "In my youth, I was never the biggest, and I grew up in the… *grittier* parts of New York. I wanted to fight for everyone's freedom, keep Earth safe and secure. To be honest, I feel like I've failed." Xavier spreads his hands out in front of him. "Every second *we're* safe is a moment everyone *else* is at risk. I know Earth's iron shield will be able to hold for a while, but we need to make Shen pay for what he did."

Frederick responds in earnest. "We *will* return, Xavier, but we need to be ready. Our only accomplishment if we return without enough force or intelligence would be to add to the list of the fallen. I won't let us end that way." Almost to emphasize his meaning, Frederick slices his knife through his remaining piece of steak.

"You might not have a choice in that," Xavier says.

Chapter Thirteen

On the bridge of the ASC Intrepid, Marcus prepares to discuss his choice to join the Pax in Lumina Dyad. The Intrepid is an older ship, designed before the Pax as a heavy cruiser for long distance patrol missions. The Intrepid is, however, only half the size of the Pax and ultimately pales in comparison. Like most Assembly warships, it has a slender, symmetric, arrowhead design with large, conventional, ballistic weapons populating the hull. There's a superstructure to the rear which gives the bridge a great view of their surroundings. Though the Intrepid doesn't sport as much new and advanced technology as the Pax, it's still considered a powerful warship.

The bridge of the Intrepid is much more compact than the Pax but has an adjacent room for the command crew to use for operational purposes. Commodore Anatoly has been using this room as his office; as commodore, he commands the Colorado sector defense fleet. The Colorado sector is one of the more populated United Coalition systems with a handful of densely inhabited planets; its population is now approaching two billion.

Anatoly knew that, with his family name behind him, he could prove to Admiralty his leadership qualities and thus quickly move up the ranks of the fleet in no time. Marcus, however, knows a different truth and hates being under Anatoly's charge. Walking into Anatoly's office, he's at first a little nervous to have this conversation. He's not sure how Anatoly will react.

Hearing Marcus's footsteps, Anatoly looks up from the screen on his makeshift desk and barks, "What do you want, Marcus?"

Marcus takes a deep breath and says, "Commodore, we just had a strange communication from Captain Langfield of the Pax."

"Oh? What did he want? I don't remember any communications on the agenda today," Anatoly says, perplexed.

"Nothing was planned," Marcus says. "He contacted us from the Lumina Dyad System."

"Strange place to be… There's nothing there of interest. Surely nothing for the pride of the fleet." Anatoly laughs a sarcastic chuckle.

"They say the Eastern League has returned and decimated the fleet at Gaia. Eastern League ships have destroyed the station, and the crew of the Pax were the only survivors." Marcus braces himself for the impact of Anatoly's incredulity.

"Marcus, have you been drinking again? That's the craziest nonsense I've ever heard!" Anatoly's chuckle has become a barrel laugh, his face turning red.

Marcus shifts his weight from one foot to the other, uncomfortable with this discussion. "Sir, I'm not sure it's a story. Frederick and the rest of the crew seemed very on edge; something wasn't right. They requested we join them and plan out our next steps."

Anatoly wipes tears from his eyes, the laughter finally subsiding. "They can request us to fly into a black hole—we aren't doing that either! It must be some sort of joke from Admiralty, or a test."

"Actually, I tried to contact Gaia after the conversation with Frederick, and I couldn't get through to fleet command at all. Don't you think that's a little odd?" Marcus asks.

Anatoly stares at Marcus in disbelief. "That's unusual but by no means unheard of, let me try and reach Pacifica." Anatoly holds up one finger and turns to his console. Marcus rolls his eyes, glad to be out of Anatoly's direct line of sight.

Using his console to open communication with Gaia, Anatoly doesn't get a connection, and stranger still, he's not able to communicate with anyone at the shipyard. He slams his console with his fist in frustration.

"The admiral *always* picks up for me," he mutters. "While that's out of the ordinary, it doesn't mean a spirit has returned from the dead and our fleet is in shambles." Anatoly shakes his head, trying to make sense of the situation.

"But what if it does?" Marcus asks. "I truly sensed the fear in Frederick's voice."

"It's a real stretch, Marcus. Are you thinking clearly? And what would you have me do? We have orders to stay and patrol the system," Anatoly says, sounding like a petulant teenager rather than a competent commodore.

"We could use it as a drill to respond to a vessel in distress. Leave one of our escorts here, maybe the Iron Wrath, and deploy the rest of the fleet. Let's meet with Frederick, and we can discuss what's happened. If it's nothing, we can come back. If there are any issues here, the Wrath can contact us, and we'll return immediately." Marcus hopes this is a clear path forward, mentally urging Anatoly to take the compromise.

"That's a tall ask," Anatoly says slowly, thinking. He rubs his chin and sits back in his chair. "Get me Frederick, I want to talk to him myself."

Marcus shakes his head. "The Pax has gone radio silent—they don't want to expose their position."

Anatoly thinks for a moment, then accepts Marcus's statement. "I suppose we haven't had much to do recently. It might be good to get the crew's blood racing!" To Marcus's surprise, Anatoly stabs the air with his index finger and points to Marcus's chest. "Very well. Sort out the specifics, but if this is a wild goose chase and it comes back to bite me, you'll be the first to know."

"Understood," Marcus says. He leaves Anatoly's office and rushes back to the bridge to arrange the fleet and organize their departure. The officers on the bridge under his command stop and stare for a second, wondering about this mysterious plan; some were eavesdropping, overhearing the conversation between Marcus and Frederick. Though they were purposefully kept in the dark, many gleaned that something terrible had happened.

Once at his console, Marcus contacts all ships at once, bringing them up on his screen so they can discuss the upcoming operation. It takes some time for the captains to complete their planning, but with persuasion from Marcus and the blessing of Anatoly, they're all on the same page. ACS Iron Wrath will remain behind and forward any issues back to the Intrepid. The rest of the fleet will proceed in formation to the Lumina Dyad system to join the Pax, just as Frederick hoped.

Although Anatoly is technically in command, Marcus is the real brains of the fleet and has gained the respect of the captains and crew. He always listens to their viewpoints and treats everyone with the same respect he wishes to receive. Anatoly, on the other hand, is more concerned with his image, reputation, and the opinions held by the higher ranks of Admiralty rather than the day-to-day operations of the fleet. Marcus contemplates this as he wonders whether what Frederick, Jane, and Xavier said is true. If it is, it means Anatoly will be forced to step up and allow the fleet to be used correctly—not just for his own selfish, self-serving needs.

Frederick would soon be flanked by reinforcements, but he still has a long way to go to collect the pieces of his crew and put them back together, Marcus thinks to himself. He'll have to inspire them to move forward with a new mission—returning to Earth and defeating the nefarious Eastern League forces.

Chapter Fourteen

Back on the Pax, Xavier organizes the bridge crew as they make their way to the flight deck; this deck is the largest section of the ship and accommodates the entire crew. He's been working to proofread Frederick's speech and thus far has been able to hide his feelings of fear and despair. Deep down, though, Xavier is afraid of what's to come. He wonders if this'll be the first of many eulogies he'll read in the next few days. Xavier straightens his uniform and plasters on a neutral yet friendly face for all to see.

Taking his position and his script from Xavier, Frederick stands in front of his command crew and prepares to speak about their fallen commander, Torrin Vale, and the future of the Pax. The solemnity of the moment is reflected in his demeanor.

"Ladies and gentlemen of the Pax Aeterna," he begins, his voice resonating with a deep sense of loss and respect, "We gather together in the aftermath of a profound tragedy. We've lost not only our esteemed Commander Torrin Vale but also brave souls who stood by him—our colleagues, crew, friends, family, and everyone on Gaia."

Frederick pauses for a moment, and his words hang in the air as the reality of his statement settles over the room. The crew shares a moment of silent mourning for those who gave their all, as well as those who were caught unaware by the onslaught of firepower from the Eastern League.

Frederick continues, "These valiant individuals who laid down their lives did so with the unshakeable belief in the preservation of the Assembly and in safeguarding peace for Earth and its colonies. Their sacrifice is a stark reminder of the price of peace and the cost of the security we strive to ensure every day."

Frederick's gaze sweeps across the room, meeting the eyes of his crew. He's met with shared sorrow and resolve. "In the face of this immeasurable loss, it might be easy to succumb to despair, to question the path we've chosen. But our fallen comrades believed deeply in our mission. They fought for a future in which humanity stands united, and peace is not just an ideal but a reality." Frederick says this last statement with passion and fervor.

"We'll honor their memory through our actions. We carry their dreams forward, as well as their hopes and unyielding spirit. Our mission continues in their name. The Eastern League, and any who threaten the peace and security we've sworn to uphold, will find us resolute and unwavering in our commitment." Frederick takes a breath, collecting himself.

"Let the memory of those we've lost be our guiding light. In their honor, we'll continue to fight for the Assembly, for Earth, and for the vision of a united humanity. This isn't the end of their story but the beginning of a renewed dedication to our cause." Frederick's voice is a solemn vow to his crew that no more blood shall be spilled without reason. A promise to those present that the many they've lost will be avenged.

"We'll return home as survivors and bearers of their legacy, champions of the peace they died defending. Together, we'll ensure their loss wasn't in vain, and in their name, we'll achieve victory," he says. "We are the Pax Aeterna, and in memory of Commander Vale and all who've fallen, we'll carry on. For them, for us, and for the future they believed in. Stand united and make them proud!"

As Frederick ends his speech, the crew erupts into applause. Eventually, the applause fades, and Frederick releases the crew to return to their duties. The flight deck is restored to its normal hustle and bustle of moving machinery. Crew members meander off, splitting into pairs and groups while chatting amongst themselves. Jane stands apart, impressed by Frederick's speech but unable to muster the courage to speak to him. Instead, she watches the perfectly choreographed dance of the flight deck: the Pax's Air Wing is on high alert, meaning combat patrols are ongoing, and the flight crew is constantly preparing aircraft and welcoming others back.

Returning craft enter the hangar on one side, and departing craft use the other. Jane watches an Eagle class fighter return, and Frederick quietly sidles up to join in her observations. Jane feels a presence next to her and, turning, sees it's Frederick.

She doesn't quite know what to say to him after everything that's happened, so she starts with, "Nice speech."

Frederick quirks an eyebrow. "Eh, not my best work, but hopefully it got the message across."

Jane nods, still not quite looking him in the eye. "I think it'll do for the moment. I haven't seen the whole crew in one place before, it's quite a sight. I always forget how many people inhabit a ship of this size." Jane glances around, gesturing at the magnitude of the hangar. She hasn't seen her team hardly at all these past critical hours. It's only been about a day since they'd arrived in Sol; her world had been much simpler twenty-four hours ago.

"And what about you, Jane, how are you doing? We haven't been able to…talk since we left Sol. Are you okay?" Frederick murmurs, lightly touching her on the shoulder. He feels her tense and quickly drops his hand.

Jane finally turns to face him. "To be honest, Frederick, I'm not sure. With everything that's happened to us, between us… I have no idea what to do." She raises her shoulders in a shrug. "I'm a scientist. My experience is theoretical, I didn't expect to actually find the Odyssey nor her crew's descendants—at least not so quickly and with a fleet of deadly weapons... I can't get over what you said to me on the bridge. You were right—I'm naive, we all are. For the first time in a long time, I feel useless." Jane's shoulders drop from a shrug to a slump, and she feels all the energy drain out of her in one fell swoop. How long has it been since she'd eaten or slept? She can't remember.

"Don't be so quick to despair, Jane." Frederick says as he brings his fingers up to touch her arm once again. This time, Jane doesn't shy away. "We're going to need your brain and your skills before this crisis is over, I'm sure. You're one of the smartest people I know, and there's so much we have yet to discover. I want—no, I *need* you to look at every piece of information you have. Maybe we've missed something." Frederick says this with as much gusto as he can muster, attempting to portray the look of a calm, collected, and rational captain; the kind of captain his crew—and Jane—need him to be right now.

A thought occurs to Frederick, and he says it out loud without really thinking. "I apologize for speaking so harshly to you on the bridge earlier, it was a tense situation. It might be time for you to formally join the crew. What do you think?" He asks.

Jane's face flushes pink, slightly excited at the prospect but unclear as to what it truly means at this point. "I'm not sure I have a choice, Frederick," Jane says, slowly but surely easing back into the relaxed tone she usually has with him. Things between them aren't the same and likely never will be again, but they're getting better. "This isn't what my team and I signed up for—not in the least." Jane's future holds danger, she knows it, and she worries not only for her own safety but also the safety of her colleagues.

Frederick reads her expression, noticing the wariness in her eyes, red-rimmed from exhaustion and sorrow. "If you want, we can find a hospitable place for them to hunker down and wait things out. There's really no need to risk anyone unnecessarily."

"That might be for the best…" Jane blows out a breath. On the one hand, she's grateful Frederick is amenable to removing her crew from the path of immediate danger. On the other hand, their departure means she'll be going on without them. "Anywhere in particular?" She asks, and with that question her mind is made up. She'll keep them safe—she can fend for herself. She'll have to, in the end.

Frederick shakes his head slowly, thinking. He's still trying to figure everything out.

"I'd love to get Marcus's opinion. Wherever we go next, we're going to need to bring additional vessels into our fleet. That's our next step. The factions might even help…" Frederick says, lost in thought as to their next move.

Their exchange is broken abruptly by the jarring sounds of the vessel's proximity alarm. Frederick's cos-link vibrates urgently, and he pulls it out of his pocket. A message is flashing across its screen: **CAPTAIN TO THE BRIDGE IMMEDIATELY**. Frederick processes the message and insists Jane join him on the bridge. The pair tear through various corridors, into and out of NovaPaths, and back to the bridge to discover the latest emergency.

The crew is tense, their focus on the monitors which display an unexpected fleet of six vessels, too far out to be correctly identified. Has Marcus been able to dispatch his fleet as planned, or has the Eastern League somehow tracked the Pax to this system? Both possibilities run through Frederick's mind, his thoughts racing. His crew is thinking the same.

Before Frederick and Jane arrived, the crew had erred on the side of caution and prepared for the worst. Though the crew has been trained in efficiency, an undercurrent of fear is palpable. This situation will require Frederick to make quick decisions with a tactical response and a leader's intuition in navigating the complexities of unforeseen encounters.

"Status?" Frederick asks the bridge at large, moving to take in the data on his console. The unidentified fleet's sudden appearance near the Pax presents Frederick with a new set of challenges.

Xavier says next to him, "Several vessels have been detected, and they're now moving towards the middle of the system. They don't seem to be moving towards us yet."

"Any idea who or what they are? Are we getting any GFFs?" Frederick asks intently.

"No idea yet, they're too far out," Marie reports from her station.

Frederick, Xavier, and Jane stand at the command console, and every other officer slips over to their respective place on the bridge, ready to respond to Frederick's orders.

"Mikhail," Frederick says, "Raise the shields and power the weapons. We need to be prepared."

Mikhail shakes his shoulders as if he's knocking off cobwebs. It's been too long since he's blown something to pieces. With a smirk, he responds, "Way ahead of you, sir. Weapons are ready, and the shield is powering up." Finally, he might get his chance at revenge.

"Good," Frederick replies.

"They're well out of weapons range, close to the edge of the system. They must've just jumped in," Leo says in wonderment.

"So, this isn't a coincidence… Maybe it's Marcus?" Jane asks with a note of hope. She's desperate to see a friendly face, especially if that face belongs to her partner.

"We can only cross our fingers," Frederick replies, looking intently at his console. He mulls over his options, trying to command with balance. His response to this potential threat must be strong, yet he can't risk overextending himself and the Pax.

Frederick gestures to Xavier to come closer; he might need more help in this fight, and so he makes a decision which he hopes will save them. "Assemble as many combat strike craft as you can, and quickly. They can provide cover if needed."

Xavier nods and furiously types at his console, preparing to contact Commander Elara and request she launch all available squadrons. He connects to her cos-link audio.

"Elara, this is urgent. Get every available craft launched. Now! We'll have company soon."

Through his earpiece, Xavier hears her answer. "Got any more details? Give me something...," she says.

"Unfortunately, we've just detected a small fleet at the edge of the system. That's all we know right now. Launch every squadron of Eagles and Hornets while we figure it out," Xavier replies. The Eagle fighters of the Pax are primarily used as space superiority fighters but can be deployed in different roles. Due to their high speed, they're perfect for scouting unknown targets while keeping their carrier vessel out of harm's way.

"Well, this day gets better and better," Elara says, and her sarcasm is evident. "As you wish, Commander. I'll personally lead Alpha squadron and be up shortly, but it'll take a few minutes to get the rest."

"Quick as you can, Elara." Xavier says, then signs off and lets Elara go.

All the while, Frederick is grasping at straws, wanting any additional information he can get. He turns to Renee for ideas. "Is there anything you can tell from our sensors? We need more intel."

"Sorry, Captain." Renee shakes her head in defeat. "From this range, we can't really tell...well, anything. They're right at the edge of our sensors, but I wouldn't be surprised if they hadn't detected us yet. Our sensors are likely more powerful than theirs.

Xavier gets Frederick's attention so they can confer. "It seems we have two choices: try and remain undetected, or turn and fight."

"Those would be the obvious choices, but maybe we can do a mixture of the two. Is Elara leading one of the squadrons?" Frederick asks.

"As always, Captain. You know her: she can't resist getting behind the controls, leading Alpha," Xavier responds.

Frederick nods in acknowledgement, and another idea strikes. "Marie, can you patch through to Elara and put her feed on the main screen? Let's see what she sees."

"Of course, Captain. One moment," says Marie.

Elara can do some quick scouting to gain the answers Frederick so desperately seeks. Frederick and Xavier's command table pulsates, and the holodisplay turns on, allowing the command crew to see Elara and her camera feed.

"You're through, Captain," Marie says.

"Elara, can you hear us?" Frederick asks, speaking up.

"Loudly and clearly, sir," Elara responds.

"Good. We need you to get a read on the small fleet that entered the system and is moving towards its center. They're too far out for us to gauge their exact location, so scout and report your findings. Primarily, we need to know: are they friend or foe? Use low power, but keep your GFF tracker on." Frederick gives Elara these instructions as clearly as he can.

"Understood," Elara replies. "I'm taking Alpha squadron out of patrol and heading out. What's the direction and how far?" She asks. Elara is used to taking on difficult missions; Frederick can always rely on her and her affinity for new challenges.

Marie says, "About a billion miles out, heading two four one from your position, Commander."

"Received," Elara replies. "Heading out." The audio crackles and the crew can hear and see her movements.

"Don't get too close, we only need you to scout," Frederick warns her, just in case. He bites his lip in worry, wanting her to stay safe.

"Understood, Captain. We won't get into any trouble," says Elara with not a hint of fear in her voice. She's back to her unflappable self, preferring this version over the mess she was earlier at the loss of Torrin. She cuts audio communication with the Pax, organizing her squadrons and her Air Wing.

She speaks directly to her squad, instructing them to follow her lead. "Beta, Gamma, Zulu, Tiger, and Lion squadrons—continue combat patrols. Alpha squadron, form up and follow me. This is a scouting mission only," Elara shouts into her mouthpiece.

She receives the nonverbal confirmations she's looking for, as she's drilled every pilot under her command to do. Elara and her flight crew proceed in the direction given by Marie. As Alpha squadron closes in on the location of the unknown fleet, six vessels appear on the sensors of the small fighters. One thing Elara knows for sure: if the mysterious fleet has them as a sensor contact, Elara and her squad will appear on their sensors, too.

"Pax," Elara says, connecting to the bridge's audio once more, "We have the fleet on sensors. Seems to be six vessels in close formation." She quickly processes this information and breaks into a grin. "The GFF is showing a confirmed signal! It's the ASC Intrepid, the Valiant, and a number of other friends."

On the bridge, the crew collectively releases a pent-up breath of anxiety. They'd been patiently waiting for news—any news, either positive or negative—and this update fills them with happiness. They're grateful to see friends rather than hostile enemies.

Frederick's smile is a mile wide. "Well, that's a relief!" He says and claps Xavier on the back.

Xavier's cheeks are flushed; it's been tense on the bridge as they watched Elara scout for answers. Now, they can at least celebrate one small victory. "I suppose Marcus was able to persuade Anatoly after all. Nice to have a few allies right about now," he says, laughter in his voice.

"Leo, move us towards them, we need to make contact," Frederick says.

Even Leo feels some of the tension leave his shoulders. "Aye, Cap. Getting her underway," he replies.

Frederick is pleased to see how his crew performed under a potential threat. They did well, still maintaining efficiency under pressure. He's sure the time will come again when they'll need to think clearly through a crisis, and soon.

He connects to Elara's audio again. "Elara, you and your pilots may return to the Pax." Shortly thereafter, the fleet shows up on the Pax's sensors, confirming the presence of the majority of the Colorado sector defense.

It's time to make contact with Marcus. Frederick asks, "Marie, can you connect us to the Intrepid?"

"Yes, sir. Putting them on your console," replies Marie.

Jane looks perplexed. She mutters under her breath, "But what about the seventh ship? Aren't they missing one…?" Frederick and Xavier overhear but neither answer.

A few moments pass before Marcus and Anatoly fill the screen of the captain's console. Xavier and Jane move in to flank Frederick.

Marcus's face is anguished. "Frederick, we need to talk," he says intently.

Frederick is perplexed by Marcus's tone but decides to ignore it for now. "It's good to see you, Marcus," he says heartily. "We're so glad you came."

Anatoly steps into view behind Marcus, pushing him to the side with one hand so he can be seen fully on screen. "We're coming over to the Pax, Frederick," Anatoly says in place of a greeting. "Prepare for our arrival, and join us on the flight deck." He cuts communication before Frederick can respond.

Frederick raises his eyebrows and looks at both Jane and Xavier. "What do you make of that scene?" So much for a friendly face; Frederick expected a different sort of greeting.

"I've never seen Marcus look so…distressed. And unhappy. He's obviously upset, and it makes me wonder what could've happened between the last time we spoke to him and now," Jane says, baffled by this exchange.

"Perhaps his worry is our worry: Gaia wasn't the only attack the Eastern League undertook today…," Mikhail says ominously from his station.

Concern—about Shen's next move, about *their* next move and how to protect Earth—grows like a weed at the back of Frederick's mind, but he can't give into the chaos that thought would surely bring. Instead, he says, "Let's not speculate too much. They'll arrive soon enough and give a reason." He rubs his chin, mulling over his options yet again.

Thankfully he has Xavier and Jane, both of whom will be invaluable in the immediate future; this he knows for sure. He turns to them both. "Jane, Xavier, let's get down to the flight deck and welcome our guests." Without waiting for an answer, Frederick makes his way towards the NovaPath. He doesn't have to look behind him to know Jane and Xavier are on his heels, and he throws one last command over his shoulder. "Mikhail, you have the bridge. Get the Intrepid's fleet in a formation around us."

"As you wish, sir," Mikhail answers, just as the NovaPath's doors close on Frederick, Jane, and Xavier, taking them out of sight.

Chapter Fifteen

Frederick, Jane, and Xavier arrive at the flight deck in time to see the Intrepid's shuttle landing. As a heavy cruiser, the Intrepid was designed to deal as much damage as possible (and as quickly as possible) to other ships, but it has very few creature comforts. Accouterments not aligned with this goal have been removed or discarded. The Intrepid doesn't even offer any strike craft coverage, relying instead on two small shuttles to move personnel from the ship to other locations throughout the stars.

Anatoly and Marcus step off the shuttle and down a short gangway. Though they're still a few yards away, Jane is experiencing a reaction to Marcus's close proximity. She's filled with a cocktail of emotions: relief, happiness, and fear. As they get closer, she reflects on the last conversation she and Marcus had—it was anything but cheerful. She's honestly not quite sure where she and Marcus stand as of now.

The three Pax crew members reach the two from the Intrepid. Finally, they're face to face. "Captain," Marcus says with a stiff nod belying his strict military training. "Permission to come aboard?" He asks.

Frederick tries to smile, but it comes out as more of a grimace. He hopes the other four don't notice. "Granted. It's good to see familiar faces."

Anatoly huffs and steps forward, slightly in front of Marcus. "I don't think you comprehend just how much we need each other now. Do you know, Frederick, after you contacted us, things went downhill very quickly," he says with a scowl.

"Maybe it'd be best for us to continue this in the operations room?" Frederick begins to usher them off the flight deck so they can speak in confidence and quiet. "It sounds like you have a lot to tell us."

Marcus purses his lips. "Yes, I think that would be best. Thank you, Frederick." He turns to Jane. "Might I have a word?" He asks quietly.

Jane nods, her thoughts swirling. Marcus turns back to the group. "Jane and I need a minute. We'll meet you there."

The three remaining men nod in acknowledgment and make their way off the flight deck. Once they're out of sight, Marcus turns to Jane and surprises her with an embrace. All at once, her emotions erupt as the feeling of human contact and warmth envelopes her. Months of distance and stress bubble up only to be washed away by the familiar scent of Marcus's uniform, his aftershave, his very essence.

Marcus murmurs into the top of her head, "I've missed you, Jane." The worries of the world—nay, the galaxy—seem far away and insignificant to them both at that moment.

"What—what about what you said last time we talked?" Jane sputters, not sure if this is really happening. Has Marcus forgotten?

Marcus pulls away so he can look her fully in that face. "Don't you understand, Jane—I was angry that we're hardly able to be with each other. It seems the universe always has other plans for us. I just want us to be happy," Marcus says.

"I wish we could go back to a time when things were simple," Jane says, placing her hands over Marcus's hands where they still linger on her shoulders. "Remember when we were both on Mars just living our lives together?" She reminisces, a wistful note in her voice.

"All I ask is that we spend some time together in the coming days," says Marcus, bending down slightly to kiss her on the cheek.

Jane is dazed; this is the most affection she's felt in months. Her mind doesn't know how to process it, but her body does. She leans into Marcus, looking up at him. "What happened before you got here? You're speaking as if we're already defeated," Jane says, and worry creeps its way back into her heart. She's trying hard not to let it in.

Marcus sighs heavily. "In short, as we left the Colorado system and headed to you, the Eastern League joined our party." Marcus lets go of her and shakes his head, running a hand over his hair. The next part is difficult for him to say. "We...we lost the Iron Wrath, one of our escort destroyers. We left it behind just in case there was an issue, but—." Marcus stops himself, remembering where he is now. "Let's get to the operations room so we can go over it in more detail."

"Okay," she demurs. "But first, I want to tell you how wonderful it is to be back together. I'll cherish every moment we have, even if it's fleeting." She reaches out to Marcus, and he takes her hand in the crook of his arm. They make their way up to deck four to join the others.

Chapter Sixteen

In the operations room, a conversation is already underway between Frederick, Xavier, and Anatoly. Marcus and Jane arrive in the middle of the discussion.

At the sound of their arrival, Anatoly turns, mid-sentence. "Ah, Marcus! Good of you to finally join us. We've been waiting, and I haven't delved into what transpired on the Iron Wrath. They're still in the dark, so let's catch them up," Anatoly says, gesturing to Frederick and Xavier who give each other a silent look of annoyance at Anatoly's words.

Jane and Marcus join the others as they huddle around the main holotable located in the center of the room. Xavier pulls the schematics of the ASC Iron Wrath up on the central console.

Marcus clears his throat and, in answer to Anatoly, begins his story. "Of course. Frederick, after we conversed, I spoke with Anatoly. He gave his approval, and the rest of the fleet followed and agreed to join you."

He pauses for a breath, then continues. "The original plan was for every ship to follow the Intrepid, apart from the ASC Iron Wrath, a Typhoon class destroyer. They were meant to stay behind and let us know of any problems, just in case," Marcus says. He opens his mouth to finish the tale when Anatoly interrupts, his demeanor rude and uncaring. Anatoly wants to ensure everyone around the table knows where he stands—and upon whom.

"Just to be clear, Captain. At this point, I didn't believe your story, but Marcus seemed certain, and I was willing to trust his request." He splays his hands out in front of himself. "And, truth be told, I didn't think it would affect me."

Frederick gazes at Anatoly and can only nod, confused as to how someone like this could actually be the commodore. He knows Anatoly has friends in high places all over the galaxy, but this man standing in front of him? This isn't the kind of man Frederick was expecting when he called for help.

"Whatever your reason, you're here now. We're very grateful for any assistance you can provide," Frederick replies.

"Indeed," Marcus says before Anatoly can jump in again. He glances sideways at his commodore before plowing on. "Prior to exiting the system, we had an… *incident*. We left the starway at the jump point and were preparing to jump, but the Iron Wrath made contact with eight vessels which closed upon them quite quickly. Before we could react and go back to the starway, they were engulfed in combat."

Marcus's words bring a mournful silence to the operations room. He lets the gravity of his statement sink in, knowing from the facial expressions of his audience that they can guess what he's going to say next. "We could tell the bridge crew were trying to do their best. It sounded like they gave them hell, but the communication went dead abruptly. Once we returned, the culprits were gone and wreckage was all that remained."

Xavier is shocked. He hangs his head, forgetting himself, and whispers, "It must've been the League."

Anatoly is standing close enough to hear Xavier's mutterings. He asks loudly, "What was that, Commander?"

Xavier didn't realize he'd been overheard. "Oh, ah, I was just thinking it must've been the Eastern League," he says, a redness creeping over his cheeks at being called out by the commodore.

"Yes, that crossed our minds, too, but come now—we have no evidence!" Anatoly says to the room at large, a skeptical look twisting his features.

Frederick holds up a single finger, asking for patience. He orders Xavier to bring up his earlier interaction between himself and Shen. Anatoly listens to the exchange with eyes wide, and his disbelief begins to diminish.

"We were able to recover the black box, and maybe we can get some answers. What I know for sure is that if we hadn't left, we might not be talking about the Iron Wrath in the past tense." Anatoly says, and his astonished look turns into a mean frown. His anger is clear to see as his small, beady eyes make their way around the room to stare at everyone in turn. Silence, heavy as a shroud, engulfs them.

Frederick breaks the standoff. "Do you actually blame *us* for the destruction?" He asks with disbelief.

"Oh no, Captain. I don't blame you, of course not. It's interesting though: as soon as you suggest we might be attacked, we lose an entire ship. Our people—gone." Anatoly snaps his fingers.

Frederick is red in the face. He's fed up with Anatoly's attitude, tone, and insinuations. He must defend his ship and his own actions. "What are you implying—that we had something to do with the attack?" Frederick nearly shouts at the commodore.

"Captain, I don't know you or what you're capable of, but I'll find out the truth." Anatoly's tone has turned menacing, and he steps close to get in Frederick's face, close enough that Frederick can see the shadow of stubble creeping along Anatoly's jaw.

Marcus, Xavier, and Jane give each other quick glances, saying silently to one another, *stay out of it*. This conversation is best left to their leaders; a battle of wits is underway.

"The only truth you'll find, Commodore, is that the Eastern League has returned, and we should prepare for the unexpected," says Frederick, matching Anatoly's tone.

"So you say," Anatoly replies, taking a step back in mock deference. "Let's look at the contents of the black box and see if we can identify the ships involved, shall we? You'll assist us." This last part isn't a question but an order.

Rage, hot and white, engulfs Frederick's chest at receiving a command on his own ship. He struggles to keep his tone civil; by a miracle, his voice remains level. "You know, Commodore, you're not the only one to lose people in the last twenty-four hours. Pain is not only your burden to bear."

"Of course, of course." Anatoly raises his hands, palms up. "Anything we can do to identify the culprits."

Turning to Marcus, Anatoly says, "Have the black box moved to the Pax."

Frederick adds, "We can analyze and cross reference it against the ships at Gaia."

"We have it with us already; it's in the shuttle," Marcus says uneasily. He knows he's allowed to speak, but he almost doesn't want to after witnessing that heated exchange. "Frederick, can someone on your team assist with analyzing the data? We can start our comparison as soon as possible."

"Jane is happy to help, and Renee would be of good use as well. She handles all the data. There should be plenty of consoles on the flight deck to plug the box into and begin the download." Turning to Anatoly, Frederick adds, "Happy with that, Commodore?"

Anatoly narrows his eyes. "As happy as I can be," he says.

"Great!" Xavier says, clapping his hands together with a little too much gusto. He's trying to diffuse some of the tension, but he's not quite accomplishing that feat. "Marcus, you can get started right away, and please let us know when you have some answers. Jane, I'll send Renee down to the flight deck to meet you." Xavier takes his coslink out of his pocket to contact Renee.

With that, Marcus nods in acknowledgement, and he and Jane leave the operations room to make their way back to the flight deck.

As they walk, Jane can't help but voice her disparaging opinion of the commodore and his prickly disposition. "I see why you're always deriding Anatoly. It makes sense to me now!" She says, smacking her own forehead.

Though he agrees completely, Marcus knows better than to belittle his own commanding officer. Speaking ill of his commodore at all, but especially on another captain's ship and in public, is taboo. In response, he gives Jane an incline of his head; it's the best he can do. She sees it and understands it as an affirmation.

Jane decides to change the subject. "It's nice to have a task to do together," she says.

Marcus is in agreement, but his thoughts are stuck on the destruction of the Iron Wrath. Jane's distraction is no match for Marcus's mind and its fixation. "I hope we find that the Eastern League forces were behind this attack. Anatoly was irate about the destruction of one of our escorts. It's never easy to lose anyone, but he took this loss very badly," he says, shaking his head.

"I'm not sure that excuses his behavior… Just because he has power doesn't mean he has to be a jerk. You should confront him," says Jane in reply.

"And what am I meant to say, Jane? He's my superior officer, and as much as I don't want to, I have to put up with it. At least until he gets a new posting. Which won't happen anytime soon." Sighing, Marcus attempts to keep his face neutral and stares straight ahead as he walks.

"I never understood why you couldn't take his place and lead the fleet. You would be so much better than that—that fool!" Jane says with feeling. Anatoly has really gotten under her skin.

Marcus chuckles lightly at her outburst before getting back to business. "You know, he's not entirely incorrect in thinking that if we hadn't left our post, we might've been able to save the Wrath."

Jane looks sideways at him. "Or think of it this way: we could be looking for the wreckage of your whole fleet." She says. "You haven't fought them—the battle at Gaia was intense. It's just as likely that even in full force, you would've been taken by surprise and suffered the same fate. I know what I'm about to say is selfish, but I'm glad you survived and made it here."

"I'd be lying if I said I wasn't glad to be alive," says Marcus as he looks at her while keeping his brisk pace. He continues the conversation, saying, "It hurts to know we could've helped. Whoever this new threat is—be it the Eastern League or some other entity— mark my words, we'll make them pay." Marcus's face has darkened now with thoughts of revenge.

Jane sees the change in his face and pulls on his arm, forcing him to stop walking. She looks him in the eye. "Protecting the Assembly means protecting its ideals of peace and prosperity, as well as the people that created it," Jane pleads, hoping Marcus can still retain his humanity. To lose that would be to lose a large part of himself, and Jane can't let that happen.

Though they're only steps away from the flight deck, Jane won't let them proceed just yet. "Promise me that no matter what happens next, you won't let this change you," says Jane, keeping her hand on his arm. "Keep a piece of the man I fell for."

Marcus looks down at her hand and covers it with his own. He takes a breath, then nods and says, "I have no idea what comes next, and I can't make a promise based on the unknown—I won't lie to you. Though I will say this: you'll always be in my heart, Jane, and your words will always be on my mind."

Jane smiles a small, tight smile. "I guess that'll have to be enough." She looks up at him and steps closer.

They embrace for what feels like mere seconds; Jane wonders whether everyone will survive the looming conflict. And if they survive, will they still remain the same as before—their personalities, their feelings and thoughts? What rules will they need to bend, promises must they break, or virtues will they violate in the pursuit of protection and peace?

Jane and Marcus break apart and resume their walk to the flight deck. Once they arrive, Marcus powers towards the shuttle, and Jane heads over to a terminal at the side of the hanger next to a collection of offices where the administration of the flight deck is performed. Crew members in these offices manage the launch and retrieval of ships, as well as other flight operations, and are affectionately known around the Pax as the "conductors"—they always seem to effortlessly conduct the movements of the strike craft.

Marcus returns with the black box, the device that holds all recorded data of the Iron Wrath. It's sizable and takes all of Marcus's strength to carry to the terminal. He sets it down on the terminal's table, wiping a sheen of sweat off his brow from the exertion. Jane connects the terminal to the black box so they can access the information they seek.

Renee strides into the flight deck and makes her way over to the terminal as Jane and Marcus fiddle with the connection. She's never met Marcus before but has heard stories about him from Jane—tales of their life on Mars and the intimacies of their relationship. Renee was quite looking forward to seeing this man for herself. Jane and Marcus's backs are turned to her, and so she has the element of surprise; she taps Jane on the back.

Jane jumps ever so slightly, forgetting Renee was meant to meet up with them, so lost was she in thoughts of the future. She turns around and looks at Renee, knitting her eyebrows together.

"Renee! What are you doing away from the bridge?" Jane asks.

"Occasionally I come out from under my rock, don't you know. And I'm here to help you two, remember? Xavier sent me," Renee answers. She turns to look at Marcus, saying coyly, "And you must be…?"

"Ah, I'm sorry—I forgot you two haven't met!" Jane gestures between the two of them. "Renee, this Marcus. Marcus—meet Renee, the Pax's scientific advisor." Introductions done, she turns around to her task.

Marcus extends his hand and says warmly, "It's nice to meet you, Renee. We can use all the help we can get." He moves to pull his hand away, but Renee holds it in a tight grip.

She looks him up and down, appraising his close-cropped hair, his eyes, his jawline. He's attractive, that's for sure. Jane's taste is impeccable—and perhaps she'd like to share? Renee decides to drop one tiny, subtle hint. "The pleasure is all mine," she says, smiling hard to show off her perfectly straight teeth. She lets go of his hand, sliding one finger across his palm as she does.

Marcus looks a bit dazed. He's not used to this much attention from women in one day. He glances at Jane to see if she's witnessed this flirtation—because that's what it is, right? He's not sure—but she'd missed the interaction, consumed with the black box. He clears his throat and turns back to Renee who continues to stare at him openly, tucking a stray strand of hair, which has fallen loose of her long braid, behind her ear.

"Let's, ah…let's see what we can find, shall we? Jane?" Marcus says loudly, hoping to get her attention.

Jane absentmindedly gestures behind her to acknowledge Marcus. Renee steps forward and brushes past Marcus ever so slightly to work on the data analysis. She begins to pull up data from the battle at Gaia, comparing it with the information located on the Iron Wrath's black box. Ah-ha! She's found a match between one of the ship configurations and the vessels that attacked the Iron Wrath.

"Look, there!" Renee cries, pointing to the holodisplay which portrays both ships' configurations.

Through one of the Iron Wrath's frontal camera feeds, they can see the ship had turned to face its unknown attacker. Because of this angle, Renee, Jane, and Marcus now have a clear view of the eight interlopers just before they struck the Iron Wrath and crippled it with an overwhelming amount of weapon fire. Renee is the first to notice it.

"At what, Renee? What are you seeing?" Jane squints, trying to see what her colleague has seen.

Renee is young and energetic, emphatic at her discovery. She allows herself a second to revel in the glory of her youth, proud that she can see things often missed by her older crewmates. "Look closely—that larger vessel in the center. The aft bridge looks similar to this." Renee points at the schematics she pulled from the ships at

Gaia. With her fingertip, she manipulates the images and overlays the schematics of the ship that destroyed the Iron Wrath with the vessels that destroyed Gaia. It's a ninety-five percent match, according to the computer.

"Do you see? It's a near perfect match!" Renee says in triumph.

Marcus looks closely, careful not to press up against Renee, and says "You're right. It's hard to refute that evidence… Though the ships that destroyed the Iron Wrath might not be the exact same that destroyed Gaia, they're at least the same class. And that class doesn't appear in the Assembly database. Very curious," he says, wondering what this could mean.

After mulling it over for a few seconds, he turns to Jane and says begrudgingly, "Perhaps there's merit to what you say about the Eastern League after all."

Jane's mouth opens in an O; a perfect look of surprise on her face before she turns smug. "Perhaps you owe Frederick an apology?" She says with a smirk.

"Ah. You might be right about that, too," Marcus says, blowing out a breath. "We need to inform Anatoly about this and hope he'll believe us when we describe to him what seems to be happening to the Assembly."

Renee looks between the pair. "Maybe we should get to the bridge?" She suggests.

"Right, I'll send Frederick a message and request he meet us there, if he's not there already." Jane pulls out her cos-link and taps at the screen.

Marcus mirrors her movement and pulls out his own cos-link, so in sync are they. He says, "I'll do the same with Anatoly. If they've been together this entire time, I'm sure they've had a, ah, less than pleasant conversation."

Both Marcus and Jane have completely forgotten Renee's presence. Renee huffs, but even that doesn't get their attention. Though she's grateful she could be of assistance, she thought she'd have a more central role in this operation, one that maybe involved her teaming up with Marcus…? She taps her foot impatiently, waiting for them both to look up from their cos-links. She wants nothing more than to head back to the bridge, under her rock and safe at her station as the Pax meanders through space.

Chapter Seventeen

Back on the bridge, Frederick and the rest of the command crew contemplate what to do next. Frederick's cos-link buzzes, and he reads Jane's message seconds after he receives it. He hides his reaction to the message from the crew, careful to keep his face blank.

Looking up from his cos-link, Frederick says, "So, now that we have the start of a small fleet, any ideas on what to do next?"

"I'm not sure we can count seven vessels as a full fleet yet, Cap," Leo says, slowly sinking back into his usual manner of speaking with Frederick. "Especially if we want to take the fight to the League. Don't we need more?" Leo asks.

Frederick considers this and asks the crew, "Alright, where do we get more help?"

"What about the emergency channel? We could use it to request other vessels join us here," Marie suggests.

"Mm, I thought about that, Marie. We can't be completely sure who's listening anymore, and we risk giving away any location we select to the League." Frederick sighs. "We can't take that risk. We should presume they know more about us than we think, so we should maintain radio silence and not transmit anything that might give us away."

"Are there any other fleets out there we can contact for support?" Mikhail asks.

Frederick drums his hands on the cool, flat surface of his console. "I've already tried to contact a few other captains that I know, but no one has answered," he says.

It's at that point Anatoly wanders onto the bridge, shouting loudly, "What have you found, Marcus?" He hasn't bothered to check whether Marcus is actually in the room but rather assumes his captain is always close, like a dog following its master.

Startled, Leo, Marie, and Mikhail look around the bridge to verify that Marcus is indeed not there. Frederick turns around and addresses Anatoly, trying with all his might to keep his annoyance at bay.

"Marcus isn't here," Frederick says. "He, Jane, and Renee are on their way back from the flight deck. We're trying to determine what to do next."

Anatoly laughs, puffing out his chest. "You were thinking without *me*? No need for that, surely. Don't worry your heads about our future plans; I'll be the one to determine what to do." Anatoly's smile is mean as he looks around the room. "As a matter of fact, I'll be the one making any and all plans from here on out."

"What makes you think that'll be the case?" Frederick asks, floored that Anatoly would push his weight around after such a short amount of time aboard the Pax. "We'd do better putting our heads together right now."

Anatoly lets out a long-suffering sigh, as if Frederick is the one making this situation harder. He walks over to Frederick, invading his personal space as he steps right up to his face. He sneers, "Because, Captain, I have a few more ranks on my arms than you do."

Frederick's face is awash in confusion. He lowers his voice to prevent the rest of the crew from overhearing this exchange. "Sir, this isn't the right time to divide our crews. We have some good ideas, and the Pax is ready to fight," Frederick says with intent.

Anatoly certainly doesn't care about subtlety, and he refuses to lower his voice to match Frederick's, instead raising it an octave. He begins a tirade, giving Frederick a piece of his mind.

"Look, Captain, I've never met you before, I have no reason to trust you. And to be blunt, I'm not sure I believe you about the League! It sounds crazy. Though whatever happens next, the Pax will be under my command, as will the rest of the fleet. Is this clear?" Anatoly asks, expecting nothing in return but an affirmative answer. His eyes are bulging, face purplish with fury.

"As you wish, Commodore." Frederick takes a step back and bows slightly, putting distance between himself and Anatoly's angry outburst. His bad attitude could ignite a fuse in Frederick, and Frederick can't let that happen now, not after everything—and certainly not in front of his crew, all of whom have been watching this episode with a mixture of interest and horror.

Frederick clears his throat. "This is my ship though, Commodore, and I feel I'm responsible for her and her crew. I won't put either in harm's way unnecessarily," he says.

"So long as you do what I say, when I say it, I don't really care how you feel," Anatoly says, eyes narrowed.

In one split second, Frederick reflects on how easy it's been to command this ship up until now. He's always preferred to be left to his own devices without the need to report back to his superiors above. His relationship with Pacifica allowed him to be slightly distant from the bureaucracy of the Assembly. Now he feels the tight shackles of micromanagement begin to weigh him down, sucking him under the current.

Jane, Marcus, and Renee choose that point to burst onto the bridge. The NovaPath opens, and Frederick looks over; his expression is dark, and the three of them can see it from their standpoint. Marcus decides to put Frederick's mood to one side for now—he needs to inform Anatoly of their findings.

Anatoly turns at the sound of the NovaPath's doors opening and sees Marcus making a beeline towards him. "Ah, there you are, Marcus! So, what did you find?"

"Commodore, there were indeed similarities between one of the ships that destroyed the Wrath and the scans the Pax crew took of the incident at Gaia," Marcus says heavily.

"Enough to be the same ship?" Anatoly questions.

Marcus makes a wry face, but Renee answers Anatoly's question before Marcus can get the words out. "It's unlikely the exact same ship, sir, but they could easily be the same class of ships," Renee says.

Anatoly waves her away. "I don't remember asking your advice, Miss…?" His mouth opens and closes. Clearly, Anatoly never bothered to introduce himself to Renee, and he certainly hasn't taken the time to remember anyone's name on the Pax.

"Uh, it's Renee, Commodore. My name is Renee."

"Yes, well, that's all very good. Marcus, is that your conclusion, too?" Anatoly says, not camouflaging the fact that he values one person's opinion over another.

Marcus looks sympathetically at Renee before answering. "Yes, they seem similar. Exactly as Frederick said—we appear to be caught up in a fight for the survival of the Assembly.

"Don't you think that's a bit…dramatic?" Anatoly asks with a grimace. If this is true, Anatoly's life is about to get much more difficult, and he isn't partial to difficult situations—not at all.

"Sir, our main shipyard and spiritual home has been destroyed, our fleet was attacked quickly afterwards. We have to presume this is happening all over Assembly space, potentially over faction space, too, and we haven't heard one distress call yet. That sounds like a fight for survival to me," says Marcus as gently as possible.

Anatoly begins to pace on the bridge, all eyes on him. Some were wondering if he might explode like a powder keg, though collectively they know it'd be hard for him to wave away this new reality.

"Always the theatrical one, Marcus," Anatoly says, still pacing. He wags his finger. "But you might be right—something bigger is going on."

Anatoly turns to Frederick and asks, "Have you made contact with any other ships or fleets out there?"

Frederick shakes his head no. He gestures for Marie to answer fully.

"Without fleet command at Gaia, there have been no communications on any of the subspace channels… It's been very quiet—eerily so," says Marie.

"They might've changed location or gone radio silent for a number of reasons." Anatoly muses, still pacing back and forth.

"Either way, we need to make contact with whomever we can before they fall into the same trap. I also recommend we strengthen our numbers," Frederick says.

"On that we agree captain, on that we agree. Now, have you tried the emergency channel yet?" Anatoly inquires.

This question triggers Frederick's irritation. After all, hadn't they just been discussing this before Anatoly barged in? And why must Anatoly ask Frederick this barrage of questions without any solutions? Frederick feels like he's being interrogated on his own ship—and why? It's clear Anatoly revels in his higher status, but the situation requires action, movement, and quick thinking, none of which are occurring right now.

"Actually, we were just discussing that when you joined us," says Frederick, pursing his lips.

"I would've expected that to be done already, but I suppose better late than never," Anatoly says unkindly.

Frederick rebuts, saying, "My concern with that option is if the Eastern League knows of that channel, we could be compromising our location."

Marcus nods and says, "I would agree with Frederick on this one, Anatoly. It'd be unwise to use a wide band channel until we know for sure it won't be intercepted."

"Nothing's going to be one hundred percent safe now, Captains. We'll need to take risks! If we can save more ships, that's a good start. Think about it," he says, tapping his temple, "The only real firepower we have at the moment is the Pax, the Intrepid, and the Valiant—what are we meant to do with three capital ships? The rest won't be able to do much in fleet-on-fleet combat. And how many vessels did the League bring to Gaia, does anyone have the number? Who knows what we could be facing," Anatoly says, still pacing around the bridge.

Mikhail pipes up from his station. "The fleet contained fifty vessels of varying sizes and configurations. Renee and I attempted to catalog them, and from what we could tell, they have a mix of small frigates, cruisers, and one large dreadnaught."

Renee chimes in with, "None of the ships composing the fleet at Gaia were the same as those in the Colorado system."

"So, it's likely we haven't seen the full force yet," Leo interjects from his seat. At this realization, he slumps further in his chair, dejected.

"Only fifty ships but probably more? Against our current fleet of seven? That sounds like good odds," Anatoly says with sarcasm oozing from every word. "Frederick, use the damn emergency channel and tell any and all Assembly ships to join us here before we lose anyone else! Use my authorization code now."

Frederick shakes his head. "I have to strongly object to this course of action," he says, feeling more incensed as the minutes pass. He's not a fan of Anatoly's command style and wonders how Marcus puts up with it.

Marcus agrees with Frederick, surprising everyone. "I do, too, sir. This is reckless!"

"Your objections are noted," Anatoly says, his mouth a hard line. He looks squarely at Frederick. "Before I have you replaced, Captain, follow my orders."

Frederick closes his eyes for a brief second. "Aye, Commodore," he says. "You heard him, Marie." He gestures for her to open the channel.

Marie proceeds to open the emergency channel on her console to send an urgent message. This channel will relay a message through subspace, similar to other communication methods, but the message is sent on a wavelength that's difficult to detect without specific Assembly receivers and decoders. The channel is used in only the direst of situations to call for support. Messages sent must include the ship's name, serial number, and the commanding officer's authorized credentials.

"I'm ready to send the message. Commodore, your authorization code, please?" Marie requests, waiting. She's worried about the repercussions of this action but is powerless to stop it.

Anatoly moves swiftly over to Marie's console. The command crew as a whole holds their breath, nervous and apprehensive. Like Marie, what can they do? Anatoly is the highest-ranking officer on board—they'd face the consequences of defying him.

Once Anatoly adds his code to the message, the communication is complete. He looks around the bridge and says, "For those of you who don't know, sending that message through the emergency channel means it's transmitted through to nearby ships every thirty minutes. Surely someone will receive it."

"But who? Friend or foe?" Frederick mutters. Whoever receives it will hopefully respond and join both ships in the Lumina Dyad system. Frederick and Marcus start praying they'll find allies rather than enemies.

Leo begins to tap his foot incessantly. "I guess, uh, now we wait…," he says.

"It'll take some time for someone to reach out to us," Frederick replies. He looks around at his battle-weary crew. He can see their exhaustion, commingled with anxiety and worry. "We should try and get some rest; it's been a long few days."

He looks to his right-hand man. "Xavier, get the night crew up here, will you? Everyone needs a break." Turning to Anatoly, he addresses the commodore as politely as he can. "Perhaps I can prepare you some quarters on the Pax? Marcus, that offer is extended to you as well. Of course, you're both free to return to the Intrepid if you wish."

Anatoly quickly declines the captain's offer, heading instead to the Intrepid. Marcus, on the other hand, watches Anatoly leave with relief. He turns to Jane quietly and asks if he might join her for the night. This is what Jane had hoped, so she accepts, and together they make their way to her quarters. Ever since Marcus stepped foot on the Pax, she'd wanted a moment alone—truly alone—with him, and she's awash with happiness to have her partner back with her, if only for a short time.

Leo looks at the clock located on the rear wall of the bridge; it displays galactic time as 22:15. He puts his console on autopilot, stands up, and heads to his meager quarters. The rest of the crew can finally sleep as well; what a relief! It's music to their ears, as they'd been at their stations for nearly two days straight. The night shift makes their way to the bridge, relieving all officers on duty. Members of the crew are weary, most dragging themselves to their rooms and collapsing on beds which feel to them like heaven. Many are asleep within seconds of their heads hitting their pillows, pure exhaustion overriding their feelings of anxiety.

Chapter Eighteen

A few hours pass on the Pax, and Leo becomes more and more restless. It's been a long time since he's had such a sleepless night. He opens his eyes and looks over at the clock on the wall next to his narrow bed, his room a far cry from the expansive VIP quarters on deck four. The clock reads 02:45, meaning he's been tossing and turning for hours, his mind running a million miles a minute. He can't seem to shut his brain off—it's like a never-ending stream of fragmented thoughts and half-remembered dreams. He's filled to the brim with unrelenting imaginings, so much so that he hasn't had a moment's worth of quiet.

He's tried every technique he knows: counting sheep, trying to empty his mind—yet nothing has the desired effect. The only item of substance filling his thoughts is one question pounding through his skull: where can he get his next fix? After yesterday's events, Leo knows it'll be difficult. He's been secretly taking Zenithar for years; he must admit he's addicted. Now, he's unsure as to where he can get more.

He's fed up with this sleepless night—maybe a change of scenery will help, he thinks. There are few decks on the Pax dedicated solely to living quarters, but those also contain conveniences the crew might need, including a twenty-four-hour mess hall similar to the one located on the observation lounge. This one, however, is missing the beautiful celestial view. Leo jumps out of bed with far more energy than he should have at this time of night. He throws on some clothes that've been carelessly tossed on the back of a chair next to a small table near his bed and heads out of his room, padding to the mess hall. He hopes he won't run into anyone on his way.

The ship has the same decor throughout, no matter the deck: dark, smooth, metal paneling inlaid with etchings that depict the ideals of the Assembly, images that make it clear that everyone must be treated equally and fairly, as no one person is above another. The carpet is thick and rich-feeling underneath his feet, featuring an interlocking golden scroll design. Leo relishes the softness now, feet sinking into its plushness. As he walks down the empty corridors, tiredness dulls his senses. This doesn't matter so much—he could make the trek blindfolded, having walked this route countless times before. He reaches the equally vacant mess hall, seeing only the chefs and other workers preparing for the start of the day. To his surprise, there's one other crew member in the mess. Mikhail must've had a hard time getting to sleep, too.

Leo is intrigued. Certainly, he's not the only person on board who suffers from sleeplessness, but he never pegged Mikhail for an insomniac. Slowly, he walks over to Mikhail's table.

"Can't sleep either?" Leo inquires, pulling up a chair and sitting down without an invitation.

"Apparently not. Though I was exhausted and thought I would succumb to sleep easily. My mind rebelled," Mikhail explains.

Leo lets his head hang a bit, almost too tired to look Mikhail in the eye as they converse. "I know how you feel, man. My mind's been running a thousand miles an hour. It's been an interesting day, to say the least."

One of the mess crew notices Leo and offers him some water. Grateful, Leo accepts and slurps it down. He drains his glass in two gulps and sets it on the table. Only then does he notice Mikhail is reading something intently.

"What's that?" Leo asks, gesturing at the digital tome in Mikhail's two large hands.

"Oh, this? It is just something I downloaded from the database—everything I could find about the Eastern League and their past. At least, everything we thought we knew…" Mikhail trails off.

"Are you trying to make us all look bad with your research?" Leo attempts sarcasm, but it doesn't have the right effect on Mikhail. His cheeky grin now feels misplaced.

"Of course not," says Mikhail seriously. "I wanted to know more about our foe. If I am being completely honest, I had not studied them heavily before. I need to be prepared for the next time we meet."

Leo gives Mikhail a skeptical look. "Uh, what can that book tell you about them as they are today? It's just history, who cares? I'm sure they've changed since then," Leo says, sitting back in his seat.

"Their history equates to who they are, what they believe, what they stand for. What kind of people they are, what they value, what they tolerate. You can learn everything about people from their history and the art they enjoy. I will study this to understand. Are they more inclined to surrender, or will they pursue us at any cost? All of these things are rooted in who they are—the knowledge of this might be life or death for us at some point," Mikhail says, some of his gruffness peeking through.

"You know this isn't all down to you, right? You're putting a lot of pressure on yourself," Leo says, not fully understanding.

"If not mine, then on whose shoulders should this burden lie? I am the weapons officer; I am meant to make sure we come home. Today, I failed," says Mikhail with sadness etched on his face, a sudden droop to his shoulders belying his tiredness and disappointment after the events of the last few days.

"What are you talking about, man? You mean with Torrin? How could you have possibly prevented that?" Leo asks, perplexed.

"I must have missed something... Maybe we are getting too lazy or we have become too complacent and blasé," Mikhail says with a sigh. "Or perhaps our feelings of superiority dulled our senses. My only guarantee is this: it will not happen again." Mikhail puts the digital book down on the table with a thump to emphasize his point.

Leo notices a fire he'd never seen before in Mikhail; anger steeped in fear. He says, "You know losing people is part of the territory, right? We're probably going to lose a lot more before whatever we do next is done." Leo looks down at the table. He wonders if he's said the right thing.

"I know that, but it does not mean I have to accept it. I will do whatever I must to ensure I am prepared so I can save as many as possible," Mikhail says, rising heavily from the table and picking up his book. His chair scrapes back, the noise a shock in the quiet, empty mess hall. "I am going back to my quarters to finish my reading in peace. Good night to you," Mikhail says with a curt nod. He walks away, back to his room. He'd come to the empty mess hall for solace, but unfortunately that's not what he received.

"See you in the morning," Leo calls to his retreating back. Now he knows he's said the wrong thing. He wonders if his anxiety over his swiftly dwindling stash of Zenithar has made him on edge, speaking out of turn to those he considers…well, if not a friend, then a close acquaintance. His leg jumps and taps of its own accord; it's been doing that for the last day. Will he even survive the rest of the week? He's not sure.

    Leo swivels his empty water glass, pondering his addiction and whether he should finally go cold turkey. He considers everything he's been able to do because of the drug: how it heightens his focus and allows his reaction times to be lightning fast. He worries about the kind of person he'd be without its help. Regardless, he may not have a choice; his supply would only last him a few more days at most…

Chapter Nineteen

Equally as awake as Leo is Commander Elara. She's still on the flight deck, now the ranking officer for both the flight crew and the marines. It's her burden and duty to select Commander Torrin's replacement, as the marines need a capable leader. The flight deck is vast—the single largest section on the vessel. It's used as a carrier and includes the equipment all marines might need for their expeditions, and it serves as the marines' training facility.

In Elara's mind, there are only a few suitable candidates to promote to commander but one that stands out as the obvious choice: Legionnaire Richard Spencer-Mosley. Top of his class but young for his rank at only twenty-five years old. He'd moved through the ranks at phenomenal speed. He's gifted with a unique mixture of skills, luck, and family name, and he's served on the Pax for the last year. Currently, Richard leads the mechanized battalion of the marines which provide the Pax with enough firepower to start a small war.

Torrin had always spoken highly of Richard, mentioning to Elara that if ever someone needed to take his place, Richard should be the one to do it. Elara moves through the flight deck, dodging the never-ending hustle and bustle as fuel is pumped into awaiting jets and strike craft taxi. Elara approaches the marine facility—it's a large, two-story structure that holds the command officers. It also contains the training center and the mechanical workshops, which are adjacent. All in all, it's a one-stop-shop for the marines' operations on the ship. As she makes her way to her destination, she admires how early the marines start their day; it's nearly 05:00 AM and already it's the first place on the ship to come to life.

Elara steps through the gliding doors of the marines' offices, but she's stopped by security. "Commander," the guard says with warmth, "What a nice surprise! And what brings you down to the pit?" He asks.

Elara smiles. "I need to speak with Legionnaire Spencer-Mosley. Do you know where he is?"

"You're in luck, Commander. He's just arrived and is heading to the ops center."

"I know the way, thank you, ensign," Elara says, nodding curtly. The security guard steps aside so she can get on her way.

The corridors of the facility continue the industrial look and feel of the flight deck; though there are metal walls, the aesthetic is practical—it makes one feel everything down here has a purpose. The walls are inset with digital displays that shine in the dim, showing those that pass lists of notices, rules, and duty rosters. No pictures for inspiration are found here. She passes workers doggedly doing their part, everyone awake, alert, and ready for the day's tasks.

Elara arrives at the operations room and spies Richard and a few other officers in a gaggle, discussing an upcoming training. She hates to interrupt, but this is important.

"Mosley," she says, stepping up to their group and breaking into their conversation. "I need to borrow you for a second." Elara has ultimate authority on the flight deck, and the other officers cease their conversation immediately. They scatter, leaving Richard and Elara alone.

Elara points to a table and chairs nestled into a corner of the room, a quiet area perfect for this discussion. She and Richard head over and sit. She begins to tell Richard her news.

"Richard, yesterday was a tough day for the crew. And, for me personally," Elara says, the pain evident in the twist of her mouth at these last words.

Richard nods and says, "Torrin was a good man. In the end, we do what we must. We knew the risks when we first signed up—there was a chance not all of us would survive. Never thought we'd lose Torrin though."

Elara smiles slightly; even now, Richard knows exactly what to say, perfectly mixing sentiment with training. She knows she's making the right choice. "Yes, of course. Now that his position is…vacant, we need to make sure the chain of command stays intact. The marines need a structure they can count on."

Richard's cheeks go pink; he's nervous as he awaits Elara's next words, hoping upon hope that she has faith in him to lead. All these years, he's worked incredibly hard to put himself in line for this position.

He swallows. "Do you have someone in mind?" He asks, now a bit timid.

Before answering, Elara thinks back to the many pranks her marines have played on her. She can't miss this opportunity for sweet revenge. She draws out her next words.

"I have a couple in mind... What do you think of Legionnaire Luter?" Elara asks innocently.

True to his training, Richard answers with, "A solid marine, never had an issue with him. I've only worked with him a bit, but he would be a good choice. Is...he who you've chosen?" Richard asks. His bright tone has deflated.

"Well, he's a good choice," Elara says, relishing the moment as Richard squirms just the tiniest bit. With a little laugh, she decides to put him out of his misery. "But I think we all know you'd be a better choice. So long as you want it," Elara says, spreading her hands out in front of her.

Richard responds so quickly, his words come out in a jumble, tripping over themselves. "I very much would!" He clears his throat and sits up straighter in his chair, attempting to regain an air of professionalism.

"Fantastic! I had a feeling you might say yes," says Elara with a grin. "We should announce it publicly now. Come with me." She gestures for Richard to follow her out of the room.

Richard scrambles up, feeling elated. Finally, all his hard work has paid off. Elara strides out and whistles for the attention of the officers in the immediate vicinity. The four officers under Richard's command walk over, along with others in the operations center.

"Alright, if I could have everyone's attention for a moment!" Elara says, raising her voice to be heard. "You all know what happened yesterday... Soon, we'll require every single marine on this ship. Our roles may change, but our service and commitment to the mission of the Pax is unwavering. To that point, I'm performing a battlefield promotion of Richard Spencer-Mosely."

Elara turns and removes Richard's current Legionnaire epaulets from his shoulders, decorated with eagles. Such epaulets are how all marines recognize the ranks of others. Elara reaches into a pocket of her uniform and pulls out two new epaulets. She replaces

Richard's older epaulets with these new ones, donned with a single large star in the middle, indicating his new commander rank.

She raises her voice once again as more marines trickle in from the surrounding corridors, pausing in their tasks to hear her address. "Attention to orders! With the power of the Assembly, I'm placing my trust and confidence in the integrity and ability of Legionnaire Spencer-Mosley, who has shown the potential to serve in a higher grade. Due to the unique position this unit finds itself, a battlefield promotion to commander has been awarded to Richard Spencer-Mosley, Assembly Combined Forces, effective immediately by the authority of Commander Elara Dorne."

A round of applause fills the room, and a tidal wave of handshakes overcome Richard as everyone rushes to touch their new commander. Richard is lost in a whirlwind of celebration and claps on the back. Cheers erupt from the crew. Elara lets them have their fun for a few minutes, stepping out of the limelight. She waits until the cheers have died down and most have gone back to their duties.

After the last handshake is complete, Elara steps forward and grabs Richard's attention with a tap on the shoulder. He turns, a big smile on his face, and absentmindedly touches his new epaulets.

"Richard, once we get through this, we can organize a formal ceremony. This'll have to do for the moment—I hope that's fine with you. Remember, the first course of action is to get the marines ready for anything. Can you do that for me? I'm putting my faith in you," Elara says in a low voice, leaning in towards Richard now that he's in her circle of confidence.

Richard quickly sobers from the high of his promotion. He nods curtly and says, "We'll be ready when we're needed, Commander."

Elara smiles. "We're the same rank now, Richard. Call me Elara."

"Force of habit," Richard says, his cheeks going pink once again. "Elara it is from now on."

"I'll leave the details up to you, but organize your forces, and let me know if there are any issues. Keep a force active around the clock until the pressure dies down," Elara says.

"Understood. We'll be ready for anything," Richard replies with confidence.

Internally, Elara releases her clenched heart. She knows she chose correctly and has faith in Richard. He can do this. The short promotion celebration is now complete, which marks the restoration of the marine's command management. Elara is free to start the day as she normally would: joining the flight leader's briefing. Today will likely be just as exciting as yesterday, and so she dismisses Richard and heads out of the flight deck.

It'll be a number of hours before the rest of the inhabitants of the vessel emerge from their nightly slumber. Some of the Pax's crew have had a challenging night's sleep—anyone who's world had been changed so dramatically would suffer the same fate. Sleep, or lack thereof, hasn't diminished the horrific events of yesterday, and though everyone has accepted that their lives are about to get infinitely harder, this knowledge is a bitter pill, hard to swallow.

Chapter Twenty

For the first time in a long time, Jane woke to what she believed was the best view in the galaxy: the face of her sleeping partner. It was a view she'd started to forget over the last few months apart from him, but she was reminded of this wonderful feeling in just one night. As she gazes at him, Marcus awakens, groggy and glazed with sleep.

"What…what time is it?" Marcus asks blearily while rubbing his eyes.

"It's 08:30 AM," says Jane softly. "The command crew will be at their posts soon, and we should get ready to join them."

Marcus murmurs, "Yes, in due time. First, can we take a minute to enjoy this moment?" He rolls over to give Jane an embrace, and they remember exactly why their partnership has flourished. In the next instant, unfortunately, they're interrupted by the ship's alarm requesting all crew to report to their stations. The alarm is relentless, a constant *bong* paired with red light that illuminates the ceiling.

Reluctantly, they pull away from each other, both with a look of longing and disappointment. Duty calls at the most inopportune moments. Within minutes, they're dressed and heading to the bridge. As they walk, they encounter other frantic crew members rushing quickly to their assigned stations. The ceilings of the hallways, NovaPaths, and corridors mirror Jane's quarters—a bright red light which reminds them of its urgency.

Marcus and Jane reach the bridge, joining Frederick and Xavier at their shared command console, and inquire as to what's happening.

"Frederick, why the alarm?" Jane asks, befuddled and admittedly still waking up.

Frederick explains, "Two contacts have emerged at the jump point on the far side of the system. We haven't received any communication from them, nor a GFF signal yet." Frederick's nervous energy is apparent. "They're moving slowly towards the center of the system, as you did, Marcus."

Marcus raises his eyebrows. "We struggled to detect your exact location in the system when we arrived... Maybe they're doing the same? With the larger fleet, they must see all our signatures."

"What do we do? Are they Assembly or Eastern League?" Jane asks, attempting to push down her panic.

"At this point, we have no idea and must assume the worst," says Xavier grimly.

Marcus nods his head yes in agreement. "Right. And we can stand down if needed," he says.

Marie breaks in, calling from her station, "Captains, there's a communication from the Intrepid... It seems to be Anatoly," she says.

Frederick knits his eyebrows together. "Put him on the command console."

Marie does as she's told, and Anatoly's bust fills the command console holodisplay.

"Marcus, I presume the Pax has detected the two contacts at the edge of the system," Anatoly says, completely ignoring Frederick's position and presence.

"Yes, they've been detected, and we'll need to verify their friend or foe status," says Marcus in answer.

"The Pax will deploy from the fleet and verify the vessels," Anatoly says this as if it were obvious.

Frederick can't stand silent any longer. "Commodore, the Pax is probably the best weapon we have against the League—we shouldn't risk her unnecessarily," he reiterates sternly.

Anatoly's hologram swivels to address Frederick. "Captain, you're also the most likely to survive contact if they're enemy vessels. I thought you had all the new toys of the fleet? Get going and report back. This isn't a discussion," Anatoly says. He doesn't give anyone else a chance to rebut or ask questions, instead cutting the connection after he utters his last words.

Frederick turns to Marcus standing next to him. He makes an exasperated noise, throwing his hands up. "Truly, I don't understand how you deal with that man. I find myself wanting to take the complete opposite course of action, just to spite him," he says.

Marcus's mouth is a flat line; he must still be careful not to disparage his commodore. "Some days are harder than others," says Marcus, hedging.

"I suppose we're going to do a reconnaissance," Frederick says, loud enough for the whole crew to hear.

"At least there are only two of them," says Leo from his station. Deep shadows have formed under his eyes; he looks the worse for wear.

Frederick notices the state Leo is in but ignores it for now. He'll get to the bottom of that later. "Get us there in one piece, would you, Leo?" Frederick requests gently.

"Aye, Cap. Getting there in one piece sounds easy enough," Leo says, piloting the ship and preparing it to move.

Eyes intense, Frederick looks at Mikhail. "Raise the shield and power the ion cannons just in case. Keep your finger on that trigger," Frederick orders.

The engines of the Pax power up to propel the vast vessel forward, moving away from the fleet that's moved into a close formation around them. The Intrepid fills the gap as the central vessel of the fleet. Within a few minutes, the Pax is in range and able to verify the unknown vessels.

"Captain, we're receiving a GFF signal from one of the ships," says Marie. She takes a few seconds to process and confirm the details.

The signal is coming from the ASC Colossus and the ASC Sovereign Sun. The Colossus and the Pax have already crossed paths, as the Colossus is usually stationed at one of the Sol jump points, a beacon of stability. Other than the Pax, it's the most powerful warship the Assembly has to offer. The Sovereign Sun is likewise a powerful warship in the Assembly's arsenal; both would be strong additions to any fleet.

"We have an incoming communication from Captain Talia Varrick," Marie says, unsure.

At that, Frederick mentally unclenches just a little. Before taking on his first command, Talia had been Frederick's mentor; she taught him everything about being a captain. The two built a strong friendship over the years but haven't seen each other in nearly a decade. Ultimately, he's glad to see such a formidable warship join his fleet with an equally competent captain at its helm.

"Put her through. It's nice to see another friendly face," Frederick says.

Marie does so, and once again the command console is filled with another holographic bust—this time of Captain Varrick. Talia is a confident captain with decades of experience, completing command after command, the first of which was a Typhoon class destroyer patrolling volatile sectors near the edge of Assembly space. During a patrol, her ship was one of the first to respond to a distress signal from a civilian evacuation convoy under pirate attack. Her decisive actions not only saved the convoy but also led to a significant reduction in piracy in that sector.

Frederick smiles as he gazes upon the holodisplay. "Captain Talia, it's good to see you—it's been too long," he says and looks at her face more intently. His smile drops to a look of concern as he notices scratches and scrapes on her cheeks and forehead. He's not certain, but he thinks she's recently been in a fight.

"Indeed, although it's been a challenging few hours," Talia drawls. "What's the condition of the Pax? From our sensors it seems you've picked up a few more allies."

"Yes, the Colorado sector defense fleet responded to our communication and joined before they were ambushed. All ships are fully operational, and we're hoping to find more vessels that survived," Frederick says.

"Does that mean Commodore Petrov is the commanding officer?" Talia asks.

Frederick's look turns wry, and Marcus answers in his stead. "He's on the Intrepid and part of our fleet, and he's the highest-ranking officer in the fleet currently. With the destruction of Gaia, it's unclear who's left and what that means for our command structure."

It's hard for Talia to shield her disappointment from the other captain's view. "And who might you be?" Talia asks, intrigued, though her expression remains emotionless.

"Marcus Harrington, Captain of the Intrepid," Marcus says and gives a short salute. He goes on to say, "We've never met, but your reputation precedes you."

Talia nods, and her face remains impassive. "Thank you, Captain. In another life—a while ago—Anatoly was my captain on a destroyer, and I was his second in command. He can be an…intriguing commanding officer." The command crew listen to Talia with interest, mentally corroborating her feelings with their own after the explosive arguments they'd witnessed between Anatoly and Frederick the day before.

Talia continues, "Putting that to one side, Captain, the Colossus is not in a good way. We sustained a large amount of damage as we left Sol… We were ambushed by a number of unidentified warships that came in guns blazing, no warning. If the Sovereign wasn't there, I'm sure you and I wouldn't be speaking. Maybe we should've asked that pirate more questions," she says, face still neutral.

"Then we're very lucky to have you both joining us," Frederick says in understanding. "What's the status of the Sovereign Sun now?" He asks.

"Also damaged but less so than us," Talia states matter-of-factly.

"We can deploy the fleet's resources to fix those scratches," Frederick offers, hoping to extend an act of kindness, and knowing he'd be asking a favor of his own in due time. "We'll need those big guns of yours soon."

Finally, a break in her non-expression. Talia allows a small smile to show through. "That's our job, Captain—to take the hits. But whatever help you can give would be appreciated. I'll have my ops officer work with yours," says Talia.

"And I'll inform Anatoly of your arrival and condition," Marcus says.

Talia's bust blinks. "I would appreciate that, Marcus. And Frederick, it's good to see you once again, I look forward to reminiscing about better times. Colossus out." She cuts the connection on her end, and her hologram vanishes from the central console.

Frederick addresses Marie, saying, "Work with the Colossus and Sovereign Sun's operation officers. See what they need for repairs, and get those vessels as operational as quickly as possible. This needs to be a priority."

Marie nods and begins tapping at her screen. "Right away, Captain. I feel a little better with their added protection," she says.

"Mikhail, you must be salivating at the sight of the Colossus again," says Leo with a light laugh.

Mikhail grunts. "She is big, but I would still bet on us in a fight. They may have more weapons than we do, but our defenses are much stronger," he says, a slow grin forming as he thinks of the power the Pax packs.

"Uh, if it's all the same to you, Mikhail, let's not put that to the test. I'm just glad they're on our side," Leo replies.

Xavier joins in, saying, "With both the Colossus and Sovereign joining us, our available firepower has increased exponentially."

Frederick nods in agreement, though he doesn't look as happy as Xavier thinks he should. "It's a nice start, but we'll need more than two ships. We have no idea how many foes we have to face—we may need hundreds of ships before we can start thinking of victory," Fredrick says.

"Give it time," says Jane, placating. "It's only been a few hours. Hopefully more will come."

"As fun as it's been, Frederick, it might be best for me to return to the Intrepid. We can assist in any operations you request, including repairs. Keep me in the loop," Marcus says.

"Of course. Head down to the flight deck, and take one of our shuttles to the Intrepid. It's the least we can do," says Frederick, imparting one last bit of hospitality. Marcus has really grown on him.

"Mind if I walk you down?" Jane asks.

"I would enjoy that very much," Marcus replies.

He and Jane head to the back of the bridge and down to the flight deck. They use this time to enjoy each other's company for a few final moments. Once they make it to the flight deck, Jane performs the necessary operations to organize a shuttle for her partner. The flight back to the Intrepid will be short since the two ships are in such close proximity to each other. They take the walk to the parked shuttle hand in hand; said shuttle is always ready to power up and fly. Gone are the days when strike craft need an hour to get flight ready; it's merely a flick of a button to power up the engines and coordinate with flight control to inform the rest of the flight deck of departure and destination.

Marcus kisses Jane on the cheek, lets go of her hand, and climbs into the shuttle. He presses the appropriate button to power up the craft and, after receiving a confirmation from flight control, pilots the shuttle to move through the flight deck to the rightmost end where launches occur; strike craft launch at low speeds and accelerate once they leave the carrier, requiring only a short takeoff. As Marcus maneuvers the shuttle to taxi on the launch section of the flight deck, Jane can't help but wonder if this is to be the last time she'll see her partner again. She sighs and turns away, headed back to the bridge. Only time will tell.

Chapter Twenty-One

On the bridge, Frederick and Xavier discuss next steps. Frederick is at the end of his tether. "I'm done with these unforeseen events, Xavier! We need to increase our sensor range and warnings." He spits out the words.

"We could deploy scouts from our Air Wing, close to the three jump points around the system," Xavier suggests.

"If the League returns, they'll appear en force. I'm not so sure waiting for imminent death is the best strategy… Maybe we can get one of the destroyers to hang at the edge of their sensor range so they can relay intel to us," Frederick mutters, thinking hard. He strokes his chin in contemplation.

Xavier nods, thinking, too. "That might work, but we'd need three vessels, and that would be a large percentage of our support fleet. Perhaps the fleet can be positioned in proximity to one of the jump points and pray nothing happens," says Xavier.

"An interesting idea—sounds like something we need to run past Anatoly, just to cover our asses." Frederick sighs. "Get a message over to the Intrepid, would you, Xavier?" Frederick requests begrudgingly.

"Of course. Though it might have more weight coming from you, sir," Xavier answers.

"It might, but it'd be good for you to take on some of these duties. I know you're considering becoming a captain one day. So, no time like the present, eh?" Frederick says with a smirk.

"As you wish, Captain," Xavier replies. He receives an affectionate chuff on the shoulder from Frederick in response. Xavier feels grateful for the opportunity to add this skill set to his repertoire. He knows Frederick enjoys helping the officers, treating it as a personal challenge to have as many as possible move on to other commands with promotions.

Frederick walks over to Mikhail's terminal and says, "I wanted to ask, as you know the strategic situation better than most of the command crew… The Assembly has hundreds of ships and plenty of facilities filling the stars. There must be others out there, right? If you were Shen and the League, what targets would be lower priority? Which fleets do you think haven't been destroyed yet and aren't important enough to be targeted first?"

"I have been looking into this, Captain." Mikhail swivels around to face Frederick and steeples his fingers together. "Shen considers himself a tactical genius, so I am sure he thinks he has taken the assembly by complete surprise." Mikhail says.

Frederick knows Mikhail respects the enemy—though he hates to admit it, so does he—but he wants to make absolutely sure. "And they did exactly that. So, we need to give our enemy the respect they've earned. Our fleet is scattered, our headquarters annihilated, and apparently, it's leaderless as well. We're far and away from mounting any sort of rebuttal," says Frederick.

Mikhail has spent every waking moment—that is, those rare moments when he isn't attempting to fire the ship's cannons—trying to further understand their enemy. He rears back in shock, so taken aback at the seeming insinuation that he hasn't respected them.

"I respect them, Captain, please make no mistake. We have all their vessels documented now, and they are only a little under par to the standards of equivalent Assembly vessels, all without having the same resources as Sol. That is quite an accomplishment," Mikhail says emphatically.

Frederick's interest is piqued. The known faction ships are weak in comparison to the equivalent Assembly vessels; they hold a one to three advantage. "How close do you think the power balance might be?" Frederick asks. He's a bit more worried than he was when he started this conversation.

"Ah. I need more time to give an official answer," Mikhail says, lifting both shoulders in a shrug. "I will also need a second opinion, but I think it is close to half. However, this does depend on what vessel we are talking about—the larger warships are closer to one-to-one of ours, but we have only seen a handful of their larger vessels. They seem to rely on small, quick vessels like the majority of the fleet at Gaia," Mikhail says slowly.

This news makes Frederick visibly concerned. His lack of real-life tactical experience is showing, despite trying to hide it. He'd naively thought the Assembly would at least have the technological and power advantage over this new adversary.

Frederick passes a hand over his face. "Well, that's unnerving, Mikhail. How did they get such powerful warships without us even knowing they existed?" Frederick asks, not sure he wants to hear the answer.

"One of the many mysteries we must unravel," says Mikhail cryptically. "But to the original point, we have to imagine that with these types of vessels, their strategy is this: hit hard and fast. We know they hit Gaia, the Colorado sector fleet, and the Colossus. The timing was relatively close together, which supports the theory," Mikhail says.

"I suppose we can presume major targets and large installations of fleets would be hit first to limit our response…?" Frederick says, thinking aloud.

Mikhail nods, corroborating Frederick's train of thought. "That would be my guess, but the question is, did they include distance in that equation? There are a number of smaller fleets further in Assembly space that might be the last hit," Mikhail muses, crossing his arms as he contemplates the questions he's raised.

"It sounds like you're going somewhere with this," says Frederick. He hopes Mikhail can shed some light on the situation.

"There are ten smaller Assembly fleets, equating to fifty vessels of various sizes. Nothing that would include a battleship like the Colossus, but every little bit helps. I can work with Marie and Xavier to get in touch with them, see who is still there," Mikhail says.

"You read my mind. Do what you need, call who you can. I'll find some other Assembly vessels," Frederick says in response.

"It will take some time, but with Marie's help, we can get started right away."

"Well then, get to it," Frederick says, clapping his hands together. "Let me know if you get a response." Frederick strides back to his station. It's already another busy day on the bridge of the Pax, and Frederick continues to dish out tasks to members of his command crew. Through the chaos and activity, he forgets he has a boss to whom he needs to report. Marie reminds him.

"Captain, we're getting communication from the Intrepid. It's Commodore Petrov," says Marie.

"Go ahead, put him through," Frederick says wearily.

Once again, Anatoly's head and shoulders float up from the holodisplay. His voice booms across the bridge, and he sounds displeased. "Captain, Marcus discussed with me the plan to dispatch the destroyers to the other jump points. That makes sense, but I'm concerned that conversations are happening without me," Anatoly says. He tuts and shakes his head. "You must understand, I can't have that. Because of this circumstance, I'll be transferring my flag to the Pax, and we'll coordinate the fleet from there. I've already communicated that to the other ships. I presume you still have some available quarters for me." It wasn't a question.

"We do and would be happy to accommodate you," Frederick says breezily, but internally he's enraged.

"Perfect. Prepare for my arrival." Anatoly once again cuts their communication abruptly, leaving no time for discussion. Frederick is starting to see a trend.

Leo quips from his station, "Another two-way conversation there, sir."

Frederick's face has a peeved expression. "You noticed that, eh? Our Commodore definitely has a particular way of conducting business," he says.

"Perhaps we'll have better luck communicating with him when he's here full time," Marie says, but her expression is skeptical.

"We might be able to act quicker at the very least. I'm surprised he didn't come over when the fleet arrived," says Renee.

"I assume he wanted to keep his fleet separate, but it's possible he sees the bigger picture now," Frederick says, and lets out a sigh. "Whatever his reason, he's coming over now, and we need to keep our opinions to ourselves—he's our commanding officer. Is that understood?" Frederick doesn't say this unkindly, but he needs everyone to be on the same page. Even if they don't fully respect Anatoly, they must at least give him a semblance of respect while he's here. He's their commodore, after all. Frederick looks at every officer on the bridge to ensure they've heard him.

Anatoly travels from the Intrepid to the Pax by shuttle, annoyed that thus far, he hasn't been the one calling the shots but somehow not recognizing he's to blame for it. Once on the Pax, he makes his way briskly to the bridge; he has a plan to lay down the law once and for all. As he enters the bridge, a harsh rebuke on his tongue for everyone, the proximity alarm goes off loudly, stealing his words before he can open his mouth. The blaring alarm signals ships in close proximity—this is becoming a familiar sound to the command crew.

"What's that racket?" Anatoly asks, shouting to be heard above the din.

Marie answers him. "More vessels have been detected, sir."

"Any idea how many, Marie?" Frederick yells out.

"I'm seeing twenty sensor pings, but I can't see any more details just yet," says Marie.

"Which jump point—is there another vessel in range?" Anatoly asks.

Leo leans forward and looks at this screen. "I see them at the northern jump point, moving slowly to the center of the system. Ah, they're moving together so it looks to be one fleet," he says.

"Seems very familiar somehow," Frederick mutters to himself. No one can hear him over the alarm, and he's glad of this.

"I'm getting a message from Shadowblade," Marie calls out.

Anatoly looks perplexed. "That's the destroyer we sent to stay in range of the northern jump point… What do they see?" He asks.

"They're receiving Assembly GFF signals," Marie says, frantically tapping at her console screen. There's an influx of information on her console, and she's trying to process it as quickly as possible.

"Alright!" Leo says and whoops. "More allies to add to the party, huh?"

Xavier turns to Frederick with a happy smile. "If those are twenty capable vessels," he says, "This might actually start looking like a fighting force!"

"I was right to open the emergency channel," says Anatoly with a smug, close-lipped smile. His eyes flash as he looks at Frederick, Xavier, and Marie in turn.

"Yes—for the moment, at least," Fredrick says distractedly. He's still concerned that this'll eventually come back to bite them all, and hard.

As the large fleet moves farther into the center of the system, the GFF identifies all vessels in the fleet; they're a mismatched collection of various sizes ranging from small frigates to larger cruisers, but unfortunately nothing as large as the Pax or Colossus. Frederick is excited to talk to the commanders and add their firepower to his ever-increasing fleet. An incoming communication is music to Frederick's ears, and he clears his throat, ready to make introductions. Marie shuts the alarm off so Frederick and Anatoly can be heard over the airwaves. She patches the call through to Frederick's console.

"Captain Ren Mallory of the Resolute Guardian contacting unknown vessels. Identify yourself," a voice says before a head and shoulders emerge on the holodisplay. Ren Mallory, a new captain in the Assembly fleet, has recently taken command of the Resolute Guardian of the Vanguard class, one of the latest heavy cruisers in the Assembly fleet. It's been used as a testbed for the improvements installed on the Pax. Unfortunately for its captain, a strong shield wasn't among them.

Frederick opens his mouth to answer, but Anatoly speaks over him. "Commodore Anatoly on the Pax Aeterna. You have quite a fleet, Captain," Anatoly says.

"Well, well—you are indeed a sight for sore eyes, Commodore! We were attacked by unknown warships that shot first, asked questions later. We survived the attack and went to corral the ships in our sector for protection until we received your message on the emergency channel. We'd decided not to use that channel ourselves, but we're glad to see allies. And some powerful allies at that." Ren's mouth quirks up in a relieved smile.

"Indeed. We hoped Assembly vessels could use this as a staging post. We have a lot to catch you up on, Captain. These ambushes are happening all around Assembly space," Anatoly answers.

Frederick chooses this moment to break in, stepping into view of the holodisplay. "In due course, we can catch you up on the events, Captain. For the moment, have your operations officers connect with ours, and we can sort out anything you might need to join the fleet formation."

"As you wish," says Ren with a nod. He's nervous, Frederick can tell—the recent ambush must've rattled him. "One thing of note—you have destroyers shadowing the jump points, and I presume your sensor range isn't large. A sensor cruiser, the ASC Specter, is a member of our fleet. If you can connect your sensors to hers, your range will be more than capable of providing coverage of the entire system. Guardian out," Ren states, his hologram dissolving as he says his goodbyes.

"That's very helpful to know, and we'll take advantage of that, surely. Now, we can pull the vessels back in safely," Anatoly says to the bridge, expecting the others to get to it.

Renee has been listening and believes her skill set could be useful at this time—finally, something else for her to do! She says boldly, "I can work with the Specter and tether their sensors to ours. That would allow for full coverage of the system."

Anatoly barely looks at her, tossing out over his shoulder, "Step to it, then. Now."

It's a busy time for the command crew; other ships continue to trickle into their fleet, which has now swelled to fifty vessels: thirty frigates and destroyers, ten light cruisers, five heavy cruisers, three battlecruisers, one battleship—the Colossus—and one supercarrier, the Pax. This now represents one of the largest fleets the Assembly has ever fielded, though they'd never had a need to muster this amount of firepower before.

The bustle of connecting with new ships finally subsides, and the crew begins to feel a renewed sense of happiness. The top of the chain of command, however, continues to be Commodore Anatoly as none of the vessels joining the fleet brought with them a higher-ranking officer. This worries Frederick; with every passing hour, he becomes exponentially annoyed with Anatoly and his style of command. Soon, both their styles would be put to the test.

Chapter Twenty-Two

As the clock on the bridge strikes 16:00, the arrival of additional vessels ceases. Leo, Mikhail, and Marie are the only ones left on the bridge. This is common practice since Mikhail is third in command and is sometimes in control for short stints while Xavier and Frederick are elsewhere.

"It is starting to get a little quiet," Mikhail muses from his station.

"At least we've got a second to think. It's been a busy day," says Marie with a hint of weariness in her voice. She's tired.

"I'll take the quiet for a while," Leo says, putting his feet up on his console. No one is around to stop him, so why not live on the wild side for a minute or two? He goes on to say, "We don't know how long it'll last before we're being shot at again."

"Keep those thoughts to yourself, young Leo—you would not want to jinx us at this critical moment of tranquility," Mikhail warns.

Renee and Jane enter the bridge, talking amongst themselves jovially, and head over to Renee's console; they've completed the integration of the ASC Specter's sensors into those of the Pax and thus can feed off their sensor details. This tethering allows the Pax's sensors to cover the entire system, providing a rare peace of mind to everyone onboard—now, there'll be no more unwanted surprises.

"You two seem happy," Mikhail says. "Can I conclude you were successful?" He asks.

Renee beams at him. "Yes, of course we were successful! The Specter and her sensors are ours—there's a few seconds delay, but we have a constant signal. If we're in the same system, they'll send their data."

Jane puts her hands on her hips, sinking into a relaxed pose. "I feel better now."

"There are always surprises to be had," says Mikhail darkly, cryptically. "We need to keep vigilant. Does Frederick know your task is complete?" He asks.

"We told him on our way up here; I'm sure we'll see him soon enough," Jane answers.

"Xavier and Frederick went down to get an overview from Elara. Richard was promoted," says Mikhail.

"Good for him!" Leo lowers his feet to the floor and swivels in his chair so he can see everyone. "It's a shame he had to get it the way he did," he says, morose.

"Torrin will not be the last we lose, I expect. You must get used to that feeling," says Mikhail, tipping his head in Leo's direction.

The glee Jane and Renee brought with them into the room has been sucked out completely. Everyone on the bridge is silent for a beat, not knowing what to say to one another.

The fleet has moved to a more central location, close to the sun at the center of the system in case the Eastern League discovers them. Little do they know it'll be but a few short hours of silence before they're once again thrown into action. Suddenly, the bridge's ceiling is flooded with that unignorable red glow, the alarm bell blaring from the speakers—something isn't right.

"What now!?" Leo yells, voice cracking. Two times in one day? How annoying, he thinks.

"Time to test our new sensors. What have they detected, Renee?" Mikhail asks, continuing to act as captain since Frederick hasn't arrived on the bridge yet.

"The Specter's sensors have picked up a number of vessels emerging from hyperspace," Renee answers, frantic.

"Where?" Mikhail barks at her, a new sense of urgency in his voice.

Renee begins tapping at her console, Jane hovering at her side. Both are astonished at the findings.

"Where, Renee—tell me where!?" Mikhail barks again, impatience getting the best of him.

"All the jump points...," Renee replies, equal parts concern and nerves.

"All the jump points? That'll severely limit our options," says Leo.

Frederick and Xavier exit the NovaPath onto the bridge, lines of worry etched on both their faces. Why is the alarm going off—and so soon after the last time? They both wonder.

"Mikhail, I leave you in command for five minutes!" Frederick says, half joking. He walks swiftly to his command console. "Status report. What do we have?" He asks.

"Vessels entering the system at all jump points," Renee says, raising her voice so she can be heard over the cacophony of the alarm and sounds of crew members reentering the bridge.

"Thankfully, you connected to that sensor cruiser," says Frederick, and Jane squeezes Renee's shoulder in support and gratitude.

"I'm not receiving a GFF signal from the vessels entering, yet the numbers are increasing," Renee says. This is curious; she looks again to make sure.

"What's the number so far?" Frederick asks.

"Let me double check… This can't be right," says Renee. She looks up at Jane. "Do you see this, too?" She asks, moving aside to let Jane peer down at her screen.

Frederick looks over. "Do you have an answer, Renee? You've got about three seconds until—."

Jane looks at Renee and nods, corroborating Renee's fear. "Captain," Renee says, "It's one hundred and twenty vessels."

Leo's jaw drops. "My god. They've found us…," he says, horror-stricken.

"Marie, get Captains Harrington, Mallory, and Varrick on a communication—we need to get out of here. Ask the commodore if he'd be so kind as to grace us with his presence," Frederick orders, barely able to restrain his frustration.

"Captain, we're receiving communication from a vessel at the eastern jump point," says Marie. She pauses, then says, "Sir, it's matching Shen's ship from the battle at Gaia."

Frederick taps his chin. Maybe Shen wants to surrender? There's only one way to find out. "In a few seconds, put him through to the command console, Marie," says Frederick as he looks around the room. "I want everyone to try and learn whatever you can about him and the fleet he's assembled. Now, Marie." The glass at the front of the bridge's holodisplay goes opaque to better display the video feed from Shen's ship.

"Captain! How good to see you again. Since I've been away, you've collected a sizable fleet," Shen drawls, smiling at his prey.

"Shen, haven't you had enough destruction already? We know your strikes weren't limited to the Solar System," Frederick says in answer.

"Oh, Captain, my Captain! You don't know the half of it," Shen says and continues, "But, you will soon. I'm in no rush, and the Assembly's fate is sealed. You simply haven't accepted the inevitability yet." Shen intertwines his fingers, completely at ease.

"Why are you doing this, Shen—why not join us and the galaxy in peace?" Frederick asks, knowing he won't get a straight answer.

"We've been watching the Assembly and the rest of the galaxy from afar. You all have an arrogance we haven't seen for centuries. Why do you think you're better than everyone else? Why must we succumb to your version of what's right?" Shen inquires.

Frederick's brow furrows, and he tries to muster some menace of his own. "You might've been watching from afar, but you don't seem to have comprehended—look at the state of humanity! We've nearly eliminated crime, removed capitalist tendencies of greed, and simply focused on doing better together as a society," Frederick explains, his emotions showing clearly in his eyes.

Shen gazes back with heavy lids, understanding now that Frederick truly believes in those ideals. He begins to chuckle. "If this is true, then why the need for your mighty vessel, why such a powerful force like the one you have before me? Was your ship truly built for your citizens' safety? No! You exist to push forward the Assembly's agenda—as far and wide as possible, making sure people conform and submit. The Eastern League will never again be anyone's pawn." Shen enunciates each word of his speech clearly, as if speaking with a child.

"So, you figured your only options were to become a vassal or eradicate the Assembly? Don't you see how extreme that is? There are options in the middle. Let's both stand down and let the diplomats work this out." Frederick pleads, hoping to appeal to Shen's reasonable side—that is, if he has one.

"Your optimism is contagious. And I do sense you believe in what you say. But you haven't suffered what we've suffered throughout history, before our evacuation from persecution. We won't allow history to repeat itself," Shen says resolutely.

Puffing and breathing hard, Anatoly finally makes his way to the bridge. He takes a minute to catch his breath since he ran most of the way here. His face is red as he watches and listens in disbelief while Frederick speaks with Shen.

"We won't let you destroy what we stand for—we'll fight you!" Frederick says, one fist clenching and unclenching repeatedly.

Anatoly strides forward; he can't let this go on any longer. He gets close enough to be seen on the display. "And who the hell might this be?" He asks, gesturing to the hologram.

"Commodore, this is Imperator Shen of the Eastern League. He's entered the system with a large fleet. Shen, this is Commodore Petrov," says Frederick, gesturing between the two. He feels a little silly making these introductions, especially in the middle of such a tense conversation.

"Oh, Commodore, you say? Such a fancy title. Are you the commanding officer?" Shen inquires, all mock civility.

"I'm the superior officer of the Assembly in this system, yes," Anatoly replies. "And you're the one to blame for all this pain." Anatoly points at Shen.

"I'm but a servant of the League," Shen says in answer to Anatoly. He levels his gaze once more at Frederick. "Do you not see? This—this 'commodore' is everything wrong with the Assembly," Shen spits out in irritation.

"You might want to be careful with your words," Anatoly says, eyes narrowed.

"As you should've been," says Shen slowly. His annoyance with Anatoly is palpable, even through the display. Normally, it takes a bit longer for Anatoly to get under someone's skin, but Shen has a knack for understanding people and their true selves.

"Superior officer, blame, pain—these are all words of your propaganda. You aren't even the superior officer in this conversation, let alone the system," Shen says.

"Are you here to antagonize me? What is it you actually want?" Anatoly asks, exasperated.

Shen's eyes bore into Anatoly. "I'm here to give you a choice: surrender or die."

"Sounds to me like less of a choice and more of an ultimatum," says Frederick.

Anatoly gives Frederick the stink eye, making Frederick feel as if his enemies are on all sides.

"However you want to perceive it," Shen says, spreading his hands out, fingers splayed. "You have a decision to make."

Anatoly squares his shoulders and puffs out his chest. "We'll never surrender to murderers like you," he says.

Shen's demeanor shifts to anger; his smirks and sarcastic chuckles are now gone. Frederick is unsure if this is due to Anatoly's wrong answer or simply because of who Anatoly is, what he stands for, and his seemingly inexplicable ability to annoy everyone around him.

"As you wish," says Shen, his mouth a straight, harsh line. He ceases communication, and the holodisplay glass returns to normal. Tension on the bridge is so thick, Frederick could cut it with a knife.

Anatoly turns and steps right in front of Frederick. He wags a finger in his face. "If you ever talk to an enemy commander without me, I'll have you demoted! Do you hear me?" Anatoly shouts, practically foaming at the mouth in his outrage.

"Sir, they contacted us and you weren't here. What was I meant to do, ignore the call? I'll run this ship to the best of my ability, and that means making decisions when needed, with or without you," Fredrick says, standing his ground.

"You'll do what I tell you, when I tell you," Anatoly says, shoving a finger in Frederick's chest. "If it were up to me, I'd have demoted you already." Anatoly breathes heavily.

"What would you have us do next, sir?" Frederick asks, though he's having a hard time staying civil, and his tone is anything but that.

"Someone—tell me how many vessels we're facing!" Anatoly yells, looking around the bridge, completely dismissive of Frederick.

"I'm seeing three hundred vessels split between the three jump points. The flow of ships has stopped," says Renee. This is an overwhelming number.

"Anatoly, we've been spending a lot of time identifying the League's classes and types of ships. Most are small destroyers and cruisers. There's still only one large warship, and it's Shen's Flagship," Jane reports as she stands by Renee's station.

Rather than thanking her for the information, Anatoly points at her and says, "That's Commodore to you."

Jane is fed up, and she can't take this disrespect anymore. Her emotions cloud her judgment, and she decides to speak her mind. "Actually, it's not; I'm a civilian, not a member of the Assembly military, and you haven't earned my respect yet. So, to me, it's just Anatoly," she says heatedly.

"I see Marcus has yet to teach you manners," says Anatoly, eyebrows raised after Jane's outburst.

"Sir, these are all members of my crew, and I'd ask you to be more professional on my bridge, or I'll have you confined to quarters," Frederick says, arms outstretched in a peacemaking gesture.

"Captain, don't push me. *I'm* the highest-ranking officer here, and you're skating on thin ice," Anatoly says.

"Sirs, we need to do something quickly. I don't need fancy sensors to know that the League's vessels are moving toward us," Leo says, inadvertently cracking the sheet of tension on the bridge.

"Confirmed. All vessels are converging on us," says Renee.

"We should charge Shen's flagship and attempt to destroy his vessel from range. Surely they'll flee," Anatoly says.

"We aren't in a position to take on that many vessels at once, sir," Xavier replies.

The crew spent the last day reviewing details from the battle at Gaia; challenging the League fleet before them would be suicide. The only person that doesn't seem to understand this is Anatoly whose tunnel vision is focused solely on the immortalization of his name should they be victorious.

"I'll be the judge of that, Commander. Have some optimism," Anatoly says, the heat leaving his voice at the thought of future praise and accolades from his peers.

"Sir, Shen's battleship is to the rear of the north group, and the east and west jump point vessels give him two flanking forces. We'll soon be in the middle of a pincer formation—they want us to go after them, and they'll annihilate us in one movement. However, they may not know we can see everything. Do you want us to attack?" Frederick asks Anatoly.

"Why do you think they're so much smarter than us? The power of the Pax and Colossus will win the day," Anatoly replies with foolish confidence.

"Sir, you're not fully thinking this through! The Colossus is damaged, but even if she were completely ready, that's only two ships—we need to tackle this fleet, but we need to do it intelligently," Frederick says.

Anatoly doesn't reply for a beat. He mulls over what Frederick has said, then asks, "Are you calling me dumb, Captain?" Anatoly sputters, enraged once more. "Frederick, I'm relieving you and assuming command of the Pax. Effective immediately."

Frederick remains at his post, completely flabbergasted. How is it that Anatoly is able to twist his words in such a way?

"Sir, we're about to enter battle... This isn't the right time," Xavier says, standing next to Frederick. The rest of the crew stands or sits mutely at their stations.

Marie breaks the silence. "We still have communications to the fleet on standby, and they're asking for orders."

Anatoly ignores this, looking at Frederick with beady eyes. "I said you're relieved, Captain," he reiterates and makes a dismissive gesture with his hand, as if to waft Frederick away like a bad scent in the air.

Frederick blinks slowly. "Yes, I heard you the first time, sir. Regardless, I need to make sure my crew and I survive for my apparent court martial," Frederick says sardonically.

"Get off my bridge—I have a frontal assault to command!" Anatoly practically screams. With this, he's successfully alienated the entire bridge crew, and they know where to place their allegiance.

Xavier must help Frederick—but what is he to do? He has only a split second to decide. He blinks, choosing a very definitive action. Moving behind Anatoly is easy; merely a few steps around the command console. The next action is much harder: he palms his coslink; the spherical top used for displaying information will do as a makeshift knuckle duster. Though it's a little large, Xavier holds it firmly. He pulls his arm back and throws an almighty punch, thrusting every Newton of force into one single strike, knowing he won't get another chance. His intent is to incapacitate Anatoly, and he hopes the blow isn't fatal. Anatoly never sees it coming. His face hits the command console cheek first, then the rest of his body follows, hitting the floor with a reverberating thud.

The bridge crew looks around at one another, confirming what's just happened. They're in shock; this is extremely uncharacteristic of Xavier. Despite this, murmurings around the bridge affirm that this was the best course of action—Anatoly needed to be stopped. Xavier remains standing in the same spot, knuckles pulsing in pain at the impact, arm dangling at his side. At the crook of Frederick's finger, one of the junior officers scurries down the stairs to determine whether Anatoly's still breathing. The officer checks Anatoly's pulse and, after a few seconds, confirms Anatoly is alive but needs medical attention.

"Take him to medical, but place him under guard and confine him to a sick bay. Get Richard to post some marines," Frederick says to the junior officer.

He turns to Xavier, placing a hand on his shoulder. Xavier's eyes are wide, and he looks down at Frederick's hand like it's a foreign object. Frederick places his other hand on Xavier's other shoulder, shaking him slightly. "Come on, Xavier, snap out of this. You did the right thing, and I thank you for it. Right now, however, you need to leave the bridge—help take Anatoly to medical." Xavier blinks and nods, and Frederick sees a spark of life behind Xavier's eyes. He pats him on the cheek and lets him go.

Xavier steps back and stoops to help the junior officer lift Anatoly's large body. Both support Anatoly's unconscious frame, his head lolling to one side as they hoist his arms over their shoulders and carry him to medical. The crew must deal with this impending crisis without these three men.

Frederick shakes his head, hoping to clear it. Instead of replaying the scene of Xavier punching Anatoly square in the face, he concentrates on what he's learned since the battle at Gaia. He addresses his crew. "Okay everyone, we need to focus. What are our options?" Frederick asks the bridge at large.

Jane clears her throat to get Frederick's attention. "The fleet doesn't have the ability to blind jump; we're unique in that. We could leave, but that means abandoning them to their death, most likely," she says.

Frederick nods in acknowledgement. "Okay, any options that don't include death for everyone?" He asks.

"We cannot take on all those vessels at once," says Mikhail in answer to Frederick's original question.

"Agreed. What if we focus on the east or western jump points?" Frederick poses this question to everyone again.

"That would significantly reduce the number of vessels we're up against, but only if we can punch through quickly…," Jane says, thinking the scenario through.

"So, we're gonna need to hit hard and fast and get as many vessels to jump—as quickly as possible," Leo says, joining in. It sounds crazy, but crazier things have happened in the last few days.

"Mikhail, I hope you weren't waiting for me to raise shields and power weapons," Frederick says.

"You wanted us battle ready!" Mikhail growls. "We are ready, sir, and I am preparing every other ship in our fleet as we speak. They will raise their weapons, too."

"Renee and Jane, answer me this: east or west jump point?" Frederick asks intently.

"Eastern seems to have fewer cruisers but a few extra ships… There'd be less firepower at the east," says Renee.

"I'd have to agree with that," Jane says, nodding.

"Right," Frederick says curtly. "Leo, you heard them—set a course for the eastern jump point. Use speed!" Frederick commands, and Leo does as he's told.

Frederick turns to Marie and addresses her at her station. "Have the majority of the fleet keep to our port rear, and have the Colossus set the pace so they're on our port side. We'll take the hits and punch through. Keep the destroyers and frigates behind us, and organize the heavy cruisers so they're on the port side of the Colossus. Battlecruisers must be on the starboard side of the fleet behind us—to protect their flank if the League tries to catch us in a pincer action." Frederick delivers these instructions matter-of-factly. He knows Marie is competent and will ensure all actions are completed.

"I'll get it done, Captain," Marie answers, and she sets to work.

The mood on the bridge is a far cry from just a day ago at Gaia. Now, the crew makes battle preparations like a well-oiled machine. Gone is their inexperience and innocence, replaced instead with a fierce determination and the hardness only loss can bring.

The League fleet is at the eastern jump point, within range of the Pax's main sensors. The command crew see what Renee and Jane see: seventy-five league vessels moving towards them. With a little luck, the northern jump point task force, including Shen's dreadnought and the majority of their forces, won't be able to contribute to the fight. So long as the Assembly fleet can act swiftly, they'll only have to deal with a minor force.

"Mikhail, take any shots you can," Frederick says. His gut rumbles with nerves as he and his ship prepare for battle.

"We are still out of weapons range," says Mikhail.

"Do what you can to limit enemy fire, especially on ships firing at the rest of the fleet. The shield will protect us for a while, but our allies need help," Frederick replies.

"As you wish, Captain," Mikhail says as he gets to work.

"Leo, keep us moving—get to the jump point as soon as you can. We don't jump until the last vessel leaves," Frederick says, making sure his instructions are clear.

"Understood. You, ah, you know we're going to be the primary target, right?" Leo asks.

Frederick nods. He must keep a brave face for his crew, but on the inside his stomach is tied in a knot, cold sweat coating his forehead. His pulse is racing. "I do. Let's see what this shield is really made of—the more vessels we save today, the better our odds against Shen in the long run," he says, arms crossed at his station.

"This is definitely better than your last plan at Gaia," Leo quips, and he has the audacity to grin as well.

"Thank you, I think…," Frederick says, turning away.

"Where are we going after this?" Marie wonders aloud.

Frederick contemplates this, but he doesn't have a definitive answer yet. "Hm. That's a good question, Marie. Any thoughts?" He asks, looking around the room.

"Marcus mentioned a station—it's called Shadowpoint—that's located at the edge of Assembly space…," Jane says slowly. "He said it's a safe space; he heard about it from Anatoly one night. Maybe he has the system name and coordinates?" Jane muses, running a hand through her hair as she thinks.

A crease forms in the middle of Frederick's brows. "I've never heard of Shadowpoint," he says. It almost sounds too good to be true.

No one on board the Pax has heard of Shadowpoint either. In fact, very few people, civilians and military personnel alike, know of its existence. It's a closely held secret, known only to the admiralty of the Assembly.

Jane says, "If you'd like, I can get the coordinates. I hate to bring the mood down, but anything we can think of, so can Shen." Jane twists her mouth into a little frown at the realization.

"Good point, Jane. We have to try, at least. Get the details from Marcus and have Marie relay them to the fleet," Frederick says.

Jane pulls out her cos-link and drafts a message to Marcus. The fleet is now fully in formation: the large Assembly vessels are protecting the smaller vessels. The Colossus and the Pax lead the charge. Marcus responds to Jane, and she forwards the coordinates to Marie who in turn communicates the plan to the fleet. Every captain is prepared to jump to Shadowpoint.

Just as everyone is lulled into a false sense of peace and security, the battle begins, and the two opposing fleets collide. The Colossus fires one of her ion cannons first, destroying one frigate from the enemy fleet in an instant. Next, the Pax and the battlecruiser Harmony's Hope, both the only other warships equipped with ion cannons, fire quickly and destroy three more warships before the League forces have fired their first shot. Shen's fleet is out-ranged by the Assembly's superior technology, but range isn't going to be the determining factor in this fight. Frederick and his crew hope the heavy warships of the Pax's fleet are able to take the brunt of the damage and shield the rest of the fleet, allowing them to retreat.

"Sir, direct hits to the enemy fleet—that is four targets down, but the Colossus, Pax, and Hope must recharge," Mikhail reports.

"You'll need to use all our weapons today, Mikhail," says Frederick, and Mikhail smiles in response. He's always wanted to show off, letting everyone know exactly what this ship can do. Today is his day to shine.

"Leo, keep us moving forward," Frederick says.

"Yes, sir. Into all those guns we go!" Leo sing-songs.

The Colossus begins to accelerate, trying to draw the fire of the entire enemy fleet. She's taking hit after hit. Though she's a sturdy ship, she can only survive so much damage for so long.

"Sir, the Colossus is taking quite a beating," Marie says.

"Our shields are taking a pounding, too," Leo says, worried. "They're failing…" He trails off, and his throat closes up with anxiety. He tries to swallow the lump that's just formed, but he can't seem to manage it. His leg begins to bounce, foot tapping out its usual rhythm.

As the shields falter, a flickering blue glow appears to grow around the ship. The Pax is losing power, her body rocked by a never-ending volley of impact from enemy vessels.

"Tell Captain Varrick to fall into the middle of the fleet—we can't lose her!" Frederick shouts, hoping one of his crew members will send the communication; he doesn't much care who, only that it gets done.

Talia Varrick has always been headstrong, never scared of a fight, preferring instead to be in the thick of the action. The majority of the time, Talia charges ahead, only thinking of the consequences later. Her typical strategy may work in this instance, as the Assembly fleet inflicts severe damage on the League fleet. The League fleet, on the other hand, hasn't been able to stop the Assembly fleet from destroying half their own. In fact, the Assembly fleet has come into point blank distance without losing one vessel. This is thanks to the Pax—she takes the majority, the rest split between the other battlecruisers and the Colossus. So far, Frederick has saved the smaller ships in his fleet, much to his relief.

"We're punching through, and the fleet is still right behind us," Leo announces with joy. Did they really come out of this victorious?

"Sir, the enemy forces—they're turning to follow us. They have a clear shot at the small vessels," Marie says, biting her lip.

In the chaos that ensued from the rush of the battle, Frederick forgot the most important part of strategic thinking: situations can change. Thinking only one step at a time doesn't allow him to plan for what would happen when they pass the Eastern League on the way to the jump point. He's put his fleet in a very precarious position—he must rectify the situation, and quickly.

Marie speaks again from her station. "We're receiving communication from the Colossus."

"I hope they have some good news," Frederick says, running both hands down his face. "Put them on my console."

The command console springs to life again, this time with the bust of a frantic Captain Varrick.

"Frederick, the enemy is at our rear! We need to move to protect it—we've sustained a large amount of damage already, and I'm not sure how much more we can take from this assault. Worst of all, our power is fluctuating. It's likely our deuterium drive can't operate fully at these levels," Talia says, breathing heavily.

"We can cover you while you make repairs; we have time before the rest of the fleet is in weapons range," Frederick says, hoping his neutral expression and calm tone give Talia strength.

Unfortunately, Frederick needs to learn hard truths in a short amount of time; Talia has already learned such lessons. "It's too late for that," she says with a weary sigh. "We weren't able to repair after the previous attack, and so the fate of the Colossus is sealed. The only thing we can do is ensure the rest of you make it through." Talia musters a brave face.

At that moment, Marie notices something peculiar on her sensors. Though she hates to interrupt, she must report this to Frederick. "Captain, the Colossus is falling out of formation," she says.

"Talia, where are you going? We need you!" Frederick demands, his neutral mask slipping away to reveal his raw fear. He bangs his hand down on the surface of his console.

Talia inclines her head. "This is how it must be, Frederick. My crew is ready. Get everyone else out of here; our sacrifice must not be in vain. I've taught you everything I can; you and the Pax are now the last best hope to save Earth. The Assembly must survive—*will* survive—but promise me you'll defeat Shen," Talia says, chin held high in determination.

"We'll do what we must," says Fredrick, numb to this impending loss.

Talia nods one last time. Frederick's screen goes blank as she cuts communication. The crew watches as the Colossus charges towards the League forces. They open fire with every gun they have available, but even a battleship of her size and strength can't survive for very long. Small destroyers circle the mighty vessel; she's played her part, stalling the Leagues forces long enough for the Assembly fleet to exit weapons range. By the time the Colossus has succumbed to damage, culminating in a huge explosion, the Assembly fleet has broken free from its pursuers.

"Captain, the Colossus…it's gone," Marie says mournfully. She puts her hand on her chest to stymie a sob.

Frederick hangs his head. "Another good vessel and crew," he says.

"I wonder when it'll be our day," says Leo, eyes welling with unwanted tears of frustration.

Frederick whirls on him. "None of that talk, Leo! We're still here, and we'll dictate our own fate. Captain Varrick and her crew gave their lives so that we might continue the fight—and we will," he says, slamming one fist down on an open palm to emphasize his point.

"We have made a dent in their forces. By my counts, the League lost thirty-five vessels to our five," Mikhail reports. Though this should be good news, Mikhail's voice is somber.

"Let's get out of here first, before we get too distracted," Frederick says. "Leo, how far are we from the edge of the system?" He asks.

"We've just arrived, ready to jump," replies Leo.

"Does every ship have the correct coordinates, Marie?" Frederick inquires.

Marie answers in the affirmative. "Yes, Captain, although I still can't find any record of Shadowpoint," Marie says, taking a deep breath and willing away the lingering sadness at losing the Colossus.

"Well, I suppose we're about to find out the old-fashioned way. Let's hope there are less guns pointed at us once we arrive. Jump the fleet out," Frederick orders. He slumps over his console, exhausted.

A few moments later, the fleet begins disappearing into hyperspace portals, leaving danger far behind. All vessels have escaped; only the Pax remains within the system. Before they leave, they receive one last message.

Perplexed, Marie says, "Captain, another communication incoming from Shen's flagship."

Frederick stands bolt upright. "Leo, cancel the jump. Let's hear what he has to say. Mikhail, how long until we're in weapons range again?" He asks.

"Not long, sir. At the current speed, it should be within minutes," Mikhail replies.

Frederick is still sick with anger at the deaths sustained on both sides today. His face portrays visible discomfort as he says to Marie, "Put him through on the main screen."

Once again, Shen, calm and collected, fills the command console holodisplay as the video feed flickers to life. His gaze pierces through, slicing Frederick's heart and nerves into pieces.

"Captain, your persistence in evasion is futile. We'll find you again. It's inevitable," Shen says, his incisors gleaming like fangs in the low light of his bridge.

"Why are you so committed to this pursuit, Shen? Can you not see what we destroyed today? Do you not care about your people?" Frederick asks, now at his wit's end.

"The League is unified, Captain. Our resolve is forged in the crucible of shared history and suffering. Every member of the League is prepared to sacrifice their life to maintain our culture and achieve what we deem just. Life is not preserved through avoidance but action," Shen replies.

Frederick rears back at this. "What life are you preserving? All I see is death and destruction."

"For centuries, Earth treated my people as lesser beings, forced into servitude, manual labor beneath your cities, treated not as people but as tools. Humanity's fear of the different, the desire to manipulate and to 'correct;' these are the traits we remember. We'll not let the memory of those who died in chains be forgotten, nor will we allow the Assembly to fall back to its baser instincts. We're a threat because we must be," Shen explains, painstakingly slowly.

"To me, Shen, you seem more of a zealot than a leader. If you negotiate with us, we can show you—humanity has evolved!" Frederick says in the hope that Shen can see reason; in the back of his mind, he knows this is futile.

"Admirable, Captain, but naive. Negotiation is a luxury for those who hold power without contest. We seek not to negotiate from a position of weakness but to dictate new terms from one of strength.

You'd do well to remember, in the grand tapestry of the cosmos, those who seize their fate dictate the future. We'll meet again, Captain, and I'll keep Earth company until then."

The screen goes dark as Shen cuts communication with the Pax. Still, his forces continue to close in, and Fredrick knows there's only one thing left to do.

"Leo, get us out of here," Frederick says.

Leo immediately sets a course and engages the hyperspace engines. His eyebrows crinkle as he says, "Captain, the engines aren't completing the power cycle…"

Frederick is aghast. He puts his hands on his hips. "How can this be happening now, just when we desperately need to get out of here?" He's tired, so very tired, and he hangs his head.

Marie reports from her station, "We've taken some damage around the engines, and it'll take a second to fix."

Renee is frantic, eyes wide. "We don't have much time, Captain! The League is closing in on our position," she says in a rush, eyes glued to the window.

"Marie…," Frederick says, his foot tapping in impatience and frustration. He feels flustered and anxious, but he tries with all his might to banish these emotions. It's not working.

"One second, Captain," Marie says shortly, just as tense as the rest of them.

Mikhail grumbles loudly, "Captain, weapons are powering down. But why…?" He's confused—he hasn't powered them down himself, and that's usually his responsibility.

Marie grunts in exasperation and holds up a hand, eyes still locked on her screen. "I need the extra power for the engines."

Frederick shakes his head. "I hope you know what you're doing," He says, shoulders tight with nerves.

After a few seconds which pass almost as slowly as eons, Leo exclaims, "I think it's starting to work!"

"I just need a little more power…," Marie mutters to herself. She continues her frantic tapping just as projectiles come within inches of the Pax's hull.

Renee pulls at her braid, fretful. "The League is back in weapons range. I see only one vessel now, but more are coming." She has to shout to be heard above the chaos on the bridge.

"It's now or never," Frederick says, voice strained.

Marie looks up. "Try it now, Leo," she says.

Leo nods and cracks his knuckles. He taps at his console and replies, "Engaging the engines." After a beat of intense silence, he whoops and yells. "Power is cycling again!" The bridge relaxes into relief at his words, and Marie slumps into her seat, glad to have this ordeal over and done.

The Pax powers up their engines and opens a hyperspace window. She leaves one danger behind while barreling full speed towards the unknown, catching up to the rest of her fleet within moments. Frederick knows they're safe in hyperspace for now, and it's time to get some much-needed rest. He sends his bridge crew to their quarters for the night, knowing tomorrow will bring more rude awakenings.

ACT III

"The Assembly's strength is forged in unity; fracture it, and all will fall."
— *Galactic Assembly Codex, Article I: Unity and Order*

Chapter Twenty-Three

    In the depths of space, the Pax and her fleet power towards the center of mysterious coordinates. Meanwhile, Earth and its citizens begin to realize the situation in which they're embroiled. Prime Director of Earth Nora Vexler has been summoned to the highest floor of San Nova's citadel for an emergency meeting. San Nova was established after WWIII and the nuclear, seismic weapon destruction of every other major city, and it held the political power of the then-newly-created Assembly. It's nestled between the ruins of San Francisco and Los Angeles, and moreover, it's the first modern city to surpass ten million inhabitants, having served as a beacon of hope for decades while Earth was rebuilt from ruins.

    The citadel is twice the size of the largest skyscrapers filling the Nova skyline. It's so tall, its pinnacle often seems to pierce the very clouds. The height and grandeur give citizens the perception that their politicians are watching them from above, protecting them from dangers beyond the stratosphere. Some wonder if the citadel is less benevolent than it seems; perhaps instead the denizens of Earth should regard it as an example of the Assembly's leadership sitting in their ivory tower without a care for commoners.

    Nora Vexler's living quarters are located on the lower floor of the citadel. As Nora ascends the citadel in a glittering glass elevator, she takes in the sprawling magnificence of the city. Over the years, it's grown to nearly fifty million inhabitants, and its expansion seems to be endless. The elevator reaches its destination—a dizzying view if one were to look down—and Nora is surrounded by a number of aides who rush her into the situation room. She's met by Fleet Consul Admiral Thane Krios, his hand outstretched to shake hers.

    Admiral Krios steadies himself, knowing time is of the essence; he'll soon explain that, in no uncertain terms, there's been a catastrophe. Krios comes from a long line of soldiers and is well-versed in the arts of war and politics. He's made a noble career for himself, consistently standing for fair practices and justice, though he's also known for being a cunning strategist. His passion and commitment for the Assembly shines through in his past work with Admiral Pacifica to refurbish the many aging space vessels at Gaia.

After a firm handshake, Krios clears his throat. "Director, I'm glad you could join me."

"You made it sound urgent, Admiral. I assume this is important?" Nora replies, glancing around the room. Its occupants have quietly gotten up from their seats and are making their exit; the windows are shuttered. After a few moments, the only occupants are herself and Krios.

The room is fully capable of seating the entire fifty-member cabinet at once, and to Nora, it seems barren with just two. She blinks as the room darkens, reaching out to place her hand alongside the large central table next to her. Nora can barely see Krios anymore; she assumes he's still standing nearby. Krios powers on the holotable, and the room fills with a display of the solar system.

"Director, I want to draw your attention to an unfolding situation. I'm not going to sugarcoat it: yesterday at approximately 20:00, we lost contact with Gaia shipyard, as well as a number of other prominent outposts throughout the system. We sent a ship to investigate, and it analyzed some of the black boxes from what remains of the station and the fleet." Krios sighs in consternation, then says heavily, "The League has returned." Though Nora can hardly see his face, shock, surprise, and worry are evident in Krios's voice—he's typically hard to read and masks his emotions with dexterity.

Nora raises an eyebrow in the dark. "They're early… We weren't expecting them for a few decades at least," she says, calm and collected at this revelation.

"Indeed. They struck Gaia first before we could redistribute our forces. They used civilian vessels to neutralize Gaia's defenses and destroyed all but one of our warships stationed there, eliminating nearly one third of our total fleet," Krios replies.

Nora takes a moment to collect her thoughts, debating what to say in response to Krios's news. She pouts a little, knowing Krios can't see her facial expression—what an inconvenience the League has become.

"I'm well aware of their existence just outside the known galaxy, but this destruction and volley of firepower? It's far more aggression than we'd planned. Which ships survived?" Nora asks slowly with both curiosity and concern.

Krios responds, a little laugh in his voice. "That's the one piece of positive news we have. The Pax Aeterna survived."

Nora moves from her space next to the table and begins to pace, careful not to bump into any chairs. She gazes at the hologram of Sol that portrays the destroyed stations—they're marked in red. Gaia wasn't the only victim of Shen's wrath.

"Well, that's something at least," Nora says, breathing out. "We can only hope they make it to Shadowpoint."

Krios continues his report of the situation, providing Nora with pertinent intel. "Jane Mitchell was on the Pax as this destruction occurred, and her partner is Marcus Harrington. He's captain of a heavy cruiser in the Colorado sector fleet under the command of Commodore Anatoly Petrov," he says.

Nora sucks her teeth, visibly irritated at the mere mention of Anatoly's name. "I met Commodore Petrov at a Gaia function a few years ago. He made quite an… *impression,*" says Nora, and her displeasure is clear. "I've never encountered someone so unaware of how his words were received," she says, shaking her head.

"He certainly wouldn't be my first choice for command, but I knew his father well, and he made me promise to look after his boy before he died," Krios says tightly, his face grimacing in annoyance.

Krios continues to speak, justifying his past choices. "He's served his purpose, you must admit. He gave the coordinates of Shadowpoint to Captain Harrington, who then gave them to Jane. And Harrington's assignment was in part to keep an eye on the Pax and provide support if ever needed. Right now, I'm glad we established those protocols," he says.

"I'm not sure I could've given that order, Thane," Nora says, and she ceases to pace, hand at her throat. "To require Marcus to keep his partnership alive just so the Pax could survive? It seems…inhuman, don't you think? I'd rather we just tell the captain our plan," Nora replies.

"Far too many people already knew the grave threat at our door—we could've told hundreds more! If we'd done that, we'd never have been able to keep the League's existence a secret," Krios says, casting both arms up in exasperation.

"Yes, but would that have been such a bad thing?" Nora asks rhetorically. She sighs, thinking to herself. She's meant to do what's best for her people.

Nora goes on to say, "Keep this in mind: there are people whose lives have been taken because of an enemy they didn't even know existed. I still think we should've told them," says Nora, frowning.

"The only thing you would've accomplished is mass panic—people are unpredictable," Krios says, tutting condescendingly. "We've kept an eye on the League from afar for decades, they won't be able to breach Earth's planetary shield. We'll be safe. Commodore Sterling of Nova Corp has his standing orders," Krios says.

"So, you've just described a grave defeat, but you're saying I should, what, trust in the plan? A plan that already seems to have failed? Should I be worried?" Nora responds to Krios's condescension in turn, tapping her foot.

Krios takes a long, deep breath; he realizes he has no agency in this battle. "What choice did we have? At this point, it's in the hands of those we've trained to do their duty…" He trails off, knowing deep down Earth will soon join the fight.

Unbeknownst to them, Imperator Shen has already set his sights on this, his ultimate objective: the annihilation of the architects of his anger. Nothing will quench his thirst for vengeance other than the complete destruction of Earth. It won't be long before he brings the full might of the League to bear. Earth's planetary shield might be able to hold the League at bay for a short period, but can Frederick and the rest of the Assembly forces respond in time to save the planets' ten billion inhabitants, shielding them from annihilation?

Chapter Twenty-Four

On the Pax, Frederick and the bridge crew have assembled, somewhat awake and alert after a restless sleep. Xavier joins the bridge crew, hurrying back from his post at the medical bay, and Frederick fills him in on the action that took place while he was attending to Anatoly.

"We're about to exit hyperspace, Captain," says Leo from his pilot's seat.

"Do you see anything in our path?" Xavier asks.

"Nothing on our sensors other than us and the fleet," Leo says. His brow furrows in confusion as he reviews the sensor's outputs. "They seem to be struggling with this system… There's definitely something scattering the scanners," Leo says.

"Just another mystery to add to our long list," says Frederick, shaking his head. He's weary and grows tired of the constant unraveling of his reality.

"Captain, we've had a few too many surprises recently—perhaps the fleet should go to battle stance? So, we're ready for whatever we're flying towards," Xavier says.

Frederick nods curtly. "Agreed. Marie, signal the fleet to go in with weapons powered as we enter the system," he orders.

"Yes, Captain," says Marie. She does as she's told.

Though it would only take another minute to travel the distance to the unknown system, it'll feel like the longest minute of their lives. It's only been a few days since the crew had their world turned upside down, Frederick thinks to himself, and he's impressed with how they've been able to acclimate to their new normal, harsh as it may be.

"Exiting to normal space in 3… 2…1…," Leo says.

As the fastest in the fleet, the Pax is the first vessel to emerge from hyperspace. It exits at the front, leading the way for the rest; they all emerge in the system within the next fifteen seconds.

"All vessels have emerged without issue, Captain." Marie says.

"What's out there?" Xavier wonders aloud. Though he knows the coordinates came from Marcus by way of Jane, an explanation hasn't yet been given as to what they'll find once they arrive.

Now that the fleet is out of hyperspace, the crew of the Pax sees a huge, green nebula that expands across the entire system, cloaking it in shadow. The murky greens almost seem to pulsate, attracting glances and stares as crew members catch a glimpse of the nebula through the window. Different hues and shades undulate around them, and it's hard to make out anything other than what looks to Jane like pea soup.

"Look at that! It's incredible…," Leo says in breathless wonder. The sight reminds him of the reason he loves to fly—to see things no one else has seen.

"Anyone know what 'that' is?" Frederick asks, turning to Jane. No one answers, caught up in the scene outside the Pax's window. He hopes Marcus has told Jane more than she's letting on, and he continues to look at her with skepticism. "Do you know where we are, Jane? You gave us the coordinates… Did Marcus tell you anything else?" Frederick inquires.

"Nothing, Frederick," Jane says, shaking her head with a shrug. She gestures to the window. "This is all he ever told me."

All the while, Renee has been investigating the nebula before them. After gathering enough information, she speaks. "Captain, it's a nebula and much denser than anything I've seen before. Our sensors are having a hard time penetrating much more than the first hundred miles," she reports.

Frederick frowns. "So, there could be anything waiting for us in there." He puffs out a frustrated breath and turns to Marie. "Get Marcus on the Intrepid for me," he says.

A short moment later, Marcus appears on the command console.

"Frederick! Looks like we've all arrived in one piece," Marcus says with a relieved smile.

"Indeed, but Marcus—where the hell are we?" Frederick asks, baffled but somehow calm. The stress has begun to ease off his shoulders.

"Somewhere we'll be able to get help. Commodore Sterling, I'm sure, will make contact soon. He'll explain everything," Marcus replies.

"What the devil is going on, Marcus? Just give it to me straight," Frederick says, imploring Marcus to make sense of the situation.

Marcus shakes his head no. "It's not for me to say, Frederick. Isn't Anatoly there to explain?" He asks, looking around the bridge through his limited view from the holodisplay.

Though Frederick may be calm, Marcus's words spark a prickle of panic at the back of his mind. He must be careful with his next words, protecting his and Xavier's positions. It's likely Marcus will be concerned for the commodore's wellbeing, and Frederick must ensure this doesn't turn into contempt for the Pax.

"Ah, yes, Anatoly. He, uh, took a knock before we left the battle. He's currently unconscious in our medical bay," Frederick says, hedging.

"Oh. Well, that's unfortunate. Send him my regards, please—but know this, Captain: you're exactly where you're meant to be," Marcus says with an unreadable expression contorting his features.

"What's that meant to mean? You gave these coordinates to Jane—what's so special about this place?" Frederick unleashes a multitude of questions without a filter.

"Sit tight, Frederick," says Marcus. "Anatoly didn't mention much to me—only that we need to arrive here if we were ever in danger. I'm sure all will be explained by the commodore." Marcus inclines his head.

With that, he closes the communication, leaving Frederick still confused. A few hours ago, as they'd left the Lumina Dyad system, Frederick felt like he was getting a grip on this situation. In that time, Marcus seems to have changed, transforming from a person who needed Frederick and his crew's help to a chess master, silently moving pieces around on a board. Was he playing dumb, or is this a bluff? Perhaps Marcus doesn't know much either, Frederick muses to himself. Maybe it's true, and Commodore Sterling *will* be able to answer the many infuriating questions that fill his mind.

"That didn't sound like the man I know," Jane says, a perplexed look clouding her features. She's just as confused by Marcus's words as Frederick.

"Perhaps it's a trap," Xavier says with raised eyebrows.

"Marcus wouldn't put us in danger by choice… If we stay here, someone will surely come to us," Jane says resolutely.

"You want us to sit here at the jump point, waiting?" Mikhail asks gruffly.

"I hate to say it, boss, but I agree with Mikhail on this one." Leo shakes his shoulders as a shiver rocks his body. It feels as though someone is walking on his grave—or maybe that's the withdrawal. "Something's not right…," he says.

"Anything at all on sensors?" Frederick asks, looking around at each of his officers. In unison, they give him a head shake: no.

"Whatever Anatoly's reason for having these coordinates, we seem to be here for a purpose. It could be important," Frederick says to the crew at large.

"The fleet should keep their battle stances at the very least," Xavier says.

Frederick nods and says, "Agreed—keep the fleet ready just in case. Get the Air Wing up and running, have them conduct patrols around the fleet nonstop for the time being. Any other vessels with strike craft should do the same. Why don't you send a few into the nebula, see what they find?" Fredrick suggests, hoping he might receive answers this way.

"As you wish," Xavier says, spreading his hands wide. "I'm sure Elara would love a chance to fly into that." Xavier quirks one side of his lip; it's a change from the morose attitude he'd adopted since laying hands on Anatoly.

"Excellent idea, Commander. I'm almost positive we aren't alone out here." Frederick looks at his crew and feels their collective tension. They're not out of the woods yet. He pushes his shoulders back, trying to appear at ease.

"Xavier, you have the bridge. Let me know if anything changes. Jane, it might be time for you and I to check on the condition of the commodore," Frederick says.

"Lead the way," replies Jane, and she follows Frederick.

Frederick gestures to the NovaPath, and they both wait to step on board. The doors slide open, and the two enter, soon on their way to deck twelve and the main medical bay.

Once the NovaPath doors close, Frederick starts asking questions. "Marcus definitely seemed different today… Is everything alright?" He asks Jane bluntly.

"I'm sorry, Frederick, I'm not sure how much I can help," Jane says with a full-bodied shrug. "I haven't been able to talk to him since he left the Pax and returned to the Intrepid."

"Did he seem different when he was over?" Frederick tries again; he's relentless.

"Nothing I can put my finger on. Why all the questions?" Jane asks, feeling slightly bewildered, like a deer in headlights. How many times must she say she doesn't know, well, *anything*?

"We're missing something, that much is clear. I'm hoping Anatoly can tell us what we need to know and fill in the gaps. But I feel it in my gut: Marcus knows more than he'd have us believe…," Frederick replies, a faraway look in his eye, lost in the mystery of their location.

"If he knew something, I'm sure he'd tell you," Jane says. She'll be loyal to her partner no matter what; she believes in him, even if he's acting strangely.

As the captain of the ship, it's Frederick's job to maintain the safety of everyone under his command—sometimes this means protecting his crew from themselves and even the people they think they can trust. History might present some insight into the here and now, so he'll have to start at the beginning but tread carefully.

"How long have you actually known Marcus, Jane? I'm not sure I've ever asked when you met," Frederick says, trying for levity.

It works, and Jane is caught off-guard, happy to spill stories of pleasant times with her partner. "We've been together now nearly ten years, ever since we met on Mars," she says, smiling to herself. "I wanted to be part of his life. We met through a mutual friend at a university event. It was a huge day for me." Jane takes a moment to reminisce about one of her fondest memories of Marcus.

"We hit it off immediately, and I really enjoyed talking to him—especially about my work. I expected him to not care; after all, he was a legionnaire at that point, in the operations department on an old cruiser. But I could tell he was different," Jane says emphatically.

Frederick whistles. "Ten years! That's a long time. I know it's been a struggle while he's been stationed away from you, you've mentioned it before. Has Marcus ever seemed this aloof?" Frederick asks, digging for information but attempting a light touch.

Jane turns her mouth down in a small frown. "Not that I remember… What are you trying to find?" Jane asks, crinkling her brow, and Frederick knows she's on to him.

At that moment, the NovaPath slows to a stop, and the doors slide open. Jane won't stop looking at Frederick, even as the two walk briskly towards the medical section of the ship.

Frederick finally breaks. "I get the feeling I'm missing something, but I can't put my finger on it," he says.

"You think Marcus isn't telling you something?" Jane asks defensively, and her expression is guarded. She doesn't appreciate these insinuations.

"I don't really know what to think," says Frederick, running one hand over his head. "Perhaps the one person that can actually shed some light on this situation is behind that door, reluctant as I am to admit it," Frederick says, pointing to the medical bay entrance.

Frederick and Jane approach the medical bay's double doors. To Jane, these are just another set of doors on the Pax; there are identical doors like these all over the ship, and they look exactly the same to her. The only way Jane can differentiate these doors from another is by looking at the screen on the wall to the left of one door. Much like other vessels in the fleet, the Pax is a maze, and it's easy for one to get lost. Somehow, Frederick always knows his way, and Jane hopes his intuition will shine a pathway into the future, too.

The Pax's medical bay is staffed around the clock; usually it's busy. Today, medical staff grapple with a few injuries from the recent battle. Frederick and Jane step through the automatic double doors and look around. They spot their target.

"James, how is our guest?" Frederick asks, striding over to Principal Medical Officer James Eastman. Patients turn to look as Frederick speaks, his entrance startling some.

Dr. Eastman has been a member of the crew for the last two years, and he's enjoying his rotation on the carrier. Frederick and

James became friends over those years, and Frederick can always count on James to give him feedback that keeps him grounded securely in humanity.

James turns his head and smiles at Frederick and Jane's entrance as he stands next to one of his bed-ridden patients. Doctors and nurses flit around the bay, tending to the cuts and bruises of other crew members who need assistance. Though medical staff bustle around the room, many of the beds are empty, and Frederick is glad of this. He and Jane reach James and look down at the bed where Anatoly lies, unconscious. Anatoly is hooked up to a remote monitoring system which displays his vitals and other information about his health status.

"Captain, nice to see you in medical," James says. He gestures to Anatoly. "He's doing well—that was quite a blow Xavier gave him, eh?" He says, stifling a laugh.

Frederick shrugs good naturedly. "Xavier may have used some, shall we say…excessive force, but you should've seen the commodore on the bridge. I find dealing with him to be very challenging," Fredrick says.

"Just because he's our commanding officer doesn't mean he's not required to earn our respect," James says, raising his eyebrows.

Frederick laughs sarcastically; he surely doesn't remember Anatoly attempting to earn anyone's respect. "I'm not sure he tried, James," Frederick says.

"Whatever he did, this might not be good for Xavier's career," James replies.

Frederick gives him a tight-lipped smile in return. "We'll see what happens. To the point at hand, we need to talk to Anatoly—that's the reason for our visit. Is it safe for you to wake him up?" Frederick asks.

"I want to let him recover for a little longer—could you come back in a few hours?" James asks, checking Anatoly's chart.

"James, please—it's important. We need some answers from him, and we can't wait," says Frederick, leaving no room for argument or disagreement.

James relents. "Fine, but keep it brief. You've got five minutes," he says and begins to work with the machines and medical devices at the head of Anatoly's bed. After a few moments, Anatoly's eyes crack open on heavy, puffed lids. He's awake, but only just.

Anatoly moans. "Argh, my head… I feel like I've been hit by a train. What happened?" He asks thickly, as if his mouth is stuffed with cotton balls.

"Commodore, you hit your head. You don't remember?" Frederick asks gently, trying to ascertain whether Xavier is in danger.

Anatoly tries to shake his head but finds the pain to be too much, so he stops moving altogether. "No, the last thing I remember is this: we were on the bridge and then…then here you both are, hovering over me," Anatoly mumbles, his usual vigor gone. He sounds weak.

"Since then, the fleet fled the Lumina Dyad System. The Eastern League was in hot pursuit, and unfortunately, we suffered some losses… The Colossus sacrificed herself," Frederick says sadly, mournfully.

A throbbing head can't stop Anatoly's temper, and he grits out, "You lost our most important asset." Though hurt, Anatoly can't hide his true, quarrelsome nature. "Where the hell are we now?" He asks gruffly, beady eyes roving the room as if he can see beyond the walls of the medical bay.

"That's why we came to pay you a visit. We don't know," says Frederick. Before he can utter any other details, Anatoly cuts in.

"Trust you to get us lost." Anatoly musters all his remaining strength to sound as irritated as possible.

"Actually, we're at the coordinates Marcus gave me," Jane pipes up from her place next to Frederick. "He gave distinct instructions: if we ever found ourselves in imminent danger with nowhere else to go, we were to use the coordinates. He said you'd given them to him. Something about a 'Shadowpoint,' but he won't go into detail. And he was adamant, he thought someday I might need them…," Jane finishes her explanation.

"Ah! Finally, he did something right." Anatoly tries to smirk.

"What do you mean, *finally*?" Jane says, emphasizes her words. "Marcus has done nothing but help you," she says, trying to keep calm but struggling—it's uncanny the way Anatoly can get on her nerves in mere seconds.

Frederick puts his arm between Jane and the bed. "Alright, let's have this out later," he says. "Commodore, where are we? Do you know where Marcus sent us?"

Anatoly sinks further into his bed; he looks almost relaxed. This is all part of the grand plan Fleet Consul created. He trains his eyes directly on Frederick to make sure his words are fully understood. "You're at a top-secret facility. It's the home of Nova Corp: Shadowpoint station. You'll be safe here." He replies cryptically.

Frederick is vaguely aware of Nova Corp, but like most of the captains and officers of the fleet, he's never interacted or even seen a Nova Corp vessel.

"I've heard whispers of Nova Corp and the people involved, but I'll admit I've never seen any evidence that they exist. When I saw the ion cannons on the freighters at Gaia, however, I thought of the stories I'd been told, and I wondered whether Nova Corp had something to do with it." Frederick tries to remember the tales he's been told of a mysterious group outside the rules and laws of the Assembly. They work from the shadows to monitor and manipulate the galaxy, ensuring the Assembly survives and prospers at any cost.

Anatoly doesn't answer, so Frederick continues. "There was a story I heard once about an older fleet sent deep into the Star Union territory for a routine patrol," says Frederick. "The mission was meant to be an easy show of power, but it resulted in the destruction of multiple Assembly cruisers by unknown assailants. Rumor had it Nova Corp sacrificed the men and women of those cruisers to rid themselves of older ships. We all dismissed this as a fantasy, a scary story circulated to keep us in line. Surely the Assembly can't be that callous about sacrificing human life, right? The stories about Nova Corp can't be real?"

"Oh, I assure you, Captain, they're very real. They're probably watching you at this moment…," Anatoly says, trailing off, his words beginning to slur.

James strides back over; their time with Anatoly is up. "Captain, I'd feel much better if we could finish this later—give Anatoly more time to rest," he says.

Frederick clasps his hands together, pleading. "A few more questions, James," says Frederick looking down at Anatoly's form, his chest rising and falling with each heavy breath.

"I'm sorry, Captain, but I must insist. He took quite a knock to the head, and I should put him under so he can get some rest. You'll be able to talk to him in a few hours," replies James as he works with the machines and puts Anatoly back to sleep.

The medical machines pump him full of drugs to increase blood flow and repair damaged cells. Within seconds, he's unconscious again. His healing is left to computers that'll remedy his ailments with both speed and efficiency, yet the doctors that manage these machines always err on the side of caution. Because of the wonders of modern medicine in the space age, it's common for people to live beyond the age of 130 years old.

Frederick glances at Anatoly's sleeping form, and annoyance washes over him. He's steaming—why is he always in the dark? It's starting to become a pattern. He looks at Jane, a scowl on his face, and gestures for her to lead the way out. They head towards the doors.

"I only ever seem to have more questions. For once I wish things were simple," he says as he walks.

"Honestly? I don't think we'll ever get the answers we want from Anatoly. Everyone's so cryptic about this place, I can't understand why...," Jane replies. She contemplates their lack of answers—between Marcus and Anatoly, neither has been direct with them yet.

They keep their voices low until they're through the double doors of the medical bay, walking slowly down the corridor. The NovaPath will take them back to the bridge.

"Some of the stories I've heard of Nova Corp... I wonder if we might be safer with Shen," Frederick muses, the tension creeping back up to his shoulders, weighing him down.

"I've never heard of them at all. What do they do?" Jane asks.

"The stories say they're on the fringe of Assembly combined forces, accountable only to their own warped sense of justice and Fleet Consul." Frederick says, using his hands to gesticulate. "They use, shall we say, less than orthodox tactics to complete their objectives, and they don't concern themselves with innocents or casualties. It's imperative they complete their missions no matter what," Frederick explains.

From behind them, they hear the heavy thump of footsteps. James calls out to them to wait. He sucks air in through his nose as he catches up.

"I overheard you both speaking about Nova Corp in the medical bay, and I wanted to provide you with what little clarity I can, for what it's worth. What you need to understand is who you're working with here; they might play military, but they operate more as spies than soldiers. Nova Corp is in the shadows for a reason; their methods aren't above board," James huffs out.

Jane whirls on him. "You've worked with them before—when?" She asks plaintively.

James replies, "The Assembly called it a 'minor insurgency' on a small backwater planet in the German Association's space. Passau, in the Munich System; a newly colonized planet that wanted to live by their own rules."

"What happened?" Frederick asks.

"Something I've tried to forget…," James says as he hangs his head and continues his bleak tale. "After a few years of service, I was contacted by a Commander White—a brute of a man who looked more like a boxer than a soldier but wore an Assembly uniform. He asked me and my squad to join his team, and I agreed. This was back when I was a special operations commander, before I decided to start healing people rather than ending them," James answers. He relives the memories in his mind's eye.

"You've never told me about this before," says Frederick, eyebrows raised. He laments the fact that James felt the need to carry these secrets on his back like a heavy pack all this time.

"I've never told anyone this story. What we did there was horrific," James says, collecting his thoughts. He blinks, and there's anger behind his eyes.

"We were taken to the planet with three other squads. There had to be at least forty soldiers, all well-trained like me, but they were Nova Corp—just without a uniform. They wore everyday clothing so you'd never know who they were, and no one talked to us throughout the entire trip. My squad and I just trained… We felt like outsiders. Only the officers would interact with us and provide me with scant updates, telling us our mission was to support 'peacekeeping' efforts on the planet and assist its population.

"The colonists had been demanding independence and wanted to be treated like the owners of their own planet. This was completely against the Assembly's wishes, and the German Association had already claimed the planet and given substantial resources to help rebuild it," James says, getting emotional at digging up these hard memories. He'd rather they stay buried.

"For the Assembly, this 'minor insurgency' couldn't be allowed to continue. When we got there, all we found were peaceful protests. I talked to some of the inhabitants, and they told me they just wanted to be left alone—to be free. They didn't need support from anyone; they wanted to have a place to call their own." James finishes his tale, shaking his head.

"Did they ever gain their independence?" Frederick asks. "I don't remember hearing anything about Passau." Frederick prides himself on his knowledge of the universe, but if the last few days have taught him anything, he isn't as well versed as he'd once thought.

"The planet's population was completely eliminated. One hundred thousand people killed in an instant." James looks away and down at the floor, the weight of his past squeezing him. Hot shame pricks the corner of his eyes, and he sucks in a breath.

"The Assembly brought us there as a ruse—they didn't want help!" James says vehemently, slashing a hand through the air. "They wanted to solve an issue as efficiently as possible."

Frederick feels a chill down his spine. "You mean to tell me they wiped out an entire planet's population to suppress a peaceful protest? How is that justified under any law?" He demands, incensed at the outrageous outcome of James' story.

"It isn't," James mutters and says, "Nova Corp operates above the law… Or perhaps without *regard* to any law. The Assembly covers up these actions with stories of tragic accidents or unpreventable disasters. They did it in Passau, and believe you me—they can do it anywhere."

Jane cringes; she feels cold all of a sudden. She wraps her arms around herself to get warm again, a reminder that she's still alive. "How did you get out of there? And why didn't you say anything before?" She asks.

"My men and I were good people, we stuck up for the inhabitants, trying to fight off Nova Corp to save the few we could.

We hid fifty in the city before Nova Corp departed. Luckily, a small freighter was left behind, and we used it to get to Planet Munich, but it took us weeks. We'd hoped they'd left us all for dead. When I checked the registry, my record listed me as deceased—killed by pirates on a freighter I'd never even heard of before. On that day, I decided my old self had died and I would forever try to be the change I wanted to see in the world. I trained and became a doctor to help people…and this is when the James you know was created; I eventually became the man you see before you," James replies, a slightly sheepish smile on his face.

Jane reaches out to place a hand on James' shoulder, saying, "We need to be very careful, in that case. Knowing what Nova Corp is capable of… I'd hate to find out what would happen if they discover you're alive," she says, giving James a squeeze, the only real comfort she can offer.

Frederick can't stand still after hearing James' story. He begins to pace, small steps in circles around the corridor. He thinks of his crew.

"We'll need to ensure our communications and movements are secure. Nova Corp can't find out about you or our knowledge of their operations. Let's assume they're monitoring us closely," Frederick says, looking at the pair.

James glances between Frederick and Jane, a faint smile breaking through despite the grim discussion. "Thank you both for hearing me out and taking this seriously. I've lived with this secret for too long, always fearing the day it might resurface," he says earnestly.

Frederick nods. "We're in this together, James. If what you say is true, they might be more dangerous than the League. Maybe, just maybe, we can get justice for those lost on Passau. First, we must eliminate our immediate foes," he says.

Frederick is interrupted as his cos-link buzzes. He pulls it out of his pocket and looks at the screen; Xavier is calling. He answers with, "Go ahead."

"Captain, you're going to want to get up here. Vessels have just been detected, and they're slowly closing in on us." Xavier's voice is frantic over the cos-link's speaker.

"I'm on my way back up," says Frederick.

"Yes, Captain," Xavier says and ends the call.

Frederick pockets the device and squares his shoulders, ready for another attack. Moments later, the ship's alarm goes off; over the last few days, this alarm has blared more times than in the entire service life of the vessel.

Frederick looks at Jane. "I'm starting to get sick of this. Let's get to the bridge and see what Nova Corp has in store for us." He and Jane bid adieu to James and make their way back onto the bridge. Finally, the NovaPath's doors slide open on well-oiled hinges, and Frederick and Jane step into a familiar scene of chaos.

"Report!" Frederick says with authority in his voice.

"Captain, we have a vessel gaining slowly on us. The nebula makes it difficult to get a fix on its exact location…," Xavier says.

"What do we know?" Frederick asks, looking around at the crew.

"It's definitely an Assembly vessel of some sort, but I'm not getting a read on which registry or class. It's big—similar in size to the Pax," Marie reports from her station.

Mikhail pipes up. "I cannot detect any power signatures from this range. Their weapons could be powered or not. I have no idea, sir," he states.

"What are the odds that this is the system's welcome party?" Frederick says, throwing his hands up. He thinks back to Marcus, Anatoly, and James' comments—didn't they all allude to the fact that Nova Corp likely had eyes on them as soon as they'd entered the nebula? Frederick ponders this; he mustn't allow Nova Corp to take advantage.

"Marie, can you establish a communication?" Frederick asks, turning to her.

"It's a little challenging, but I think so. Give me just a moment," replies Marie.

Frederick turns to Renee and says, "Get as much information about the system and the vessel as possible."

"Of course, Captain." Renee stares intently at her console.

Eager to be of service, Jane says, "I'll help you." She strides over to Renee.

"Leo, take us in closer, but go as slow as you can… Make it look casual," Frederick says to his pilot.

"Uh, how the hell do I fly casually?" Leo asks sardonically.

Frederick places his hands on his hips and begins to pace. "I don't know, just don't make us look like an easy target!" He says.

"Yes, sir. Casual it is…," Leo mutters.

"Captain, I have a connection with the other vessel," Marie calls from her place on the bridge.

"Patch them over to my console. Everyone, keep your eyes open and stay alert—prepare for anything," Frederick says. The bridge crew work like a well-oiled machine: the past week's experiences have taught each member a lesson in life and combat. The biggest lesson of all has been to have faith in their captain.

A new face appears on the holodisplay, shrewd and calculating. Frederick and the rest of the crew meet the gaze of small yet intimidating eyes, and Frederick is intrigued—perhaps it's time to finally get some answers.

"This is Captain Frederick Langfield of the Pax Aeterna. Identify yourself," Frederick says sternly.

"Hello Frederick. I'm Noia Sterling, captain of the Justice. Lots of vessels on my sensors for a man that calls himself a captain," says the voice.

"We've picked up some allies along the way while looking for a safe space. Can you…offer that?" Frederick asks haltingly. He treads as carefully as possible.

"Why would you need a safe space, Captain Langfield? I hope you don't mean to say trouble has followed you," Noia's hologram says.

"No more trouble than any captain should expect. Have you heard about the Eastern League and their return?" Frederick asks, feigning nonchalance.

"We're aware of the League and their plan, yes," the hologram says and nods. "We're also aware of Gaia's destruction. I hope you didn't have anything to do with that, Captain. Truth be told, I'm wondering how you got these coordinates—this is a highly classified system." Noia's eyebrows crinkle.

Frederick sighs. Might as well tell the truth. "Yes," he says, "We were at Gaia when everything happened. We were the only ones to survive the battle—orchestrated by an Imperator Shen and his fleet. Afterwards, we regrouped and united our forces with the fleet you see before you. Shortly thereafter, we were once again forced to go on the run, and Commodore Petrov gave us these coordinates to use in case of extreme emergency. To us, this definitely counts as extreme."

"And where is the commodore now? I don't see him on your bridge," Noia's hologram says, looking around at what he can see of the Pax.

"Currently, he's in our medical bay resting. He, ah, received an injury. As I said, the League drove us from the Lumina Dyad System while we were regrouping," Frederick answers.

"So, that was your signal we detected? Hm, a risky strategy, Captain, but I'm glad it worked for you." Noia's holographic eyes look at the officers in his line of sight on the bridge of the Pax. He takes his time observing what he can, giving everyone a second of direct eye contact as he continues to speak.

"Captain, you and your fleet don't have clearance to be here, but these are strange times. Join us at Shadowpoint and let's continue this conversation," Noia states, a dark gleam in his eye.

"Any safe harbor you can give to the fleet would be appreciated," Frederick says, relief flooding through him. He's optimistic, though cautiously so; all isn't what it seems.

It's as if Noia has read Frederick's mind. He says in reply, "You're perfectly safe here—in fact, there's only one way in and out. We're sending coordinates to the base, but be aware that your sensors may struggle. We'll update your fleet vessels to ensure they're able to see in the future. Follow us, Captain, and keep close. Dock with the station when you can, and have the rest of the fleet orbit. Unfortunately, we can't accommodate everyone at once," Noia explains.

"I would ask that the Intrepid also docks. I'd like Captain Marcus Harrington to join us," Frederick says.

"As you wish," Noia says with a gentle smile. He closes the communication.

Frederick looks around as the holodisplay screen disappears. The crew can see the nebula in every direction now.

Xavier decides to break the silence first. "Noia doesn't seem so bad," he begins.

Frederick raises his eyebrows. "I fear, in this case, looks can be deceiving. We should still keep vigilant," he says. Frederick can't shake the feeling that this has all been too easy, and he remains wary.

"Should we cancel our battle stance, at least?" Xavier asks.

In response, Frederick nods in agreement. "We should—no need to draw unnecessary attention. The people at Shadowpoint are members of the Assembly, and we should treat them with respect. That being said, let's keep one eye open," he says.

Xavier understands. "Marie," he says, "Cancel the battle stance across the fleet, and tell them to stand down and follow us to the coordinates. As a matter of fact, have we received those coordinates from Noia's vessel?" He asks.

"As you wish, Commander. Yes, we've just received them," Marie replies, glad to have a task to occupy her mind rather than leaving it to dwell on the unknown of their situation. This was meant to be her last mission, what will become of her now?

"Let's get to it then," Xavier says, clapping his hands together. He turns to Leo and points, saying, "Set a course."

Leo glances at Xavier and asks with a tiny huff, "Do I need to fly casually this time?"

"Perhaps there'll be another opportunity," says Xavier with a grin.

The bridge settles down from the excitement, leveling out into ordinary operations. Frederick is delighted to see his first officer take a more active role in running the vessel; Xavier has begun to take charge in a good way. Frederick pulls him aside, beckoning him to one side. Xavier complies and joins Frederick by the window so they can have a quiet word together. In their periphery, the nebula glows in green hues.

"You don't need me today, Xavier," says Frederick, turning his head to the side to view his first officer in a new light. Xavier is coming into his own on this ship.

"Really?" Xavier sputters at first but quickly regains control of his emotions. "Well, you might need to spend more time with the fleet and the commodore. Since I'm your first officer, I should get into the practice of commanding the Pax more often," Xavier says, squaring his shoulders.

"I agree, Commander," says Frederick, crossing his arms. "Whatever happens in the future, it'd be good for you to step up and into a captain's role now. If anything, our experiences here will prepare you for your first command—you're more than ready. With everything that's happening, however, I don't know *when* you might take command of your first ship, but my advice is to perform your duty to the best of your ability," Frederick says.

"Understood, Captain. I appreciate your confidence," Xavier replies, beaming.

Frederick returns the smile with one of his own and gently pats Xavier on the shoulder. They walk back to their shared station on the bridge. Once Xavier reaches their station, Frederick continues past him and heads to the NovaPath at the back of the bridge.

"I'm off to the observation lounge," Frederick announces to the crew at large. He says to Xavier, "Commander, you have the bridge," and nods curtly, pressing the button for the NovaPath. He turns and steps into it.

Behind him, he hears Xavier say, "Yes, Captain," with pride and hope in his voice.

Chapter Twenty-Five

An hour has passed since Noia and his flagship initially made contact. The Pax and her fleet are now in sensor range of Shadowpoint station. No one on board has any expectation as to what Shadowpoint might look like; as the Pax brings them closer, crew members look out of windows and see a huge metal structure—the size rivals that of Gaia. Hopefully the Pax and her crew will find the answers they seek rather than more questions.

"This must be Shadowpoint," says Frederick, having returned from a short rest in the lounge. He strokes his chin, turns to Leo, and asks, "What's its bearing?"

"Dead ahead, around a million miles out," Leo replies.

"We are well within weapons range of anything they might have," Mikhail muses from his place on the bridge.

"We're all on the same team, Mikhail, remember that. Get your finger off the proverbial trigger, please," Frederick reprimands, and Mikhail holds his hands up in surrender.

"Marie, anything else out there, any other ships?" Xavier asks.

"I'm detecting some power signatures, but this nebula is causing issues with the sensors. I can't tell you definitively," Marie responds.

"Any GFF signals at all?" Xavier presses, hoping for more intel.

"Yes, but they're distorted… Strangely, the distortion doesn't appear to be caused by the nebula," Marie says.

"Someone… or some*thing*, I should say, is distorting the signatures," Frederick says, perplexed. The gears begin to turn in his mind as he thinks. Who or what could be causing this interference?

"Seems that way, sir," Marie confirms.

"We'll have to be on our best behavior—we don't want to aggravate our hosts," Frederick says, letting out a breath. The pressure is on once again.

"Captain, we've received a message from Noia's vessel. They're requesting the fleet hold formation at least five miles from the station, but you've been asked to join Noia on the flight deck of Shadowpoint. He sent landing instructions," Marie states, looking up from her screen.

Frederick pauses for a beat before saying, "Ah, well, let's not keep our hosts waiting. Xavier, you have the ship and the fleet—keep it in one piece until I get back." He begins to mentally prepare himself for another meeting with Noia.

Xavier nods. "I'll do my best, Captain," he says.

Before heading towards the NovaPath which will take him to Shadowpoint, he thinks of something. "Jane, it might be best if you join me," Frederick says, turning to face her. "I'll need your input. And Mikhail, you'll join us too," he says, directing his gaze at each of them in turn.

Both Jane and Mikhail step away from their places on the bridge to follow their captain to the NovaPath. Before they can reach it, however, Frederick stops himself mid-step. It dawns on him that he'll need all the support he can get, and he remembers his request to Noia.

"Marie, send the landing instructions to the Intrepid and ask Marcus to join us as well," Frederick orders, and Marie nods in acknowledgment.

"I'll have Elara prep a shuttle for you, and I'll do my best to take care of the Pax while you're away," says Xavier.

"Very good, Xavier," Frederick says, tipping one corner of his mouth down. He's grateful that his first officer is so forward-thinking. "And something tells me Earth is the League's final target…"

As the doors of the NovaPath shut behind Frederick, Jane, and Mikhail, they resolve to finally get some answers—at this point, they're desperate for knowledge. Frederick also decides to create a plan of attack to fight the forces of the League; he's determined to deny them their objective.

The flight deck is busy as ever, and the NovaPath deposits its occupants right in the middle of it. Elara and Richard are waiting at the NovaPath's doors, ready to assist.

"Xavier sent me the flight instructions. We have a shuttle ready for you," Elara says, gesturing to a waiting spacecraft.

The cohort walk across the flight deck to the waiting transport. At this moment, Richard decides to share his concerns.

"Captain, I'd feel better if you'd let me join you. I've heard stories… Well, rumors mostly," Richard says to Frederick, biting his lip in concern.

"If they wanted us dead, we wouldn't be having this chat right now. Besides, Richard, I'm not sure having a squad of marines with us sends the right message," Frederick replies.

"I strongly insist that I join you." Richard tries again.

"I applaud your initiative, Richard, really, I do. Regardless, I have enough Assembly personnel here with me, so you may stand down," Frederick replies, though not unkindly.

"Yes, sir," Richard says with a short salute. "If you need us, just call." He backs away and allows Frederick, Mikhail, and Jane to proceed to the shuttle.

"Rest assured, if we need extraction, you'll know," Frederick says over his shoulder as he strides to the transport. Mikhail and Jane flank him.

The mammoth opening of the flight bay typically displays a multitude of colors because of the radiant and vivid hues of hyperspace, backlit by stars below. Today, however, the nebula provides an undulating green backdrop which unnerves some of the pilots who've never before flown in such conditions. The entourage arrives at the shuttle, and Frederick enters first, followed by Jane, and then Mikhail. All three strap themselves into their seats.

Elara takes command of the shuttle and will be the one to move her VIPs around. She climbs in last and looks at her cargo. "Ready back there?" She asks.

"Let's get going," says Frederick, eager to be underway.

The shuttle engines power up and begin to hum, pulsing loudly with increasing frequency until the shuttle lifts slightly. It hovers meters from the deck of the Pax. Elara navigates the shuttle through the flight deck, communicating with flight deck control. The shuttle arrives at the designated launch section, and Elara accelerates to flight speed in the blink of an eye.

The Pax remains stationary so small craft like the shuttle can operate safely. It's rare for shuttles to operate at high speed as the gravitational forces can cause damage over extended periods of time. These skips, hops, and jumps take ships thirteen hours, at worst, to make a trip from, say, Earth to Pluto; luckily, the starways cut that down to mere seconds. This trip should take the shuttle even less time, and Marcus will meet them at Shadowpoint forthwith.

The shuttle departs, and the Pax is soon nothing but a speck in their rearview. Flying inside the nebula is like wading through a thick, viscous liquid, and visual navigation is all but impossible. Sensors on the shuttle act as eyes, the only way Elara is able to see and navigate. She must trust in the machine.

"Commander, what do you see out there?" Frederick yells from his seat.

"Plenty... I just can't tell you what, exactly," Elara responds, squinting to see through the cloying atmosphere.

Restless, Frederick gets up from his seat and moves to the front of the shuttle to join Elara in the cockpit. A vacant copilot seat is available, and Frederick invites himself to take possession. Jane and Mikhail remain seated, lost in their own thoughts.

"Not many people know this, but I used to be a pretty handy pilot back in my academy days," Fredrick says, leaning back comfortably in his new seat. He feels the overwhelming need to bond with Elara. She's the commander of the flight deck, after all, though with all the chaos on the bridge, Frederick often forgets.

"Really? Huh, you've never mentioned that," Elara says as she raises her eyebrows in disbelief. "Well, you'll have to come down to the simulators and show us what you've got."

"Absolutely," Frederick says and nods his head towards the window. "Anything on sensors yet?" He asks.

"There's a lot of interference," Elara says slowly, "We have a read on the station, but nothing other than that. There are a significant amount of power readings coming from all around… It's likely several hundred ships are here with us."

Frederick peers out the window intently. Elara's words are ominous, and he feels a twinge of nerves. He leans forward in his seat and glances around the green nebula, hoping to catch a glimpse of something, anything.

"But, sir—we're amongst friends, aren't we?" Elara asks, a note of alarm in her tone.

Frederick quirks his mouth to one side in a small frown. He's not sure he can answer that question as confidently as he'd like to at the moment. After a beat of silence, he says only, "Time will tell."

It doesn't take long for the shuttle to complete the journey from the Pax to Shadowpoint station. The hangar bay of the station is located on the very bottom, so Elara points the shuttle in that direction. Shadowpoint itself is a marvel to behold, and while Frederick may have thought Gaia was the crowning feat of the Assembly, he wonders anew how the Assembly could've possibly hidden such an achievement. And *why* would they hide it? James's story still runs through Frederick's mind, and he thinks they may be flying straight into the lion's den. They have little choice in the matter now.

"Captain, you'd better go and take your seat before we land," Elara says, glancing at him out of the corner of her eye.

Frederick accepts, and he moves to take his seat once again at the back of the shuttle. Jane has closed her eyes in the meantime, but Mikhail is staring intently out the window at the looming structure that is Shadowpoint.

The hangar is smaller than the Pax's bay, but it's still capable of handling numerous shuttle craft. Elara sees eight other shuttles perfectly lined up in as many stalls. She maneuvers the shuttle until she sees one vacant slot with a few personnel ready to receive her. She slows the shuttle engines until they're emitting only a low rumble. The shuttle descends towards the deck, kissing the hangar bay gently. Elara smiles to herself; she enjoys showing off her professional skills.

Jane's eyes flutter open, and Mikhail stretches his arms and cracks his knuckles. Frederick senses the shuttle powering down, and he instructs Jane and Mikhail to remove their shoulder restraints. The doors of the shuttle open, and they make their exit, Frederick in the lead. Elara keeps her pilot's seat and remains on board; she'll stay here and await their return when they're ready to fly back to the Pax. Frederick, Jane, and Mikhail wonder what they'll discover today. As Frederick steps down the small set of stairs which lead from the shuttle to the floor of the hangar, he sees three officers waiting to meet him; one face in particular is familiar.

"Captain Noia, I presume?" Frederick sticks his hand out to shake the other man's already outstretched one. He gestures to Jane and Mikhail and begins to introduce them, but before he can give Noia their names, the conversation takes a turn.

"Sorry, Captain, I didn't mention it before, but I'm a commodore. I simply enjoy captaining the Justice so much—she's the pride of my fleet and a good ship to use during a first meeting. You should know," says Noia with a wink. Frederick smiles in return. The commodore has a miraculous ability to put everyone at ease. Frederick is powerless but to feel safe and secure in Noia's presence.

"Sir, you should have said—," Frederick says, astonished. His military training kicks in, and he remembers to act formal. Before he can finish, Noia cuts him off mid-sentence. He appears to be holding back a laugh, eyes dancing.

"Captain, where do you think you are?" Noia asks, spreading his hands wide and gesturing around him. "This isn't the Assembly Admiralty. We live outside those regulations, and ranks don't mean anything here. Respect means far more," he says, a grin splitting his face.

"You can call me Commodore, but I'm only such because I have the loyalty, commitment, and trust of those in my charge. Nova Corp functions better like this. In fact, every single officer under my command is expected to lead and discuss with me any objections. I'm hardly perfect," Noia finishes, inclining his head in a show of deference.

"What do you mean, 'this isn't the Assembly'? Are you not part of the Assembly fleet?" Frederick asks, curiosity at its peak.

"There's a lot you don't know, Frederick. Let's get to the operations room—I can explain everything there. But first, where's Anatoly? I was hoping he'd join you," Noia says, a furrow in his usually smooth brow.

"Unfortunately, he's still recovering on board the Pax. It'll take some time, and I expect we'll be on our way before he's healed," Frederick answers.

Noia notices Frederick's intense eye contact; it's as if Frederick hopes he believes this story. Unfortunately for Frederick, Noia's years of experience have taught him to see through such flimsy facades. He goes along with the ruse anyway. "Ah, that's a shame. I would've loved for him to be part of our conversation, but no matter." Noia claps his hands together and turns, gesturing for Frederick, Mikhail, and Jane to follow. He and his officers lead them out of the hangar and away from the shuttle.

As Noia walks, he turns his head to look back at Frederick. "You said earlier you were leaving... Somewhere you need to be, Captain?" He asks.

"With your help, Commodore, yes. You see, I was hoping to take the fight to the Eastern League." Frederick quickens his pace to keep up with Noia's long strides.

"You do, do you? Well, I'm sure we can sort something out," Noia replies.

The cohort moves from the hangar bay through thin, winding corridors. As they do, they notice the station is far more industrial than the Pax, closer in appearance to Gaia. Large, metal panels make up the ceilings, walls, and decks of Shadowpoint Station, emphasizing Nova Corp's preference for function over form.

"Commodore—," Frederick starts. Once again, he's interrupted.

Noia holds an arm out. "Frederick, if you don't start calling me Noia, I'm going to throw you in the brig," he says.

"Force of habit, I'm afraid. Let me start again: Noia, do you command all of Nova Corp, or do you have a boss, too?" Frederick hopes he can use humor to create a rapport.

"We all have our masters, Frederick, you should know that by now," Noia says somberly. "Yes, in short, I lead all the forces of Nova Corp, but I report directly to Admiral Krios. When he's in need of our particular skill set, he lets us know."

Jane jogs to keep up with the two conversing men. "It's quite an impressive station you have here. Most of us have never even heard of it," she says.

"You weren't meant to know. We're a secret organization, Jane—it's key to remain a secret," Noia responds with a sardonic look.

"You...know my name?" Jane asks, perplexed.

"Again, it's my job to know most things about everything, and your research has been very important to our work," Noia says by way of an answer.

Jane looks away and wonders how her life might've been used by others. Eventually, they arrive at the operations room, and Noia leads them to its center where a table sits. He begins the conversation, darkening the room while pulling up a map of the known galaxy. The room is filled with dots resembling star systems, and longer shapes representing the fleets hang in the air along with them.

"Here's the situation: from what we can ascertain, the League has returned en force, conducting a coordinated assault across all Assembly space and even into fleets in faction space. Well, I guess you already knew that." Noia looks around the room and sees a smattering of nods from his guests. He continues.

"What you might not know is the extent of their attack. Nearly ninety percent of all warships are unaccounted for as of right now, which is far more than we were expecting," Noia explains.

Frederick is taken aback, focusing on Noia's very last words. "What do you mean 'more than we were expecting'?" He asks incredulously. Though he's physically in the dark, watching the holographic shapes and dots float through the air, he realizes just how metaphorically in the dark he's been from the beginning. A terrible leaden weight drops into the pit of his stomach, and his gut churns. "Did you know this was going to happen?" Frederick asks Noia point blank.

"There isn't much we don't know, Frederick. It's our job to monitor threats," Noia says steadily, as if he's speaking to someone slow to understand.

Noia's condescension makes Frederick's blood boil. He's still dealing with the residual feelings of despair from the loss of his crew members and compatriots, and this revelation makes his struggle all the more difficult. Frederick's tone turns uncharacteristically intense. He points to Noia, a murky figure in the darkness. "You just mentioned ninety percent of the fleet has been lost—that's millions of people! If you knew you could've saved them, why didn't you warn anyone? I don't understand. How can you be so calm about that?" Frederick demands, his tone thick with indignation and fury.

Noia sighs as if this is but a minor concern. "It's not my job to be emotional; my job is to make sure the Assembly survives another day," he says quietly, "I have to be okay with losing some so more may survive."

"I've watched crew members get sucked into space, my mentor sacrificed herself so I might be here with you today. This isn't a game you're playing—we're not chess pieces to be moved!"

Frederick retorts, his voice steady and firm. He narrows his eyes, now distrustful of someone he was hoping to call a friend.

"That's exactly what you are, Frederick! Why do you think you're sent on missions? Do you think large carriers are dispatched to help settlers without ulterior motives? Know this: you're sent on missions from Admiralty. Everything you do is because someone else willed it. You think bad of me for calling water wet?" Noia responds, irritation evident in his every word.

"What good did you hope would come from this galaxy-wide destruction—what could you possibly have gained?" Frederick sputters. There's a note of disbelief in his voice.

"The admiral's plan was to sacrifice a significant percentage of our older fleet to make the League feel in control. We expected the League would then commit their entire force to the destruction of Earth, allowing us to strike hard and fast. Reducing them to rubble in one stroke. The League seems to be over achieving," Noia says, taking care to control his emotions. He won't allow Frederick to get under his skin; he's been in the hot seat before. "We've never been able to find their home system, unfortunately. We need to damage and capture one of their vessels so we can interrogate the crew, ending the League once and for all. If we don't, they'll scurry away like cockroaches, only to return once again."

"That sounds an awful lot like genocide," Frederick says. He thinks back to his conversations with Shen, and he starts to wonder if there might be truth to Shen's words. Frederick has always been a man of integrity and compassion. Looking across the table, he doesn't see these principles mirrored in this Assembly officer. In fact, he sees something entirely different masquerading in a costume.

Frederick's gut is still churning, sounding an alarm bell. He's uncertain, though, and must continue to probe Noia. "Since the destruction of Gaia, we haven't been in contact with Admiralty. We should report back on the situation," he says, trying to buy some time.

"I'm Admiralty to you, and I've given my orders. That should be enough," Noia states matter-of-factly.

"Pacifica was my Admiral—more than that, he was my friend—and he never mentioned any of this," Frederick sputters.

Noia rolls his eyes, unnerved that he has to explain himself, to prove anything at all. "While you're here, Frederick, you'll follow my command," he says curtly, and makes to move on from this line of conversation.

"I don't know you, Noia, and up until yesterday, you were just a phantom. Can't you see this from my perspective? I don't trust you, and this stands against everything I believe in, what I thought the Assembly stood for—in fact, I think it's time the Pax and our fleet send a report to Fleet Command and update them as to our status," Frederick says, still stalling.

"You're talking to your commodore—what about this can't you understand?" Noia asks. He's visibly rankled at Frederick's obstinacy.

"Earth still exists, doesn't it? I'll contact Prime Director Vexler if I must, but I'll get answers one way or another!" Frederick raises his voice in exasperation.

"Do you expect them to tell you something different?" Noia asks, raising his eyebrows.

"I pray they do—what I've just heard worries me. This goes against everything I've stood for in my entire career," Frederick says, aghast.

"If it'd make you feel better, wait just a moment. I'll contact Admiral Krios right now," Noia says, finally relenting. He signals to one of his officers standing adjacent to him. In moments, the darkness ascends and the star cartography vanishes. In its place appears Fleet Consul Admiral Krios's hologram.

"Commodore, what do you have to report?" Krios's holographic head says.

Noia steps forward. "Admiral, we've connected with the Pax and her fleet. They're now safely at Shadowpoint, and I have Captain Langfield here with me. He has some questions for you." Noia looks over at Frederick.

"Oh? Well then, spit it out, Captain." Krios swivels his eyes to take in Frederick.

"Admiral, the commodore has explained, in no uncertain terms, that the destruction of a vast percentage of our fleet is part of some grand plan," Frederick says, throwing his hands up in frustration.

"That's correct. What's the question, Captain?" Krios asks, his tone steely.

"My question is this: why? We've been attacked by the League—their commander introduced himself as Shen, mentioned this was retaliation for the grievances his people endured in the past. They want their pound of flesh, yet our plan seems to be to find their new homeworld and wipe them from existence. Is that really how we deal with this problem?" Frederick asks.

"Perhaps Noia hadn't finished his brief," says Krios. "Did he explain that, just a few hours ago, six hundred warships appeared in Earth's orbit? They've started an orbital bombardment. The planetary shield was raised and has been repelling the assault, but without assistance, it'll fail. Calculations predict the shield will run out of power in roughly ten days. Do you think the League will stand by the same moral code as you?" Krios's voice is flinty and cold, daring Frederick to respond.

"They're acting out of rage, a blinding emotion!" Frederick says as he begins to pace, passing a hand over his head. "They've been isolated for hundreds of years, fostering this desire for revenge. If we behave exactly as they think we will, then we're no better than them," he finishes.

"We'll be alive, *that* will be the difference, Captain. Our job is to keep the galaxy safe. What do you think would happen if the Assembly just dissolved?" Krios asks rhetorically. His voice is a crescendo, echoing around the silent operations room.

He goes on. "We've been holding the galaxy together. Under our guiding hand, we've had two centuries of growth, expansion, and prosperity because of our overwhelming amount of power. Without us, I guarantee that within days, the factions would be fighting over the scraps of the Assembly, dissecting our technology to use against each other," Krios says with intent.

Frederick shakes his head. "Those two centuries you've just mentioned—they weren't merely about growth in numbers but also in improvements that can't be measured. We refined our moral positions, removed greed, and abolished homelessness." Frederick pokes himself in the chest. "To me, those stand as far greater accomplishments—accomplishments the Assembly was founded to protect. Every human life is considered important, and I find it hard to accept that we now turn away from these values in the face of fear… Condemning an entire people to death over a possibility! At least give me some time to think of a plan that doesn't include slaughter." Frederick breathes heavily.

"I do hear your words, Captain, and I understand now why Pacifica liked you and gave you command of the Pax. But the plan stands." Krios cuts his eyes to Noia and says, "Commodore, continue as we agreed. I want the location of the League's homeworld, and you have ten days to get to Earth and defeat the forces in orbit before they break through the shield. Captain Langfield, I'll give you an opportunity. If you can persuade Commodore Noia as to an alternative action, then you may deviate from our plan," Krios says.

"Yes, Admiral." Noia acknowledges Krios's order.

"Has something happened to Commodore Anatoly?" Krios asks.

Frederick blinks, then nods. "Yes, sir. He was injured during our last engagement, and it'll take him some time to recover," he responds.

"Shame. In that case, the Pax's fleet will need a new commodore. Captain, I have no choice but to promote you to the rank of commodore for the duration of this mission. And please—don't screw it up. You'll need to lead the mission to save Earth. Noia, fill the commodore in on everything relevant," Krios says, changing the course of Frederick's life in just a few sentences. He doesn't seem to feel the weight of this quick promotion, but Frederick does.

As the admiral's holographic bust falls from view, Frederick remains nervous and uneasy. Regardless, it's clear he's but a small pawn on a larger chess board. The room is silent, and Frederick looks at the stunned faces of Mikhail and Jane; they're both in shock. He's unable to speak with them now, of course, but he can't wait to debrief with them when they're back on the Pax.

Frederick decides to break the silence. "Noia, what else don't I know that I need to?" He asks.

Before he can answer, Noia receives a message on this cos-link. He reads it: another guest has arrived.

He looks up from his device. "The other shuttle has landed. We're expecting Captain Harrington, is that right?" Noia asks.

"Oh yes—Marcus Harrington will be joining us. He's the captain of a heavy cruiser in the Colorado sector defense fleet. He and his crew came to our rescue," Frederick says, gratitude evident on his face. He glances at Jane. "As a matter of fact, Jane and he are partners," and Jane ducks her head at the comment.

"I thought he might help us plan our next steps, but it seems those steps have already been laid before us," Frederick finishes, spreading his hands out, palms up.

"If you and he will join me for dinner tonight, we can discuss our options further. I've organized some accommodations for you all, and I've asked my officers to take Marcus to his quarters; you can debrief him later. On another note, we have a fleet available for you, so once you're ready to defend Earth, they'll follow your orders," Noia says, and Frederick thinks he detects a slight hint of nervousness beneath Noia's placid expression. Could he be worried about something?

"How many vessels are part of this fleet?" Frederick asks.

"I'm not going to lie to you, Captain. I don't think it'll be enough, but it's close to two hundred warships, mostly destroyers and cruisers. Only a handful of heavy capital ships are ready for action; Gaia was meant to provide more ships for the assault. Obviously, that isn't happening anymore," Noia says with a frown.

Jane pipes up from her place in the room. She's taken all this information in stride and, though she's shocked at what she's learned, she still hopes to be of help. "Plus, the fifty or so we brought with us," she says.

"Mikhail, based on your knowledge of our firepower and that of our enemy, what are our chances?" Frederick asks, looking to Mikhail for some sense of clarity.

Mikhail clears his throat. He doesn't answer straight away; instead, he takes a minute to remind himself of the technical details from previous engagements. He knows instinctively that this is going to be a challenge.

"Captain, it depends on which warships comprise the new fleet, and if they match the forces we have seen before. It is likely we will be at a substantial disadvantage, so I recommend a minimum of one ship for every two of the Eastern League's if we are to be victorious," Mikhail says.

Jane replies, "That would match Renee's and my findings, too. Their vessels are close in capabilities to our own, but their reliance on smaller vessels might give us an edge."

Frederick gazes around the room. He feels the tension ebbing, and they all, including himself, seem to be settling into the beginning of an alternate plan. Since their home is now on the line, they must find a way to match the League's larger fleet. They can't allow the League's superiority in numbers to get the better of them.

"We have a few days to come up with a better plan," Frederick says in response.

"We might not have the firepower to destroy the fleet entirely, but if we can take out key components of the fleet—especially Shen's flagship—it might create enough chaos for us to take advantage," says Mikhail.

"We wouldn't have a lot of time to take advantage of the situation, though, would we? I mean, we'd have to strike hard and fast to have a chance," Jane says.

"Ah, but Frederick, we don't have a choice. Our mission is to support Earth, defeat the fleet in orbit, and remove the Eastern League threat, one way or another," Noia says.

"One way or another, yes." Frederick nods his agreement. He's beginning to feel a little more confident about their next move.

"Preferably something that avoids so much death…," Jane says.

"We still have to find the location of their homeworld, in case you can't come up with another solution. Perhaps the Pax's new captain—whom you'll need to select quickly, by the way—can retrieve a few crew members for us. We have the location of a supply station they used as a staging post before the invasion. Plus, we think it'll be lightly defended, an easy target for the Pax," Noia says, placing his hands on the smooth surface of the center table.

Frederick says, "If it buys me time to think, then we can do that. Mikhail, you and Jane return to the Pax. While you head out, I'll contact Xavier; he'll command the mission."

Two Shadowpoint officers have been in the room the entire time, silent. At this remark, they step forward, seemingly appearing out of nowhere, and one says, "We can show you the way—it's a labyrinth." The two officers turn and begin to head towards the door, leading Jane and Mikhail back to the hangar. Once they leave, only Frederick and Noia are left in the room.

"Frederick, before we sort out the future, we need to talk about the present. And now that it's just the two of us, I must confess something of a…personal matter," Noia says. His voice is low, denoting the gravity of his next statement.

"Have we not had enough surprises for one day?" Frederick says and sighs deeply.

"There are plenty left, especially if you wander the halls of this station. It might be best to keep an open mind at the very least." Noia leaves his place at the center table and walks slowly to one of the large windows along the side of the room. He turns his back to the room and looks out; from this vantage point, he sees a number of warships docked with Shadowpoint, though the nebula obscures much of the view. He can just make out a few berthed destroyers.

Noia doesn't turn around but says from the window, "This one concerns your colleague, Marcus. I must admit, I know who he is, but what I don't know is how you two came together."

"Once we left Gaia, we contacted the Colorado sector fleet, which included Marcus, and requested a rendezvous. Then, Commodore Anatoly assumed command of all vessels in our makeshift fleet before he was incapacitated," Frederick answers from across the room.

"I've worked with Anatoly before, and I know he's a difficult person to get along with…a challenging personality, to be blunt. It might be best if he were relieved of his command, though I worry you might not have the stomach for what comes next." Noia turns around but remains at the window.

"I'd worry less about my stomach and more about our mission," Frederick says, shaking his head. He looks at Noia squarely—better to rip the band-aid off now. "You mentioned something about Marcus?" Frederick probes.

"Jane's research in the starways, as well as in the history of the Eastern League, has been very interesting to us. We knew she might try and rope someone into her crusade to find out the truth— honorable people and their moral compasses are so predictable." He turns back to the view out the window, gazing at the nebula. A scowl clouds his features for a brief moment; if Frederick had been able to see it, he would've gotten a glimpse into Noia's true personality. Little does Frederick know, Noia is used to playing by his own rules, and the goodness in people sickens him.

"You've been spying on Assembly personnel," Frederick says, more of a statement than a question; he knows it to be true.

"You really don't understand the gravity of our mission, do you?" Noia laughs lightly, a chilling chuckle of mirth, and turns back from the view. "We have eyes and ears everywhere. Without knowledge, we're nothing—we're a drum without a beat. We must listen to the music of the universe. That way, we keep everyone safe, secure," Noia says with a slight fanatical glint to his eye.

"And all we have to do is forgo our freedoms in return," Frederick says.

"A small price, but I'm not here to debate ethics with you. Yes, we've been keeping a close eye on Jane," Noia says slowly, cutting his eyes to Frederick. He knows this is going to be a challenging conversation.

"I don't really know how to say this easily, so I'll just say it. Marcus has been working for us for the decade he and Jane have been together. We promised him a rapid career path advancement to captain in return for his…*cooperation*. He was reluctant at first, but as he learned to love his partner, things settled naturally," Noia says, finally revealing the truth.

Frederick is incredulous once again, and in such a short span of time. "Are you saying you're playing cupid nowadays, too?" He asks. His eyebrows are raised so high they're in danger of getting lost in his hairline.

"They were star crossed lovers, Frederick, they just needed help! In the end, it all worked out perfectly, you know as well as I do that it's true. Partnerships aren't prescriptive; so long as it works for the couple, that's all that matters," Noia replies.

"There's a difference between having a relationship that fits the needs of the individual and manipulating one side to suit your will," Frederick says, beginning to pace again.

"We aren't the bad guys here, Frederick!" Noia gesticulates for emphasis. "We needed Jane to find out about the ruins, we needed her to continue on the path she herself set in her crusade to find the truth. Marcus allowed us to help from afar when needed. Really, all Marcus had to do was stick it out for the long run. This was his choice. If you're angry with anyone, I might suggest having a word with him," he finishes.

"What do you suggest I say to Jane? Hey Jane, a quick word: your partnership is a lie," Frederick says sarcastically.

"I wouldn't recommend you say anything," Noia says plainly. "Blissful ignorance is best at this point—what good would come of telling the truth?" He asks, not expecting an answer.

"You're giving moral advice?" Frederick asks, rubbing his forehead. He's tired, so tired.

"I'm a pragmatist, Commodore, what do you think will happen if you share this?" Noia asks.

"It just doesn't sit well with me... It's her life, she deserves to know," Frederick says vehemently. Jane means a lot to him, and he hates to see her bamboozled, lied to, and hurt.

"That's your call. It's the burden of command, and you have to decide what people know and what isn't relevant," Noia answers.

Frederick is starting to wonder what he's signed up for, and he shakes his head in disbelief. In his eyes, the Assembly is meant to be the guiding light of the galaxy. Now, however, it feels like they're more than a guiding hand, manipulating everything they touch. Is this truly for the good of everyone? Or maybe the Assembly's good will is more selective than he first thought.

"One problem at a time," Frederick says, bone-weary. "I should contact Xavier and inform him of his mission." He makes to leave the room, assuming Mikhail and Jane will be back on the Pax soon.

Noia stops him before he can exit through the door. "You can call him from here when you're ready, though you might want to get some rest. I'm sure it's been a long day for you. There are quarters for you just down the corridor, room 187. I have everything prepared. The system we're looking for is close by—the Lauderact System.

"It should only take a few hours by hyperspace, and the Pax alone will be enough. We sent a civilian ship there a few days ago and found an operational station with two frigates defending. I have duties to attend to, unfortunately, but let's have dinner tonight." Noia takes his cos-link from his pocket to check the time. He sighs. "Time is getting away from me today. Meet me in the officer's mess hall at 20:00; the location is in the station computer—you can access that from your quarters," Noia says, opening the operations room door. He motions for Frederick to exit first.

Noia exits the room after Frederick and heads in the opposite direction. Frederick waits until Noia has turned a corner before he makes a move to call Xavier and inform him of his orders. Now that Noia is out of sight, Frederick feels he can speak openly. He retrieves his cos-link from his pocket and opens a communication with Xavier.

Frederick says through his cos-link speaker, "Xavier, I have a short, and hopefully easy, mission for you."

"Understood, Captain. Are you not coming back to the Pax? Elara just returned with the shuttle, and we thought you'd be on it," Xavier's voice says through the cos-link.

"Not just yet… It's best I remain here for the moment. There's, ah, more to everything than we initially thought. Once you return from your mission, I'll fill you in. Go to the Lauderact System. When you get there, you'll find an Eastern League outpost. Capture as many of their personnel for questioning as you can," Frederick says.

"I have a few points of clarification first—," Xavier begins, but Frederick breaks in before he can finish.

"As do I, and getting answers is what I'll be doing while you're away. Jane and Mikhail might be able to shed some light in the meantime," Frederick says in a rush. The next part of this conversation will be harder. "I spoke with Fleet Consul Admiral Krios from Earth, and they're under assault by the League. The planetary shield has about ten days left, and we're meant to lead the defense. First, we need to gather more intelligence on the location of their homeworld." Frederick takes a breath before continuing.

"I've been promoted to commodore, and I need you to command the Pax for this mission. Earth is the League's final target… As I said, a lot has happened since we arrived," Frederick finishes.

There's a moment of silence before Xavier responds. When he does, he says, "If you think this is best…though I didn't realize we were kidnappers now."

"Before this situation is over, I fear we'll be called far worse than that." Frederick sighs before continuing. "Commodore Noia suggested the Pax would be more than adequate for this mission, but I'm not sure I trust anything that comes out of his mouth. Take the

Intrepid, Sundancer, Valiant, and Resolute Guardian with you as backup," he says.

"I see. Of course, I'll do as you command, but I wonder if it would be better for you to return to the Pax," Xavier responds.

"I wonder, too, but I feel I can do more good here right now. Good hunting, Commander, and bring her back in one piece. Don't get too comfortable while you're in charge, I'm going to want her back," Frederick says, only half joking.

"No promises, Commodore," Xavier says before signing off.

The pieces on the chess board are moving, and Frederick thinks of his future. He'll need to continue his mental sparing with Noia, and for that he must use all his strength and fortitude. Retiring to his new quarters seems like a prudent next step, so Frederick heads vaguely towards his assigned room—he's already forgotten the directions Noia gave him. It takes a few minutes for him to find the correct quarters, and once he does, the door slides open, sensing his presence.

Frederick steps into his temporary quarters and stares; it's fit for a king. A large, spacious living area with ample room to sit and entertain is the first thing he notices, and a bedroom is off to one side. Frederick takes the liberty of using this bedroom and its bed now, setting an alarm on the room computer so he can get a few hours of sleep. He lets his mind drift away, hoping his dreams might provide inspiration for a better plan to stop the Eastern League.

Chapter Twenty-Six

While Frederick tries to relax for a few hours, Imperator Shen stands at the helm of his flagship, overseeing what he considers his magnum opus. The fleet stretches behind him, a harbinger of doom, and Earth trembles before his gaze. Generations of meticulous planning are converging into this singular, devastating moment. Shen takes small steps back to his throne and sits upon it, watching his fleet start a precise orbital bombardment, each calculated impact chipping away at the planetary shield in a mesmerizing display of destruction. The beautiful mix of colors above Earth would be a bewitching sight to behold if not for their destructiveness.

Juan's steps echo as he approaches Shen's throne. "Imperator, the last of the fleet has given their reports, and all stations in the system have been neutralized. The system is secure; Earth's destruction is imminent," he states.

"Excellent. Have them regroup with us here. We mustn't grow complacent. Remember, Juan, the Assembly will retaliate. We've struck a grievous blow, but they still have sharp teeth," Shen replies, his voice a measured, icy calm.

"We have them on the run now. We've crippled their fleet, destroyed their stations. Surely, they're powerless against us," says Juan, insistent.

"Don't underestimate them," Shen cautions, rising from his throne again and approaching his trusted prime. "History is replete with tales of seemingly insurmountable odds overcome by sheer determination. We're close, but don't let the illusion of victory cloud your judgment."

"Of course, sir. Something of import: one of our supply convoys from Lauderact is overdue. They were meant to arrive in Sol hours ago, but we still haven't picked them up on our sensors," Juan says.

"Curious indeed, that system is a long way from anywhere. It's unlikely to be a coincidence. We must start guarding the convoys, or we'll quickly dwindle our reserves," Shen says in response. He passes

Juan and continues to walk slowly to the rear of the bridge once more. Juan follows. The relics hanging on the Harbinger's walls hold more than physical importance to the League's heritage; they also hold philosophical and cultural significance to Shen.

These relics allow Shen and his people to learn from the past failures of many civilizations on Earth. One of Shen's favorites is an ancient Japanese samurai katana. He picks this up from the wall now and brandishes it in both hands carefully as if it were his newborn child. "Do you know what this is, Juan?" Shen asks, looking at the sword.

Juan responds, "It's a katana from an ancient civilization on Earth."

Shen nods, proud. "Very good. But what is it, and what does it do?" He asks Juan.

"It's a sword, used for fighting," Juan says, hoping he isn't missing some important detail. He's eager to please his imperator.

"Essentially, yes, it's both of those things. Though it's far more," Shen says in barely subdued awe. "It was owned by Musashi, one of the most famous samurai in feudal history. Samurai were the fiercest of fighters, and Musashi was a titan. He became a prolific calligrapher and painter, and he focused on mastering skills and committing wholeheartedly to everything he did."

Shen continues to brandish the sword. "This katana," he says, "is simple in appearance, but it requires absolute skill to wield—but that's not enough. You have to understand what a samurai master is, what their culture means. Even the slightest movement is a planned action." Shen runs his finger against the sharp blade, and he cuts himself slightly. Blood runs down his finger, but he doesn't cry out nor show any sign of pain.

For a moment, he falls deep into his own thoughts of science and history; both overtake his consciousness. He rouses himself from his musing with a little shudder. He grabs a corner of his robe and cleans the sword, then he returns the katana to its prized location. "We must make sure our enemy likewise doesn't defeat us with a thousand cuts. We've had no communications from the Pax?" Shen asks Juan.

"No, nothing, sir," Juan says, hands clasped behind his back.

"Hm. In that case, dispatch a taskforce to see what's occurring in the Lauderact System," Shen orders. With that, he returns to his throne and continues his subjugation of the Assembly.

Chapter Twenty-Seven

Xavier prepares for the mission to which he's been assigned. His first solo command! He's feeling trepidation and anxiety at the thought. Instead of focusing on his fears, however, he decides to channel his nervous energy into ensuring the command goes smoothly. He stands at his console table on the bridge and places his hands, palms flat, against the cool surface. Its familiarity helps calm his nerves, and he breathes deeply.

"How long until we arrive, Leo?" Xavier asks.

"Shouldn't be long now, just a few minutes. I can see a system jump point on the sensors now—it looks clear," Leo answers, keeping his eyes glued to his screen.

"Maybe we'll get lucky today," Xavier says in response, feeling a little less worried.

"We're due some luck, after everything that's happened," Marie says from her usual station on the bridge.

"Remember, no matter what, we need to capture at least a few high-ranking officers," Xavier says to the crew within earshot. "They'll know the location of any important installations and, most importantly, their homeworld. That's our primary mission."

"Captain, if we could hack into their computers, we might be able to download their data, including any cartography data," Mikhail says. He's settled back into his seat on the bridge and is ready to be of service after the revelations he was privy to while at Shadowpoint.

"A good suggestion! Please pass that along to Richard and his team, and make sure their first target is the command center—tell them to try and capture as many officers as possible and download what they can," Xavier says, heart thrumming at giving his first official order on this command.

Marie's spirits are high; she's optimistic that this mission will go off without a hitch. "I'll update Richard now, Xav—uh, still not used to calling you *captain* yet, sir," Marie says with a slight laugh.

"As soon as Frederick returns, I'll be glad to relinquish the title back to him," Xavier says with a wry grin. This is more an operational title, and Xavier still retains his old rank of commander. On this mission, however, he's inheriting the title of captain and all the responsibilities it entails.

"Captain, we're exiting hyperspace now," Leo says as he guides the Pax into normal space.

"Anyone see what's out there?" Xavier asks the bridge crew.

"I'm seeing a small station, a few hundred thousand miles off our bow and further in the system. I'm not seeing anything else," says Renee as she makes a cursory scan of her screens.

"An easy target," Mikhail says with an expression of satisfaction.

"Don't get ahead of yourself, Mikhail. It's never that easy…," Xavier says, absentmindedly rubbing his chin. "Leo, get us close. Marie, did our escorts drop out of hyperspace with us?" Xavier asks.

"All ships accounted for, sir, and we're good to go," Marie responds, tapping away at her console.

"Let's make this quick," Xavier says, clasping his hands together.

"Under sublight one, it would take us two minutes to get there," Leo reports.

"That should give us enough time to alert our troops. Marie, get the flight deck ready to dispatch the strike force—once we enter position and make it safe for them, they can start their approach," Xavier responds.

"Alright, Captain, and I'll inform Elara, too. She can provide protection," Marie says.

"Do we have a general idea about the station? As in, is it armed? Should we expect some, ah, gifts from the League?" Xavier asks.

"I cannot detect any power signatures that might indicate weaponry, but we should be prepared," Mikhail says.

"Get the shields on—just in case. And relay to the fleet to go to battle stations," Xavier orders, flexing his leadership skills.

"Captain, I'm noticing something strange… A short distance from the station, there's a large amount of debris. My best guess is that it's from a number of transport vessels," says Jane looking over Renee's shoulder at her screen.

"So, we aren't the first to get here. I was expecting more of a welcome from the League. This is all too easy," Xavier says with a wrinkled brow. He's suspicious.

"You had to go and say it now, didn't you!" Leo says, throwing his hands up.

"Let's hope I can't jinx us any further, but we should investigate and recover whatever we can. Renee, can you get scans from this range?" Xavier requests.

"I can do the basics. If we get closer, I can get even more," Renee says. She's doing all she can on her end.

"I don't like this, something's wrong… Let's get in and out as quickly as we can," Xavier says uneasily.

"Yes, Captain. Seems like a few vessels—maybe it's a convoy, but it's hard to know at this point. I'll keep at it," Renee says.

"Captain, we're fifteen miles away from the station. I'm powering down the engines to a minimum," reports Leo.

"Deploy the strike force," Xavier says resolutely.

The bridge abounds with activity. Renee and Jane work together to gain as much information as possible on the wreckage, and Leo makes sure the ship is in the right position. Marie organizes all the local forces, and Mikhail places his finger on the trigger, waiting for any bombshells. It's only been a few days since the initial shot of this conflict was fired, but it feels like a lifetime ago for the crew. In the last few days, they've learned much from each situation, and they've turned into a well-oiled machine.

Xavier is proud of himself and of the crew's response so far. He watches the multiple shuttles and fighters moving in formation from the Pax to the station; all is going well. Almost too well. The shuttles find a landing bay, and the strike team disembarks, led by Richard.

Marie puts Richard's video feed up on the main screen of the bridge so the crew can hear him and see through his camera. The audio pops to life, and Richard's voice comes through.

"Captain, we're deployed on the station, and we found many unarmed crew. We have it secured, and we'll continue to scout the station and see what we can find. We'll look for the bridge," Richard says.

"Good hunting, Commander. And be quick. I'm sure there are more than a few shocks in store for us," Xavier responds.

"Copy, Captain. I'll report back when we have more information. Out," Richard says, then breaks the connection.

A few minutes of peace pass, and Xavier's mind races with possibilities. He wonders if the strike force will run into any unexpected resistance—will they find what they need? Soon enough, he has his answer.

"Captain, there are a number of hyperspace portals opening at the jump point," Renee states from her seat.

"Which jump point? Any idea who and how many?" Xavier demands with a whisper of worry in his voice.

"There seems to be only one jump point in the system, the same one we used. I'm sensing five ships emerging, but no GFF signatures yet," says Renee, "The ships are well within sensor range, but I'm not detecting any weapon power signatures."

Jane pipes up and says, "Two of the vessels match the configurations from previous engagements with the League." Her eyes are wide.

"Our five against their five—I will take those odds," Mikhail grumbles.

"Leo, bring us around to face the enemy. Marie—have the fleet flank us left and right," Xavier orders.

"Captain, we're receiving communication from the lead vessel," Marie says.

"Maybe they want to mock us before attacking…," Leo says sarcastically, running his hands through his hair.

"It's text only, but they mention not believing in their cause and wanting to discuss options with us…?" Marie says, confused.

"Why would they want to talk now? They're winning," Renee says, a skeptical look on her face. Her brows furrow as she scans her screens.

"That'll be my first question…" Xavier thinks a moment before coming to a decision. "Invite their captain over. We'll meet them in the hangar bay," He orders.

"As you wish, Captain," Marie says and gets to work completing her tasks.

"This smells like a trap," Mikhail deadpans from his seat.

"Then why would they come to our ship? Their fleet is no match for ours. If it's a trap, you might want to give them some pointers for next time," Xavier quips.

"At least let me come with you. Just in case," Mikhail says.

"So long as you bring an open mind, then yes, of course. Another option for finishing this conflict might've just presented itself to us. Frederick will be pleased if we can facilitate that," Xavier says, nodding at the thought.

"Their vessels are still closing and are well within weapons range. We won't have too much time to react if they decide to open fire," Leo says.

"Are their weapons still powered down, Mikhail?" Xavier asks.

"From what I can see, yes, but we're trying to understand their vessels and systems. I could be wrong," Mikhail says.

Xavier gives out orders in rapid fire. "Renee and Jane—keep an eye on their power readings. If there are any changes, let me know immediately. And let's keep the fleet at battle stations but communicate that they're only to fire if fired upon. Apprise the captains of the current situation, and keep Richard over there until we're done… The less they know about our mission, the better," Xavier says.

Xavier and Mikhail head to the NovaPath which will take them off the bridge. Once safely in the NovaPath, Xavier receives a message on his cos-link. He takes it out of his pocket to review.

"A small craft has left their fleet and is making its way towards us," Xavier states.

"I would love to have an up-close look at their schematics, but something seems…off to me," Mikhail says in response.

"I'll do the talking, but keep an eye on them, will you? We might be inviting them in, but it doesn't mean I trust them," Xavier says as the NovaPath doors slide open.

Mikhail nods his assent, and Xavier knows he has his back. They head to the hangar bay, and within a few minutes they're on the appropriate deck for the designated meeting space with the Eastern League representatives. The journey down the corridor to the hangar is quick, but in the past, Xavier always relied on Frederick to take the lead. Somehow, this walk feels different, every step just a little harder, as if the ground is soft and unsteady.

Considering the activity on the hanger, it's a safe place for a meeting with enemies, at least from Xavier's point of view. When they enter, Xavier senses an abnormal atmosphere—the hustle and bustle isn't as energetic as it normally is since a number of craft are away at Shadowpoint. The rest of the strike craft are currently awaiting orders to launch, and so the hangar seems to Xavier almost quiet.

"I presume those are our guests," Mikhail points to a solitary inbound craft, similar in size to their own shuttle. This one is much more aggressive in design, with sharp, jagged edges and a dark, almost black coloring.

"Well, let's get this party started," Xavier breathes and clears his throat. He attempts to puff his chest out in a show of confidence, but Mikhail sees through it right to Xavier's nervous core.

"Whatever happens here, we must complete our mission and get what we need," Mikhail says under his breath.

The arriving shuttle begins to hover, then lands, its engines slowly winding down as its occupants step from an open hatch. Two officers emerge, both small in stature and adorned in elaborate uniforms. As soon as they reach Xavier and Mikhail, Xavier steps forward to introduce himself.

"Captain, I presume?" Xavier asks as he extends his hand to his enemy in greeting.

One of the officers steps forward as well, shaking hands with Xavier. "Marshal Kenji Blackwood. I'm the commanding officer of the battlecruiser Iron Phoenix and task force twelve. And you are…?" Kenji gestures to Xavier.

"Commander Xavier Reynolds," Xavier answers. "I'm the acting captain of this vessel, and this is my second in command, Commander Mikhail," Xavier answers.

"Acting captain, I see… And what happened to your last captain? Or do I want to know?" Kenji says with a sardonic twist of his mouth. He seems like an inscrutable man.

"He was called away on another mission, leaving me in command," Xavier says matter-of-factly. He'll remain guarded until he can get a better read on Kenji.

The Shadows of Peace 227

"Well, you'll have to do for now," Kenji says, brushing invisible dust from his impeccable uniform. "I'll cut to the chase, Commander. My fleet and I desire to defect. I can't support Imperator Shen Sato and his barbaric idealistic crusade. We surrender unconditionally." Much to Xavier's surprise, Kenji lowers himself to one knee, presenting his sidearm and placing it in front of him. His compatriot follows suit.

Xavier's mouth drops open, and his eyebrows shoot up. He waves his arms in a stopping motion, gesturing for the two to rise. "All right, please get up. What's the meaning of this? Do you expect us to believe the League is so fractured, entire fleets would defect?" Xavier asks, dubious.

"Have we not presented ourselves to you? We've come to your warship of our own accord. You're orbiting one of our supply stations—we're well within our rights to blow you out of the sky, yet we're here with open arms, hoping for a similar response," Kenji says as he and his companion rise from their knees to once again stand before Xavier and Mikhail.

"If you wanted to blow us out of the sky, you should have brought a bigger ship," Mikhail starts to say, but Xavier cuts him off with a motion of his hand.

"I'm sure there will be more than enough time for that. So, what say you? Will you accept my proposal?" Kenji asks with an optimistic look, his eyebrows raised.

"Other than surrender, what's your exact proposal?" Xavier asks, still guarding his expression. He tries to keep his tone neutral.

"My proposal is this: we join you in the defense of Earth, but after that, you let us go our own way, under our own banner. This is all we want, Acting Captain. The quiet life is what we desire, we want to live not filled with hatred and revenge but with something more. Something better," Kenji says and takes a breath. He changes the subject abruptly. "Have you met anyone from the League before?" He asks.

"We've had a few conversations with Imperator Sato, and he's tried to end us on more than one occasion. He and Captain Frederick have had words over the last few days," Xavier admits.

"So, you know he's consumed by his own hatred for Earth and the past transgressions of its inhabitants?" Kenji asks, crossing his arms.

"Yes, that sentiment is hard to miss. He seems hell bent on making sure the past remains in the present," Xavier replies.

"It's more than that—he's determined to have his pound of flesh. Ever since we left Earth, we've tried to build a utopia, a world away from the problems of the past that focuses on the future. We were so close…" Kenji thinks back to his younger years and his favorite school lesson.

"I remember my history classes so vividly," Kenji continues, "From the early days of our home on Sonnara, our founders tried to set up a balanced government run entirely by the council, despite the hardships they encountered." Kenji explains how his ancestors established the planet centuries ago when they arrived on the Odyssey. The inhabitants of today have built cities and civilization, and Sonnara is now their capital. In the beginning, every founding member had an equal voice.

"Back then, ten members oversaw each area of our society, and we had nearly one hundred years of progress before the military took over. We went from harmony to hatred so quickly," Kenji says, shaking his head and looking down at the floor.

"I joined the navy thinking I'd be able to make a difference. Maybe I'd help my people return to a better path. This is the only way I can do that," Kenji finishes and raises his eyes to meet those of Xavier and Mikhail.

"Does everyone in your fleet want this too? That must be a few thousand people. Do they all feel the same as you?" Mikhail asks.

"Just under two thousand. There are a few that are resistant to our change in course, but we were able to make sure they didn't present an obstacle," Kenji replies.

"You mean you killed them…?" Xavier tries to clarify with a note of disappointment. He'd hoped for better from those standing before him.

"They were a threat, and the rest of us needed to make sure we had a future." Kenji uncrosses his arms and spreads them wide. He speaks as though killing these people was the only obvious and logical option.

"How many had to suffer and die so you could have a future?" Mikhail grits out.

"Too many," Kenji says, hanging his head in shame. "Although now we can show others from the League that there's another way."

"Marshal Kenji, I'm not sure I approve of your methods. If you truly want to part ways with the League, we'll entertain your offer, but you and your crew must surrender your vessels to our command. We can accommodate everyone—it'll be cramped but safe until we decide what to do next," Xavier explains.

"We'd hoped you'd allow us to crew our own ships and join you. Please, we pose no threat to you," Kenji says, imploring.

"In my books, you need to prove your trustworthiness—it's not simply *given*, it's earned." Now it's Xavier's turn to cross his arms. "These are my terms. If they aren't acceptable to you, well… You can take your chances on your own, and we'll see who'll blow each other out of the water first," Xavier says, his face a blank mask. His eyes are dark and shining, daring Kenji to make a wrong move.

Kenji takes a moment to mull over his options. Truth be told, he and his crew aren't in a position to fight, especially with the two fleets so close. His one battlecruiser and four destroyers are no match for the Pax and her escorts.

Kenji sighs in defeat. "We don't have much of a choice, it seems, nor do we have many shuttles." Kenji holds his hands palm up in surrender. He knows this is the right thing to do, but his pride is bruised and he feels like he's been bested.

"I would ask that our ships' bridge crew remain. They know how everything works, and they might be of value to you," Kenji says.

Xavier leans in close to Mikhail so they can quietly confer. Mikhail starts. "Captain," he says, "We could use some help on the vessels, surely, but we should be careful. We know nothing about them." Mikhail retreats to his previous position.

Xavier looks at Kenji squarely. "You can keep your bridge crew and a few engineering staff, but we'll deploy marines to your vessels," he says.

"If that would make you feel safer, I suppose we have a deal," Kenji says. His expression opens up and Xavier spies a slight upward tilt of Kenji's mouth. He seems relieved.

Happily, Xavier extends his hand in newfound friendship. He still worries that this might be a ruse, but he senses Kenji truly wants to do good—a desire mirrored in Xavier's own heart. As Kenji and his officer surrender to Xavier, he wonders if the Pax will actually have enough space to hold their new guests. This might be just what Frederick wants, and Xavier is ecstatic to complete his first command so successfully. The captured vessels represent a treasure trove of knowledge, but a new option in the fight for freedom is infinitely more valuable.

Mikhail gestures to Kenji and has a discussion with him in a private corner of the bay. As he does, Xavier takes one last look around the hanger before recommending that everyone return to the bridge to organize and plan. He gathers Mikhail, Kenji, and Kenji's associate into the NovaPath, and the entourage return to the bridge.

Chapter Twenty-Eight

The doors slide open, and the four men meet a sea of staring eyes. Xavier steps off the NovaPath first. "Listen up," he says, raising his voice so the entire bridge crew can hear him. He gestures behind him as the rest of the men step off the NovaPath. "This is Marshall Kenji. He and his fleet are defecting. The deal is this: their personnel will be relocated to the Pax and our vessels, and several officers will stay on the League ships to maintain key systems.

"Their bridge crew will also keep their original posts. To that end, we'll need to move the majority of their crew to the Pax and other vessels in our fleet for transfer back to Shadowpoint. It's going to be cramped, but it's only a few hours in hyperspace, so we can cope. We need all marines to secure the vessels and any crew members left—everyone is to be supervised," Xavier finishes and looks around the bridge at the astonished expressions of his crew members.

"I guess they're scared," Leo says slowly, hoping to diffuse the tension. It doesn't work.

"We aren't scared—," Kenji feels insulted, but before he can fully explain, he's cut off mid-sentence.

Xavier says coolly, "It's a long story, and all will become clear in time. In short, they have a difference of opinion to other members of the League." He's hoping for no further questions.

"Better be a big difference," Marie says, a fierce expression of distaste on her face.

"All we want is peace," Kenji replies as he tents his hands together in front of him.

"Less people shooting at us is okay in my books," Leo quips.

"Let's not get too ahead of ourselves," Xavier says, hands outstretched with palms down in a placating fashion.

He turns to Marie. "We're going to need Richard back here, pronto," Xavier orders.

"I assume we can get everything we need from our hosts at Shadowpoint," Marie says as she gets to work.

Xavier looks back at Kenji but addresses Marie. "I assume so, too, but let the fleet know what's happening. We'll need them to take some crew members and definitely supply any marines or non-critical personnel to provide muscle."

"How many people are we talking about?" Jane asks from her seat next to Renee.

Kenji replies, loud enough for everyone to hear. "A little under two thousand."

"We'll spread them around the ship; some of the larger areas can accommodate that amount of people. And we can set aside space in the hangar bay and the marines' area," Renee says.

"Agreed. Head down to the hangar and start organizing," Xavier says to Renee, and she gets up from her seat to follow orders.

"If they're friendly, I can get us a little closer. Even with our landing ships and shuttles going around the clock, we can only transport seventy-five, maybe one hundred per round trip. It's going to take twenty or thirty trips to get everyone. The shorter the trip, the quicker we can do this," Leo says.

Xavier nods. "Good idea. Have the rest of the fleet take up positions close to the League's fleet. We'll need their help," he says.

As the fleet starts to move, the Pax enters the middle of the formation. To many on the bridge, it feels like they're heading into the lion's den: more than enough firepower surrounds them and could cause major damage should their new allies prove to be less than honest. The League is in a perfect position to cause more destruction to the remaining Assembly forces.

It takes hours to complete the transfer, but in the end, everything goes smoothly. Lady Luck has finally decided to smile on the Pax and her crew. A few junior Assembly officers are thrust into command positions, and Kenji is allowed to stay on the bridge of the Pax. The marines are fully deployed throughout the fleet, and other crew members have been given weapons and will now assist in guard duty—for some, this is their first time using weapons since academy training. It's clear this is an unusual situation.

"Captain, the last of the remaining crew in the landing craft are leaving the Iron Phoenix. This should be the last round, then we'll be finished," Marie reports. Now that the assimilation of League vessels into the Assembly fleet has been completed, it's time to leave the Lauderact System.

"We sent a message to Frederick, and he's working with Shadowpoint to take the crew off our hands until our mission is complete," says Jane.

Kenji turns to Xavier with a baleful look. "Just remember that my crew are not your prisoners. We're here to defect, not spend time in your cells," he says.

Xavier acknowledges Kenji with a curt nod. He says to Leo, "Signal the fleet and set a course for the jump point. Let's get out of here."

"It's a small system, shouldn't take long…," Leo responds. The fleet falls in line with the Pax, the large vessel once again leading the charge to the jump point. Leo prepares the ship to jump back to Shadowpoint with their trophies.

"Captain, more hyperspace portals are dead ahead at the jump point. Fourteen ships are emerging," Marie reports.

"Were you expecting anyone else?" Xavier turns to Kenji.

"No, they must be here to investigate the missing convoy," Kenji says, uneasy.

Xavier knits his brows together. "Missing convoy? What missing convoy?" He taps his chin and thinks back. Only a few hours ago, they were investigating another mystery, and this thought comes back to him now.

"Ah, you mean the wreckage in the system. That might've been something to mention earlier," Xavier says severely.

"It was a hectic moment, and it slipped my mind," Kenji says. "However you want to deal with this, it's imperative they don't report anything back. We need to keep our newly-formed alliance a secret. Perhaps you should destroy those ships, and quickly," he warns.

"I would be inclined to agree, Captain, and they are well within weapons range now. I am detecting elevated power readings," Mikhail calls from his station.

"In that case, battle stance across the fleet. Mikhail, charge all weapons and target the vessels," Xavier orders.

"This fleet is different from the rest, Xavier. The fleets at Gaia and the Lumina Dyad contained smaller vessels," Renee says, frantically studying the sensor data as she tries to find any information that might help her captain.

Kenji leaves Xavier's side to join Renee at her station. He leans over her shoulder and stares at her screen, intent. "Hm. Looks like eight of our cruisers, four destroyers, one carrier, and a battlecruiser. That's a lot of firepower for a fleet investigating a missing convoy," he says.

"Jane, can you add that information to the targeting computers?" Mikhail asks.

"Yes, one moment, Mikhail," Jane says. She looks up at Kenji. "Which is which?" She asks. Kenji helps her update the data. This'll make communication and targeting much more effective in the future.

"I am seeing the vessel classifications now, Captain. Which do we target first?" Mikhail asks.

Xavier considers, then says, "Let's see what we can do about that battlecruiser first. Target it with the ion cannons, and lock the others on the nearest cruiser," he commands.

"Leo, get me a clear shot, please," Mikhail requests.

"Don't miss this time though, right? One moment," says Leo as he positions the Pax parallel to the incoming fleet. This maneuver allows Mikhail to fire a devastating broadside salvo. The ion cannons glow blue as they charge up, accelerating hydrogen ions close to the speed of light. The cannons unleash power beams that strike the League fleet's most powerful ship in mere seconds; two beams from the top turret hit mid ship, and the other two beams from the lower turret hit the engines.

Both cause large explosions as the battlecruiser is ripped apart from the inside. With this one strike, the enemy fleet is far less dangerous. The League's weapons aren't an immediate risk now, but with the destruction of the battlecruiser, the rest of the vessels turn to the jump point.

"One down, thirteen to go," says Xavier as he rubs his hands together. "Mikhail, keep firing. Marie, have the Assembly ships focus on the destroyers. We'll take care of the rest."

"They're turning tail and running," Leo says with a smirk.

"Their power signatures are increasing, they must be powering up," Renee states.

"It'll take them five minutes to charge up completely after their recent jump, and their capacitors will be fully depleted. We have some time, but not much," Kenji rejoins.

"Good to know. So, we have a ticking clock—we need to wrap this up. Leo, get us closer," Xavier responds, staring intently out the bridge windows.

"Oh, I'll get ya so close, you'll be able to see the enemy commander on their bridge. That's how close we're gonna get," Leo says, a cocky grin on his face.

"That'll put the rest of the fleet in harm's way, especially the League ships—they can't do much with a skeleton crew, and our ships are understaffed now," Jane says, her words sounding an alarm bell around the bridge.

"If we want to keep this a secret, we need to make sure they can't report anything. Have we detected any communications yet?" Xavier asks.

"Nothing yet, but we can flood the system with electronic counter measures," Marie suggests.

"It will make our targeting more challenging, but I can accommodate this," Mikhail says.

Xavier breathes heavily. "Do it," he says with finality.

"The Valiant is taking heavy hits… They won't be able to take much more," Renee says, her tone tinged with remorse.

"The Sundancer isn't doing well either. They should both disengage," Marie reports with urgency.

"Have them fall back behind us so we can protect them," Xavier says. He's feeling antsy, beginning to second guess this maneuver.

"It might be too late, the Valiant isn't moving," Renee says, looking up from her screen.

"Leo, can you shift to protect them?" Xavier asks in a last-ditch effort to salvage this mission.

"Not if we want to keep most of our weapons on target," Leo responds, shaking his head.

"We can't let any of them escape," Kenji says vehemently.

"All they'll know is that we've captured a few vessels, won't they?" Xavier asks.

"Shen knows there are people that don't agree with his direction for the League, and he'll hunt us down at all costs," Kenji says, putting his head in his hands.

"They're not here for us, are they—they're hunting *you*. You needed our protection to survive… You used us," Xavier says, finally realizing the truth. He puts a hand to his forehead.

"Can we talk about this another time? We have more important issues to deal with right now," Jane says sharply.

"The Sundancer is suffering from secondary explosions, and her crew are evacuating. The Valiant isn't doing much better. On another note, most of the enemy vessels have been destroyed—only the carrier remains," Renee reports, half hopeful.

"The main cannons are charged, ready to fire," Mikhail grunts.

"Fire at will. Just…make it go away," Xavier says, still in shock.

Another thunderous volley from the Pax causes critical damage to the enemy carrier, yet she still stands. Very few vessels in the galaxy can withstand four direct hits from multiple ion cannons, but the carrier is more armored than the rest of the League's fleet. The remaining League forces have now been destroyed, thanks to the combined fire of the Pax's new defecting allies.

"Concentrate fire on that carrier," Xavier orders all officers. He watches from the bridge as the Pax's weapons continue to fire every second; a flash from each of the barrels signifies when a slug is sent downrange towards its target. Under the weight of the fleet's fire, the carrier falters, destroyed. The Pax has won the first victory for the Assembly—even a small one such as this indicates a shift in the war. This win provides a spark of hope for the bridge crew.

"All enemy vessels defeated, sir," Marie says, grinning from ear to ear.

"Good work, everyone. When we get back to Shadowpoint, the first round is on me tonight!" Xavier says with a little whoop. His gesture is warmly received by the crew; though currency was eliminated decades ago, it's the thought that counts.

"Make sure the crew of the Intrepid and Valiant get picked up, then get us out of here, Leo," Xavier says, releasing a pent-up breath.

"With pleasure. Spooling up the hyperdrive engines now," replies Leo.

The Pax and her fleet head back to Shadowpoint; they enter the jump point, open a hyperspace portal, and proceed through. Though this mission was a success, they lost two cruisers in the process. The loss weighs heavily on Xavier now that the adrenaline of battle has worn off—not only from a strategic standpoint, but the loss of human life, too—and he feels the need to lick his wounds. He heads to his quarters for some peace and quiet.

He ruminates on an off-hand conversation he'd had with Captain Hale Rodriguez at an All-Commanders meeting during their journey to Lauderact. Rodriguez gave him some advice about putting the mission first, especially in times of conflict. It wasn't clear who survived the destruction of the two Assembly cruisers, or if Rodriguez was among them. Xavier hopes most of the crew were able to evacuate. The Pax blazes through hyperspace faster than the speed of light, but Xavier's mind is still faster, contemplating what he could've done differently. If he'd changed course, would those vessels still be part of the fleet—would their crew still be alive?

Pacing in his quarters, Xavier moves to his console and pulls up the database record and crew manifest for the Valiant. The names of three hundred crew members scroll across the screen, and Xavier notices Rodriguez's entry. He touches his name to expand his service record; the screen displays his headshot followed by a detailed biography and his service record. The bio details his numerous preceding commands, culminating in captain of the Valiant. At the end of the report are large red letters which read MIA.

Xavier takes a deep breath, but he feels his heart rate increase. The room starts to spin around him, and Xavier gasps for air. The walls close in second by second, and he falls back into a chair, unconscious from a panic attack. After what feels like a few minutes but has actually been a number of hours, Xavier's eyes crack open slowly. He wakes to concerned faces belonging to Dr. James Eastman, Jane, and Frederick standing over him. Their expressions are worried.

"Xavier, are you alright? You weren't responding to comms, so we came to check on you and found you lying like this," Jane says, gesturing to his prone body sprawled on a chair.

A disorientated Xavier tries to reply, but all that comes out of his mouth at first is a series of uhs and ums. He clears his throat, trying to get his bearings. Finally, he's able to explain his muddled state. "I was just, ah, looking at the console and must've gotten light headed… It's been a long day," Xavier says, clutching his head.

Frederick has an idea, and he wanders over to look at Xavier's console. He sees the screen and thinks he understands what's going on. Frederick decides not to say anything about it in front of the onlookers, so instead he walks back to the circle of concerned crew and addresses James.

"Is he okay?" Frederick asks.

James examines his patient. He can't find any obvious cause for concern. "Yes, I believe so. Although, Xavier, I recommend you get some fluids in you, and perhaps a hearty meal. Do let me know if you have any other symptoms," James says, packing up his medical tools, and Frederick is happy and relieved to hear that Xavier isn't badly hurt.

As James finishes collecting the small amount of equipment he brought with him and moves to leave the room, Frederick stops him. They walk to the doorway as Jane still hovers over Xavier. "How's our other patient?" Frederick asks James.

"For the moment, Anatoly is still sleeping peacefully in the medical bay, but I can't keep him sedated for too much longer—maybe another day, max. You might want to find a more permanent home for him," James replies.

James exits Xavier's quarters, leaving Jane and Frederick to help their colleague.

"Were you looking over Captain Rodriguez's file, Xavier? It's quite a read; numerous commendations and commands under his belt," Frederick says, returning to Xavier's screen. He swipes through the captain's page.

"I was…looking over the crew roster of the Valiant, sir," Xavier replies weakly.

"Drop the 'sir,' would you? I'm just interested in what you were doing before you collapsed," Frederick says, feigning an easy-going attitude.

Still a little groggy, Xavier responds with, "Of course, sir—I mean Frederick. Yes, I wanted to browse through the names of their crew." Xavier sits up and looks around. "We must be back at Shadowpoint now, yes?" He says, still a bit bewildered by all this information.

"Indeed, you arrived thirty minutes ago. When you didn't report to the bridge after the Pax entered the system, Jane came and found you like this. She asked that I come to assist, and she also filled me in as to the events of your mission. You've been very busy," Frederick says.

"…It went a little different to how we expected," Xavier responds.

"When I sent you on this mission, I wasn't expecting you to bring back a fleet of captured vessels. Honestly, I wasn't even sure you'd come back with the information we needed," Frederick says.

"I also informed Frederick about Kenji and the reason his fleet joined us," says Jane.

"I thought we could at least give them a chance to prove themselves," Xavier says, still optimistic.

"Commander, don't worry—you did the right thing. Just because we're at war doesn't mean we forget our humanity. They handed themselves over to you. Now we might have friends that can help spread light in these dark times," Frederick says, walking over to place his hand on Xavier's shoulder.

"You had the bridge's support, Xavier. Though we were, of course, nervous at first—as I'm sure you were, too—it didn't take long for us to realize that your choice was the right one," Jane says.

"We lost both the Valiant and Sundancer," Xavier says with a hangdog expression.

"Half the crew were saved in the escape pods. They were spread over the fleet. In fact, we're continuing to locate them," Jane informs him.

"Between the two vessels, that sounds like three hundred people," Xavier replies, his face brightening.

"Commander, considering the conditions, you did well to keep the number of losses down," Frederick says.

"I…I lost two out of the five ships we had when we first began this mission," Xavier replies. He's unable to get out of this dark spiral in his mind, his thoughts sinking into a deep depression.

Frederick scoffs good naturedly. "You returned with five more, and by the sounds of it, two thousand people that were being hunted. Sometimes we must see when we've done good, even if it's not perfect," he says.

Xavier is still visibly shaken, and his heart is beating at a rapid pace in his chest. He can feel it pounding; it's a wonder Frederick and Jane can't see it through his uniform. When he finally replies to Frederick, he struggles to choke back a sob. "You say that so casually, but we've already lost too many…"

Frederick can sense his second in command struggling with his emotions. He must do something to get him back on track, make him realize he's done good today. Frederick turns to Jane and says quietly, "Would you mind giving us the room?"

She nods and, with one last look at Xavier and squeeze of his shoulder, she leaves. Xavier's quarters are finally empty, save Xavier himself and Frederick, and Frederick hopes Xavier feels this is a safe space for them to speak openly with each other.

"Xavier, my friend," Frederick starts. "It's never easy being in command. Leadership has its luxuries, but you're now feeling its true pressure, and in the hardest way possible. We don't get to choose our missions; we must only do the job that needs to be done. You completed your task, and no one could've predicted what was going to happen. You did exactly what I would've done," Frederick says with real feeling. He hopes his words will thaw Xavier's cold thoughts toward himself and his past actions.

"But… you would've brought the Sundancer and Valiant back…," Xavier replies, his speech still stilted.

"Well, I *might* have been able to bring them back, or I might've lost many more," Frederick says and steps forward to lower himself in front of Xavier, still sitting in the chair he fell upon.

Frederick continues. "We don't get the luxury of playing the game of what-if because we have to live in the present. Our decisions determine the direction of thousands, and those in our charge—those relying on us—matter more. We also don't get the opportunity to drill into every decision we make, as sometimes we must make those decisions in a split second.

"In the cold void, you're alone. You can be gone for hours or days, even years, as you know. And when you're out there, you're the

Assembly's ambassador, general, and diplomat, all rolled into one; that's the burden you carry, so you must have faith in yourself and your crew. Harder still is that you have to hold your values firmly and with both hands. That way, you'll be able to sleep at night after all is said and done," Frederick finishes, looking up at his first officer.

Xavier takes a deep, deep breath and passes a hand over his face. His heart seems to have slowed down, and his vision is clearing. "I'm glad you're back, Frederick. I'm not sure I was ready to jump into the deep end just yet," he says with a weak smile.

"Maybe not, but how would you have known? I need to be honest with you: this isn't your last solo command, and I need to know you if you're up to the task. Judging by your past performance during our missions together, I'm sure you are, but with this panic attack… I wonder if *you* think you're up for it. Can you keep going? It'll get harder before it gets easier," Frederick says carefully.

Xavier hangs his head for a moment, looking at the floor and avoiding Frederick's eye. He's ashamed of his reaction, but he must be strong. Hasn't he been training for this for a while now? The events at Gaia, the battles fought and narrowly won afterwards—they've all tested his might and mental strength, but he's had Frederick to lean on. Can he do this, carry the weight of such responsibility on his own? He takes a moment to summon his shredded confidence and finally says, "Yes, sir. I'll be there for you, the Pax, and the Assembly."

Frederick smiles encouragingly and says, "Good to hear. Give yourself some time, then head to the bridge. We have a lot of work to do." He stands up and pats Xavier on the back before walking to the door. As he approaches, the doors slide open, and he turns back to Xavier one last time. "I'm glad you're staying by my side… I'm not sure I can do this without you." He turns back to the doors and exits, hoping his last words provide enough inspiration in Xavier to extinguish any feelings of self-doubt. The doors close behind him.

Chapter Twenty-Nine

Now in the corridor, Frederick makes his way back to the bridge when he spies Jane lingering nearby. "Nice of you to wait," says Frederick, and Jane joins him as he moves towards the NovaPath at the end of the hall. They step inside and start their journey.

While inside the NovaPath, Jane starts up a conversation. "I thought you might want to talk. How's Xavier doing?" She asks, concern and empathy evident in her tone. She doesn't like seeing Xavier in such a state, and she still has residual unease about the condition in which she found him.

Frederick gives her a full-bodied shrug in response. "He'll be fine, I think. Just had his nerves rattled a little," he says.

"Understandable. Though it might be best for him to recover before we get underway again," Jane replies.

Frederick purses his lips. "I'm not sure we have enough time for that… I fear we'll all need to be comfortable being uncomfortable," he says.

"How much further do you think he can be pushed, if at all?" Jane asks in reply.

"I want the best out of my crew, and that means I need to push them, take them to their breaking point. Hopefully we can all survive to see everyone we hold dear one more time," Frederick says, leaning back against the NovaPath wall. He feels tired all of a sudden under the weight of his command; sometimes the crown is heavy upon his head.

"Do you have a plan?" Jane asks plainly. She can be blunt rather than coy when she wants to be.

"Maybe," says Frederick with another shrug, "but let's see if Noia has a softer side."

"If you're betting on his humanity, maybe we should get Mikhail to run diagnostics on the combat systems," Jane says with a small smile. She feels like she hasn't been able to crack a joke in quite a while—everything has been so tense and uptight.

At that moment, the NovaPath reaches its destination, and Jane and Frederick emerge to a quiet scene on the bridge. Mikhail, Leo, Renee, and Marie are present and working at their stations. Kenji, Richard, and Elara are deep in conversation at the command console in the middle of the bridge.

Leo turns around at the sound of the NovaPath doors closing. "Commodore! We heard about Xavier, is everything okay?" Leo isn't one to show his feelings—or at least, he tries not to show them—though in this instance, he can't help but question the condition of his friend and colleague. Xavier means a lot to Leo and the rest of the command crew.

Frederick nods and decides to address the entirety of the bridge, everyone within earshot. He raises his voice to make the announcement. "Xavier will be fine, though he's struggling with the loss of the Valiant and Sundancer, particularly since this loss happened under his watch. I don't believe he made any improper decisions, so if anyone disagrees, please take it up with me privately. I asked him to return to the bridge once he's had a chance to compose himself."

Frederick looks around at each officer individually, searching for any indication of an opposing viewpoint. He doesn't see any glares or frowns, so he assumes the crew agrees with his statements.

Frederick says sadly, "We don't have the luxury of time at the moment; Noia's plan will be for the detriment of the League and the Assembly, everyone will lose. I'd rather come up with a better way, one that avoids as much death and destruction as possible." He looks at the small group gathered at the central console. "Kenji, we need your help," he says.

"I'll assist however I can," Kenji says from his place at the table. "And my crew will surely be willing as well."

"On that note—Marie," Frederick says, turning to face her, "What's the status of the League's transfer?" He asks.

Now that the Pax has returned to Shadowpoint, there are more options available to the League's defectors. A single large marine transport, called the Horizon, handles the entire fleet's crew; this vessel has a singular focus: to accommodate troops. Therefore, it's well-suited to hold the crew while a decision is made as to their future.

"A few more trips and they should all be placed on the Horizon. Once that's complete, it'll take time for the marines and other crew members to return to their home base," Marie answers.

"We still have a deal though, Commodore? We aren't prisoners," Kenji says.

"Jane caught me up on the particulars. Yes, you and your crew are under my protection until we come up with a more permanent solution, but this isn't easy for us," Frederick says in return.

"I understand that, so long as we have your word," Kenji says with an incline of his head.

"You have it. Though we need a plan to present to Noia," Frederick states.

"Did you have anything in mind, Commodore?" Mikhail asks.

"That's what we need to do now—let's figure this out," Frederick says, walking over with Jane at his side. He motions for everyone to follow.

Leo, Mikhail, Marie, and Renee move from their stations, and more junior officers in other positions around the bridge relieve their senior officers' posts. Kenji, Elara, and Richard are already in place and shuffle around the table. It's cramped as everyone congregates, but they make room for one another.

Once they're all assembled, Frederick begins explaining. "So, we know our one objective: currently, Earth is under siege, and the shield has enough power for eight or nine days. We've been in touch with Earth recently, and they now count eight hundred attackers—including a number of heavy warships, not just the small vessels we've fought so far," he says.

"Even with the Assembly fleet at full strength, that is a challenge. Even before Gaia was destroyed," Mikhail grumbles.

"Shen must've gathered his full strength for this assault, which means he must assume his targets have been neutralized and the Assembly poses no real risk to his plans…," Kenji says, thinking out loud.

"What's his full plan—do you know it?" Jane asks, ever hopeful.

"His end goal is to ensure destruction of the Assembly; he wants vengeance for the past. While the Assembly remains, it's a stark reminder of past struggles, and so he hopes to wipe you from the map and begin anew—this time, under his control. He'll eliminate every ship and station in his way and annihilate any Assembly planet to remove their interference. With this, he believes removing you physically will remove you in spirit, too," Kenji says, eyes downcast.

"It sounds like Earth is only the start… If he wants to go after every Assembly member, that's around one hundred billion people across countless worlds, and Earth is the only one that currently has a planetary shield; they would be sitting ducks," Jane exclaims, putting a hand to her heart. This is terrible news.

"It won't matter—we have to stop him before he gets through Earth's shield," Frederick says, and his voice is strong.

"How? That is eight hundred ships—we do not have enough firepower to take them head on!" Mikhail sputters. Even his beloved ion cannons can't outlast this many attackers.

"Kenji, you said this could be the League's entire fleet. Does that mean Shen left important or strategic locations undefended? Could be softer targets," Frederick says, tapping his chin in contemplation.

"We have many facilities. There's a shipyard and other outposts that could be inviting targets. What might be more lucrative, though, is our homeworld and primary systems. If you were to threaten that, he might be inclined to pull forces from Earth in defense," Kenji replies.

"Do you have the coordinates of those targets?" Frederick asks.

Before Kenji can reply, the bridge's NovaPath doors open, and Xavier emerges. He stops short at the sight of everyone gathered around the center console table, and Frederick sees him falter. He moves forward to greet him, hoping to assuage any feelings of embarrassment Xavier may still be harboring.

Once he reaches Xavier, Frederick says, "Are you ready to return to duty? I want to make sure… It's okay to say no."

Xavier gives him a sheepish look. "I appreciate the concern, really—as well as your words earlier. They meant a lot to me. I feel well enough to get back to work… I want to help," Xavier says in earnest.

"That's good to hear, Xavier, good to hear!" Frederick says and claps him on the back. "We need your brain. Come." Frederick nods his head toward the table and beckons Xavier forward.

They return to the rest of the team, and everyone makes space, welcoming them into the fold once more. The conversation is still ongoing.

"It would be helpful for your officers to identify weak points in your warships," Mikhail says to Kenji.

"I'm not sure how I feel about giving you details that can get my people killed…," Kenji responds, hedging and looking uncertain. He's made his choice, no turning back, and he's pledged his allegiance to the Pax and her fight. Why, then, does he look so unsettled?

"If you want your people to take the peaceful path, you'll need to fight for it," Frederick responds. The irony isn't lost on him.

Kenji looks both reluctant and nervous to give away such information. "Let me think about this one, Commodore," he finally says.

Jane senses his discomfort and steers the conversation in another direction. "So, we need to move as many vessels away from Earth as possible, somehow split the League's forces—that'll give us the best chance," she says.

Mikhail replies, "We need to do this while not stretching our forces too thin. They will still keep the majority of their forces around Earth, and Shen will want to capture his prize."

"There's another problem," Leo says, sticking one finger up. "Sol is large, and it'll take a few hours, even at maximum speed, to get from the jump point to Earth."

Renee huffs and shakes her head. "That'll give them plenty of time to detect our approach."

"We need a way to hide ourselves for as long as possible," says Marie, tapping her chin while thinking.

"Or we could try and lure Shen's forces away and across the system. We cannot fight their fleet one on one, but we can tackle them throughout the system in bite sized chunks," Mikhail says, his gruff attitude peeking through as usual.

"You want to run guerrilla style hit and run attacks to whittle them away?" Xavier questions Mikhail.

"They have a numerically superior force; one way or another, we cannot fight it all at once," Mikhail shoots back.

"I wonder whether Shadowpoint can provide assistance in concealing our numbers—or at the very least, help us delay detection," Frederick muses.

The officers murmur and chatter amongst themselves, discussing different options. Frederick catches snippets of their conversation and hopes they can come up with a plan to succeed. Perhaps this is finally the beginning of a path forward—a plan that ends with saving Earth. And the League...how can he save *them*?

Frederick breaks in and asks above the chatter, "How do we protect the League from Shadowpoint's forces?"

"What do you mean, Commodore?" Kenji inquires, perplexed.

A shadow passes over Frederick's face; how can he best explain this to Kenji? He doesn't want to break their new and fragile alliance, so he chooses his words carefully. He wets his lips before saying, "My orders are to eliminate all other League forces and settlements once Earth is saved and Shen's fleet is destroyed. I've been told to...remove the threat for good."

"Ah, I see. So that explains why you wanted all my coordinates," Kenji says, and the truth finally dawns on him.

"Yes—I mean, that was my mission, but I was given the opportunity to present an alternative," Frederick says, imploring everyone, but especially Kenji, to understand. He pauses for a moment before continuing, then says, "That's where you come in; the universe dropped you into our lap for a reason."

"You think I can help you do this?" Kenji says, pointing to his own chest. "How?" He asks heatedly.

The room is now silent, hanging on the words of their newly minted commodore and a defector from their worst enemy. They listen with bated breath.

Frederick says, "That all depends on how many others follow you and your cause."

Kenji gives him a wry look across the console table. "There aren't many. My fleet is loyal, but many members of the greater fleet are zealots nowadays. I know of a few high-level officers that I can rely upon. If you include my ship, in total, my cause has around thirty vessels," Kenji replies.

"If we were to eliminate the rest of their forces, could you and your ships secure the League's territory?" Frederick asks.

"Not quite, but we could protect Sonnara. If we can secure the system, we can overthrow the ruling military leadership and reestablish the council's return to the good path. Perhaps one day we can rejoin the galaxy. That is, when we're ready," Kenji says, a hopeful look on his face.

"You're talking about a coup... Do you have the civilian support to manage this?" Jane asks.

"That's one thing I can guarantee. Many of the castes feel the same way—like they've been pushed aside by the military, and there's nothing they can do about it," Kenji explains.

"A coup may be a smoother process than annihilating an entire planet from orbit," Mikhail deadpans.

"Yeah, uh, let's *not* do that..." Leo says, scrunching his face at the thought of blowing up a planet. He taps his foot and puts his hand on his hips, seemingly uncomfortable in his own skin. Jane surreptitiously watches him as she stands at the console table. He shifts again, scratching at his arm, then his neck. Something is going on, she thinks, but decides to focus on it later—they've got more important issues to deal with now.

Frederick rubs his hands together. "This is starting to sound like a plan," he says.

"Even if we're able to pull some forces away from Sol and use hit and run tactics, we're still outgunned," Renee says. She's not as optimistic as the rest of the crew.

"Marie, have you identified all the ships here at Shadowpoint?" Frederick asks.

"No, sir, but there are around one hundred to two hundred power signatures," Marie answers.

Frederick nods his acknowledgment. "I think it's time for Noia to join us. He wasn't particularly happy to have you and your crew at the station," he says while looking toward Kenji. "Maybe we can improve his mood."

"We'll continue to work on the particulars, then you can discuss our revised plan with Commodore Noia," Xavier suggests.

"My thoughts exactly," Frederick says. "Kenji, why don't you join me in the observation lounge? Let's get some food."

Turning to Marie, Frederick says, "Signal the commodore and invite him over to the Pax. If he asks why, let him know we'd like to explain our revised plan." Marie nods and leaves the center console table to begin her tasks.

Frederick inclines his head in Xavier's direction. "When he arrives," Frederick says, "receive him and bring him to the operations room. Kenji and I will meet you there, just let us know once he gets here."

There are nods around the command console, and everyone scatters to complete their tasks. Frederick feels he might've found a way to settle this conflict; he hopes to persuade Commodore Noia to see things from his point of view. Frederick leaves the bridge with a sense of accomplishment, Kenji in tow. As he and Kenji head towards the observation lounge, he wonders if Kenji will be able to persuade Noia, too—after all, the fate of his people is resting on the shoulders of Shadowpoint's commanding officer. They exit the bridge and are soon out of sight.

Marie contacts Shadowpoint and communicates with Noia. As Frederick advised, she invites Noia to the Pax; he's delighted at the opportunity and travels over, hopping onto a shuttle. Xavier makes his way down to the landing bay to meet him in anticipation; he only waits about ten minutes before Noia's shuttle arrives. Once the shuttle has landed and Noia steps down a short gangway and onto the Pax, he strides over to Xavier.

At Noia's approach, Xavier extends his hand and says, "Commodore, welcome to the Pax Aeterna. I'm Xavier Reynolds, it's a pleasure to meet you." He smiles congenially.

"Thank you, Captain. Or—well, I suppose it's Commander now. Congratulations on your recent success! I never thought you'd bring us so many new toys to play with," Noia says, clasping both of Xavier's hands in his and shaking heartily.

Xavier frowns. "They're defectors, sir, not playthings," he says.

"I know, but I definitely prefer them in our care rather than in our sights, don't you?" Noia says and laughs, not expecting an answer.

"Now, where is Commodore Langfield? I thought he'd be here as well," he says, looking around the bay.

"He's waiting for you in the operations room, and he's very much looking forward to discussing the plan," Xavier explains.

"Ah, he is, is he? Well, let's not keep him waiting. Though before we head to the operations room, I thought I might pop into the medical bay. I wanted to say hello to the doctor on board—James is his name, right? He and I go back a ways, and I haven't seen him in a while," Noia says. His smile seems forced to Xavier.

"He is indeed still our doctor," Xavier says, nodding, "However, I was asked to take you right to the operations room…" He looks at Noia's peeved face and says in a rush, "I'm sure we can stop by quickly."

"Excellent. I do appreciate you accommodating my request, Commander," Noia says with a tight expression.

Xavier leads Noia to the medical bay, through long corridors and into a NovaPath. It takes them a few minutes to arrive, but they finally stride towards the medical bay doors. As they walk, Xavier feels his cos-link buzzing and takes it out of his pocket. Frederick has sent him a message asking if Noia is on board. Xavier answers in the affirmative but notes that he and Noia have taken a quick detour.

Noia stops walking and looks to Xavier. "Is that Frederick wondering where we are?" He asks.

"Yes sir," Xavier says, looking up from his cos-link. "We should make this a short interlude before heading to the operations room."

"We'll be in and out in a jiffy, I assure you," Noia says.

"If you know James from before, perhaps I can leave you with him? I could use a moment to meet with a crew member," Xavier says distractedly, fiddling with his cos-link.

"Of course! I'll drop in for just a moment, and you can come get me in a few minutes," Noia says.

"Thank you. It's just through there," Xavier says, pointing to the double doors on the left. Xavier walks down the corridor to meet with Legionnaire Felicity; he'd been meaning to drop in on her as she's one of his direct reports, but with so much going on, he'd neglected his usual check-ins. Since Noia knows James, Xavier figures this is the perfect opportunity to kill two birds with one stone and catch up on his overflowing to do list. He turns on his heel, leaving Noia to meet with James alone.

Noia pushes through the double doors slowly; they glide closed behind him with a thud. The medical bay is practically empty. The staff have treated many of the minor injuries from the most recent skirmish and discharged their patients. Noia's footsteps echo on the metal floors, then he stops and looks around, taking in his surroundings. Since there aren't any staff milling about, there's no one to stop him from walking to his target: the one occupied bed. Next to it stands James, administering drugs to Anatoly's prone body.

At the sound of footsteps, James turns, and his face blanches. His eyes are wide, and he stops his hands, now slightly shaking—he doesn't trust himself to continue his medical duties at this moment. Noia walks over with long, slow steps, hands behind his back.

"Hello there, Troy. It's been a long time," Noia says, a sinister grin splitting his face in two. His incisors are showing, and they gleam in the harsh light of the medical bay.

James blinks in surprise, taken aback to hear a name he hasn't been called in years. He'd know that voice anywhere.

"Commander White. It's been a while," James says, clearing his throat. His mouth has suddenly gone dry. "I was wondering if you'd pay me a visit at some point."

"Ah-ah, it's Commodore Noia now," Noia says, wagging a finger. "And how could I not pay a call to you? How did you get off Passau, that forsaken planet, and leave your work behind?" Noia asks, reaching James and stopping at the foot of Anatoly's bed. He places his hands in the pockets of his uniform, affecting a casual stance. His posture is just the opposite.

James raises his chin. "I suppose there's something in this world that'll always remain a mystery to you," he says defiantly.

"Fine, keep your mystery—it's irrelevant now," Noia says with a shrug. "I wonder, though… Do you think Frederick would be interested in some of our past missions? I'm sure you haven't told him everything," Noia says, that sinister smile still playing on his lips.

A slight sheen of sweat has broken out on James's forehead. He doesn't wipe it away, for fear Noia would see the gesture as a weakness. "What do you want, Noia? Why are you here?" James asks, his heart pounding in his chest.

Noia takes his hands out of his pockets and places them on the railing at the foot of Anatoly's bed. He gestures to him and asks, "How's he doing? I hear he was injured, that he's been out for a while." His eyebrows are raised.

James is confused by Noia's concern and cocks his head in surprise. "He'll be fine… He just needs more rest," he answers.

"See now, here's the issue," Noia says, tapping his chin with one hand and continuing to look at Anatoly's sleeping form. "I need only one person to lead the fleet against the League, and I can't do it myself for various reasons. So, it's either Anatoly or Frederick. One of those officers seems to have a plan, and the other is lying in front of us. And that one knows far too much about me and what happens here at Shadowpoint. That's a problem." Noia says all this so casually, as if he's describing a minor inconvenience. It has a chilling effect on James, and he grimaces.

"I'm not going to like where this is going, am I?" James asks, heaving a heavy sigh.

Noia chuckles without humor. "Hm, I wonder if the old you would? Certainly not this new version. Don't worry about it—all I need is for you to leave, immediately. Give me just two minutes with my friend here, and your past will be safe with me," Noia says, stepping closer to James and patting his shoulder, that wicked grin back on his face.

James looks down at Noia's hand and closes his eyes. He considers his options in a split second; he doesn't really have a choice in the matter. He knows he's not strong nor capable enough to fight this battle.

Noia stares at James, boring a hole into his very soul, and waits. James takes a step back, opening his eyes and letting Noia's hand fall. "So long as this is the last time we ever meet," he says, and walks backwards for a few steps. Then, he turns around and heads briskly for the medical bay doors.

As he walks, he hears Noia call out, "Never say never, my friend!" Without turning back, James pushes through the doors of the medical bay and strides down the hall, far away from the scene playing out at Anatoly's bed.

Noia waits for the doors to close, signaling James's retreat. He looks at the medical machines connected to Anatoly's body, watches as his chest rises and falls with each breath. He blinks, then pushes a few buttons on the screen of the medical machines, causing the pumps to add unneeded air to Anatoly's bloodstream. With a few clicks, he deactivates all other devices keeping Anatoly sedated. It doesn't take long for Anatoly's body to start shaking, then convulsing as if he were having a seizure. Anatoly's eyes fly open, and even in his groggy state, he recognizes the blurry face in front of him.

"Noia? What are you doing?" Anatoly chokes out. Each word is a struggle.

Noia tsk-tsks. "You've failed me for the last time, Commodore. You were meant to bring me the Pax, not unleash Frederick, this fool of a man, on me," he says harshly.

Anatoly grips his chest, and groans. He can feel the life oozing out of his body, but he hangs on as hard as he can. "I—I brought you your prize," he wheezes.

Noia is calm as he replies, his eyes slitted. "I expected better from you, but perhaps that's *my* failure. Earth is now on the brink of collapse, and the League is the target of Frederick's focus, meaning all my puppets have played their part. Soon, Earth will be nothing more than a burning rock, and the League will be decimated."

"You used me…," Anatoly slurs out, and the last of his strength is spent speaking these final words. He blinks slowly, gazing up at the face of his murderer.

Noia towers over him with a devilish look. "You're pathetic—you were nothing more than a tool, and honestly, dying is the only thing you ever did right. The Assembly is weak: they fought for peace, but peace is just another word for control. True power—*real* power—comes from strength. Nova Corp is the future, and we'll bring unity to both the factions and the galaxy, but on *our* terms! Just as it should've been from the start." Noia sighs and looks down, glad Anatoly has held on long enough to hear his rant.

Anatoly's eyes suddenly roll to the back of his head. His mouth opens and he gasps, begging for a breath that'll never come. In just a moment, the movements cease, and his body is completely still once more. A final gasp escapes, then his face goes slack. Noia watches all this with a blank depression, feeling nothing.

"Goodnight, sweet prince. I'll see you soon," Noia says. He smiles to himself, proud of a job well done. He strolls out of the medical bay calmly, leaving the scene for someone else to find. He waits for Xavier in the corridor, leaning against the wall without a care in the world.

Xavier walks briskly into view after a few minutes. "Ah, Commodore Noia! Did you find James, sir?" He asks.

"Yes, I did," Noia says. "It was wonderful to see him again. He's just left, so I thought I'd wait here for you. Shall we get to the operations room? I can't wait to hear this plan of yours," he says almost cheerily. Noia doesn't have to try hard to ignore his actions from the last few minutes. To him, they're already gone—poof. It's all just a means to an end. Xavier motions for Noia to follow him down the hall so they can continue their journey.

Acknowledgments

I would like to first and foremost thank my partner, Chelsee Dickson, from the bottom of my heart. She has been my guiding light on this endeavor, providing me with the wealth of experience she has to help bring my world to reality. Words cannot express how thankful I am to you.

I'd like to thank my parents—especially my father—who endured numerous revisions and reviews, as well as provided their overall support for this creation.

Lastly, my heartfelt gratitude goes to everyone who encouraged me along the way. Your belief in my project kept me going.

About the Author

John Gibbons is a science fiction (sci-fi) fanatic and has been his entire life. He's passionate about bringing his story and the Stellar Universe to life through novels, games, and other outlets, and he's taken inspiration from television shows and movies like *Star Trek: The Original Series*, *The Expanse*, and *Stargate*. John's appetite for a diverse array of sci-fi mediums allows him to create a universe that takes a unique spin on the genre.

At an early age, John was diagnosed with dyslexia, and he faced many difficulties with reading and writing. *The Shadows of Peace* represents not only his love for sci-fi, but also his determination to overcome personal boundaries. He strives to be a role model for other dyslexics and hopes his journey will spark others to believe in themselves no matter the challenges they face.

John lives in Atlanta, Georgia with his partner. He's hard at work creating new and innovative content for the Stellar Universe. *The Shadows of Peace* is his first novel.

For updates about the Stellar Universe, please visit: www.StellarDigitalStudios.com

Printed in Great Britain
by Amazon

1f2b23ba-a40d-41e9-9029-b1fed0176835R01